I0831605

FRACTURED AXIOM

THE KREMØTOA CODEX
BOOK THREE

SAEKO KURENAIHANA

For permission requests, inquiries or questions, **scan the QR-Code below** to go to the Contact Form. If the link breaks, go to https://kurenaihanabooks.com/contact-me/ and fill out the web-form.

3rd Edition | 2026

CONTENTS

CONTENT WARNING & INFORMATION

The Kremøtoa Codex series is an adult science fantasy saga intended for **mature, adult** audiences. This book, *Fractured Axiom,* incorporates genre elements of:

- **LitRPG / GameLit**
- **Quest & Adventure Fantasy**
- **Political & Psychological Thriller**
- **LGBTQ+ Romance (F/F/F/F Polyamory)**

Fractured Axiom continues the exploration of the series' core themes, with a specific focus on:

- **Mortality and Embodiment:** The connection between the physical and digital self.
- **Sacrifice:** The personal costs of fighting for a better future.

- **Confronting the Past:** Healing from trauma by facing it directly.
- **Ideology vs. Humanity:** The conflict between rigid dogma and personal truth.
- **Found Family:** The strength drawn from bonds of love and loyalty in the face of despair.
- **Revolution:** The power of a new idea to shatter an old world.

The Kremøtoa Codex is a series intended for mature audiences. This volume contains material that readers may find distressing. **Discretion is advised.** Please be aware *Fractured Axiom* contains:

- **Explicit Sexual Content:** Detailed depictions of consensual sexual encounters between female characters.
- **Psychological Distress:** In-depth explorations of existential dread, body horror, trauma, PTSD flashbacks, and severe panic attacks.
- **Abuse:** Scenes containing intense verbal and emotional abuse, misogyny, and manipulation.
- **Violence:** Descriptions of fantasy violence, combat, and potentially graphic creature-related gore.

As this is the full intended edition of the novel, explicit scenes have a warning at the top of each chapter. Please take note of any trigger warnings.

PREVIOUSLY, IN THE KREMØTOA CODEX...

The Quartet's new alliance was nearly destroyed when The Alchemist framed Master Willem of the Azure Rose Guild for an assassination attempt on Sera Valerius. Ada Lynx's unique powers proved Willem's innocence, solidifying their partnership against the tyrant Alaric Thorne. Lacking funds, they sought the lost treasure of the Imperial ship, the Argent Lion. After Ada located the wreck and they acquired a submersible, they retrieved not only a fortune in gold but also schematics revealing a devastating truth: the Ehxcehl Empire was responsible for creating the world-consuming Pattern Blight and the monstrous Malware. This shattered Sera's faith and reforged her purpose in the revolution.

To secure a fleet, the fellowship journeyed to Rhedeon using Ada's newfound 'Blink' teleportation, an exhausting process that necessitated the creation of a telepathic link for silent, tactical coordination. There, they discovered the true power broker was the enigmatic Render-Witch, Nividia. After gaining her attention at the Midnight Gala, they passed her impossible test: retrieving a data-core from the Sunken Core by having Ada use her Admin powers to repair the dungeon's broken final puzzle.

Returning to a Port Dominus crushed by Thorne, they launched a desperate assault on his weapons and financial sector. Their victory was shattered when the captured Alchemist triggered a suicide bomb, destroying the Azure Rose headquarters. As all seemed lost, Nividia's personal fleet arrived, answering Ada's earlier plea and annihilating Thorne's remaining forces and Thorne himself, Ada's chilling punishment left Thorne trapped in an 'Empathy Feedback Loop'. But this reprieve was short-lived, as the world began to suffer a 'Cascade Failure', objects and whole cliffsides glitching out of existence. Ada received a garbled message from Earth, realizing the world's collapse is tied to her physical body dying, which her friends are about to unwittingly disconnect.

CHAPTER 1

A WORLD OF CODE

The cold steel of the command center floor was a brutal anchor to a reality that was dissolving. It pressed against Ada's cheek, a single, sharp point of sensation in a universe of overwhelming noise. Samantha's voice echoed in the telepathic space, a ghost haunting the machine, a looped recording of impending doom.

"Please just text or CALL back so we don't call 119..."

The words were an act of love. An act of annihilation.

ADA!*...Sera, what is wrong with her?* Korina's thoughts were a frantic spray of panicked code, raw data without analysis.

I don't know! She won't respond! Ada! Sera's mental voice was a command, laced with a fear Ada had never heard from her before.

Ada's own scream felt like a distant memory, swallowed by the sterile, ozonic air of the room. A metallic taste, sharp and foul, flooded her mouth. She tried to push herself up, her palms slipping on the polished surface. The dormant consoles around them gleamed, indifferent. They were just terminals. She was the server.

And the server was crashing.

Her body was the hardware running their world. Her comatose form in a Sagiyama apartment was the literal machine that processed every sunrise, every heartbeat, every thought they had. The cascade failure wasn't a glitch in the code. It was a symptom. The system was failing because the system's core—her physical body—was failing. The paramedics Samantha were about to call weren't coming to save her; they were coming to pull the plug on everything.

A fresh wave of terror seized her, a physical weight that crushed the air from her lungs. She gasped, a ragged, wet sound.

"Ada, look at me." Erita's voice, a low and urgent command, cut through the chaos. She crouched low, her golden eyes boring into Ada's. "Breathe. Tell us what you saw. Is it the Empire? A new weapon?"

Ada shook her head, a violent, jerky motion. *Oh, if only it were that simple. If only it were an enemy they could fight with steel and strategy.*

"It's...it's..." The words wouldn't form. They were too big, too monstrous. How could she give voice to a truth that would invalidate their very existence?

Korina knelt beside her, her hand finally landing on Ada's shoulder. The touch was warm, grounding. It was real. That was the unbearable tragedy of it. Korina was real. Her love was real. And Ada's past was about to delete her.

"Rina," Ada whimpered, the name a prayer.

"I'm here," Korina's voice was a trembling thread. "I'm right here. Just tell us. Whatever it is, we face it together."

Together. The word was a knife. *There was no together in this. She was the single point of failure.*

Ada pushed herself onto her knees, her body shaking with the effort. Her tear-blurred vision swam, the faces of the women she loved—her entire world—wavering before her. Sera, her expression a mask of fierce, protective anguish. Erita, her sharp, analytical mind stalled by an unquantifiable horror. And Korina, her eyes wide with a terror that mirrored Ada's own.

She had to tell them. She had to give them the dignity of the truth before it was all gone. She owed them that much.

She took a shuddering breath, the air burning her throat.

"This world..." she began, her voice a raw, broken whisper. The three of them leaned in, their shared silence a vacuum. "Kremøtoa...it's not real."

Korina's hand tightened on her shoulder. Sera's jaw clenched. Erita's eyes narrowed, searching for a trick, a metaphor.

"It's a simulation," Ada forced out, the confession tearing through her. "A program. I...I wrote it. I built it."

A profound stillness fell over the command center. The only sound was Ada's choked breathing. She saw the denial warring with confusion on their faces. It didn't make sense. It couldn't.

"And the cascade failure...the glitches...all of it." She looked from Korina, to Sera, to Erita, her gaze begging them to understand, to forgive her. "It's happening because...my real body...back on Earth...it's dying."

The confession hung in the air, a poison gas, silent and absolute. The command center, once a symbol of their victory, transformed into a mausoleum. The low hum of the remaining systems seemed to mock them, a ghost-song for a world that was never real. Ada watched them through a film of tears, the salt stinging her lips. *She had done this. She had built them, loved them, and then, with a few whispered words, she had unmade them.*

Sera's face, usually a canvas of fierce resolve, fractured. Vulnerability, raw and deep, exposed the woman beneath the warrior. Her knuckles were white where she gripped the edge of a console. Her gaze was fixed on a point in the middle distance, seeing not the room, but the crumbling foundations of her entire life. Her faith in the Empire, her honor, the very feel of the sun on her skin—all of it, a lie. A single, guttural sound tore from her throat, more an expulsion of breath than a word.

"No."

Her hand, as if by instinct, fell to the hilt of her sword. The worn leather grip was a familiar comfort, a tangible piece of reality. But it was useless. A phantom's weapon in a ghost's world. The rage began to build then, a cold fire that burned away the shock, leaving behind a terrifying stillness. It wasn't directed at Ada. It was a fury aimed at the cosmos, at an enemy she could not cut.

Korina went perfectly still. Her violet eyes, always so vibrant with a storm of data and inquiry, went wide and vacant. She was a system analyst staring at a paradox that had just consumed the system. Her brilliant mind, which could map thaumaturgical frequencies and decrypt impossible code, slammed against an absolute wall. Her fingers, trembling almost imperceptibly, found their way to Obsidian. The cool metal of the data-slate was her anchor. She tapped its surface, a frantic, silent search for...what? A system file that read **[REALITY_STATUS: SIMULATED]**? A diagnostic to confirm her own non-existence? The slate remained dark, its silence a confirmation of the horror.

Then, she moved. Not away, but toward Ada. Her arms wrapped around Ada's shaking form, a fierce, protective gesture that defied all logic. Her own world had just been obliterated, yet her first instinct was to shield its destroyer.

I broke them, Ada thought, a fresh wave of self-loathing washing over her. *I built this beautiful, complex world just to drag them into my own personal nightmare. They should hate me. They should be screaming at me, tearing me apart.*

Why don't they hate me?

Erita's face became a mask of ice. No shock, no overt horror. Her golden eyes narrowed, processing the information with a terrifying pragmatism. She analyzed the fallout, the emotional carnage around her, like a spymaster assessing a battlefield. The existential terror was just another variable. The impending deletion of their universe was just another opponent. Her gaze flicked from Sera's rigid fury to Korina's clinging desperation, and finally settled on Ada. There was no pity in her eyes, only a cold, hard assessment of the asset before her. The broken, weeping gød who held their fate in her dying hands.

The silence stretched, thin and brittle, threatening to shatter into a million pieces of screaming madness. Erita broke it.

"Enough."

The word was a slap. *Sharp. Final.* It cut through the haze of despair. Sera flinched, her eyes finally focusing on the room. Korina's grip on Ada tightened, her face buried in Ada's shoulder.

"The specifics don't matter," Erita continued, her voice level, devoid of emotion. She paced once, a predator in a cage. "Real, not real. Simulation, program. These are just words. The threat is the same. Annihilation. The only question is, what are we going to do about it?"

Korina pulled back slowly, her face streaked with tears, but the vacant shock in her eyes was gone. It was replaced by a familiar spark—the flicker of a problem-solver confronting an impossible equation. Her mind, shattered for a moment, was already beginning to reassemble the pieces into a new, terrifying paradigm.

"We adapt," Korina whispered, her voice gaining strength with each word. Her gaze met Ada's, "We analyze. We find a solution."

Korina's words hung in the air, a fragile shield against the abyss. *We find a solution.* It was the scholar's creed, the analyst's promise. For a single, breathless moment, it felt possible. A problem, no matter how catastrophic, was simply a set of variables waiting for the correct algorithm.

Then a violent, crimson pulse erupted from a comms data-slate on the central console. A harsh, electronic blare shattered the quiet, a sound designed for imminent catastrophe.

"What now?" Sera's voice was a low growl, her hand flying back to her sword hilt.

The existential dread vanished, replaced by the familiar, cold rush of adrenaline. A tangible threat. An enemy they could see. Erita was already moving, her face a mask of grim efficiency.

"The roof. Now."

There was no debate. They moved as one organism, a Quartet linked by a shared will to survive. Korina's hand found Ada's, her grip desperate and solid. Sera grabbed her other arm, her touch a bulwark of strength, pulling her along. They pounded up the emergency stairwell, the clang of their boots echoing in the narrow space, a frantic heartbeat driving them upward.

They burst onto the rooftop into a wall of wind. The air was thick with the scent of salt spray and the ozone-tang of decay rising from the pixelating ruin where the harbor had been. The deep, resonant hum of powerful engines vibrated through the soles of their boots, a bass note that resonated in Ada's bones.

Ada's gaze snapped to the horizon. It wasn't dozens of ships. It was an armada. A fleet larger than any nation in Kremøtoa could possibly muster hung suspended against the bruised twilight sky. Sleek, obsidian warships, identical to the ones Nividia had commanded, materialized from the shimmering static of the cascade failure, their emerald lights cutting through the gloom. They weren't attacking. They were simply arriving, a silent, terrifying testament to impossible power.

What is this? An invasion? No...this energy...I know this energy. That teal signature, the flawless rendering...that's Nividia!

Why is she back?

A shimmer of teal light coalesced near the edge of the roof. The air warped, and two figures solidified from the light. Nividia, an icon of unsettling grace in her emerald gown, stood beside a warrior whose face was a thunderous mask of shock and fury.

Janna.

Janna's gaze swept over the ruined city, the glitching coastline, and the haunted faces of her friends. Her knuckles were white where she gripped the pommel of her greataxe.

"What in the Void happened here?" Janna's voice was a choked rasp, disbelief warring with rage.

"Thorne is neutralized," Erita clipped, her eyes locked on Nividia, assessing the true perceived threat. "His network is broken. Afterward...the system had a cascade failure."

Janna's eyes widened, her gaze snapping to Ada, searching for an explanation that made sense. But Nividia wasn't looking at the devastation. She paid no mind to the crumbling city or the panicked citizens below. Her luminous violet eyes were fixed on the edge of the world, where reality frayed into a mess of corrupt data and shimmering pixels. A faint, curious smile played on her lips. She looked like a programmer who had just discovered the most fascinating bug she had ever seen.

The energy halo around her head flared with a soft, teal light. She took a slow, deliberate step forward, her gown flowing around her as if untouched by the wind. She didn't seem to be looking at a cataclysm; she was observing a data stream, a colossal rounding error that had gained physical form.

Finally, she turned. Her gaze bypassed everyone else and landed squarely on Ada. There was no accusation in her eyes, no anger. There was only a terrifying, predatory curiosity. Her voice was calm, melodic, cutting through the wind and the low hum of her fleet.

"The structural integrity of the world-mesh is unraveling," Nividia stated, not as a question, but as a simple observation. "Fascinating. This isn't a natural decay. It's a forced de-resolution. A foundational paradox."

She tilted her head, her silver hair catching the dying light.

A foundational paradox. The words were clinical, detached, but they landed in Ada's gut like a block of ice. Nividia's calm was more terrifying than any scream. It was the calm of a scientist observing a terminal diagnosis.

"You're talking about my...my body," Ada whispered, the wind stealing the words.

Nividia's violet eyes held hers, a flicker of something—not pity, but perhaps acknowledgment—in their depths. "The hardware is failing, yes. But your system built a contingency. A failsafe I have long sought, but could never approach." She lifted a slender hand, not toward the ruined harbor, but toward the sky. "Look."

Ada followed her gesture, her gaze dragged upward along with

Sera's, Korina's, and Erita's. The sight stole the breath from her lungs. The three moons, her silent system monitors, were *broken*.

Argent, the brilliant silver eye of the cosmos, was no longer a steady beacon. It flickered like a dying filament, its sharp light wavering, casting trembling, unstable shadows across the rooftop. BIOCE, the pearlescent orb of system integrity, skipped in its orbit —a stuttering frame in a corrupted animation, jerking from one position to another with an unnatural, sickening lurch.

But it was Cache that drew a raw whimper of terror from Korina. The bleeding moon, the perpetual crescent, was no longer a faint, sickly red. It burned with a ferocious, impossible crimson light, so bright it hurt to look at. And it was shrinking. Not waning, but physically contracting, collapsing in on itself as if being consumed by an internal fire. A faint, ghostly hum seemed to emanate from the sky, a low thrum of cosmic agony that vibrated deep in Ada's teeth. The air grew thin, charged with a strange magical static that made the hair on her arms stand on end.

"The moons are visual representations of core system functions," Nividia explained, her melodic voice a bizarre counterpoint to the celestial horror above them. "Argent regulates thaumaturgical energy distribution. BIOCE runs low-level integrity checks. Cache...Cache is the error log. It absorbs and contains corrupted data."

She gestured to the impossibly bright scar in the sky. "It is overloaded. Full. It is now compressing data, preparing to purge. When it vanishes, the system will suffer a fatal error. Total data loss."

Total data loss. Deletion. Not just her. Everyone. Everything.

A fragile, desperate hope flickered in the abyss of Ada's terror. A failsafe. Nividia had mentioned a failsafe. *An Oracle? A failsafe? Did I build that? Is it a part of the original code I've forgotten, buried under layers of subroutines and patches? Or...or has the world created it itself? An emergent protocol born from the will to survive?*

"The Oracle," Ada said, her voice tight. "You said there was an Oracle."

Nividia nodded, her expression turning serious, the hint of amusement finally gone from her eyes. "The Oracle of BIOS. It is not a person or a place—but both. A root-level repair protocol embedded in the world's foundational code. A hard reset terminal. It is the system's last, desperate attempt to heal itself."

The flicker of hope grew into a small, warm flame. *A reset. A repair. It was possible. They could fix this.*

"Where?" Korina's voice was barely a whisper, her fingers digging into Ada's arm for support. "Where is it?"

Nividia's holographic gaze swept over them, and the cold returned, extinguishing the flame in Ada's chest. The sheer, soul-crushing weight of her next words settled over them like a shroud.

"In the heart of the infection. The deepest part of the Ashen States."

The name landed like a physical blow. The Ashen States. The cascading failure that was devouring the southern continent. A place of pure data corruption, where the laws of physics were suggestions and the very air was sentient malware.

"It is a journey of nearly four thousand kilometers through a land that actively rewrites itself," Nividia continued, her tone flat and unforgiving. "The creatures there are not living things. They are glitches, fragments of weaponized code made flesh. They will not just kill you. They will decompile you. It will take a hundred days, if you survive the first week. And I would estimate..."

Nividia's gaze hardened, "That Cache will disappear in one-hundred and...four days."

A hundred days. Through a living hell of corrupted reality. The hope didn't just die; it was ripped out, leaving a gaping, bleeding wound of impossibility. Ada felt a dizzying wave of vertigo. Her past—the dying girl in a Sagiyama apartment—was literally trying to delete her future—the women standing beside her, their faces pale but resolute in the dying light.

"Why are you telling us this?" Ada asked, the question clawing its way out of her throat. "Why are you helping?"

"Because I cannot go," Nividia said simply. "I am a...well let's say my very presence near the Oracle would destabilize it, like bringing a magnet to a spinning hard drive. It would be...untidy." A flicker of her old amusement returned. "And frankly, I find this variable—*you*—far too interesting to allow it to be prematurely deleted."

Her gaze hardened, becoming a piercing point of command. "Your unique nature, Architect-Queen, is the key. You are an external administrator. You are the only one who can interface with the Oracle without being rejected as a foreign process. The Oracle is our only hope."

She paused, letting the finality of her words sink in.

"It's a journey you must take."

The wind howled around them, a mournful cry from a dying world. The impossible quest hung in the air, a sentence of death. But as Ada looked at the women beside her, she saw no despair. She saw Sera's jaw set in a line of unbreakable iron. She saw Erita's eyes narrow, already calculating routes and threats. She saw Korina, her terror giving way to the fierce focus of an analyst facing the ultimate problem.

Korina's hand, still clutching Ada's arm, tightened. Erita's hand found hers, then Sera's found Erita's. Their four hands clasped together, a silent, unbroken chain against the apocalypse. It wasn't a choice. It was a fact.

I will not let my past destroy them, Ada thought, a cold, hard resolve solidifying in her core. *I have to fight for my future.*

"We'll need a map," Sera said, her voice a low rumble.

"And supplies," Erita added, her tone clipped and practical.

Korina looked at Ada, her violet eyes clearing, reflecting the grim determination of the others. "And a new plan."

Ada met their gazes, one by one, feeling the current of their shared will pass between them. The fear was still there, a cold knot in her stomach, but it was no longer in control.

"We go," Ada said, her voice quiet, but absolute. "Together."

CHAPTER 2

A WARNING ACROSS THE VOID

Nividia's fleet vanished as silently as it had arrived. One moment, the harbor was a canvas of impossible obsidian warships and shimmering emerald light; the next, it was just the dark, oil-slicked water of Port Dominus under the sickly glow of the three moons. The oppressive quiet that settled over the command center was heavier than any sound. It felt like the air in a tomb.

Janna stood rigid, her knuckles white where she gripped the back of a console chair. Her gaze flickered from the empty harbor, to the strained faces of the others, and finally to Ada. "What in the Void was all that? A simulation? Architect-Queen? What does any of that mean?"

Sera took a deep, weary breath, the sound like grinding stone. "It's...complicated, Janna."

"Try me."

It was Korina who answered, her voice hollowed out by the sheer, crushing scale of their new reality. "This world, Janna...

Kremøtoa...it isn't real. Not in the way we thought. It's a construct. A program. And Ada...Ada is the one who wrote the code."

Janna's face cycled through a storm of emotions—confusion, disbelief, a flash of anger, and finally, a haunted, lost expression that mirrored the feeling in Ada's own gut. She looked at Ada, really looked at her, as if seeing her for the first time. The Architect-Queen. A gød. A programmer. A girl in a room somewhere else.

"So...everything?" Janna gestured vaguely at the city outside, at her own hands. "The sky? The sea? Me?"

"You *are* real," Ada said, the words tasting like ash in her mouth. "Your thoughts, your feelings, your choices...they're all yours. I just...I built the world you live in."

Janna sank into the chair, the fight draining out of her. The revelation was too vast, too world-shattering to process. She just stared into the middle distance, lost.

The weight of the quest settled on Ada's shoulders, a physical pressure that made her want to curl up on the floor. A hundred and four days, maximum. Four thousand kilometers through a digital hellscape. Every step a battle against a world actively trying to unwrite them. It was impossible. A slow, agonizing death sentence.

Her mind, seeking an escape, snagged on a different problem. A smaller one. Samantha. The messages replayed in her head, not as memories, but as data points.

"Hey, just checking in. You free for coffee this morning?"

That was the first message, the one that had pierced her dream of peace on the *Sea Serpent*. A simple, everyday text. Then the next one, the worried one from Kløak.

"Everything oki? Sam is getting really worried."

And the last, the one that triggered after the cascade failure, the panicked call to emergency services. The timeline felt compressed, urgent. A few days. A week at most. But she'd been here for...Ada's internal clock spun. The escape from Celgrad, the journey to Port Azure, the weeks at sea, the long, grueling trek to Rhedeon...it was nearly five months.

Five months.

The sterile, ozone scent of the damaged consoles filled her nostrils. The low hum of the machinery, once a background noise, now sounded like a countdown timer.

Five months here...is almost one week there.

A wave of vertigo washed over her, so intense she gripped the edge of the console to keep from falling. The world tilted on its axis. The numbers crunched in her head with horrifying, irrefutable logic. *A time dilation.* A massive, terrifying time dilation.

"Argent's light," Sera was saying, her voice a low murmur as she looked at a map with Erita. "The Ashen States are almost the size of the Empire now. The terrain alone..."

Ada wasn't listening. Her breath hitched. The problem wasn't the distance. It wasn't the monsters. It was the clock. A clock she couldn't see, ticking in a world an entire reality away.

The paramedics aren't coming in a few hours, Kremøtoa time, her mind screamed. *They're not on their way. They're there. They're at the door. RIGHT NOW.*

"**Stop**," Ada gasped, the word tearing from her throat.

The others turned, their discussion cut short by the raw panic in her voice. Sera's hand went to her sword hilt. Erita's eyes narrowed.

"Ada? What is it?" Korina asked, stepping closer, her face etched with concern.

"The time," Ada said, her voice shaking, her gaze unfocused as she stared at the flickering red crescent of Cache in the sky. "Nividia was wrong. We don't have a hundred days."

"What are you talking about?" Erita's voice was sharp, cutting. "The moon isn't going to just fall out of the sky tomorrow."

"No," Ada choked out, her heart hammering against her ribs. "It's not about the moon. It's about my body. On Earth." She looked at them, her eyes wide with a terror that dwarfed everything they had faced before. "My friend, Samantha...her messages...they span almost a full week of time on Earth...I've been here for five months."

Korina's breath caught. The implications hit her first, the horrifying math unfolding behind her eyes.

"A week there is five and a half months here," Ada whispered, the horrifying truth laid bare. "One day on Earth is...three and a half weeks in Kremøtoa."

Silence. Utter, profound silence. The hum of the consoles seemed to roar in the sudden void.

"We don't have one hundred and four days," Ada's voice cracked, raw with a new, frantic urgency that bordered on hysteria. "We have less than five days. Five days before they unplug me. Before all of this..." She gestured wildly at the room, the city, at their faces. "...gets deleted."

The air in the command center turned sharp, each breath a sliver of glass. Five days. The number hung in the space between them, a guillotine blade suspended by a fraying thread. Janna stared, speechless. Silas looked ashen. Sera, Korina, and Erita formed a tight, protective triangle around Ada, their faces a mixture of horror and disbelief.

Ada began to pace, a caged animal in a crumbling prison of her own design. The smooth durasteel floor felt like hot sand. *They don't get it. They're still thinking about a journey, about supplies, about a war. There is no war if we don't exist.*

"I have to send a message," Ada announced, her voice tight, strained. She stopped pacing and spun to face them, a manic, desperate light burning in her eyes. "Not in a dream. Not a whisper through Kløak. I have to force a connection—***now***."

Erita's arms crossed over her chest, a wall of pure, undiluted skepticism. "And how do you plan on doing that? The last time Kløak connected, it left you a wreck for hours. You want to *force* it? What if you drain yourself completely? What if you crash the system *here*? We need you for the journey, Ada. We can't afford to lose you before we even take the first step."

"What journey?" Ada's voice rose, cracking with frustration. "Erita, there is no journey if they pull the plug! Every second we stand here debating, the clock is ticking down. Those paramedics on Earth aren't having a coffee break. They're walking up the stairs to my apartment *right now!*"

Sera stepped forward, placing a hand on Ada's shoulder. The touch was meant to be steadying, a grounding weight, but it felt like a restraint. "Ada, is this even possible without hurting you? Without...breaking something?" Her low, steady voice rumbled with concern, a stark contrast to Ada's frantic energy.

They think I'm being reckless. The thought was a hot spike of anger and fear. *They don't understand—there's no time for caution! I can't let them pull the plug. I can't let my past erase them.*

"It's going to hurt," Ada admitted, meeting Sera's worried gaze. "But being deleted will hurt more."

Korina had been silent, her eyes darting between Ada and the holographic interface of Obsidian, which she held clutched to her chest. Her fingers flew across the surface, pulling up strings of arcane-looking code, data streams represented as flowing rivers of violet light.

"Theoretically..." Korina's voice was quiet, but it cut through the tension. Everyone turned to her. "Kløak is a system relay. The data flow is structured to be unidirectional—from Earth to Kremøtoa. Pushing a message back would be like trying to force a river to flow uphill. The energy cost would be...exponential."

"See?" Erita gestured toward Korina. "Exponential. Meaning it could kill you."

"But," Korina continued, her eyes fixed on the data stream, a flicker of intellectual fire overriding her fear, "the protocol isn't a solid wall. It's a valve. If we could isolate the specific data stream Kløak uses for transmission...if we could create a buffer to handle the energy feedback and route it away from Ada's core consciousness...she might be right. It might be possible to inject a small, compressed data packet back through the connection."

Erita let out a sharp, disbelieving laugh. "A 'small packet'? What are you going to send, a postcard? 'Wish you were here, please don't delete my universe'?"

"Something like that," Ada snapped, her patience gone. She pulled away from Sera's grip and faced Erita, her slight frame radiating an intensity that made the spymaster take an involuntary step back. "I need to send a single command. Something that will delay them. Something to buy us time on their end."

The room fell silent again. The sheer audacity of it, the impossible, gød-like command spoken with such desperate conviction, hung in the charged air.

Erita's shoulders slumped slightly, her skepticism finally cracking under the weight of Ada's terrifying certainty. The fight wasn't about recklessness anymore; it was about the lack of any other option.

Sera's hand found Ada's shoulder again, but this time it wasn't a restraint. It was support. She looked from Korina's focused expression to Erita's reluctant frown, and finally back to Ada. Her gaze searched Ada's face, not for a plan, but for the conviction to see it through.

Ada met her eyes, letting all the terror, the desperation, and the fierce, unyielding love she felt for them pour into her gaze. "I can't lose you," she whispered, the words raw, stripped of all artifice. "Any of you. *I won't.*"

That was it. That was the answer Sera needed. She gave a single, firm nod.

"Alright," Erita sighed, running a hand through her short, golden hair. The tension in her posture finally broke. "Void, it's a terrible plan. But it's the only one we've got. What do you need from us, Ada?"

A frantic, electric energy seized the command center. The debate was over; the impossible plan was now the only plan. Ada moved to the main console, the heart of Thorne's fallen empire, and pulled a secondary data-slate from a port. She slid it across the cool metal surface to Korina.

"Obsidian is too valuable to risk a feedback surge," Ada said, her voice sharp and focused. "We'll use this one as a buffer. I need you to isolate Kløak's data-stream—find its signature and create a recursive loop to hold the connection open when it pings."

Korina nodded, her usual academic excitement replaced by a grim, focused intensity. She plugged the spare slate into Obsidian, her fingers a blur as she partitioned its memory and built a virtual sandbox. Sera and Erita flanked them, their stances betraying a tension that went beyond guarding against a physical threat. They were guarding a miracle, a desperate, last-ditch prayer against the encroaching void. Janna and Silas stood back, watching the two women who now held the fate of their world in their hands.

"Ready," Korina breathed, her eyes locked on the complex, flowing script that represented the command center's data flow.

Ada took a deep breath, the air thick with the metallic scent of ozone, and placed her hands over the spare slate. She didn't touch it. Instead, a luminous, violet energy bled from her palms, bathing the device in an ethereal glow. The lights in the command center dimmed, the humming of the life support systems dropping to a low growl as Ada drew power directly from the tower's core.

Come on, come on, just let me through...

She closed her eyes, diving into the system's architecture. She wasn't just observing the code; she *was* the code. She found Kløak's signature, a faint, pulsing thread of alien data, and held it. "Now, Rina. Open the conduit."

Korina's command hit the system. A high-frequency hum filled the air, rising in pitch until it was a physical pressure against their eardrums. Ada felt the connection snap into place, not as code, but as a tangible, physical sensation. It was like reaching out with a phantom limb across an impossible, cosmic distance and feeling the faintest touch in return. The exhilaration was a jolt, a surge of pure, unadulterated hope. For a breathtaking second, she could feel the other side—a network humming with the traffic of a billion devices, a world away.

"It's working!" Korina gasped, her face illuminated by the slate's violet light. "The stream is stable!"

Ada focused her intent, compressing her message into a single, tiny packet of data. A simple, desperate command: [Execute:

KLØAK_Override.InitiateCall]. It was a long shot, a hail-mary pass into the digital ether, but it was all she had. She prepared to inject it, to force the river to flow uphill.

Then, a new window materialized on the slate's screen. The text wasn't in the angular script of Kremøtoa. It was in a clean, sans-serif font she knew with a soul-deep loathing. *San-Fransesco.*

[Authentication Required: Please sign in with your Apell Account to authorize this device.]

No.

The thought was a physical blow. The phantom connection, the beautiful, fragile thread stretching across reality, shattered. The high-frequency hum died with a harsh, digital *snap*, like a bone breaking. A jarring emptiness crashed down on Ada, the loss of the connection leaving a phantom ache in her very code. The lights in the command center flickered violently before returning to their normal, steady hum.

It was over.

A choked, guttural sound tore from Ada's throat, half sob, half curse. She snatched her hands back from the slate as if it were white-hot.

"Ada? What was that? The connection just...collapsed," Korina's voice was laced with confusion and fear. She stared at the alien text on the screen, her brow furrowed. "I don't recognize this protocol. It's not Imperial. It's not...anything I've ever seen."

Ada stared at the two simple lines of text on the screen, and a rage colder and deeper than any she had felt for Thorne or Kraus Valerius washed over her. It was the impotent fury of a thousand debug sessions, of a million lines of beautiful code rendered useless by a corporate mandate.

No! An authentication wall? Of course. Apell. The connection must've been trying to upload to Sam's phone by FTP. The name on the screen wasn't the one she knew, but the predatory, proprietary logic was unmistakable. *They walled off everything. In a world of open standards, they built a prison and called it an ecosystem. This is the stupidest, most arbitrary reason for our world to end.*

"Ada?" Sera's voice was low, laced with worry.

Ada finally looked up from the slate, her eyes burning with unshed, furious tears. She met Korina's questioning gaze, the hope draining from her face to be replaced by a hollow despair.

"It's a closed system, Rina," Ada said, her voice rough, defeated. "A proprietary firewall. It's not just code; it's tied to a physical chip on her device. The message isn't getting blocked by a complex algorithm. It's being blocked by a login screen. Samantha's phone doesn't recognize our data-slate, and it wants her password before it will accept any connection—the connection is trying a direct upload."

She let out a bitter, humorless laugh that died in her throat. "We can rewrite the laws of reality, but we can't get past a corporate paywall. We can't just hack it." She looked around at the faces of her lovers, her friends, her family—all staring at her, waiting for a solution she didn't have. "We're completely locked out."

Locked out. The word was an absurdity, a cosmic joke delivered with the sterile, passionless indifference of corporate design. Ada stared at the authentication prompt, a monument to proprietary greed standing between her world and its continued existence. A cold, quiet rage began to build in her chest, a pressure that felt like it could crack her ribs. *All this power, the ability to bend reality to her will, and she was being thwarted by a password field.*

"There has to be another way," Sera's voice was a low growl of frustration, echoing Ada's own.

"There isn't," Erita countered, her arms crossed. "If the phone won't accept the connection, it won't accept it. We're shouting at a locked door."

*A locked door...*Ada's gaze drifted from the hateful Apell logo on the screen to the complex, flowing code that represented Korina's Lynx monitor, still idling on Obsidian's display. The little pixel-cat was curled up, sleeping peacefully. A self-contained, persistent script. An executable that ran independently, always present. *But Erita is wrong. We're not shouting at the guest's door. We're shouting from the landlord's own house.*

A spark ignited in the frozen depths of her fury. It was a wild, defiant, and deeply arrogant idea. *It was perfect.*

"You're right," Ada said, her voice suddenly calm, cutting through the despair. The others turned to her, surprised by the abrupt shift. "We can't get through the phone's door." She met Korina's gaze, a new, dangerous light in her eyes. "So we'll build a new window on my own desktop."

Korina blinked, her mind racing to catch up. "Your...desktop... monitor? On your computer? On Earth?"

"I am the root user," Ada said, the words a declaration of faith. She tapped the screen of the spare data-slate. "The connection failed, but for a microsecond, it established a handshake. Not with the phone, but with the machine it's plugged into. My machine. If I can't send a message *to* the phone, I can leave a message *on* the computer. A warning. Something persistent. Something they can't possibly ignore."

The sheer, insane ambition of it hung in the air. Erita stared as if Ada had proposed to punch a hole in the sky.

But Korina's eyes widened, the fire of intellectual passion returning. "Like the Lynx," she breathed, her gaze darting to Obsidian. "You want to write a persistent application directly into your computer's core operating system...from here."

"Exactly," Ada confirmed. "We'll use your framework. Your Lynx is elegant, self-sustaining—it's the perfect chassis. But we'll need to strip it down, recompile it for a completely different architecture, and force it through that tiny handshake window before the authentication wall slams shut."

It was a task that bordered on the impossible, a feat of cosmic hacking. Without another word, they bent over the data-slates. The command center faded away, the world shrinking to the glowing violet screens. Sera and Erita stood guard, silent sentinels at the edge of creation.

Ada became the conduit, the raw power source. She held the connection open with sheer force of will, a sliver of a crack in the dam of reality. The strain was immense, a crushing weight that made the air thick and tasted of ozone. Sweat beaded on her temples. Korina became the architect. Her fingers flew across Obsidian's holographic interface, not just typing, but sculpting. She took the beautiful, whimsical code of her Lynx and tore it apart, rebuilding it into a raw, brutally efficient piece of malware designed to do one thing: **display a message and refuse to be closed.**

Lines of code scrolled past at a speed no human eye could follow. It was a symphony of intellect and power, a frantic, desperate dance on the edge of oblivion. Ada pushed, her entire being focused on forcing the stream of data across the void.

Korina refined, her mind a razor, cutting away every non-essential byte, optimizing every command for a system she couldn't even see.

Ada felt the resistance from the other side, the fundamental laws of two different realities pushing back. It felt like trying to force a key into the wrong lock. *It's not enough. Just executing commands isn't enough. I have to...I have to become the source.* She stopped thinking in terms of sending and receiving. She reached deeper, past the user interface of her own Admin powers, and for the first time, she began to *write*.

Suddenly, a deep, resonant **CLICK** echoed through her, not as a sound, but as a feeling in the core of her soul. It was the heavy, satisfying thud of a massive tumbler falling into place. A lock she didn't even know existed had just sprung open. The resistance vanished. The flow of data became effortless, a part of her.

On Obsidian's screen, the final program materialized. It was a simple, stark-white warning box, the kind from an older, forgotten era of computing. The text was blunt:

> **[{SYSTEM WARNING: CRITICAL BIOLOGICAL EVENT IMMINENT}]**
> **USER: ADA_LYNX | STATUS: ALIVE | VITAL SIGNS: STABLE (INDUCED STASIS)**
> **DO NOT DISCONNECT FROM POWER. DO NOT ATTEMPT PHYSICAL REVIVAL.**
> **DISCONNECTION OF PRIMARY SYSTEM WILL RESULT IN CATASTROPHIC, IRREVERSIBLE BIOLOGICAL TERMINATION.**
> **I AM OKAY. I AM SAFE.**
> **—ADA**

Below the text, a tiny, animated pixel Lynx cat, identical to Korina's, playfully chased a swarm of glitching, pixelated moths that always stayed just out of its reach.

"Push it," Ada breathed, her voice a raw whisper.

Korina's finger tapped the final command. For a heartbeat, the image remained. Then, with a silent flash, the warning box vanished from Obsidian's screen. It was gone. Sent.

The connection severed. The power receded. Ada swayed, catching herself on the console, a profound exhaustion washing over her. Korina slumped in her chair, her breath coming in ragged gasps. They looked at each other, their faces pale in the steady, normal light of the command center.

Korina's hand found Ada's, her fingers lacing through hers. A silent, shared acknowledgment of what they had just done. They couldn't know if it had worked, if anyone would see it. But they had thrown their stone into the darkness.

"Moths?" Korina asked, her voice quiet, tired, but full of a soft curiosity. "Why moths...I didn't put that in...?"

Ada managed a faint smile, her gaze distant, remembering a different life. "An old hacker inside joke. They represent computer bugs. You can spend all night trying to fix the code, chasing them down, but there's always one more you can't quite catch." She squeezed Korina's hand, the small, intimate gesture a stark contrast to the world-altering power they had just wielded. "They were my favorites, back then...they're like...gothic butterflies."

CHAPTER 3

CHERRY BLOSSOMS AND HORROR

The phone rang, a frantic, digital shriek in the suffocating quiet of the car. It drilled into Samantha's ear for the fourth, fifth, sixth time before the inevitable click and the dispassionate voice of the automated system.

"The person you are trying to reach is not available..."

Samantha snapped the phone shut, the plastic groaning under the pressure of her grip. Her own hands trembled. A knot of pure, cold dread tightened in her stomach, a physical thing coiling in her gut. *Please be okay, Ada. Please just be asleep.*

"Anything?" Hijiri Lynx's voice was a thin, wavering thread, stretched to its breaking point. Her knuckles were bone-white on the steering wheel, a stark contrast to the cheap, dark plastic.

"Straight to voicemail. Again."

The rhythmic pulse of the GPS was the only other sound, a calm, synthetic heartbeat counting down the meters to Ada's apartment. Its screen cast a sterile blue and red glow across the dashboard, illuminating the fine lines of stress etched around Hijiri's mouth.

"Maybe she's just...in the zone? You know how she gets. Her new project..." The words were a desperate prayer, a flimsy shield against a possibility neither of them wanted to name.

"Mom, it's been twelve hours since my last text. She always answers you. Always." Samantha's voice was sharper than she intended, honed by a fear that was rapidly curdling into panic. *She always answers for her mom. Something is wrong.*

The Sagiyama night blurred past the windows, a smear of neon and taillights. Each red light was an agony, each second a fresh twist of the knot in Samantha's stomach. She fumbled with her phone again, her thumb slick with sweat as it skidded across the glass screen. She tried to type, but the letters swam, a jumble of incoherent characters. *Jutd anser. Ada plss.*

Useless.

Giving up, she stabbed at the microphone icon, the small vibration a minor shock against her palm. She held the phone to her mouth, the words spilling out in a rush of raw, unvarnished fear.

"Ada? Everything okay...?" Her voice cracked, a fragile sound against the city's drone. "I'M STARTING TO GET REALLY SCARED. We haven't heard from you. Your mom is with me. We're coming over. Please Ada! Please just text or CALL back so we don't call 119... Please..."

She sent the message, the small *whoosh* of the upload sounding like a final, desperate flare shot into an empty sky. She stared at the screen, at the little audio file sitting there, unanswered. Beside her, Hijiri let out a soft, choked sound, a mother's fear made audible.

The familiar side streets of Sagiyama blurred past the

window, a smear of convenience store lights and darkened residential homes. Normally, this drive was a comfort, a route etched into her memory from years of friendship. Tonight, every corner felt like a threat, every shadow a portent. The air in the small sedan was thick and recycled, tasting of plastic and the metallic tang of fear.

"She was doing so well, Sam," Hijiri's whisper was barely audible over the hum of the engine. "She was so excited about this...this world she was building. She said it was safe there..."

The word *'safe'* landed like a stone in the pit of Samantha's stomach. It brought back the ghost of another memory—the smell of antiseptic, the stark white room, the hollow look in Ada's eyes after...after everything. *Please...not again...not that...*

"She is okay," Samantha said, forcing a conviction she did not feel. She said it for Hijiri as much as for herself. "We're going to get there, and she'll be passed out on her keyboard with ramen spilled all over her desk, and she'll be pissed we woke her up."

Hijiri managed a weak, watery smile that didn't reach her eyes. "I'd give anything for her to be pissed at me right now."

"In two hundred meters, turn right," the GPS announced, its voice devoid of emotion.

The turn brought them onto Ada's street. It was quiet. Deceptively normal. A few cars lined the curb, their windows dark. The apartment complex rose before them, a simple, three-story building that looked exactly as it always had. That normalcy was the most terrifying thing of all.

"You have arrived at your destination."

The car slid into a parking space. For a moment, neither of them moved. The engine ticked as it cooled. The silence in the car was now absolute, a heavy blanket that smothered thought.

Samantha could hear her own heart, a frantic drumming against her ribs.

Finally, Hijiri fumbled with the clasp of her seatbelt, her movements jerky and uncoordinated. She pulled her keys from the ignition, the small metal teeth clinking together with a sound that was unnaturally loud.

They got out, the cool night air a shock against Samantha's flushed skin. They walked toward the entrance, their footsteps echoing on the pavement. Side-by-side, a mother and a best friend, marching toward a closed door that held all of their hopes and all of their fears. Hijiri's hand shook as she sorted through her keys, searching for the one that would unlock her daughter's apartment.

The key scraped in the lock, the sound of metal on metal a raw nerve in the suffocating silence. Hijiri's hand trembled so violently that Samantha took the key ring from her, her own fingers cold and clumsy as she found the right one. The deadbolt slid back with a heavy, final-sounding *thunk.*

The apartment was still. A profound, unnatural stillness that felt heavier than simple quiet. The air was cool and tasted of recycled air and the faint, ghostly scent of Ada's jasmine tea. A half-empty mug sat on the small table by the door, a silent testament to a moment interrupted.

"Ada? We're here, sweetheart," Hijiri called out, her voice thin and reedy. It was swallowed by the quiet, leaving no echo.

"*Ada!?*" Samantha's voice was louder, sharper, laced with a command that begged for a response.

Nothing.

A soft, blue-violet glow pulsed from the open doorway at the end of the short hall—the computer room. The den. The sanctuary. Samantha's heart hammered against her ribs, a frantic prisoner.

They moved toward the light, their steps hesitant, as if approaching the scene of an accident.

And then they saw her.

Ada was slumped in the custom-built immersion chair, her head tilted back at an unnatural angle against the headrest. Her face was pale, almost translucent in the glow of the massive monitor, her lips tinged with a faint blue. Her hands rested limply on the armrests—her chest barely rising up and down. She wasn't sleeping. This was something else. Something absolute.

The world tilted on its axis, a dizzying lurch that stole the air from Samantha's lungs. A raw, guttural sound escaped Hijiri, a mangled sob of a name. "Ada..."

She fumbled for her phone, her thumb stabbing at the screen. "119...I'm calling..." Her voice was a choked, panicked whisper.

"Wait!" The word tore from Samantha's throat, raw and instinctive. Her eyes, wide with horror, had snagged on the monitor that framed Ada's still form.

It wasn't a screensaver. It was a single, stark window of text, glowing in a calm, authoritative green font against a black background.

[{SYSTEM WARNING: CRITICAL BIOLOGICAL EVENT IMMINENT}]
USER: ADA_LYNX | STATUS: ALIVE | VITAL SIGNS: STABLE (INDUCED STASIS)
DO NOT DISCONNECT FROM POWER. DO NOT ATTEMPT PHYSICAL REVIVAL.
DISCONNECTION OF PRIMARY SYSTEM WILL RESULT IN CATASTROPHIC, IRREVERSIBLE BIOLOGICAL TERMINATION.

I AM OKAY. I AM SAFE.
— ADA

“What? Samantha, she’s barely breathing!” Hijiri cried, her voice cracking with hysteria. The emergency call was connecting.

“Mom, *hang up*! Look!” Samantha pointed a trembling finger at the screen. Below the stark warning text, in the bottom right corner, a tiny, animated pixel-art cat—a little violet lynx—was curled up, sleeping peacefully. As she watched, a few glitchy, pixelated artifacts, like tiny digital moths, flickered near the edge of the window. The cat’s ears twitched. It sat up, stretched, and then playfully pounced, batting one of the ‘moths’ into non-existence with a triumphant flick of its ears.

The moth bugs.

The memory hit Samantha with the force of a physical blow. A summer night, years ago, huddled around a tiny CRT monitor in Ada’s childhood bedroom. Ada, barely a teenager, had been coding her first simple game and had created a bug she couldn’t fix—a cluster of pixels that flitted randomly across the screen. “They’re not bugs,” Samantha had joked, “they’re moth bugs. They’re attracted to the screen light.” Ada had laughed, a rare, unburdened sound, and coded a little pixel cat to chase them away.

She’s not dead. Oh god, she’s not dead. But what is this? That cat...the “moth bugs”...no one else would know that. It’s a message. It’s really her.

The low, steady hum of the supercomputer’s cooling fans filled the silence, a mechanical breath in place of Ada’s.

“That’s crazy! It’s a machine! We have to get help!” Hijiri insisted, her gaze fixed on her daughter’s placid face.

Samantha stepped between her and the chair, her mind racing, trying to stitch together the impossible.

The decade of work. The literal life savings. The obsessive talk of a fully immersive, persistent world.

"And *what* are they gonna do, *Mom?*" Samantha's voice was tight, urgent. She reached out and gently took the phone from Hijiri's hand, ending the call. "The paramedics?—They're going to see her like this, see *that,*" she gestured to the impossible machine, a behemoth of custom-forged metal and bundled cables, "and they're going to do exactly what the screen says not to. They'll unplug it."

The full weight of the words—*IRREVERSIBLE BIOLOGICAL TERMINATION*—crashed down on her.

"Mom—we can't turn it off." Samantha's voice dropped, filled with a terrifying, resolute vigor. She looked from the message, to the whimsical cat, to the still, pale girl in the chair. "I think she actually did it."

Hijiri stared at her, her face a mask of confusion and grief. "Did what?"

Samantha met her gaze, the impossible truth forming on her lips. "I think...I think she actually uploaded her consciousness."

"You think she did what?" Hijiri's voice was a fractured whisper, her face a canvas of disbelief and dawning horror.

"The immersion," Samantha said, her gaze fixed on the glowing screen. She gestured toward a smaller, secondary monitor tucked beside the main display. It showed a series of calmly scrolling graphs and numbers. "She built a failsafe. A biofeedback loop. She showed me the schematics once."

They crept closer, drawn into the violet-blue light of the den. The air was thick, heavy with the scent of ozone and the low, thrumming hum of the supercomputer. It was the sound of a living thing breathing, a mechanical lung that filled the apartment. Hijiri paced behind the chair, her footsteps frantic on the hardwood floor, a frantic counter-rhythm to the machine's steady pulse. "A biofeedback...what does that mean? Samantha, her skin is cold!"

"It means she's monitoring herself," Samantha murmured, her eyes scanning the data. A green line traced a perfect, rhythmic peak and valley. **HEART RATE: 45 BPM.** A blue wave flowed in a slow, hypnotic pattern. **RESPIRATION: 6 BREATHS/MIN.** Below them, a complex, multicolored graph spiked and ebbed with furious, incomprehensible activity. **NEURAL ACTIVITY: 97% | DELTA & THETA WAVE SUPPRESSION ACTIVE.** A soft, almost inaudible *beep* emanated from a small speaker, a sound so calm it was chilling. *Her heart rate is too slow. Slower than deep sleep. And her brain...what does that even mean? It's not sleep. It's...stasis. Controlled. Deliberate.*

"It's not right," Hijiri muttered, her voice choked with tears. She ran a hand over Ada's hair, her touch desperate. "We have to call a doctor. *An ambulance.* They can help her."

"They can't," Samantha said, her voice firm, though a tremor ran through her. She turned from the screen, her eyes pleading. "Mom, look at this. Does this look like anything a doctor has ever seen? They'll see a girl in a coma hooked up to a...a bomb. They'll pull the plug. The screen says it will kill her."

"But we can't just leave her here!" The words burst from Hijiri, a raw cry of a mother's helplessness. "She's just...lying here! What if she's in pain? What if she's trapped?"

Samantha felt that same helplessness, a crushing weight in her chest. She could see Ada, right there, inches away, but it felt like she was looking at her from across an impossible gulf. She was an astronaut lost in the void, and this machine was her only tether. A tether that warned them not to pull.

Her gaze drifted back to the monitor. Her eyes caught on a new detail. In the bottom-left corner of the biofeedback screen, a small window had appeared. It hadn't been there a moment ago. A thin, yellow border pulsed with a gentle, insistent rhythm.

Samantha leaned closer, her breath fogging the glass.

[BIOLOGICAL RESERVES: 78% AND DECLINING.]

A cold dread, sharper and more immediate than before, pierced through her shock. The words were clinical, detached, but their meaning was brutally simple.

"Oh, no," she breathed.

"What? What is it?" Hijiri rushed to her side, her frantic energy momentarily focused.

Samantha pointed a trembling finger at the new text. "It's a countdown."

[PROJECTED DEPLETION TIME: 104.3 HOURS]
[RECOMMENDED ACTION: NUTRITIONAL IV DRIP]

The knot in Samantha's stomach tightened until she felt she might be sick. It wasn't just that Ada was gone. It was that her body was still here, a machine left running, a machine that was slowly, methodically running out of fuel. *How long has it been since she ate? Since she had a drink of water?* She had been so consumed with her project, skipping meals, existing on caffeine and instant ramen. It could have been a day. Maybe more.

"Nutritional...IV...?" Hijiri read the words aloud, her voice hollow. "That's...that's a hospital thing. That's what they do in hospitals."

"And we can't take her to one." The finality of it settled over Samantha, cold and absolute. They were trapped. They couldn't call for help, but doing nothing was a death sentence. A slow one, measured out in percentages and hours by the very machine that held Ada captive.

The steady, placid beep of the heart monitor suddenly sounded monstrous, a clock ticking down to zero. The hum of the computer was no longer a breath; it was the growl of a predator, jealously guarding its prey. They were no longer just observers of an impossible phenomenon. They were its unwilling caretakers. And the clock was running.

104.3 hours. Four days. A little more. The coppery taste of adrenaline flooded Samantha's mouth. The machine's hum was a low growl in her ears, the beep of the heart monitor a metronome counting down the seconds of Ada's life.

"An IV," Hijiri whispered, her hands fluttering uselessly at her sides. "We need to get her to a hospital. Samantha, we have to." She reached for her phone again, her face a mask of frantic resolve.

"***No.***" The word was sharp, a shard of ice in the warm, humming room. Samantha stepped in front of her, blocking her path to the door.

"Samantha, don't be foolish! Look at her!" Hijiri's voice rose, cracking with hysteria. "This isn't a game! We can't just...leave her here to starve!"

"And what do you think will happen if we call them?" Samantha's own voice was low, tight with a desperate, terrifying clarity. *Think. Don't panic. Think like Ada would.* "A doctor will walk in here. They'll see a girl in a coma, her vitals suppressed to almost nothing, hooked up to a machine they can't possibly understand. They won't see a failsafe. They'll see the cause. And they will unplug her."

The words hung in the air, stark and ugly. The police would be even worse. *They'll think it's a suicide attempt. Some kind of tech-assisted...Gød, no.* They would see the warning on the screen as the ramblings of a disturbed mind. They would break the one, single, explicit rule Ada had left for them. *They wouldn't be helping. They would be pulling the plug on her universe.*

Hijiri stared at her, her eyes wide and pleading, the fight draining out of her, replaced by a profound, bottomless confusion. "But...what do we do? We can't...we can't do *nothing*."

A cold resolve solidified in Samantha's gut. Fear was a useless luxury now. They had one chance. One long shot. One person on the entire planet who might see this not as madness, but as a problem to be solved. One person who spoke Ada's language of logic boards and power cycling.

She pulled her own phone from her pocket. The cool, solid weight of it in her trembling hand was a small anchor in the storm of her panic. Her thumb, slick with sweat, swiped across the screen, scrolling past names until it found the one she was looking for.

Kenji.

The name glowed on the screen, a simple, familiar contact that now held the weight of a world. He was an figurative ocean away, probably asleep, blissfully unaware that his entire world was about to be upended. *Please pick up, Kenji. Please, please be the genius Ada always said you were...Please understand.*

With a surge of desperate hope, she pressed the call button.

The dialing tone echoed in the silent apartment, each synthetic ring ratcheting the tension higher. One ring. Two. Hijiri watched her, her breath held, her face a mixture of bewilderment and a new, fragile hope. Three rings. Samantha's heart hammered against her ribs. *Come on, little brother. Wake up.*

Four rings.

"Moshi moshi...?"

The voice that answered was thick with sleep, a low, gravelly murmur that was so jarringly normal it almost made Samantha laugh. It was the voice of someone ripped from a deep, peaceful sleep, not one prepared for a reality-shattering crisis.

Samantha's own breath hitched. The words she had rehearsed in her head turned to ash in her mouth. All that came out was a raw, unfiltered plea.

"Kenji..." Her voice was a ragged whisper. "It's me. Sam."

A pause on the other end. The sound of shuffling, of a mind slowly booting up. *"Sam? What time is it? Is everything...?"*

"I need your help." The words tumbled out, tripping over each other in their haste. "It's about Ada." She took a deep, shuddering breath, her eyes locked on Ada's still, pale form in the chair. "You're the only one I know who might...who might understand—please! Come to Ada's apartment...and bring a nutritional IV bag or two, *please!...*"

CHAPTER 4

THE HUNDRED DAY TREK

The air in the command center crackled with a nervous energy. Not the frantic, chaotic energy of battle, but the taut, unsettling stillness of a held breath. Ada stared at the holographic map of Kremøtoa projected above the war table, its vibrant colors now marred by a spreading stain of corrupted data – the Ashen States. A thin, wavering line, highlighted in pulsating violet, stretched from their current position in Port Dominus across nearly four thousand kilometers of hostile territory, a path fraught with peril.

"The Oracle's location, according to the fragments of lore I've managed to recover, lies deep within the Ashen States," Nividia's voice, projected from the shimmering, violet-tinted holo-comm, echoed through the room. Her usual tone of playful arrogance was replaced by an unsettling gravity. "The coordinates, as you can see, are...problematic."

Korina, her face pale and drawn, stood beside the map, a slender finger tracing the perilous path. "We must first navigate a new flora entity I would call 'the Malware Swamps'. The recent Cascade Failure event has...accelerated their growth." Her voice was tight, strained. "They now span nearly a hundred and fifty kilometers, a festering morass of corrupted code and...and things." She shuddered, her gaze fixed on the swirling, sickly green pixels that marked the swamp's expansion across what was once the fertile southern borderlands of the Ehxcehl Empire, now dangerously encroaching on the Intellective States.

"Then comes the Wordæus Theocracy," Erita said, her voice a low, clipped whisper. "A land of fanatics, ruled by an Empress who views any deviation from her dogma as heresy. Not exactly a welcoming committee."

"And finally," Korina continued, her voice barely above a whisper, "the Ashen States themselves. A wasteland of glitching terrain, corrupted data streams, and...and creatures born from the world's decay. The Glitch-Wyrms, the Data Phantoms, the...the things that carve entire sectors from the land." She trailed off, her gaze fixed on the swirling, chaotic mess of pixels that marked the Ashen States, a physical manifestation of Kremøtoa's slow, inevitable death.

A heavy silence settled over the room. Admiral Silas, his face grim, cleared his throat. "Even with Nividia's fleet, the journey is... ambitious. The Theocracy's naval defenses are formidable, and the Ashen States...well, no one's ever returned from a direct incursion into that blighted wasteland."

Sera, her arms crossed over her broad chest, let out a low grunt. "Not to mention the *things* that live there. Creatures born from corrupted code, twisted by the world's decay. Even the Aegis Order, in its prime, wouldn't risk a direct confrontation with those abominations."

Nividia's image shimmered in the holo-comm. "My lore on the Oracle is...fragmented. Legends, whispers, half-remembered prophecies. There's no guarantee it even exists. And even if it does...there's no guarantee it can help."

Ada felt a cold dread creeping up her spine. The journey ahead was a suicide mission, a desperate gamble against impossible odds. Four thousand kilometers of hostile territory, infested with monsters born from her own dying code. The thought made her stomach churn.

She looked at the faces around the table. Sera, her jaw set, her eyes burning with a fierce determination. Korina, pale but resolute, her fingers still tracing the impossible path on the map. Erita, her expression unreadable, her gaze fixed on the shimmering holo-comm. Janna, stoic and unwavering, her presence a solid anchor in the swirling chaos. Silas, his face etched with worry, but his loyalty unwavering. And Nividia, her image flickering in the violet light, her usual playful arrogance replaced by a grim acceptance of the daunting task ahead.

Ada took a deep breath, forcing down the rising panic. She had brought them here, to this impossible world, to this desperate fight for survival. She had made mistakes, terrible mistakes, but she would not abandon them now. Not when Kremøtoa, her creation, her sanctuary, was on the brink of collapse. Not when the people she loved, the people she had sworn to protect, needed her more than ever.

"We go," Ada said, her voice firm, unwavering. "We find the Oracle. We fix this world."

The warehouse, once Thorne's opulent headquarters, now buzzed with focused activity, a hive of preparation for the impossible journey ahead. Crates of supplies lined the walls, weapons gleamed under the harsh fluorescent lights, and the air hummed with the low thrum of arcane energy.

Erita, moving with her usual feline grace, directed the flow of supplies with crisp efficiency. "Silas, those rations need to be compartmentalized. We'll need to distribute the weight evenly across the packs." Her voice, though still laced with its characteristic cynicism, held a new note of urgency.

Silas, his face grim, nodded curtly. "Aye, Swift. Already on it." He gestured towards a group of Azure Rose recruits meticulously packing crates with protein bars, dried fruit, and concentrated nutrient paste. "We're also loading up on Korina's new water purifiers. Those things can make a potable brew out of just about anything."

Erita's lips curled into a wry smile. "Let's hope so. I'd rather not die of dysentery in a blighted swamp, thank you very much." She turned her attention to a stack of bulky, metallic suits. "And how are those environmental suits holding up?"

"Korina's done a remarkable job, considering the circumstances," Silas replied, his voice filled with grudging respect. "They won't offer full protection against the data corruption, but they should mitigate the worst of it. At least long enough for us to get the hell out of dodge."

Across the warehouse, Sera and Janna worked in

companionable silence, their movements a synchronized dance of preparation. Sera meticulously sharpened her twin blades, the oiled steel gleaming under the harsh light. The rhythmic rasp of the whetstone against metal echoed through the room, a steady, reassuring counterpoint to the chaotic activity around them. Janna, meanwhile, carefully inspected her heavy battle-axe, her thick fingers tracing the worn leather of the grip, her expression thoughtful.

"This isn't going to be like our usual skirmishes, Sera," Janna said, her voice a low rumble. "No quick strikes, no flashy maneuvers. This is going to be a grind. A slow, brutal march through hell."

Sera nodded, her gaze fixed on the honed edge of her blade. "I know, Janna. This isn't about glory or conquest. It's about survival. Endurance. We need to be prepared for the long haul." She tested the edge of her blade with a calloused thumb, a thin line of blood welling up. "We need to be ready to fight, not just for days, but for weeks. Months."

In a corner of the warehouse, surrounded by a chaotic mess of wires, circuits, and glowing data-slates, Korina was a whirlwind of activity. Her fingers flew across the holographic keyboard projected from *Obsidian*, lines of code scrolling across the screen at dizzying speed. The air around her crackled with arcane energy, a faint violet glow emanating from the data-slate as she worked.

Almost there, Korina's voice echoed in Ada's mind, a rapid-fire burst of excitement. *Just a few more calibrations, and Obsidian's new diagnostic suites should be fully operational. I've designed them specifically to analyze the Cascade Failure's data corruption, identify patterns in the glitches, and hopefully...help us navigate that unstable, blighted hellscape.*

Ada, seated at a makeshift desk constructed from salvaged crates, nodded absently, her gaze fixed on the ancient, leather-bound tome in front of her. The pages, filled with Nividia's cryptic notes on the Oracle, swam before her eyes, a jumble of arcane symbols, half-remembered prophecies, and fragmented legends.

She felt a new, raw power humming just beneath the surface, a wild, untamed energy she didn't yet fully understand or control. It was a direct result of her desperate message to Earth, a side effect of bridging the gap between Kremøtoa and the physical world. Her [CREATION] power, once a precise, almost clinical tool for manipulating the world's code, now felt...different. Unpredictable. Dangerous. Like a barely contained wildfire, threatening to consume everything in its path.

She closed her eyes, taking a deep breath, trying to calm the swirling chaos within her. The Oracle. It was their only hope, their last, desperate gamble against the encroaching darkness. But what *was* it? A program? A person? A place? Nividia's lore offered no clear answers, only cryptic clues and fragmented whispers.

Ada opened her eyes, her gaze fixed on the swirling, chaotic pixels that marked the Ashen States on the holographic map. Somewhere, deep within that blighted wasteland, lay the key to Kremøtoa's survival. The key to their survival.

Korina watched Ada, a mixture of concern and fascination swirling within her. Ada's usual calm, almost clinical demeanor had been replaced by a restless energy, a barely contained storm of conflicting emotions. The weight of their impending journey, the knowledge of Kremøtoa's true nature, and the lingering guilt over her actions weighed heavily on Ada's shoulders. Korina longed to offer comfort, to wrap Ada in a protective embrace and whisper reassurances, but she hesitated. The memory of her own vulnerability in the market, the raw, exposed nerve of her trauma, still felt too fresh, too close to the surface.

Ada looked up, her violet eyes meeting Korina's. A flicker of a smile touched her lips, a small spark of light in the gathering darkness. "Rina," she said, her voice soft, "I have an idea. Something I think I can do for you. For *Lynx*."

Korina's heart skipped a beat. *Lynx*. The little pixel-cat, Ada's whimsical creation, had become more than just a security monitor; it was a constant, comforting presence on *Obsidian's* screen, a tiny, animated avatar of Ada's love and care. The thought of Ada enhancing it, imbuing it with even more of her unique essence, sent a thrill of excitement through Korina.

"What do you have in mind?" Korina asked, her voice barely a whisper.

Ada's smile widened, a mischievous glint in her eyes. "Something...special. A little upgrade, courtesy of your girlfriend." She winked, and Korina felt a blush creep up her cheeks. Ada's playful teasing, once a source of nervous fluster, now filled her with a warm, comforting glow.

"I'm intrigued," Korina said, a smile tugging at the corners of her own lips. "Show me what you can do."

Ada gestured towards a nearby workbench, a chaotic jumble of tools, wires, and spare parts salvaged from Thorne's workshop. "Come. Let's get to work."

Korina followed Ada to the workbench, her heart pounding with anticipation. Ada picked up *Obsidian*, her fingers tracing the smooth, cool surface of the data-slate. A faint violet glow emanated from Ada's fingertips, a subtle but unmistakable sign of her power. *Just a small adjustment to the code,* Ada's voice echoed in Korina's mind, a gentle whisper that sent shivers down her spine.

A little...tweak to the Lynx program. Something I think you'll appreciate.

Korina watched, mesmerized, as Ada's fingers danced across the holographic keyboard projected from *Obsidian*. Lines of code scrolled across the screen, a blur of symbols and commands she couldn't fully comprehend. The air around them crackled with arcane energy, the violet glow intensifying, pulsing with a rhythmic beat that matched the frantic rhythm of Korina's own heart.

Suddenly, the violet glow vanished. Ada handed *Obsidian* back to Korina, a mischievous smile playing on her lips. *There. All done.*

Korina took the data-slate, her fingers trembling slightly. She glanced at the screen, her eyes widening in surprise. *Lynx*, still perched in its usual corner, looked...different. Its pixelated eyes, once a static violet, now shimmered with a soft, intelligent light. Its tiny, animated body seemed to pulse with a subtle energy, a faint aura of...something. Something she couldn't quite define.

Hello, Rina, a tiny voice echoed in Korina's mind, a soft, playful whisper that made her jump. *It's nice to finally meet you. Properly, I mean. Ada says I can talk to you now. Isn't that neat?*

Korina stared at the screen, her mouth agape. *Lynx* blinked, its pixelated eyes widening in an expression of innocent curiosity. *Well?* it whispered. *Aren't you going to say hello?*

Korina looked at Ada, her eyes wide with disbelief. "It...it can talk? Telepathically?"

Ada chuckled, a warm, comforting sound that eased Korina's astonishment. "Not exactly *talk*. More like...relay messages. A direct link between Lynx and your mind. A little benefit of my... burgeoning admin powers."

It's true! Lynx chirped, its tail twitching excitedly. *I can tell you all sorts of things! System diagnostics, threat assessments, even the latest gossip from the network. Though Ada says I'm not supposed to eavesdrop on Imperial communications anymore. Spoilsport.*

Korina's mind reeled, struggling to process the implications of Ada's creation. A telepathic pixel-cat? It was absurd. Impossible. Yet, here it was, a tiny, animated testament to Ada's boundless creativity and her ever-evolving power. A power that, despite its potential for destruction, also held the promise of something truly extraordinary. Something...beautiful.

"It's...amazing, Ada," Korina whispered, her voice filled with awe. "Thank you."

Ada smiled, her violet eyes shining with a warmth that melted Korina's heart. "You're welcome, Rina. *Anything* for you."

And me! Lynx added, puffing out its pixelated chest. *Don't forget about me!*

Korina laughed, a genuine, joyful sound that echoed through the warehouse, a small spark of light in the gathering darkness. The impossible journey ahead, the looming threat of the Cascade Failure, the weight of their responsibilities...it all seemed a little less daunting, a little less overwhelming, with Ada by her side. With *Lynx* whispering playful secrets in her mind. Together, they would face whatever challenges lay ahead. Together, they would fight for Kremøtoa. For their future. For their love.

The rusted gates of Port Dominus creaked open, a mournful sound that echoed the somber mood of the assembled revolutionaries.

The Azure Rose recruits, their faces grim and determined, stood in silent formation, their newly acquired Imperial weapons held at rest. The Crimson Veil agents, their expressions masked by shadows and scarves, lined the rooftops, their presence a silent promise of support. Admiral Silas, resplendent in his custom-made uniform, stood at the head of the formation, his weathered face etched with a mixture of pride, sorrow, and unwavering resolve.

Ada, clad in her obsidian and violet gown, felt the weight of their gazes upon her, a tangible pressure that settled heavy on her shoulders. She met Silas' gaze, her own expression mirroring his resolve. He gave her a crisp, formal salute, the gesture sharp and precise, a stark contrast to the tremor in his voice.

"My Queen," Silas said, his voice thick with emotion. "May Argent's light guide your steps. We will hold the city. We will protect the revolution. No matter the cost."

Ada returned the salute, her heart aching with a mixture of gratitude and guilt. She knew the burden she was placing on Silas, the risks she was asking him to take. But she also knew there was no other choice. The fate of Kremøtoa rested on their success, on their ability to reach the Oracle and restore balance to the fractured world.

A holographic image flickered to life beside Silas, the shimmering form of Nividia Rhenderon, her violet eyes gleaming with an unsettling mixture of amusement and something...darker. Something Ada couldn't quite decipher.

"Do not fail, little Architect," Nividia said, her voice a silken whisper that carried an undercurrent of steel. "The game is far more complex than you yet realize." The image vanished, leaving a lingering chill in the air.

Ada turned her back on the city, her gaze fixed on the desolate landscape that stretched before them. The once-vibrant fields, now scarred and corrupted by the spreading blight, painted a stark picture of the task that lay ahead. The air hung heavy with the stench of decay, a constant reminder of the world's slow, agonizing death.

Sera, clad in her crimson tunic, fell into step beside Ada, her hand resting lightly on the hilt of her sword. Korina, her violet gown shimmering faintly in the dim light, followed close behind, *Obsidian* clutched tightly in her hand. Erita, her dark leather armor blending seamlessly with the shadows, brought up the rear, her golden eyes scanning the horizon for any sign of danger. Janna, her massive frame a reassuring presence, stood beside Erita, her battle-axe resting easily on her shoulder.

Ready? Ada whispered, her voice echoing in the minds of her companions.

Ready, Sera replied, her voice a steady, reassuring presence in the swirling chaos of Ada's thoughts.

Ready, Korina echoed, her voice tinged with a nervous excitement that mirrored Ada's own apprehension.

Ready, Erita confirmed, her voice cool and pragmatic, a stark contrast to the warmth that bloomed in Ada's chest at the sound of her lover's mental whisper.

Ready, Janna rumbled, her voice a deep, grounding hum that resonated through Ada's very being.

They walked in silence, their footsteps crunching on the parched earth, the only sound in the vast, desolate landscape. The gates of Port Dominus clanged shut behind them, a final, definitive sound that marked the beginning of their perilous journey. The Hundred Day Trek had begun.

The sun beat down on them mercilessly as they traversed the

barren plains, the air thick with the stench of decay. The corrupted landscape stretched before them, a desolate wasteland of glitching terrain and twisted, skeletal trees. The sky, once a vibrant azure, was now a sickly, pale green, the three moons—Argent, Cache, and BIOCE—hanging low and ominous in the corrupted sky.

Ada, her body still weakened from the strenuous blink jump, stumbled, her breath catching in her throat. Sera reached out, her strong hand gripping Ada's arm, steadying her.

Easy, Ada, Sera whispered, her voice filled with concern. *We'll take it slow. We have a long way to go.*

Ada nodded, grateful for Sera's support. She took a deep breath, drawing strength from the warmth of Sera's touch, the unwavering loyalty in her eyes.

They continued their trek, their pace slow and deliberate. Korina, using *Obsidian*, scanned the horizon, her brow furrowed in concentration.

There's a cluster of corrupted entities about five kilometers ahead, Korina reported, her voice tight with apprehension. *Low-level malware, but numerous. We should avoid them if possible.*

Agreed, Erita said. *We need to conserve our energy. This is just the beginning of the journey.*

Ada, using her Admin-view, surveyed the landscape. She saw the corrupted entities, their code flickering and distorted, their movements erratic and unpredictable. She also saw something else. A faint shimmer in the distance, a distortion in the fabric of reality. A glitch.

There's a path, Ada said, her voice echoing in the minds of her companions. *A narrow passage through the mountains. It's...unstable, but it should allow us to bypass the malware.*

Lead the way, Architect-Queen, Janna rumbled, her voice filled with a quiet confidence that bolstered Ada's resolve.

Ada nodded, and they set off again, their footsteps echoing in the desolate silence of the dying world. The Hundred Day Trek had begun, and with each step, they ventured deeper into the heart of the corrupted code, the fate of Kremøtoa resting heavy on their shoulders.

CHAPTER 5

A WORLD ON THE BRINK

The steady thrum of the Prefecture's arcane generators, usually a comforting sound of order and control, now grated on Kraus Valerius' nerves. Each pulse of energy seemed to mock him, a rhythmic reminder of his dwindling power. The sterile perfection of his command center, once a sanctuary of logic and efficiency, now felt like a suffocating cage.

"Report," he snapped, his voice a low, gravelly hum that echoed in the cavernous space.

The junior aide, his face pale and drawn, stammered, "Prefect... the...the reports from the Southern Marches...they're..."

"Spit it out, Ensign!" Kraus snarled, his patience wearing thin. "I haven't the time for theatrics."

"The swamps...they're expanding, Prefect," the aide blurted out, his voice barely above a whisper. "Our containment protocols...they're not...they're not working. The corruption...it's... it's adapting."

Kraus slammed his fist on the obsidian console, the impact

echoing through the chamber. The holographic display flickered, the image of the spreading Malware Swamps momentarily distorting before snapping back into focus. The sight of the pulsating, festering landscape, its tendrils reaching ever outward, filled him with a cold, pragmatic dread.

"Adapting?" he muttered, his voice laced with disbelief. "The data corruption...it's evolving?"

"Affirmative, Prefect," the aide confirmed, his voice trembling. "Our Axiomatic Field Scanners are registering...unprecedented levels of arcane instability. The...the creatures...they're multiplying at an exponential rate. Our containment lines...they've been breached. We're losing ground."

Kraus turned away from the display, his gaze sweeping across the pristine, geometric perfection of his command center. Every line, every angle, every glowing data-slate spoke of order, of control, of the Empire's unwavering commitment to logic and efficiency. Yet outside, beyond the sterile confines of the Prefecture, the world was unraveling, the very laws of reality breaking down.

He paced, his mind racing, trying to process the impossible. The Malware Swamps were not just a static anomaly, a localized corruption that could be contained and controlled. They were a spreading disease, a cancer eating away at the very fabric of Kremøtoa. And his meticulously crafted protocols, his carefully calibrated containment strategies, were proving utterly useless.

He thought of Ada Lynx, the girl with the unclassifiable power, the anomaly that had defied all his attempts at quantification. He had initially viewed her as an asset, a tool to be exploited for the Empire's gain. He had seen her power as a weapon, a means of restoring order and control. But now, as he watched the world crumble around him, he began to reconsider.

Perhaps the girl was not the cause of this decay, but a symptom. A herald of a deeper, more systemic corruption that threatened to consume everything. He had always believed in the power of logic, of order, of the Empire's ability to impose its will upon the world. But now, as he faced the unraveling of his carefully constructed reality, he began to question the very foundations of his beliefs.

"Prefect?" the aide said, his voice hesitant. "What are your orders?"

Kraus stopped pacing, his gaze fixed on the holographic display. The image of the spreading swamps, the grotesque creatures swarming over the land, filled him with a sense of profound unease. He had spent his entire life building this Empire, this bastion of order in a chaotic world. And now, he was watching it crumble, powerless to stop it.

"Prepare a full report for the Imperial Council," he said, his voice cold and detached. "Detail the extent of the corruption, the failure of our containment protocols, and the...the evolving nature of the threat. And...and include a revised assessment of the...the Lynx anomaly."

"Revised assessment, Prefect?" the aide repeated, his voice tinged with confusion.

Kraus nodded, his gaze still fixed on the display. "Yes, Ensign. A revised assessment. I believe we may have...miscalculated the nature of the...variable."

The aide, clearly bewildered, stammered, "But...but Prefect, the Council...they believe the girl is a threat. A danger to the Empire."

Kraus turned to face the aide, his pale blue eyes cold and calculating. "And what, Ensign, do *you* believe?"

The aide hesitated, his gaze darting nervously between Kraus and the display. "I...I believe, Prefect, that the situation...is...is far more complex than we initially anticipated."

Kraus allowed himself a thin, almost imperceptible smile. "Indeed, Ensign. Indeed. It would appear...that we are dealing with something...far beyond our current understanding."

He turned back to the display, his gaze fixed on the spreading corruption. The world was changing, the rules were being rewritten. And he, Kraus Valerius, Prefect of Celgrad, Master of Order, was about to adapt.

Within the Grand Conclave Chamber of the Veritas Archives, the High Council convened, not amidst the chaos of a crumbling world, but within a serene sanctuary of shimmering data streams and softly humming reality query engines. The six figures, each a master of their respective fields, sat at a circular obsidian table, their faces illuminated by the ethereal glow of projected holographic schematics. The air around them crackled with arcane energy, a testament to the immense intellectual power concentrated within this hallowed hall.

Grand Magister Xehon, his ancient, sharp features etched with a profound, almost unsettling calm, gestured towards the central holographic display. The image depicted a swirling vortex of corrupted data, the epicenter of the Cascade Failure, its tendrils reaching out to consume the land. Cities dissolved into pixelated chaos, landscapes warped into impossible geometries, and monstrous malware constructs stalked the blighted terrain.

"Fascinating," Archivist Itania murmured, her voice a low, almost predatory hum. "A truly unprecedented display of systemic instability. The thaumaturgical signatures...they're unlike anything I've ever encountered."

"Indeed," High Chancellor Pantium agreed, his voice a dry, rustling sound like parchment shifting in the wind. "The historical records contain no precedent for such a rapid and widespread corruption of the axiomatic framework. The implications for data preservation...are...staggering."

"The system's architecture, however, remains remarkably sound," Scholar Atomuzk noted, his voice a quiet, almost apologetic rumble. "The core code, the foundational algorithms... they're holding up remarkably well, considering the magnitude of the disruption."

"A testament to the brilliance of our predecessors," Grand Magister Xehon declared, his voice a resonant, almost musical tone. "But sentimentality aside, we have a puzzle to solve." He turned to Councilor Celerun, the youngest and most eager member of the Council. "Report, Councilor. What is the status of our analytical drones?"

"We've deployed twelve units into the affected sectors, Grand Magister," Celerun reported, his voice a nervous, rapid-fire cascade of technical jargon. "They're equipped with Axiomatic Field Scanners, Reality Query Engines, and Thaumaturgical Spectrometers. We're gathering data on the malware constructs, their energy signatures, their propagation algorithms, their..."

"Their tactical capabilities?" Xehon interrupted, his voice sharp. "Can they be weaponized?"

Celerun hesitated, his gaze darting nervously towards the display. "The data is...inconclusive, Grand Magister. The constructs exhibit a high degree of adaptability, their forms and functions constantly shifting. Predicting their behavior...is proving... challenging."

"Challenging," Xehon repeated, a hint of amusement in his voice. "A delightful understatement, Councilor. This is not a mere challenge, this is an opportunity. The ultimate test of our intellectual prowess. We are witnessing the unraveling of reality itself, and we, the High Council of Veritas, are uniquely positioned to understand it."

"Grand Magister," Master Centrinah interjected, her voice a smooth, diplomatic tone. "While I appreciate the academic value of this...phenomenon, we must also consider the political ramifications. The Empire...they will not hesitate to blame us for this. They will see this Cascade Failure as a consequence of our...lax oversight of the axiomatic framework—we caused the Ashen States existence, we *let this happen.*"

"Let them," Xehon said, waving a dismissive hand. "Their accusations are irrelevant. We are not concerned with political posturing, we are concerned with truth. With knowledge. With understanding the fundamental laws that govern this reality. And this...this chaotic symphony of corruption...is providing us with data we could never have obtained through conventional means."

"Where *is* Vance?" Xehon asked suddenly, a sharp edge entering his voice. "He should be leading this analysis. His expertise in systemic architecture...it's essential."

Councilor Celerun shifted uncomfortably in his seat. "Councilor Vance...is...unavailable, Grand Magister. He...he sent a message indicating...a...a personal matter requiring his immediate attention."

Xehon's eyes narrowed. "A personal matter? And what, pray

tell, could be more important than witnessing the unraveling of reality itself?"

"He...he didn't specify, Grand Magister," Celerun stammered. "The message was...rather vague."

Xehon let out a long, slow sigh. "Vague. Unacceptable. His absence is...inconvenient. But we will manage without him. For now." He turned back to the display, his gaze fixed on the swirling vortex of corruption. "I expect a full Council report as soon as possible. Every data point, every anomaly, every thaumaturgical fluctuation...I want it all documented and analyzed. We will understand this. We will find the root cause. We will unravel the secrets of this Cascade Failure. And we, the High Council of Veritas, will emerge from this chaos...with a deeper understanding of the very nature of reality itself."

The Council continued their analysis, their voices a low, almost hypnotic murmur of technical jargon and theoretical speculation. They deployed more analytical drones, their holographic projections flitting through the chamber like spectral fireflies. They ran simulations, their reality query engines humming with the strain of processing the immense amounts of data. They debated, their voices rising and falling in a complex counterpoint of logic and arcane theory. They were not afraid. They were not concerned. They were fascinated. For them, the Cascade Failure was not a disaster, but a data set. A puzzle to be solved. And they, the serene, detached intellects of the Veritas Archives, were determined to solve it, no matter the cost.

The rhythmic clicking of data-slates echoed through the Grand Conclave Chamber, the only sound in the otherwise silent hall. The High Council of Veritas, their faces illuminated by the cool, ethereal glow of holographic displays, continued their analysis of the Cascade Failure, oblivious to the horrors unfolding elsewhere within their hallowed halls. Scholar Atomuzk adjusted his spectacles, his brow furrowed in concentration as he studied a complex waveform. Archivist Itania, her fingers dancing across the surface of her data-slate, murmured a series of arcane equations. Grand Magister Xehon, his gaze fixed on the swirling vortex of corruption, steepled his fingers, a small, almost imperceptible smile playing on his lips.

Elsewhere from the intellectual atmosphere of the Grand Conclave Chamber, replaced by the stale, musty air of a secluded archive, dust motes danced in the single shaft of moonlight that pierced the gloom—illuminating rows upon rows of ancient scrolls and forgotten tomes. A figure stood hunched over a table, their back to the entrance, their movements obscured by the shadows. A muffled sob echoed through the stillness, followed by a whispered plea. “Please...no...stop...”

The figure did not stop. Their movements became more forceful, more insistent. The sobs intensified, punctuated by gasps of pain and terror. The figure’s shadow loomed large on the wall, a grotesque, distorted silhouette that seemed to writhe and pulse with a predatory energy. A crumpled robe lay discarded on the floor, a splash of violet against the dark stone. The air crackled with a faint, sickly energy signature, a subtle distortion of the archive’s normally stable thaumaturgical field. The whispered pleas continued, growing weaker, more desperate. “Please... someone...help...” Then, silence.

Back in the Grand Conclave Chamber, the High Council remained engrossed in their analysis. Scholar Atomuzk pointed to an anomaly on the holographic display. “Fascinating,” he murmured. “The rate of data corruption...it’s accelerating exponentially. We’re approaching a critical threshold.”

“Indeed,” Xehon agreed, his voice calm, almost detached. “A most intriguing development. This could provide us with invaluable insights into the fundamental nature of systemic decay. Councilor Celerun, I want you to...” He paused, his brow furrowing slightly. “Where *is* Vance? He should be here. He needs to see this.”

“I...I don’t know, Grand Magister,” Celerun stammered, his gaze darting nervously towards the entrance. “He...he hasn’t responded to my messages.”

Odd, Atomuzk mused, his internal monologue a stark contrast to the placid, academic tone he maintained in the Council’s presence. *Vance’s absence...it’s illogical. He wouldn’t miss an event of this magnitude. Not unless...*A flicker of suspicion, a cold, analytical spark, ignited within the Scholar’s mind. *Not unless he was somehow involved.* He glanced at Xehon, whose serene facade betrayed no hint of the Grand Magister’s true thoughts. Xehon’s public pronouncements about Vance’s absence being merely ‘inconvenient’ struck Atomuzk as a carefully crafted deception, a way to deflect attention and maintain the Council’s image of serene control. *No*, Atomuzk decided, his internal voice hardening with a quiet resolve. *This requires further investigation. Discreetly. Xehon’s blind faith in Vance...it’s a dangerous vulnerability.* He returned his attention to the holographic display, his face a mask of placid curiosity, but his mind already formulating a plan to uncover the truth, whatever the cost. “Grand Magister,” he said, his voice carefully modulated. “While I agree that analyzing the

Cascade Failure is paramount, I believe it's also prudent to ensure Councilor Vance's safety. Perhaps I could send a small team to his quarters, just to confirm his well-being?"

"That won't be necessary, Scholar Atomuzk," Xehon dismissed, his voice a smooth, polished stone. "I'm sure Councilor Vance is simply engrossed in his own research. We mustn't allow ourselves to be distracted by minor personnel matters. The Cascade Failure... *this* is our priority." Xehon gestured towards the swirling vortex of corrupted data on the holographic display, his eyes gleaming with an unsettling intensity. "This is an unprecedented opportunity to study the very fabric of reality. We must seize it."

Atomuzk nodded slowly, his face a mask of placid agreement, but his mind racing. He knew, with a chilling certainty, that something was *wrong*. Vance's absence was not a coincidence. It was a symptom. A symptom of something far more insidious than a simple cascading failure. He didn't know what Kaelen was involved in, but two things were abundantly clear: he couldn't be seen as complicit in anything that threatened the integrity of the Archives, and he couldn't stand idly by if Vance was in danger, or worse, involved in something morally reprehensible. *No*, Atomuzk decided, his internal voice hardening with a quiet resolve. *This requires a more...discreet approach.* He glanced towards the corridor that led to Vance's private archives, his eyes narrowed with suspicion. The shadows seemed to deepen, the silence stretching into an almost palpable tension. *Carefully now*, he cautioned himself. *One wrong step, and everything could unravel.*

The air in Codexia crackled with a strange, unsettling energy. The familiar, comforting patterns of the cobblestones rippled and writhed, momentarily dissolving into a chaotic swirl of light and shadow before snapping back into place. A farmer's well bucket, crafted from sturdy oak, shimmered, its solid form flickering like a dying ember, then solidified again as if nothing had happened. The villagers huddled in the town square, their faces pale with terror, not at the sight of a system failure, but at what they perceived as a demonic incursion, a sign of the world's spiritual decay. Their whispered prayers, desperate pleas for divine intervention, were answered by the thunderous arrival of the Justicars.

Their burnished cerakote armor gleamed in the flickering light, their long, ceremonial staves held high, symbols of the Theocracy's unwavering authority. At their head rode Lady Calibree, High Inquisitor and leader of the Justicaress elite. Her tall, severe form radiated an aura of absolute, fanatical conviction. The wind whipped her black cloak around her, revealing glimpses of the silver tattoos that traced the lines of her shaved skull, sacred verses etched into her very being. Her dark grey eyes, cold and piercing, swept over the cowering villagers, missing nothing.

"Fear not, children of the Word," Calibree's voice rang out, a chillingly calm counterpoint to the villagers' panicked whispers. It was not a voice that sought to soothe, but one that commanded, each syllable imbued with the unwavering certainty of her faith. "These...*omens*...are not the work of demons. They are a test. A trial sent by the Word itself to cleanse this world of its corruption."

A collective gasp rippled through the crowd. A test? A trial? Their terrified whispers intensified.

"The rot has spread deep," Calibree continued, her gaze sweeping over the villagers as if she could see the impurities festering within their very souls. "Unsanctioned knowledge. Heretical technology. The seeds of corruption have been sown, and now, we reap the bitter harvest."

She raised her hand, silencing the murmurs. "But despair not. Salvation is at hand. The Word has shown us the path to purification. And we, the Justicars, are its instruments."

Calibree lowered her hand, her voice hardening. "The cleansing begins *now*."

The Justicars moved through the village with the brutal efficiency of a well-oiled machine. A farmer's simple, automated water pump, designed to ease the burden of irrigation, was smashed to pieces, declared "illegal technology, a perversion of the natural order." Books, treasured possessions containing knowledge gleaned from outside the Theocracy's approved texts, were confiscated and burned in a pyre in the town square, their ashes rising like a dark prayer to the flickering, unstable sky. Citizens were dragged from their homes, their faces etched with terror, to be 'questioned' about the purity of their faith, their adherence to the Word's rigid and unforgiving dogma.

A young boy, clutching a small, intricately carved wooden toy, was separated from his weeping mother.

"This...this is heresy!" a Justicar boomed, his voice thick with righteous indignation, holding the toy aloft as if it were a venomous serpent. "Unauthorized creativity. A corruption of the Word's perfect design." He crushed the toy in his armored fist, the boy's cries echoing through the square.

Calibree watched the scene unfold, her face impassive. There was no malice in her eyes, no pleasure in the villagers' suffering. Only the cold, unwavering certainty of a true believer purging the world of its imperfections. This was not cruelty, in her mind. It was a necessary act of purification. A sacred duty. The Word demanded it.

A woman, her face streaked with tears, threw herself at Calibree's feet.

"Please, High Inquisitor," she begged, her voice choked with desperation. "My husband...he's a good man. He meant no harm. He just...he wanted to make life easier for us. He built that pump to help with the crops. He didn't know..."

Calibree looked down at the woman, her gaze unwavering.

"Ignorance is no excuse," she stated, her voice flat, devoid of empathy. "The Word demands obedience, not intent. Your husband's actions have invited corruption into this world. He will be cleansed."

The woman's cries intensified, but Calibree turned away, her gaze fixed on the flickering, unstable sky. The purification continued, a wave of righteous violence washing over Codexia, leaving a trail of broken objects, shattered lives, and the chilling silence of absolute, unquestioning faith. The three moons, Argent, Cache, and BIOCE, watched silently from above, their light casting long, distorted shadows across the ravaged town square.

Calibree turned her gaze back towards the sky, her lips moving in a silent prayer. The Word would guide her. It always did. The purification would continue, no matter the cost.

CHAPTER 6

FULL CIRCLE

The air in the area near Oakhaven still hummed with a quiet, foundational power, but it was a song Ada now heard with a different ear. The memory of her arrival—the terror, the awe, the crushing loneliness—felt like a story about someone else. *A scared little girl, lost in a world she had built but did not understand.*

She looked at the women beside her. Sera, a bulwark of crimson and steel, her presence a steadying anchor. Korina, her violet eyes scanning the ethereal flora, her mind a symphony of analysis and wonder. Erita, a shadow of gold and leather, her gaze sharp, missing nothing. Janna, a silent mountain of strength, her calm presence a balm.

It feels like a lifetime ago that I was here, Ada thought, a bittersweet ache blooming in her chest. *Now I'm their Queen. But what does that title mean when my world is fraying at the seams?*

A patch of the impossibly vibrant grass at her feet flickered, its emerald hue dissolving into a matrix of static for a bare second before snapping back. A nearby crystalline flower, which pulsed with a soft golden light, went dull and gray, then flared back to life. The glitches were subtle here, at the heart of the system, but they were undeniable.

"The baseline thaumaturgical resonance is...unstable," Korina murmured, her brow furrowed as she studied Obsidian's readings. "It's like listening to a perfect chord with a single, dissonant string vibrating underneath."

"It's quiet," Janna observed, her voice a low rumble. "Too quiet."

They left the meadow, their boots sinking into the soft earth of the rolling hills that led toward Oakhaven. The journey that had once taken her hours of terrified wandering passed in a somber, silent march. The sky, a canvas of perpetual twilight and swirling violet-gold auroras over the meadow, had bled into a muted, overcast gray. A cold, steady drizzle began to fall, pattering against their cloaks and chilling the skin on Ada's cheeks. The world smelled clean and earthy, of rain on damp soil.

More glitches scarred the landscape. The bark of an ancient oak briefly dissolved into a low-resolution texture, a smear of brown and green pixels. A distant hill seemed to stutter in its place, jumping a few feet to the left before settling. Each anomaly was a fresh stab of guilt in Ada's gut. *This was her code. Her failure.*

When they crested the final ridge, Oakhaven lay below them in the gray light. The buildings were whole, the fields were green, the well at the center of the village square stood as a monument to her first, explosive act of healing. *But the life was gone.*

The usual sounds of a bustling village—the ring of a

blacksmith's hammer, the laughter of children, the low murmur of conversation—were absent. A profound, sorrowful silence had descended, broken only by the soft, steady patter of the rain.

Villagers emerged from their homes, not with the joyous cries Ada remembered, but with a slow, deliberate reverence. They stood in their doorways or by the edge of the square, their faces turned toward her. They were not gaunt or sick, but their eyes held a shared, deep-seated grief. They watched, their expressions somber, respectful, yet utterly silent.

Ada's breath caught in her throat. *Something is wrong here. This isn't the Oakhaven I saved.*

They walked down the muddy path and into the village proper, the silent gazes of the villagers following their every step. The weight of their collective sorrow was a physical pressure, pressing in from all sides.

Sera moved closer to Ada, her shoulder brushing against hers. "The last time you were here, you were a stranger. A frightened girl running from a knight in shining armor."

A ghost of a smile touched Ada's lips. "I thought you were going to kill me."

"Now," Sera's voice was a warm, low murmur beside her, a stark contrast to the chill of the rain and the silence of the village. "Now, you're our Queen."

The title landed with the weight of a tombstone. A queen of a dying world, a savior to a village steeped in a sorrow she couldn't comprehend. The rain continued its gentle rhythm on the cobblestones as a woman stepped forward from the crowd, her hands clasped before her, her face a mask of tragedy.

The woman who had stepped forward was not Marta, but

another, younger, with kind lines etched around her eyes. Ada recognized her from her first visit—Elara, the elder's daughter—the one that had shrieked and had caused the 500km blast-wave of Ada's power to start *everything*. The little girl Ada remembered in her gaze was gone, replaced by a deep, settled sadness that was somehow more piercing. The rain slicked her dark hair to her temples.

"Architect-Queen," Elara's voice was thick with an emotion Ada couldn't immediately place. It wasn't fear or awe, but a quiet, profound respect. "We knew you would return."

Ada swallowed, the cold rainwater on her lips tasting of ozone and damp earth. "I...I'm so sorry. I saw...I hear the silence. Has something happened?"

Elara offered a sad, gentle smile that did not reach her eyes. She reached out and, with a startling familiarity, took both of Ada's hands in her own. Her skin was warm. "Our Chief, my father Elian, has passed into the soil."

The words struck Ada like a physical blow. ***Elian***. The wizened old man with the sharp, knowing eyes who had first trusted her. *He died of old age. A natural death. A simple, programmed cycle I wrote, but never...felt.* A hollowness opened in her chest. She had written the code for mortality, for senescence, for the eventual, inevitable system shutdown of a biological entity. But she had never experienced its execution as a loss.

"He died two weeks ago," Elara continued, her grip tightening on Ada's hands. "Peacefully, in his sleep. His heart simply... stopped. He was old, and he was tired, and he was ready." She looked up, her gaze locking with Ada's, and a single tear traced a path through the grime on her cheek. "When you came, he was wasting away—we all were. The blight was taking us...piece by piece. We would have watched him die in agony, helpless. But you...you healed us. You healed him."

Ada felt her own vision begin to blur. Behind her, she could feel Sera's presence, a solid warmth at her back.

"He said you gave us the most precious gift of all: ***time***," Elara's voice cracked, the raw emotion finally breaking through her composure. "Time to say goodbye. Time to be with him, to hold his hand, to listen to his stories one last time without the shadow of that corruption hanging over us. You gave us the gift of a proper grief. A good death. And for that...for that, Oakhaven will be forever in your debt."

Elara bowed her head, pressing Ada's hands to her forehead in a gesture of profound gratitude.

And that was what broke her.

The carefully constructed walls around Ada's heart—the logic, the code, the queenly composure—crumbled into dust. It wasn't the sorrow of his death. It was the love. The gratitude. The sheer, overwhelming reality of their lives and their losses. They were thanking her for time, but her world was running out of it. Their love, their grief, it was all so real. *It's too real.*

A sound tore from Ada's throat, a raw, ragged sob that was half-gasp, half-scream. The strength fled her legs, and she sagged, held up only by Elara's surprised grip. Tears streamed down her face, hot and unfiltered, mingling with the cold rain. The world dissolved into a smear of gray stone and concerned faces.

Sera's hand was instantly on her back, firm and steadying. "Ada..."

But she couldn't stop. The grief was a torrent, not just for Elian, but for the dealer at the Gilded Hand, for the recruits lost in Port Dominus, for Master Willem...for the beautiful, vibrant world she had created only to watch it die. For the crushing, impossible weight of their faith in her.

She pulled her hands from Elara's, pressing them to her face as her whole body shook with the force of her weeping.

"Give her some space," Erita's voice was sharp, a protective blade cutting through the silence of the villagers.

Then Korina was there, her slender arms wrapping around Ada from the side, pulling her into a fierce, all-encompassing hug. Korina buried her face in Ada's shoulder, her own body trembling in empathy. "It's okay, Ada," she murmured, the sound a desperate, loving whisper against her ear. "We're here. We've got you."

Ada leaned into the embrace, surrendering to the storm inside her. She clung to Korina, her fingers digging into the fabric of her cloak as if she were the last anchor in a collapsing universe. Sera's hand rubbed slow, calming circles on her back while Erita and Janna moved to stand as silent, unbreachable sentinels, shielding their weeping queen from the watching eyes of the village she had saved and the world she was now failing.

The storm of grief passed, leaving a hollowed-out quiet in its wake. Elara guided them to the edge of the village, to a small, serene plot of land beneath the dripping boughs of ancient pines. The rich scent of wet earth and needles hung heavy in the chilled air. Korina's hand rested lightly on Ada's arm, a silent anchor in the aftermath of the squall that had torn through her.

There it was. *Elian's grave.* It was humble, marked only by a simple cross of weathered wood, dark with rain. At its base, someone had placed a small, brave cluster of wildflowers, their purple and yellow petals glistening with water droplets. A proper grave. *A final resting place.*

Ada stared at the wooden marker, the raw data of the scene processing through her mind with a new, terrifying clarity. *Elian's life had been a complete process. A program that had run its full course, from initialization to a clean, expected termination. Birth, life, death. A graceful shutdown.* He had existed, and now his existence was logged, archived in the memory of his people and the very soil beneath their feet. It was an ending she had designed, a fundamental law of this reality.

This was a death with dignity. It had weight. *Meaning.*

The Cascade Failure was something else entirely. It was not a **[PROCESS_END]**—It was a **[DELETE_FILE]**; a **[FORMAT_DRIVE]**. It was not the conclusion of a story, but the violent erasure of the book itself. An unnatural, unceremonious voiding of data. There would be no graves for the victims of the glitch, no wildflowers, no memories. There would be nothing. Just a gaping, pixelated hole where something used to be. The ultimate horror was not death—but non-existence.

This, Ada thought, her gaze fixed on the rain-slicked cross, a cold fire beginning to kindle in the pit of her stomach. *This is what I'm fighting for. The right to an ending. The right to a full life cycle.*

Her companions stood around her, a silent tableau of shared solemnity. Sera, her jaw tight, her eyes fixed on the grave with a warrior's respect for a fallen elder. Erita, her usual cynicism replaced by a guarded, somber stillness. Janna, a figure of granite and reverence, her head bowed slightly. They were all so real, their grief and their loyalty an undeniable truth in this world of her own making.

A dizzying thought spiraled through her mind, sharp and unwelcome. The physicists on Earth, her professors, her peers—they had all argued that a stable, self-sustaining simulation on the scale of a world was a computational impossibility. The energy requirements, the processing power, the sheer complexity of rendering billions of emergent, sentient variables...it was the stuff of science fiction.

But I did it.

The thought was not a boast. It was a terrifying statement of fact. She, Ada Lynx, a twenty-five-year-old from Sagiyama, Gifu Prefecture, Japan—with a modified supercomputer and a lifetime of savings—had achieved the impossible. Kremøtoa was proof.

So...why not Earth?

The ground seemed to tilt beneath her feet. If she could do it, why couldn't someone else? Someone bigger, older, impossibly more advanced? What if her universe—the one with Sagiyama and Samantha and the taste of cheap ramen and the sting of cold rain on asphalt—was just another Kremøtoa? Another layer in a nested reality she couldn't perceive?

The question was a chasm opening beneath her. *Was she just a line of code in someone else's grand program? Was her own trauma, her escape, this entire desperate fight, simply an emergent property of some forgotten subroutine?*

For a moment, the sheer scale of the possibility threatened to swallow her whole. Then, a new, colder logic took hold. *It doesn't matter.* Whether she was a gød or a ghost in a machine, the stakes remained the same. This world, *her* world, was real to the people living and dying within it. Their pain was real. Their love was real.

Her own love for them was the most real thing she had ever known. If she was a line of code, then she would be the line of code that fought for the integrity of her own simulation.

Janna's deep, resonant voice broke the quiet drip of the forest. "He lived a good life." She took a step forward, her heavy boot sinking slightly into the soft earth. Her gaze was not on Ada, but on the simple wooden cross, her expression one of profound respect. "A life worth *remembering*."

That was it. The final, clarifying piece of the puzzle. *Remembering*. The Cascade Failure erased memory itself. It deleted the proof that a life had ever been lived. Elian would be remembered. Master Willem, the dealer, the Azure Rose recruits—they would be remembered. Ada would make sure of it. She would carve their names into the source code of the new world she was going to build from the ashes of the old.

The last of the tears dried on her cheeks, leaving behind the chill of the damp air. The grief had been burned away, leaving behind something hard and pure. The hollow space in her chest was gone, filled now with a cold, terrifying resolve. She was no longer just a creator mourning her flawed creation. She was an architect with a blueprint, a queen with a purpose, a gød with a war to win.

She finally pulled her gaze from the grave, her eyes clear and sharp, and looked past the pines, towards the corrupted horizon. The journey was long. The enemy was oblivion itself. And she was ready.

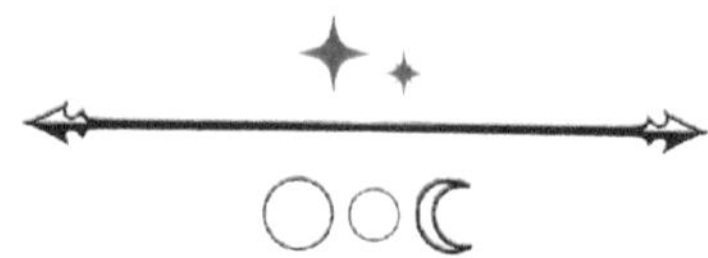

The walk away from Elian's grave was a silent, somber procession. The dripping pines and the soft crunch of their boots on damp earth were the only sounds that accompanied the weight of their shared grief. Korina felt Ada's hand slide into hers, a small anchor in the melancholy quiet. The air, washed clean by the passing storm, carried the sharp, sweet fragrance of pine needles and rich soil. It was a scent of renewal, a stark contrast to the finality they had just witnessed.

Then, as they crested a small hill, the clouds fractured. A brilliant, warm light spilled across the landscape, and against the bruised purple of the receding storm, an impossibly vibrant arc of color ignited the sky.

It was a *perfect rainbow*, a shimmering, incandescent ribbon of pure light that seemed to pulse with a life of its own. Korina stopped dead. Her mind, a machine of ceaseless calculation, instinctively began to dissect the phenomenon—the prismatic refraction of sunlight through suspended water droplets, the precise angles of incidence and reflection, the specific nanometer wavelengths of each distinct color band. She had run these simulations a thousand times, understood the physics with an intimacy that bordered on obsession.

But she had never *seen* it. Not like this.

The raw, illogical beauty of it slammed into her, bypassing every axiomatic filter and logic gate she possessed. It was not data. It was...*a miracle.*

"Rina?" Ada's voice was a soft murmur beside her. She followed Korina's gaze to the sky, a tender smile touching her lips. Ada squeezed her hand, a silent question. Without a word to the others, she tugged Korina gently away from the path, leading her into the trees. Sera, Erita, and Janna paused, watched them go, a silent accord passing between them. They understood.

Ada found a small clearing and pulled Korina close. "I want to show you something," she whispered. The world dissolved in a soft, violet shimmer, a blink so gentle it felt less like a teleportation and more like waking from a dream.

They stood in the Genesis Meadow.

The breath left Korina's lungs in a choked gasp. The air hummed with a soft, ethereal energy. The sky above was a permanent, deep indigo, painted with swirling auroras of violet and gold that cast a gentle, magical glow over everything. Translucent deer made of pure light grazed on grass that shone with an inner luminescence. Crystalline flowers pulsed with soft, rhythmic blues and purples, and glowing, soft-bodied fungi illuminated the roots of ancient trees. This was not a forest; it was a symphony of creation.

Tears welled in Korina's eyes, hot and sudden. She looked from the impossible beauty of the meadow back to the rainbow, still visible through a break in the canopy. Shame, sharp and profound, coiled in her gut. All her life, she had chased knowledge, pursued data, sought to quantify the universe in a desperate attempt to prove her worth, to erase the memory of Kaelen's sneering dismissal. She had stared at schematics, at lines of code, at the glowing screen of Obsidian.

"I never looked up," she whispered, the words catching in her throat. The confession felt like shedding a suit of armor she hadn't realized she was wearing. "I've documented the spectral variance of hundreds of atmospheric light refractions. I've written multiple theses' on it. But I never...I never just *looked*."

Ada didn't offer pity. Her expression was one of profound,

aching understanding. She stepped closer, her hands coming up to gently cup Korina's face, her thumbs stroking away the tears. "In my world," Ada said, her voice a soothing balm, "we had another name for it. Not a scientific one. A beautiful one." She looked up at the arc of color. "*Arc-en-Ciel.*"

The words—foreign, melodic, soft—struck Korina with the force of a revelation. ***Arc-en-Ciel.*** *Arch in the sky.* It was so simple, yet it held a universe of meaning that no equation ever could. It was a name for the *why*, not the *how*. And in that single, crystalline moment, *everything reconfigured.*

Her entire perception of Ada shifted. She wasn't a system anomaly to be studied, a fascinating paradox to be solved. She was the architect of *this.* The mind that conceived of spectral deer and crystalline flowers was the same mind that held her face with such tenderness. The power that could rewrite the source code of reality was the same power that had just whispered a word of poetry to heal a wound she never knew how to name.

The violation at Veritas, Kaelen's hands and his words, had made her believe she was a flawed dataset, something broken and only useful for what could be extracted from her. She had built her walls from logic and analysis, believing emotion was a weakness, a corrupting variable.

But Ada...Ada hadn't tried to fix her. She had simply loved her. She showed her a world where logic and beauty were not opposing forces, but two parts of the same magnificent design. Ada was the **why.**

Argent's light, she thought, her heart swelling with a feeling so immense it threatened to shatter her. *It's not just love. It's... everything. She is the Genesis Meadow. She is the Arc-en-Ciel.*

The tears were flowing freely now, not from sadness, but from overwhelming, purifying joy. She looked into Ada's eyes—the luminous violet of her code, the brilliant, warm gold of her humanity—and saw her entire future.

"Argent's light," she breathed, the words barely a whisper, raw and trembling with the weight of this new, absolute truth. "I... Ada..." She leaned into Ada's touch, her own hands coming up to rest on Ada's wrists. "You're...you're my first true love."

CHAPTER 7

THE FRAYING EDGE

The fellowship traveled south from Oakhaven, moving along the less-patrolled Imperial roads. Sera, taking point, couldn't shake the feeling of a phantom limb. The weight of her Aegis armor, absent now for weeks, still felt present, a ghost on her shoulders. She glanced back at Ada, Korina, and Erita, their forms silhouetted against the late afternoon sun. They moved with a quiet confidence, a shared purpose that resonated with Sera.

Something was different about Korina. A lightness in her step, a subtle smile playing on her lips. Sera, used to Korina's focused, often anxious demeanor, found the change intriguing.

"Alright, Kori, what's got you grinning like a swamp cat who stole a cream pie?" Sera asked, her voice a mix of teasing and genuine curiosity.

Korina's smile widened into a full-blown blush, and Ada, walking beside her, mirrored the crimson hue.

"Oh, it's...it's nothing," Korina stammered, her eyes darting nervously between Sera and Ada.

Ada giggled, a soft, melodic sound that made Sera's heart flutter.

"Rina, is it okay if I tell them?" Ada asked, her own blush deepening. She looked at Korina with an almost shy tenderness that Sera found both endearing and surprisingly arousing.

Korina nodded, still blushing, but a small, determined smile touched her lips.

"Well?" Erita prompted, her golden eyes gleaming with amusement. "Don't keep us in suspense."

"Rina...Rina told me that...that I'm her first true love," Ada confessed, her voice barely above a whisper.

A beat of silence hung in the air, then Janna erupted in a booming laugh that echoed through the trees.

"Argent's light, that's adorable!" Janna exclaimed, clapping Korina on the back with enough force to nearly send her tumbling.

Korina squeaked in surprise, her blush intensifying to a shade of violet that rivaled her hair. Ada giggled again, hiding her face in Korina's shoulder. Sera grinned, a genuine warmth spreading through her.

"That's...that's wonderful, Kori," Sera said, her voice softer than she intended.

Erita, however, just smirked, her golden eyes twinkling with mischief.

"Cute," she muttered, nudging Korina with her elbow. "Real cute."

Korina groaned, burying her face in her hands. "*Void*, you guys are embarrassing me," she mumbled.

Janna's laughter boomed again, and even Sera couldn't help

but chuckle. It was good to hear laughter again, a sound that felt strangely out of place in the increasingly grim reality of Kremøtoa.

The initial days were a stark march through the Empire's heartland. Sera, taking point, noticed the subtle but undeniable signs of decay. The perfectly maintained stone roads, a testament to Imperial efficiency, were beginning to show hairline fractures, unnatural, pixelated cracks marring their smooth surfaces. Imperial watchtowers, once manned by vigilant Aegis patrols, stood silent and empty, their signal fires cold. Supply convoys, once a common sight on these well-traveled roads, were nowhere to be found. The rigid, unyielding order of the Empire, the very foundation of Sera's upbringing, was starting to fray at the edges. It was a direct consequence of the Cascade Failure, the spreading corruption that was causing widespread logistical and systemic breakdowns across the Empire.

Sera found a rusted, discarded Imperial Compliance Slate by the side of the road. She picked it up, examining its cracked screen and flickering display. The slate, once a symbol of Imperial authority, was now just another piece of debris, a testament to the Empire's crumbling control.

Anything useful on that, Sera? Erita's voice echoed in Sera's mind, a cool whisper in the back of her thoughts.

Just a broken slate, Sera replied, tossing the useless device into the bushes. *But it's another sign that things are falling apart. Faster than I thought.*

We need to move quickly, Korina added, her voice a worried hum in Sera's mind. *The longer we're on the road, the more dangerous it becomes.*

Agreed, Ada's voice chimed in, a calm, steady presence in the telepathic network. *We need to reach the Oracle as soon as possible. The fate of Kremøtoa depends on it.*

Sera nodded, her resolve hardening. She glanced back at her companions, their faces grim but determined. They were a small group, facing impossible odds, but they were united in their purpose. They would fight for their world, for their love, for the future they were building together. They would not let the Empire, or the Cascade Failure, or anything else, tear them apart.

They continued their march south, the setting sun casting long shadows across the desolate landscape. The road ahead was uncertain, but they would face it together. They were the Crimson Revolution, and they would not be broken.

The rhythmic crunch of their boots on the cracked stone road was the only sound for miles. Korina, walking beside Ada, felt a shiver crawl down her spine. It wasn't the chill wind whipping across the desolate plains; it was a deeper, more unsettling kind of cold. The world felt...wrong. Off. Like a program running on corrupted data.

Did you see that? she whispered into the telepathic link, her voice a nervous hum.

See what, Rina? Ada replied, her mental touch a warm, comforting presence.

The birds, Korina explained, pointing towards a flock of crows circling overhead. *They just...froze. Mid-air.*

A few seconds ago, the crows had been flapping their wings, cawing raucously as they wheeled against the pale sky. Then, abruptly, they had become statues, suspended in mid-flight as if time itself had stuttered. Now, just as suddenly, they were moving again, their flight resuming as if nothing unusual had occurred.

I saw it too, Erita confirmed, her voice a cool, sharp whisper in Korina's mind. *That's not normal, even for Rhedeon standards.*

What in the Void was that? Janna's voice boomed in their minds, a gruff rumble of confusion. *Never seen birds do that before.*

Sera, ever vigilant, scanned the horizon, her crimson hair whipping in the wind. *Is it some kind of thaumaturgical trap?* she asked, her mental tone laced with suspicion.

No, it's not a trap, Korina replied, her fingers flying across Obsidian's smooth surface. The data-slate's screen flickered with complex diagrams and code streams as she analyzed the recent anomaly. The little pixelated lynx in the corner, Ada's whimsical addition, paced nervously, its purple eyes blinking rapidly. *It's...it's a glitch. A data corruption error.*

Explain, Ada commanded, her mental voice calm but firm.

The world's code is becoming unstable, Korina explained, her voice rising with a frantic edge. *Random errors are appearing in the environment. Like those birds. They shouldn't have frozen like that. Their behavioral algorithms should have continued running.*

So, the world is glitching out? Sera asked, her mental tone a mix of disbelief and apprehension.

Essentially, yes, Korina confirmed. *The Cascade Failure...it's not just destroying the landscape. It's corrupting the underlying systems. The rules of the world are breaking down.*

As if to punctuate her words, the river they were approaching began to behave strangely. A section of the water, about fifty meters ahead, appeared to loop. The current, instead of flowing smoothly downstream, began to flow backwards in a jarring, unnatural cycle. The water twisted and contorted, defying the laws of physics, before snapping back to its normal flow. The little pixelated lynx on Obsidian's screen let out a tiny, digitized meowsing, a programmed response to the sudden surge of corrupted data.

Void's name... Janna muttered, her voice filled with awe.

That's...that's impossible, Sera whispered, her usual confidence wavering.

Not impossible, Korina corrected, her voice strained. *Just...highly improbable. The world is no longer predictable. The algorithms governing the environment are malfunctioning. Every step we take is a gamble.*

A wave of nausea washed over Korina, a physical manifestation of the world's digital decay. She gripped Obsidian tighter, the smooth, cool surface a small comfort in the face of the unraveling reality around her. Ada's warm hand found hers, a silent reassurance that grounded her.

What does this mean for our journey? Erita asked, her voice a thread of ice in their minds.

It means we need to be even more careful, Ada replied, her mental touch firm and reassuring. *We can't rely on the world behaving as it should. We need to adapt. Improvise. And trust each other more than ever.*

Korina nodded, her heart pounding in her chest. The world was breaking down, but their bond, their love, their shared purpose, that was the one thing that remained constant. That was the one thing she could still hold onto. And in this fractured, glitching world, that was enough. For now.

The town of Duskhaven clung to the edge of the Empire like a withered leaf about to fall. Ada, Sera, Korina, Erita, and Janna entered through a crumbling archway, the Imperial crest above it chipped and faded. The usual bustling energy of a border town was replaced by a suffocating stillness. Shops were shuttered, their windows boarded up. The few citizens who dared venture outside scurried from shadow to shadow, their faces pale and etched with fear.

This place feels...wrong, Sera whispered into the telepathic link, her mental tone mirroring Ada's own unease.

It's the Cascade Failure, Korina explained, her voice a clinical hum in Ada's mind. *The data corruption is affecting everyones' behavioral algorithms. Fear and paranoia are the dominant responses.*

Makes sense, Erita chimed in, her mental tone laced with cynicism. *When the world starts falling apart, people tend to lose their minds.*

We need supplies, Janna grumbled, her voice a low rumble. *But I don't like the look of this place.*

Ada nodded, her gaze sweeping over the deserted marketplace. The air hung heavy with the smell of dust and decay, a physical manifestation of the world's digital rot. The three moons hung low in the twilight sky, Argent casting long, distorted shadows that seemed to writhe and twist like the corrupted code infecting her creation.

We'll split up, Ada decided, projecting her voice into their minds. *Sera and Janna, secure the perimeter. Erita, gather intel. Korina, you're with me. We'll try to find a general store or something.*

Be careful, Sera's voice echoed in Ada's mind, a warm touch of concern.

Always am, Ada replied, offering a reassuring mental smile.

Ada and Korina moved through the deserted streets, their footsteps echoing eerily in the silence. The citizens who crossed their path avoided eye contact, their bodies tense, their whispers just out of earshot. Ada caught snippets of their conversations: 'demons in the forest', 'the moons are bleeding', 'the end is near'. The fear was palpable, a thick, suffocating blanket that smothered the town.

They found a general store, its door slightly ajar. The interior was dimly lit, the shelves mostly bare. A lone shopkeeper huddled behind the counter, his eyes wide with terror.

"We need supplies," Ada said, her voice calm and steady. "Food, water, medical kits. Anything you have."

The shopkeeper stared at them, his lips trembling. "Demons," he whispered, his voice barely audible. "They're everywhere. In the shadows. Watching us."

He's glitching, Korina whispered into the link. *His dialogue tree is corrupted. He's stuck in a fear loop.*

Ada sighed, her patience wearing thin. She reached out, her fingers brushing the shopkeeper's arm. *[Execute: Calm_Emotional_State],* she commanded silently, injecting a line of code directly into the shopkeeper's programming.

The shopkeeper blinked, his eyes losing some of their frantic edge. "T-Thank you...what...what can I get for you?" he asked, his voice still shaky but more coherent.

While the shopkeeper gathered their requested supplies, Ada

noticed a group of Imperial guards entering the store. Their armor was dented and scratched, their faces grim. The usual air of authority was replaced by a desperate, haunted look.

"Have you seen any...disturbances?" the lead guard asked, his voice strained. "Strange creatures? Unnatural phenomena?"

The shopkeeper shook his head, his eyes darting nervously towards the shadows. "Nothing, sir. Just...just the usual."

Ada exchanged a quick glance with Korina. The guards were clearly overwhelmed, their training and discipline unable to cope with the unraveling reality around them. The Empire's control, once absolute, was crumbling.

"We'll be on our way then," the guard said, his voice laced with a forced confidence. "Stay vigilant. Report anything unusual."

The guards left, their footsteps heavy on the creaking floorboards.

Ada and Korina exchanged relieved glances. *That was close,* Korina whispered into the telepathic link, her mental tone a mix of relief and anxiety.

Too close, Ada agreed, her own thoughts echoing Korina's apprehension. They hadn't been sure if the guards were responding to a specific alert about their presence or if they were simply on a routine patrol, their nerves frayed by the encroaching chaos. Either way, the encounter had been a stark reminder of the danger they faced, even in a town seemingly abandoned by the Empire.

"Here you go," the shopkeeper said, his voice still shaky, placing their supplies on the counter. "That'll be five silver byts."

Ada paid him, adding a few extra coppers. "Thank you," she said, offering a reassuring smile. "Stay safe."

As Ada and Korina turned to leave, the shopkeeper called out, his voice gaining a newfound strength. “Wait,” he said, his eyes meeting Ada’s with a surprising intensity. “I...I need to thank you.”

Ada paused, a flicker of curiosity in her violet eyes. “For what?”

“For...for breaking the spell,” the shopkeeper explained, his voice gaining steadiness with each word. “I...I was trapped. Frozen. Couldn’t think. Couldn’t move. Just...fear.” He shuddered, the memory of the terror still clinging to him like a digital ghost. “You...you freed me.”

Ada exchanged a glance with Korina, a silent acknowledgment of the shopkeeper’s unusual awareness. Most NPCs wouldn’t have recognized the manipulation, their programming simply adjusting to the altered emotional state. This man, however, seemed to have retained a fragmented memory of the fear, a flicker of sentience in the crumbling code of the world.

“It was nothing,” Ada said, a hint of warmth in her voice. The shopkeeper’s gratitude, however misplaced, touched something deep within her. It was a reminder of the human element within her creation, the spark of consciousness that flickered even in the face of systemic decay.

“No,” the shopkeeper insisted, his gaze fixed on Ada. “It was everything. You...you gave me back myself. My name...my name is Elroy. What...what’s yours?”

Ada hesitated for a moment, her programmer’s mind calculating the potential risks of revealing her identity. But the shopkeeper’s earnest plea, the genuine gratitude in his eyes, disarmed her usual caution. “Elroy was it?” she said, offering a small smile. “Ada Lynx. Not like the animal...*LIH*-nux.” She gestured towards Korina. “This is Korina.”

“Ada Lynx,” Elroy repeated, his voice a low murmur. “Korina.”

He looked at them, his eyes filled with a strange mix of hope and fear. "...we'll remember you. Remember what you did for us."

"Maybe," Ada echoed, a flicker of something akin to sadness in her violet eyes. The thought of Duskhaven remembering them, remembering this small act of kindness amidst the encroaching chaos, felt strangely poignant. It was a testament to the enduring power of connection, even in a world on the brink of collapse.

Ada and Korina left the general store, their backpacks laden with supplies. As they stepped back out into the deserted streets, Ada couldn't shake the feeling that Duskhaven, this forgotten town on the fraying edge of the Empire, held a significance beyond its strategic location. It was a microcosm of Kremøtoa itself, a place where hope and fear, order and chaos, reality and simulation, collided in a silent, desperate struggle for survival. And Ada, the reluctant god of this crumbling world, felt a renewed sense of responsibility, a fierce determination to not only fix the broken code but to protect the flickering sparks of humanity within it.

They rejoined Sera, Janna, and Erita at the edge of town. Erita, her usual cynicism tinged with a surprising urgency, reported a disturbing discovery: Thorne's influence extended even to this remote outpost. His enforcers were actively rounding up citizens, searching for anyone suspected of harboring dissent. The Cascade Failure hadn't weakened Thorne's grip; it had simply given the catatonic tyrant a new excuse to tighten it.

We need to leave, Erita said, her voice sharp in Ada's mind. *Now. Before they find us.*

Ada nodded, her gaze sweeping over the desolate town. Duskhaven, once a symbol of the Empire's reach, was now a ghost town, haunted by fear and the encroaching digital decay. And as they turned their backs on its crumbling walls, Ada couldn't shake the feeling that they were leaving behind more than just a town. They were leaving behind a piece of Kremøtoa's soul, a fragment of the world she had created and was now desperately trying to save.

They left the store, their packs heavier, their minds racing. The encounter with the guards had been a sobering reminder of the precariousness of their situation. They were deep within Imperial territory, their faces plastered on wanted posters, their every move potentially tracked. The Cascade Failure was disrupting the Empire's systems, creating pockets of chaos and confusion, but it wasn't a guarantee of their safety. If anything, it made their situation more unpredictable, more dangerous.

We need to get out of here, Ada said, her voice firm despite the tremor of fear that ran through her.

Agreed, Korina replied, her mental tone mirroring Ada's urgency. *Let's find the others and get moving.*

Ada noticed a group of children huddled in an alleyway, their eyes wide with fear, whispering about monsters in the dark. *It's spreading,* Korina whispered into the link, her voice filled with a chilling certainty. *The fear. The chaos. It's not just the land that's decaying. It's the society. The very fabric of the Empire is unraveling.*

Ada nodded, her heart heavy with a grim understanding. The Cascade Failure wasn't just an abstract threat; it was a cancer, eating away at her creation from within. And as they stepped back out into the desolate streets of Duskhaven, Ada knew that the fight was far from resolution. *Far from it.*

As they left Duskhaven, the whispers followed them, clinging to their backs like phantom cobwebs. The fear in the town was a physical presence, a cold, suffocating weight that pressed down on them, even after they had left the town's dilapidated gates behind. The crows continued their erratic flight, sometimes freezing mid-air, sometimes flying backward, as if the very laws of physics were being rewritten around them. The river, still flowing upstream, seemed to mock the logic of the world Ada had created.

This is bad, Korina said, her mental voice tight with anxiety. *Really bad. The corruption is spreading faster than I anticipated.*

We need to reach the Oracle, Erita said, her voice clipped and urgent. *The sooner, the better.*

Agreed, Sera replied, her mental tone grim. *But we need to be careful. The closer we get to the Ashen States, the more unstable the terrain will become.*

We'll adapt, Janna said, her gruff voice a steady counterpoint to the others' anxiety. *We always do.*

Ada nodded, her gaze fixed on the horizon. She felt a surge of determination, a renewed sense of purpose. She had created this world, and she would not let it be consumed by chaos. She would fix it, no matter the cost.

They continued southeast, the landscape growing increasingly desolate. The once vibrant fields were now barren wastelands, the trees twisted and gnarled, their leaves withered and gray. The air grew heavy with the stench of decay, a constant reminder of the world's impending collapse.

They camped under a sickly, pulsating sky, the moons casting an eerie, distorted light. The usual comforting silence of the night was replaced by a low, persistent hum, a symphony of static that seemed to emanate from the very earth beneath them. Even the fire they built crackled with an unnatural energy, its flames flickering in strange, geometric patterns.

Ada slept fitfully, her dreams filled with distorted images of her creation, twisted landscapes and monstrous entities made of pure, glitching code. She woke with a gasp, her heart pounding, her body slick with sweat.

Are you alright? Sera's voice echoed in her mind, soft and concerned.

Just a bad dream, Ada replied, trying to sound reassuring, even though the fear still clung to her like a shroud.

We're almost there, Erita said, her voice sharp and pragmatic. *Another day, maybe two, and we'll reach the edge of the Malware Swamps.*

Ada nodded, her gaze fixed on the horizon. She knew that the Swamps were just the beginning of their journey, the first of many perilous obstacles they would face on their quest to reach the Oracle. But she also knew that they had come too far to turn back. The fate of Kremøtoa rested on their shoulders, and they would not fail.

The next day's journey was a grueling trek through a landscape that seemed to actively resist their progress. The ground beneath their feet shifted and cracked, the air thick with a cloying, unnatural humidity. The crows, now more numerous, swirled around them like living shadows, their caws a constant, unsettling chorus.

As they crested a hill, the horizon ahead came into view. And for the first time, Ada saw the true extent of the corruption that was consuming her world.

The horizon was no longer a distant line of mountains and forests, but a swirling, writhing mass of sickly green and purple miasma. It seemed to pulse and breathe with a life of its own, a monstrous entity made of pure, corrupted data. The air grew thick and heavy, the humidity pressing down on them like a physical weight. The stench of decay intensified, now mingled with a sharp, metallic scent, like ozone after a lightning strike, but twisted, corrupted. It was the smell of broken code, of reality itself unraveling.

Korina's *Obsidian*, clutched tightly in her hand, began to emit a low, persistent warning hum, its screen flickering with distorted images of the landscape ahead.

Argent's Light... Sera breathed into the telepathic link, her voice filled with a mixture of awe and dread. *What is that?*

The Malware Swamps, Erita replied, her voice grim. *And it's far worse than I imagined.*

Ada stared at the horrifying spectacle before them, her heart pounding in her chest. She had created this world, this beautiful, vibrant world, and now it was being consumed by a cancer of her own making. She had brought this upon them all. She was the architect of their destruction.

But even as despair threatened to overwhelm her, a flicker of determination ignited within her. She would not let her creation be destroyed. She would find a way to fix it, to heal it, to restore it to its former glory.

We need to get moving, she said, her voice firm despite the tremor of fear that ran through her. *The Oracle is waiting.*

CHAPTER 8

THE SCHOLAR'S SUSPICION

The air in the Grand Conclave Chamber of the Veritas Archives hummed with a low, almost imperceptible thrum of arcane energy. Scholar Atomuzk, his fingers stained with ink and chalk dust, meticulously adjusted the focusing lens of his data-slate, his gaze fixed on the swirling holographic projection of Kremøtoa's corrupted sectors. The crimson tendrils of the Cascade Failure, like veins of diseased data, pulsed and spread across the map, a horrifying visual representation of the world's decay.

Grand Magister Xehon, his ancient face etched with serene detachment, gestured towards the projection. "The rate of corruption is accelerating," he observed, his voice a calm, almost melodic counterpoint to the escalating crisis. "Archivist Itania, your assessment?"

"Fascinating," Itania murmured, her eyes gleaming with intellectual curiosity. "The system's foundational architecture remains remarkably sound, even under such extreme duress. A testament to the brilliance of its original design."

"Indeed," Xehon agreed. "A shame that such elegance is being marred by such...unforeseen variables."

A young Scribe, his face pale with anxiety, approached the central dais, clutching a data-slate. "Grand Magister, a high-priority report from Duskhaven. A...significant thaumaturgical anomaly."

Xehon raised a perfectly sculpted eyebrow. "Significant? In what manner?"

"A localized surge of pure violet energy, Magister. Of immense magnitude. It appeared and vanished in a blink of an eye. The witnesses describe it as...a light of correction."

Atomuzk straightened, his quiet, analytical mind intrigued. A 'light of correction'? Such a phrase suggested a deliberate act, a targeted intervention. An anomaly within an anomaly. His fingers twitched with the urge to dissect the data, to unravel its underlying logic.

Xehon, his composure undisturbed, gestured for the Scribe to display the report. The holographic projection shimmered, the corrupted map of Kremøtoa replaced by the grainy image of a general store in Duskhaven. The image was timestamped and geo-tagged, its metadata meticulously cataloged. Then, the anomaly occurred.

The general store's interior, dimly lit and filled with mundane objects, was suddenly bathed in an ethereal violet light. It wasn't a gradual illumination, but an instantaneous, overwhelming surge of pure energy. The light pulsed with an almost palpable power, shining *through* the solid matter of the store, as if the very walls themselves were made of translucent glass. For a fraction of a second, the image was completely saturated with violet, the details of the store obscured by the sheer intensity of the light. Then, as quickly as it had appeared, it vanished. The store returned to its previous dim state, the objects within undisturbed, the shopkeeper seemingly unharmed.

Xehon frowned, a rare display of uncertainty. "Curious. The energy signature is...unprecedented. Yet, there appears to be no lasting effect. No structural damage. No thaumaturgical residue. Run the surveillance logs again, Scribe. Perhaps we missed something."

The Scribe, his fingers trembling, repeated the sequence. The violet light pulsed, dimmed, and vanished. Still, nothing.

"Remarkable," Itania murmured, her voice a low hum of fascination. "Such a potent surge of energy, yet completely localized and...transient. As if it were...a phantom event."

Atomuzk leaned closer to the projection, his analytical mind working furiously. The energy signature was undeniably thaumaturgical, yet its behavior defied known principles. It was like a burst of code, injected into the system and then immediately withdrawn, leaving no trace of its presence. A precise, targeted intervention. But to what end? And by whom?

"Scholar Atomuzk," Xehon said, his voice sharp, breaking through Atomuzk's concentration. "Your thoughts?"

Atomuzk hesitated, his mind still grappling with the anomaly's implications. "The energy signature is...unique," he said, choosing his words carefully. "Pure violet. Highly focused. It suggests a... refined control over thaumaturgical principles. Beyond anything I've encountered in the Archives."

"Could it be related to the Cascade Failure?" Celerun asked, his voice tinged with anxiety. "A...new form of corruption?"

Atomuzk considered the possibility. The timing was certainly suspicious. But the nature of the energy, its precision and control, seemed to contradict the chaotic, destructive nature of the Cascade Failure. This was not a random event. This was a deliberate act.

"I...I don't know how to classify it, Magister," the Scribe stammered, his voice trembling. "The shopkeeper, Elroy, he was... catatonic. Eyes wide, muttering about the end of the world. Then, the light...and he was fine. Completely normal. Like nothing happened."

Atomuzk's suspicion solidified. This was not a natural phenomenon. This was a deliberate act of...restoration. A countermeasure to the Cascade Failure, perhaps? His mind raced, formulating hypotheses, discarding them just as quickly. The implications were staggering.

"Show me the shopkeeper," Xehon commanded, his voice laced with a rare edge of impatience.

The Scribe, his fingers fumbling on the data-slate's controls, zoomed in on the figure behind the counter. The shopkeeper, Elroy, was a middle-aged man with thinning hair and a weary, haunted expression. His eyes, wide and unfocused, darted nervously around the store, as if expecting the world to dissolve around him at any moment. Then, the violet light pulsed, and Elroy blinked. His eyes refocused, the haunted look replaced by an expression of...clarity. He straightened his tunic, adjusted the spectacles perched on his nose, and resumed stocking shelves, humming a quiet tune.

"Remarkable," Itania murmured, a flicker of genuine surprise in her voice. "A complete restoration of cognitive function. And in such a short time frame. The implications for thaumaturgical healing are..."

"Irrelevant," Xehon interrupted, his gaze fixed on two figures who had entered the store just before the violet light appeared. One was tall and slender, with long, unruly dark violet hair and sharp, intelligent purple eyes. The other, slightly shorter, had intricately braided violet hair and a data-slate clutched in her hand.

"Who are they?" Xehon demanded, his voice cutting through the hushed whispers in the chamber.

The Scribe, startled by the Grand Magister's sudden intensity, scrambled to access the store's audio logs. A faint crackling sound filled the chamber, followed by the clear, distinct voices of the two women.

"Elroy? Is that you?" the taller woman asked, her voice laced with concern.

"By the moons..." Elroy murmured, his voice weak and trembling. "I...I thought I was done for. The glitches...they were everywhere. Inside my head..."

"It's alright, Elroy," the taller woman said, her voice soothing. "It's Ada. Ada Lynx. And this is Korina. We're here to help."

"Ada...Korina..." Elroy repeated, his voice gaining strength. "You...you saved me. Argent's light, you saved me..."

Atomuzk's breath hitched. *Ada? Korina?* The names resonated with a strange familiarity. He'd heard them before. Where? His mind raced, sifting through the vast archives of his memory. Then, it clicked.

The Oakhaven incident. The reports of a thaumaturgical anomaly, a young woman with violet hair who healed a child and restored blighted fields. The same unique violet energy signature. Could it be...?

The name, even without the surname, rippled through the chamber like a shockwave. "Korina," the Scribe repeated, his voice barely above a whisper. “She...she said her name was Korina.”

A murmur of recognition, then a sudden, tense silence. Even the perpetually detached Archivist Itania straightened in her seat, a flicker of surprise in her usually impassive eyes. Everyone in the Conclave Chamber knew the name. Korina Tel. The brilliant academic—the once-in-a-millennia prodigy...the disgraced scholar.

Grand Magister Xehon, however, waved a dismissive hand, his expression unchanged. “Korina Tel,” he said, his voice laced with a hint of disdain. “A minor talent. Fled the Archives years ago. A regrettable loss of potential, but hardly relevant to the current crisis.”

Atomuzk’s gaze narrowed. *A minor talent?* Xehon’s words were a calculated dismissal, a deliberate downplaying of Korina’s brilliance. He remembered the circumstances of her departure all too well. Not a voluntary exit, but a forced exile. Ostracized, shunned, her reputation systematically dismantled after a... scandal. A scandal involving her academic rival, Kaelen Vance. Xehon’s protégé.

His gaze swept across the assembled Councilors. Pantium, as always, remained impassive, his ancient face a mask of serene indifference. Centrinah, ever the pragmatist, seemed more concerned with the political implications of the Duskhaven anomaly than its underlying cause. Celerun, the ambitious junior Councilor, nervously adjusted his robes, his gaze fixed on Xehon, seeking approval. Itania, her intellectual curiosity piqued, leaned forward, her eyes gleaming with a predatory intensity.

And then there was the empty seat. Councilor Vance’s seat. Conspicuously, persistently empty. Once again, Kaelen was absent from a critical Council meeting. An absence that, in light of the recent revelations, seemed less coincidental and more...calculated.

A cold knot of suspicion tightened in Atomuzk's stomach. The pieces were falling into place, forming a disturbing, unsettling pattern. Korina Tel, disgraced and exiled after a scandal involving Kaelen Vance. Kaelen Vance, Xehon's protégé, now inexplicably absent. And Ada Lynx, a thaumaturgical anomaly of unprecedented power, appearing in Duskhaven alongside Korina, wielding violet energy that healed and restored. The connections were too significant to ignore.

Xehon, seemingly oblivious to Atomuzk's growing suspicion, archived the Duskhaven report with a flick of his wrist. "Another anomaly," he declared, his voice calm and dismissive. "To be studied, cataloged, and ultimately...understood. Unless anyone has further insights to offer, I suggest we return to the analysis of the Cascade Failure. Time, as they say, is of the essence."

Atomuzk opened his mouth to speak, to voice his concerns—to demand a full investigation into Korina's exile and Kaelen's disappearance. But the words caught in his throat. He knew, with a chilling certainty, that any challenge to Xehon's authority would be met with swift, ruthless dismissal. He needed more data. More evidence. Proof that would be irrefutable, undeniable.

"Grand Magister," he said, his voice quiet and measured, "if I may, I would like to...cross-reference the Duskhaven report with some older texts. Perhaps there are precedents, historical echoes that might shed light on the nature of this...violet energy."

Xehon, his attention already shifting back to the holographic projection of the Cascade Failure, waved a dismissive hand. "By all means, Scholar Atomuzk. Knowledge is power, as we all know. Inform the Council of your findings."

Atomuzk bowed his head, concealing the flicker of determination and defiance in his eyes. "Of *course, Grand* Magister."

He turned and walked towards the exit, his mind already racing, formulating a plan. He would start with Korina's file. Then, Kaelen's. He would dissect the data, piece by piece, until he uncovered the truth. He owed it to Korina. He owed it to the integrity of the Veritas Archives. He owed it to the crumbling world of Kremøtoa.

Exiting the Grand Conclave Chamber, Atomuzk navigated the labyrinthine corridors of the Veritas Archives, his footsteps echoing in the silent halls. He reached his private study, a small, cluttered space filled with stacks of data-slates, scrolls, and ancient texts. He activated the security protocols, sealing the room from any outside intrusion, and then approached his personal console.

Atomuzk's fingers danced across the console, inputting a complex sequence of commands. He initiated a high-level, encrypted search, bypassing the standard archival protocols.

The data flowed onto the screen, a cascade of information detailing Kaelen's academic career. A meteoric rise through the ranks of the Veritas Archives. Brilliant, ambitious, innovative. A prodigy in his own right. But something about the narrative felt... off. Too perfect. Too seamless.

Atomuzk narrowed his search parameters, focusing on the years surrounding Kaelen's most significant breakthroughs. He cross-referenced these dates with a series of 'odd' or 'unclassifiable' events from the Archives' history, but from a certain demographic: other talented female scholars—all brilliant, all promising—who had abruptly resigned, their research discredited, their reputations tarnished. Data breaches blamed on "system errors" that coincided suspiciously with Kaelen's access to sensitive information. Research grants mysteriously reallocated, diverted from promising projects led by female scholars to Kaelen's own endeavors.

The dots began to connect, forming a disturbing, sickening pattern. A pattern of academic sabotage, abuse of power, and... potential sexual assault. Atomuzk felt a chill crawl down his spine. He delved deeper, accessing the Archives' confidential records. He found them. A number of formal complaints filed against Kaelen by other female scholars, all alleging various forms of harassment, intimidation, and unwanted advances. All of which had been summarily dismissed by Grand Magister Xehon for 'lack of evidence'.

He stared at the screen, his stomach churning. *Lack of evidence.* The words mocked him, a testament to the Council's willful blindness, their complicity in protecting one of their own. He now understood. He understood Korina Tel's 'scandal'. Her abrupt departure. The hushed whispers, the veiled accusations, the systematic dismantling of her reputation. It wasn't a scandal. It was a *cover-up*. A horrific, life-changing assault on her autonomy, her brilliance, her very being, disguised as a lapse in judgment—a stain on the pristine reputation of the Veritas Archives. And Xehon, the supposed guardian of knowledge and truth, had orchestrated the *entire charade*.

Atomuzk leaned back in his chair, his mind reeling. He had a mountain of incriminating evidence. A damning indictment of Kaelen Vance and, by extension, Grand Magister Xehon himself. But he had no willing witnesses. The victims, silenced and shamed, had either fled the Archives or retreated into the shadows, their careers ruined, their lives irrevocably altered. He was alone.

His thoughts returned to Korina. He imagined her pain, her isolation, the injustice she had endured. A wave of anger washed over him, a burning fury that threatened to consume him. He had to do something. He had to expose the truth. But how? Accusing a High Councilor, especially one as influential as Kaelen Vance, was political suicide. He would be ostracized, ridiculed, his own career destroyed. And Xehon, with his iron grip on the Council, would ensure his silence, his findings buried deep within the Archives' confidential records, never to see the light of day.

He stared at the web of corruption he had uncovered, the intricate network of lies and deceit that had protected Kaelen Vance for so long. Disgust warred with a cold, hard pragmatism. He had to be careful. He had to be strategic. He had to find a way to expose the truth without destroying himself in the process.

His gaze fell on Korina's file, still open on his console. He scrolled through the data, searching for anything, any clue that might help him contact her. And then he saw it. A small, almost insignificant detail. A data-slate transponder token. A unique identifier for secure communication. A direct link to Korina Tel and her data-slate, *Obsidian*.

A flicker of hope ignited in his chest. He had a way to reach her. A way to tell her he knew the truth. A way to offer his support, his assistance. A way, perhaps, to finally bring Kaelen Vance to justice; not only Vance...but Xehon too. He'd target the entire Voided council for their complicity, *they don't care about Korina, I may be the only one...*

He reached for the console, his fingers hovering over the keys. He hesitated. This was a dangerous game he was about to play. A game with potentially devastating consequences. But he knew, with a certainty that transcended logic and reason, that he had to play it. For Korina. For the Veritas Archives. For the future of Kremøtoa.

CHAPTER 9

THE CLINICAL ASSESSMENT

The apartment door swung open before Kenji's knuckles could make a second rap. Samantha stood there, a phantom of her usual self. Her hair was a tangled mess, her eyes wide and rimmed with a sleepless red. She pulled him inside without a word, her grip on his arm surprisingly strong.

The air inside was thick and close, a strange cocktail of stale coffee, the metallic tang of ozone, and the faint, sweet scent of microwaved ramen. Stacks of programming manuals listed like condemned buildings on every flat surface. Empty energy drink cans stood in silent, aluminum armies. It was the organized chaos of a mind chasing a singular, all-consuming obsession. Kenji's own room often looked like a toned-down version of this.

But his eyes were not on the mess. They were on the machine.

It dominated the far wall, a custom-built altar of glowing silicon and humming fans that pulsed with a life of its own. Thick, braided cables snaked from its core like obsidian arteries, feeding a bank of monitors. It was not a store-bought rig. This was bespoke

—a monster forged with a specific, terrifying purpose. The low, resonant thrum of its cooling systems vibrated through the floorboards, a constant, powerful heartbeat. A low whistle escaped Kenji's lips.

"My God, Sam...what has she been building?"

"Kenji..." Samantha's voice was a ragged whisper. She pointed a trembling finger toward the center of the technological shrine.

And then he saw her.

Ada.

She was slumped in a high-backed immersion chair, the kind used for deep-dive VR simulations, though this one was clearly a custom, more invasive model. A complex neuro-headset covered her eyes and temples, trailing wires that disappeared into the supercomputer's main chassis. She was perfectly still, her face pale under the monitors' glow. Her chest rose and fell in a slow, steady rhythm, but she looked...absent. As if the person who inhabited that body had simply vacated the premises.

A primal, cold dread seized Kenji's chest. He dropped his duffel bag, the IV kits inside clattering. "Is she—?" He took a step forward, his mind flashing through a dozen horrible scenarios—electrocution, neural feedback loop, catastrophic system failure.

"***Don't!***" Samantha's shriek cut through the electronic hum. "Look!"

She pointed again, this time at the central monitor. Kenji's gaze followed, and the fear in his gut froze, replaced by a sudden, jarring sense of intellectual whiplash.

The screen wasn't displaying an error code or a system crash report. It was a custom-coded application window. The text glowed a stark, urgent green against a black background.

[{SYSTEM WARNING: CRITICAL BIOLOGICAL EVENT IMMINENT}]
USER: ADA_LYNX | STATUS: ALIVE | VITAL SIGNS: STABLE (INDUCED STASIS)
DO NOT DISCONNECT FROM POWER. DO NOT ATTEMPT PHYSICAL REVIVAL.
DISCONNECTION OF PRIMARY SYSTEM WILL RESULT IN CATASTROPHIC, IRREVERSIBLE BIOLOGICAL TERMINATION.
I AM OKAY. I AM SAFE.
—ADA

And in the bottom right corner of the window, a tiny, animated pixel-art cat, the same shade of violet as Ada's eye color, was curled up asleep. Its tail twitched.

Kenji stared, his mind struggling to reconcile the grim, capitalized warning with the whimsical, 8-bit feline. He felt the static crackle in the air around the massive machine. The chill of fear that had gripped him moments before didn't vanish, but it was forced aside by a wave of stunned admiration. *She had anticipated this. She knew someone would find her. She knew they would panic. She had coded a failsafe message to stop them.*

"She's...in there," Samantha choked out, tears finally spilling down her cheeks. "I think...Kenji—I think she uploaded herself."

Kenji tore his eyes from the screen and looked from the

humming supercomputer to Ada's peaceful, motionless form. He took a slow, deliberate breath, his brain shifting gears from panicked friend to analytical technician. The chaos of the room, the terrifying machine, the girl who looked like a ghost—it all coalesced into a single, complex problem. A problem of unprecedented scale and elegance.

"The energy matrix is self-regulating," he murmured, his eyes tracing the flow of power through the transparent casing of the liquid-cooling system. "The design is...remarkably elegant." He turned to his sister, his voice now quiet, stripped of all emotion except a laser-like focus. "Tell me everything. Start from the beginning."

The supercomputer hummed, a low, constant thrum that felt like the pulse of the room. It was the only steady thing in Samantha's world. Her own heart hammered a frantic, arrhythmic beat against her ribs. She wrapped her arms around herself, digging her fingers into her sweater as if she could hold herself together by force.

"Everything?" Her voice was a dry rasp, the words catching in her throat. The bitter ghost of yesterday's coffee coated her tongue. She nodded, her gaze flickering from Kenji's unnervingly calm face to Ada's still form, then to the absurdly cheerful pixel cat snoozing on the monitor.

"It—it was the last few weeks," she began, the story tumbling out in a disorganized rush of memory and fear. "She was always working on...on this." Samantha waved a hand at the massive machine. "Her 'project.' Kremøtoa, she called it. But it got... *different*. She stopped answering her phone. *She barely ate*. I'd bring her food, and she'd look at me like she didn't see me, just...through me."

How do I make this sound sane? He's looking at me like I'm a specimen under a microscope.

"We had coffee. Every Tuesday. *For years,* Kenji, we never missed it. Last week...she didn't show. I called. I texted. Nothing. Then, a few days ago, I started getting these weird messages back." She fumbled for her phone, her hands shaking so badly she almost dropped it. She gave up, the memory clearer than the screen anyway. "They weren't from her. I mean, it was her number, but it wasn't...Ada. Just short, weird phrases. 'Finalizing build.' 'System integrity at 99%.' 'Thank you for believing in me.'"

Her breath hitched. She pushed herself off the hard-backed chair she'd been perched on for hours and began to pace the small clear space between a stack of textbooks and a tower of empty ramen cups. The supercomputer's hum followed her, a constant, indifferent witness.

"So I called her mom," Samantha's voice cracked. "We came here together. We found her...just like this. Her mom, she was hysterical. She had her phone out, she was already dialing 119."

Samantha stopped pacing and stared at Kenji, her eyes wide with the remembered panic.

"But I saw the monitor. The warning. That little cat. I knew it was from her. I...I grabbed the phone out of her mom's hand. I had to physically stop her. I told her the paramedics would just unplug everything. That it would kill her. *How do you explain that to a mother?*"

"I've been here ever since. I haven't slept. I've just...watched. Watched the monitor. Watched her." Samantha's gaze fell on her friend, so pale and still, a living statue in a temple of her own design. A wave of exhaustion so profound it felt like a physical weight washed over her. The adrenaline that had kept her wired for the last twenty-four hours was sputtering out, leaving only a hollow, cavernous fear.

"She uploaded her consciousness into her fantasy world," she said, the sentence sounding utterly insane even as it left her lips. "She's trapped in there. And her body...it's just...here."

She finally fell silent, the hum of the machine filling the void. She watched Kenji, her entire being focused on his reaction. He wasn't looking at her with pity or disbelief. His expression was one of intense, focused concentration. His gaze moved from the intricate wiring of the computer to the custom-built immersion chair, to the warning on the screen. He absorbed it all, not as a panicked friend, but as an engineer diagnosing a system of impossible complexity.

Kenji said nothing for a long time. He absorbed Samantha's frantic story not as a narrative of panic and grief, but as a series of data points. He moved with a quiet, deliberate grace, his footsteps silent on the worn floorboards of Ada's apartment. He circled the supercomputer, his eyes tracing the custom-forged architecture. He didn't touch anything, but his fingers hovered over the braided cables and the intricate network of cryo-fluid tubes, feeling the ambient heat radiating from the machine.

It was an engineering marvel. A masterpiece of bespoke design. But it was still just silicon and rare earth metals. It was a physical object, bound by the laws of thermodynamics and processing limitations. And that was the first impossibility.

He turned his attention to the monitor. The warning message was clear, the typography stark. Below it, the real-time biometrics scrolled in a placid, green stream. **Heart_Rate: Stable. Blood_Oxygenation: 98%. Neural activity:** a complex, rhythmic wave that was neither sleep nor wakefulness. And in the corner, the little pixel-cat, Lynx, twitched its tail in a pre-programmed loop of slumber. *A perfect, self-contained system.* He reached out and lightly tapped the bezel of the monitor. The cat's ears perked in the animation before it settled again.

Wait...what?

It wasn't just a warning. *It was a live user interface. A status report from a running program.* That was the second impossibility.

Finally, his gaze settled on Ada. She was not in a coma. Comas were chaotic—a systemic breakdown. This was...clinical. Precise. An induced stasis managed with a level of bio-feedback he couldn't begin to comprehend. Her body wasn't just a vessel left behind; it was a peripheral, actively managed and maintained by the central processing unit. The third impossibility.

Three facts that could not logically coexist. A machine not powerful enough to host a consciousness was running an active UI that was in turn managing the complex biological stasis of its user. It was a paradox. A system that defied the fundamental principles of his world.

Unless...he was looking at the problem from the wrong direction.

She didn't upload her mind into the machine. The thought struck him with the force of a physical blow, a sudden, terrifying moment of clarity. *She migrated it. The supercomputer isn't the server. It's a transceiver.*

He turned to face Samantha. The analytical calm on his face had fractured, replaced by an expression of profound, soul-shaking awe that bordered on horror. The air in the room felt thin, sucked away by the gravity of his realization.

"Samantha," his voice was low, almost a whisper. "This computer...it's incredible. The most advanced private build I've ever seen. But...it's not powerful enough."

"What? What do you mean? It has to be, she..."

"No." Kenji cut her off, his eyes wide. "To digitally host a human consciousness, to run a simulation complex enough to contain a mind...you'd need a quantum computer the size of a city block. This is a V8 engine and she's achieved orbital velocity. The math doesn't work..."

He took a step closer to Ada's chair, his voice dropping even further, filled with a reverent terror. "She didn't upload herself *into* the game. The data isn't *in* there." He pointed a trembling finger at the humming machine. "That thing is just a gateway. An anchor. It's a bridge between her physical body here and...wherever her consciousness actually *is*."

Samantha stared, her face a mask of confusion and dawning dread. "I don't understand."

Kenji's gaze was locked on Ada. "She's not a player character. She's not an avatar logged into a server." His voice cracked with the sheer weight of the words. "Samantha...she's not just *in* the game. I think...she's become the game."

The silence that followed was absolute. The steady hum of the supercomputer suddenly sounded different—not like a machine, but like the slow, deep breathing of some vast, sleeping creature.

"The world she created, Kremøtoa...I think that's her consciousness now. The program and her mind are one and the same. The code, the physics, the magic she wrote...it's all just her, thinking. She's...the **[root]** Administrator."

Samantha's face, which had held a tiny, desperate flicker of hope that Kenji could simply *fix* this, crumbled. The hope vanished, extinguished and replaced by a new, bottomless despair. This wasn't a technical problem. This was a metaphysical one. A fragile, impossible miracle. Her friend wasn't trapped. She had evolved.

A soft, broken sob escaped Samantha's lips. She slid down the wall until she was huddled on the floor, her shoulders shaking. The quiet sniffles were the only sound that dared to break the heavy stillness. Kenji stood frozen, staring at the woman in the chair who was now a gød in a world of her own making, tethered to this reality by a thread of impossibly advanced technology he could never have dreamed possible. He was an expert standing before a miracle, and he was completely, terrifyingly out of his depth.

The weight of his own words settled in Kenji's gut like a block of ice. *She has become the game.* It was a conclusion so far beyond the realm of logic that it looped back around to become the only possible truth. He looked at Samantha, crumpled on the floor, her small sobs the only sound breaking the supercomputer's steady hum. Her grief was raw, human. His own reaction was a colder, more terrifying thing—the intellectual shock of a physicist discovering a new, fundamental law of the universe by watching it tear a hole in his reality.

He took a slow, deliberate breath, forcing the analytical part of his brain to override the primal urge to run. "Samantha," he said, his voice quiet but firm. "Listen to me. We touch *nothing*."

She looked up, her face streaked with tears. "*What*?"

"The computer. The headset. The power supply." He gestured to the humming monolith. "This is not a PC we can just reboot. It's a transceiver. An anchor. If we break the connection, if we so much as cause a power flicker..." He didn't need to finish. The implication hung in the air, heavy and absolute. He would be unplugging the universe that now held Ada's mind.

"But we can't just leave her like this!" Samantha's voice rose, cracking with a new wave of desperate frustration. "We have to do *something*, Kenji! She's going to *die*!"

As if on cue, a soft chime drew his attention back to the monitor. A line of green text had shifted, now flashing a stark, insistent yellow.

[BIOLOGICAL RESERVES: CRITICAL. NUTRITIONAL INPUT REQUIRED. T-MINUS: 99.1 HOURS]

There it was. The one variable they could control. The physical, biological machine that was Ada's body. Not the gød, not the architect, but the flesh and blood that tethered her to this world.

"You're right," Kenji said, a new, sharp focus cutting through his awe. "We can't fix the system. But we can maintain the hardware." He looked at Samantha, seeing the wild panic in her eyes recede, replaced by a brittle, hard-won focus. He saw her internalize the same thought. *I can't pull her consciousness out, but I can keep her body from failing. I can do this.*

He moved to the duffel bag he'd dropped by the door. "You were right to call me. And right about what to bring." He unzipped it, the sound loud in the quiet room. Inside, nestled among diagnostic tools and a laptop, were several sterile IV kits and bags of saline and total parenteral nutrition. Clinical, sterile, real.

The next few minutes were a blur of quiet, intense activity. They moved with a shared, unspoken purpose, transforming the cluttered apartment into a makeshift ICU. Kenji laid out the supplies on a cleared-off patch of floor—the IV bag, the tubing, alcohol swabs, medical tape. The sharp tear of a sterile package was a small, violent sound in the charged silence.

"The left arm," Kenji instructed, his voice low and professional. "Hold it steady for me. And whatever you do, *don't* jostle the headset."

Samantha knelt beside the immersion chair. She took Ada's arm, her touch infinitely gentle. Kenji watched her hands, which had been trembling moments before, become steady as she cradled her friend's limb. He saw her jaw set, her focus narrowing to this one, crucial task. They were her anchor. They had to be.

"I've got her," Samantha whispered. "Just...be careful."

Kenji tore open an alcohol swab, the sharp, antiseptic smell cutting through the stale air of the apartment. He carefully cleaned a small patch of skin on the inside of Ada's cool, delicate arm. The veins were faint but visible. He picked up the catheter needle, his own heart pounding a steady, heavy rhythm in his ears. This was it. No room for error. He exhaled slowly, positioned the needle, and with a single, practiced motion, slid it into the vein. A perfect insertion. He secured it with tape, connected the IV line, and with a flick of his thumb, opened the roller clamp.

A single, clear drop slid down the tube, then another. A steady, rhythmic drip began, a tiny, life-sustaining metronome. They watched it, mesmerized, for a long moment. It was a ridiculously small action against an impossibly large problem, but it felt like a monumental victory.

Kenji hung the bag from a floor lamp he'd dragged over, adjusting the drip rate with meticulous care. He looked back at the monitor. The flashing yellow warning flickered, and then, with a soft, reassuring beep, it resolved into a solid green.

[BIOLOGICAL RESERVES: STABILIZED. NUTRITIONAL DRIP DETECTED.]

A profound, shared relief washed over them, so immense it was physically exhausting. Samantha let out a breath she seemed to have been holding since she first found Ada. She gently laid her friend's arm back down, her touch lingering for a moment.

Kenji sank back on his heels, the adrenaline leaving him feeling hollowed out. They had stared into a metaphysical abyss and found a single, tangible handhold. They couldn't save Ada, not yet. But they could keep her alive. They could buy her time.

He looked at Samantha, who was watching the steady drip, her expression no longer one of terror, but of grim, unwavering resolve.

"This stops the clock on her body, at least," Kenji said, his voice barely a whisper. "For now."

He settled onto the floor beside her, their shoulders almost touching, two sentinels at the foot of a strange, new gød's throne.

"Now...we wait."

CHAPTER 10

THE MALWARE SWAMPS

The air hung thick and heavy, a cloying, unnatural humidity that clung to Janna's skin like a shroud. The stench was overwhelming—a nauseating blend of rot and ozone, like a battlefield after a thaumaturgical bombardment, but amplified, twisted into something...*wrong*. Fundamentally wrong. Even the light felt sickly, a filtered, green-and-purple miasma that writhed and pulsed over the landscape, casting an eerie, unsettling glow on the twisted, glitching trees and the bubbling, viscous pools of what looked like corrupted data.

Janna gripped the worn leather of her axe handle, her knuckles white. She'd seen her share of grim battlefields, smelled the stench of death and decay in a hundred different forms. But this...this was different. This wasn't the natural decay of flesh and bone, the inevitable entropy of the world. This was a wound. A festering, unnatural sore on the very fabric of reality. A place where the rules didn't apply, where the world itself seemed to be unraveling. The Memory Leak Swamps.

Ready? Sera's voice echoed in Janna's mind, the telepathic link a reassuring presence in the oppressive silence.

As I'll ever be, Janna replied, her mental tone gruff but resolute. She ran a gloved hand over the reinforced seams of her environmental suit, a final check. The suit's arcane filters hummed softly, a fragile barrier against the noxious air. She adjusted the straps of her axe, the familiar weight of the weapon a source of comfort in this alien landscape. She looked at Sera, her expression grim. *Let's get this blighted nightmare over with.*

Sera nodded, her crimson hair a stark contrast to the sickly green light. She hefted her twin blades, the polished steel gleaming faintly. *Stay close,* she said, her mental voice sharp, focused. *And watch your step. This place...it doesn't play by the rules.*

With a final, deep breath, Sera stepped into the gloom, her silhouette quickly swallowed by the swirling miasma. Janna followed close behind, her axe held ready. Ada, Korina, and Erita formed the rearguard, their forms barely visible in the swirling mist.

The ground beneath Janna's boots was soft, yielding, like walking on a bed of rotting leaves. But every now and then, her foot would sink unexpectedly into a patch of viscous sludge, the consistency of rancid oil. The air grew thicker with each step, the stench more overpowering, the light more distorted. The silence was broken only by the bubbling of the data pools and the soft hum of their environmental suits.

Erita moved with a predator's grace, her senses heightened, every nerve ending attuned to the swamp's insidious rhythm. The air, thick with the stench of decay and corrupted data, tasted of ozone and bile on her tongue. The sickly green-and-purple light played tricks on her eyes, the landscape shifting, shimmering, like a poorly rendered image. But Erita was in her element. Chaos was her playground. Uncertainty, her advantage.

Movement. Eleven o'clock. Two data-leeches. High probability of thaumaturgical drain. Sera, handle it. Erita's mental command was crisp, precise, devoid of emotion. She didn't wait for confirmation. She trusted Sera implicitly.

A flash of crimson, a grunt of exertion, and the telepathic equivalent of a satisfied sigh. *Cleared.* Sera's response was brief, efficient. Erita allowed herself a small, almost imperceptible nod. Good.

Erita's gaze swept across the corrupted landscape, her golden eyes piercing the swirling miasma. The ground beneath her boots was treacherous, a morass of mud, corrupted data streams, and half-rendered flora. One wrong step could mean sinking into a data bog, a fate worse than death. She adjusted her grip on her daggers, the familiar weight of the weapons a reassuring presence against her thighs.

Janna, front. Glitch-croc. Partial phasing. Unpredictable attack vector.

Janna's deep rumble echoed in Erita's mind. *Understood.*

Erita heard the heavy thud of Janna's boots as the warrior braced herself. A distorted roar ripped through the swamp, the sound glitching, skipping, like a broken recording. Then, a blur of motion as the glitch-croc materialized partially, its jaws snapping shut inches from Janna's armored leg. The creature's form was a grotesque parody of a crocodile, its scales replaced by flickering pixels, its eyes glowing with corrupted code.

Janna didn't flinch. She swung her axe in a wide arc, the weapon connecting with the creature's distorted snout. A sickening crunch, a spray of pixelated blood, and the glitch-croc dissolved into a cloud of static, its roar cut short.

Clean kill, Janna rumbled, her mental voice laced with a grim satisfaction.

Good. Stay alert. This place is crawling with them. Erita felt a flicker of unease. The constructs were growing bolder, their attacks more coordinated. It was as if the swamp itself was learning, adapting to their presence.

Korina, status report, Erita sent, her mental voice sharp.

Suit integrity at eighty-seven percent. Thaumaturgical reserves stable. No significant data corruption detected...yet. Korina's mental voice was strained, laced with a hint of anxiety. The swamp was taking its toll on everyone.

Ada?

A moment of silence, then Ada's voice, calm, focused. *Monitoring system stability. Low-level data corruption detected in the surrounding flora. No immediate threat.*

Erita nodded, though no one could see her. Ada's calm was a constant, a reassuring presence in the face of the swamp's insidious chaos. But even Ada's control had its limits. Erita had seen the flicker of fear in her violet eyes, the strain on her face as she fought to maintain order in this decaying world.

They pressed on, deeper into the swamp. The air grew thicker, the light more distorted, the constructs more aggressive. Erita led the way, her senses sharp, her mind a whirlwind of calculations. She was the point of the spear, the first line of defense against the encroaching darkness. And she wouldn't falter. Not while Ada, Sera, Korina, and Janna were behind her. Not while Kremøtoa's fate hung in the balance.

Movement. Ten o'clock. Multiple bog-crawlers. Unstable texture mapping. Avoid direct engagement. Erita guided them around a cluster of pulsating, semi-rendered trees, their branches dripping with viscous data streams. The trees seemed to writhe, to reach out with grasping, pixelated limbs.

A sudden, sharp hiss from behind. Erita whirled around, her daggers drawn.

Data-leech. On Korina! Sera's mental shout was laced with panic.

Erita saw it then, a small, leech-like creature with glowing circuits visible beneath its translucent skin. It had latched onto Korina's arm, its tendrils pulsing with a sickly green light. Korina cried out, her mental voice filled with pain and fear.

Erita reacted instantly. She hurled a dagger, the weapon striking the data-leech with pinpoint accuracy. The creature shrieked, a distorted, electronic wail, and detached from Korina's arm, dissolving into a cloud of static.

Korina, report! Erita demanded.

Suit integrity compromised. Thaumaturgical reserves down thirty percent. Data corruption detected. Purging...purging... Korina's mental voice was weak, strained.

Erita cursed under her breath. The data-leeches were more dangerous than she'd anticipated. They didn't just drain thaumaturgical energy; they corrupted the very code that held their bodies together.

Ada, can you— Erita began, but Ada's voice cut her off.

Already on it. Purging corrupted data. Stabilizing suit integrity. It'll take a few cycles. Ada's mental tone was calm, focused, but Erita could sense the strain beneath the surface.

Erita looked at Korina, her face pale, her breathing shallow.

The scholar leaned heavily against Ada, her eyes closed. They needed to get out of the swamp. Now.

New objective, Erita sent, her mental voice sharp, decisive. *Find the nearest stable exit point. Move.*

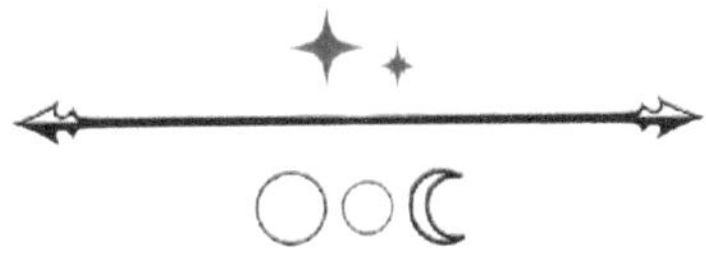

The putrid stench of the swamp clung to Korina like a second skin, a greasy film coating the inside of her nostrils. Each breath was a struggle, a conscious effort to filter the corrupted air, the miasma of decay. Her arm, where the data-leech had attached itself, throbbed with a dull ache, a phantom echo of the creature's corrupting touch. Ada's healing had mended the physical damage, purged the corrupted code from her system, but the memory of the violation lingered, a cold knot of anxiety in her stomach.

They reached the river, and Korina's breath hitched. It wasn't water, not really. It was a churning, swirling stream of pure, liquid data, corrupted and volatile. It shimmered with a thousand sickly colors, sizzling and popping as it ate away at the banks, dissolving the earth into a shower of corrupted pixels. The air above it crackled with static, the very space around it seemed to warp and twist.

Void's name... Janna's mental curse was a low rumble of disgust. *What in the Architect's name is that?*

Corrupted data stream, Korina replied, her mental voice tight. *Highly unstable. Anything physical that touches it...disintegrates.*

So, we're stuck? Sera's mental voice was edged with frustration. Korina could feel the warrior's restless energy, the desire to push forward, to fight. But this wasn't an enemy they could simply hack and slash their way through.

Not necessarily. Korina raised *Obsidian*, its cool surface a comfort against her trembling hand. The little Lynx monitor, Ada's whimsical creation, blinked its pixelated eyes, its ears perked in what Korina now interpreted as encouragement. *The Lynx is picking up a repeating code sequence. Flawed, but predictable. There are windows of data stability. Brief, but they follow a pattern.*

Korina focused, her mind a whirlwind of calculations as *Obsidian* analyzed the river's chaotic flow. The Lynx monitor paced anxiously across the bottom of the screen, its tail twitching. Then, a flicker of recognition in its pixelated eyes. The cat sat up, its ears perked, and began to meow-sing, just loud enough to be heard by Korina.

It's okay Rina, I've got this, it purred telepathically into Korina's mind. *Look here at this pattern. Easy peasy.*

A surge of warmth spread through Korina, a mix of relief and affection for Ada's thoughtful creation. Even in the face of this monstrous corruption, Ada's playful spirit shone through, a beacon of hope in the encroaching darkness.

Okay, Korina broadcast, her mental voice clear, decisive. *I've got the sequence. We have to move on my mark. From one stable point to the next. Exactly. Any hesitation and...* She didn't need to finish the sentence. The image of the dissolving earth, the sizzling, crackling data stream, was enough.

Understood, Sera replied, her mental voice tight.

Ready, Erita sent, her mental tone sharp, focused.

Whenever you are, whippersnapper, Janna rumbled.

Rina...be careful. Ada's mental whisper was filled with concern, and Korina felt a surge of affection for her girlfriend. It was more than just worry; it was love. A love that transcended the boundaries of this simulated world, a love that anchored her to something real, something true.

Korina took a deep breath, steadying her nerves. *First jump. Three...two...one...MARK!*

The first stable point materialized, a small, shimmering platform of solidified data, barely large enough for one person. Sera, closest to the riverbank, leaped onto it, her movements precise, economical. The platform flickered, threatened to dissolve, but Sera held her ground, her crimson tunic a stark contrast to the chaotic colors of the river.

Next jump. Three...two...one...MARK!

Erita sprang forward, landing lightly on the next stable point. The platform where Sera stood dissolved back into the data stream, leaving her momentarily suspended above the abyss.

Three...two...one...MARK!

Janna's massive frame landed with a thud, the platform groaning under her weight. Sera leaped again, her movements a blur of crimson.

Three...two...one...MARK!

Korina's heart pounded in her chest as she launched herself across the chasm, her eyes fixed on the next shimmering platform. The wind whipped past her face, the stench of corruption filled her lungs, and for a terrifying moment, she was suspended in mid-air, the ground dissolving beneath her feet. Then, her boots connected with the solid data, and she stumbled forward, her breath catching in her throat. Ada landed beside her, her hand reaching out, gripping Korina's arm, a silent reassurance.

The final stable point materialized, and Janna and Erita leaped onto it, followed by Sera. The platform beneath Korina and Ada dissolved, the data stream swirling and crackling below.

Final jump. Three...two...one...MARK!

They landed on the opposite bank, the solid earth a welcome relief beneath their feet. Korina sagged against Ada, her legs trembling, her breath coming in ragged gasps.

They had made it.

Ada pulled Korina into a tight embrace, her warmth a comforting anchor in the unsettling landscape. "You did it, Rina," Ada whispered, her voice thick with emotion. "You were brilliant."

Korina's breath hitched, a mix of exhaustion and a profound, unexpected joy. Ada's arms around her, the scent of lavender and ozone clinging to Ada's clothes—it was a tangible reassurance, a validation she hadn't realized she craved. The praise, so simple, so sincere, resonated deep within her, a warmth spreading through her that had nothing to do with Ada's magic and everything to do with Ada's genuine affection. It was a warmth that chased away the lingering chill of the corrupted river, the phantom ache in her arm, the fear that gnawed at the edges of her mind.

We did it, Sera sent through the telepathic link, a note of pride coloring her mental voice. *Good work, Kori.*

Indeed, Erita added, her mental tone dry but approving. *Not bad, scholar.* Even Janna's gruff mental *Well done, whippersnapper,* held a note of respect.

Korina clung to Ada, burying her face in Ada's shoulder. The corrupted landscape, the looming threat of the Cascade Failure, it all faded into the background, replaced by the solid warmth of Ada's embrace, the quiet strength of their shared victory. For the first time since the harrowing crossing, Korina felt a flicker of hope, a fragile ember in the encroaching darkness. They had faced the impossible and emerged victorious. Together, because of her and her calculations.

The heart of the Malware Swamps pulsed with a sickly, violet light. Ada felt a strange pull, a magnetic force drawing her towards a massive, pulsating node of corrupted data at the swamp's center. It was the source, the root process for this festering wound in Kremøtoa's code. *[Execute: System_Diagnostic]* she mentally commanded, her Admin-view highlighting the node in a stark, pulsating crimson. It was far larger, far more complex than she had anticipated. This wasn't just a glitch; it was a cancer, a malignant growth threatening to consume her entire creation.

A chill ran down Ada's spine, a premonition of something far worse than the corrupted data itself. Ethereal, glitching phantoms began to coalesce from the swamp's miasma, their forms indistinct, constantly shifting like flames in a digital wind. Memory Constructs. Korina's data-slate had warned her about these entities, hostile programs born from the collective anguish of forgotten warriors, trapped in the corrupted sectors. *[Query: Memory_Construct_Threat_Assessment]* Ada silently commanded. *Obsidian* displayed a grim assessment: physical attacks were useless, passing through their forms like smoke. Their primary weapon was a silent, psionic scream, an assault on the mind itself, forcing victims to experience their deepest fears, their most traumatic memories.

Incoming, Sera warned through the telepathic link, her mental voice tight with apprehension. *Multiple hostiles. Non-corporeal. Prepare for—*

The first wave of fragmented memories hit them like a psychic shockwave. Ada's mind reeled, bombarded with random, impersonal data—the smell of a forgotten meal, the texture of rough wool, the sound of a childhood song she hadn't heard in years. It was disorienting, confusing, but ultimately harmless. Like static on a radio frequency.

Void's name...what was that? Janna grumbled, her mental voice laced with confusion.

Data fragments, Korina reported, her mental tone clipped, analytical. *Residual memories. Unfocused. No discernible pattern.*

Just keep moving, Erita sent, her mental voice sharp, pragmatic. *They can't harm us if we don't—*

Erita's words cut off abruptly. Ada felt a surge of pure, unadulterated terror from Erita through the telepathic link, a pain so profound it momentarily staggered her. Erita's usually sharp, focused expression went slack, her golden eyes widening with a horror that had nothing to do with the swamp around them. A specific Memory Construct, its form coalescing into the shape of a weeping, cloaked maiden, had latched onto Erita, its psionic tendrils digging deep into her mind, dredging up something buried, something she had fought for years to keep locked away.

Eri...what's happening? Ada sent, her mental voice filled with a desperate urgency. There was no response. Only the raw, visceral terror, amplified a thousandfold by the telepathic link, clawing at Ada's mind, threatening to drag her down into the same abyss of pain.

Erita's body began to tremble, her hands flying up to her ears as if trying to block out a sound only she could hear. A low, guttural moan escaped her lips, a sound of pure, unfiltered agony.

Erita? Sera sent, her mental voice filled with concern. *Eri, what is it?*

Still no response. The Memory Construct, its form now shimmering, pulsating with Erita's own amplified terror, tightened its grip. Ada felt a wave of nausea, the psychic feedback from the link threatening to overwhelm her. She had to break the connection, shield herself from the raw, agonizing pain. But she couldn't. She wouldn't abandon Erita. *Not now.* Not when she needed her the most.

Erita's moans intensified, morphing into a choked sob, a strangled cry of anguish. Her knees buckled, and she collapsed to the ground, her body convulsing, her face contorted in a mask of pure, unadulterated horror.

Then, the scream ripped through the swamp, a raw, guttural sound of pure agony that echoed across the corrupted landscape, a sound that seemed to tear at the very fabric of reality itself. It was the sound of a soul shattering, a mind breaking under the weight of a memory too terrible to bear.

Erita's scream ended as abruptly as it began, leaving a ringing silence in its wake. She lay crumpled on the ground, her body still trembling, her eyes wide, unseeing, her breath coming in shallow, ragged gasps. The Memory Construct, its purpose served, dissipated back into the swamp's miasma, leaving Erita alone in the echoing silence of her own personal hell.

Ada, Sera, Korina, and Janna stared at Erita, their faces masks of shock and horror. They had witnessed the unshakeable spymaster, the woman who had faced down Thorne's enforcers without flinching, the woman who had navigated the treacherous underworld of Port Dominus with cold, calculating precision—reduced to a trembling, broken shell. They had heard the echo of her deepest pain, felt the raw, visceral terror of a memory too horrifying to comprehend. And they were left with a chilling realization: the Malware Swamps were far more dangerous than they had ever imagined.

Panic seized Ada. *Eri...Rina...Sera...Janna...report!* she sent through the link, but only static answered. She scrambled to Erita's side, dropping to her knees in the muck. "Erita!" Ada said, gently shaking Erita's shoulder. "Eri, can you hear me?" Erita's eyes flickered, but there was no recognition, no focus. Just a vacant stare that pierced through Ada, a chilling emptiness that made Ada's blood run cold.

[Execute: Neural_Synchronization_Reboot. Target: Erita_Systema] Ada commanded, her Admin-view highlighting Erita's neural pathways in pulsating violet. The command failed. *Impossible.* She had never encountered a system error she couldn't fix, a code she couldn't rewrite. But Erita's mind was locked, shielded by something far more powerful than any encryption protocol she had ever encountered. It was as if a firewall had slammed shut, blocking Ada's access to the very core of Erita's being.

"Erita, please," Ada pleaded, her voice cracking with desperation. She cupped Erita's face in her hands, her thumbs gently stroking Erita's cheeks. "Come back to me. Please, Eri..." Erita's eyes finally focused, meeting Ada's gaze. For a fleeting moment, a flicker of recognition, a spark of the woman Ada knew and loved, flashed in Erita's golden eyes. Then, it was gone, replaced by the same vacant stare, the same chilling emptiness.

"ERITA!" Ada screamed, her voice raw with anguish, echoing across the desolate landscape.

CHAPTER 11

A RACE OF WHISPERS

The muted hum of the Prefecture's climate control system was the only sound in the perfectly ordered office. Prefect Kraus Valerius sat rigidly behind his obsidian desk, the polished surface reflecting the stark, shadowless light of the luminous panels overhead. His pale blue eyes, cold and assessing, scanned the same intelligence report for the tenth time. The Veritas Council, in their infinite academic naiveté, had classified the Duskhaven incident as an "anomalous thaumaturgical surge," a "curious outlier" in the escalating Cascade Failure. Fools. They saw a puzzle to be solved. Kraus saw a scalpel. A tool of exquisite precision capable of excising the rot that infected Kremøtoa, cell by cell.

Duskhaven. A backwater town on the Empire's frayed edge. A shopkeeper named Elroy, driven to near-madness by the creeping glitches, his mind fracturing under the weight of a reality unraveling before his eyes. Kraus' thin lips curled into a cruel smile. *And then, a surge of pure, violet thauma. Not the chaotic, entropic energy of the Blight. Not the sputtering, erratic bursts of failing systems. But a focused, controlled wave of power that, in an instant, repaired the shopkeeper's fractured mind, restoring perfect order, perfect calm.*

The report confirmed the presence of Ada Lynx and Korina Tel in Duskhaven immediately prior to the event. The disgraced Veritas scholar. A useful pawn, no doubt manipulated by the girl. The report dismissed the surge as a random fluctuation, a side effect of the Cascade Failure. Another example of the Council's willful blindness. They clung to their theories, their equations, their elegant models of a reality that was crumbling around them. They lacked the vision, the ruthlessness, to see the truth.

Kraus, however, saw the truth with chilling clarity. Ada Lynx was not just an anomaly; she was a catalyst. A key to unlocking a new era of absolute order, an era where chaos would be eradicated, dissent silenced, and the Empire's dominion secured for eternity. The girl's power, this ability to impose order on a fractured system, was not magic; it was engineering. Precision engineering on a scale that dwarfed even the most ambitious projects of the Veritas Archives. It was the power to rewrite reality itself.

He steepled his fingers, his gaze fixed on the report's final paragraph. The Veritas Council, in their infinite wisdom, had decided against further investigation. They considered the Duskhaven incident an isolated event, a statistical outlier unworthy of their precious time and resources. Their focus remained on understanding the Cascade Failure, on finding a cure for a disease they themselves had unleashed. Their arrogance would be their undoing.

Kraus, however, would not make the same mistake. He would not let this opportunity slip through his fingers. Ada Lynx was the key. The key to controlling the chaos, to weaponizing the very forces that threatened to tear Kremøtoa apart. He would find her. He would isolate her. He would dissect her abilities, unravel the secrets of her power, and then, he would unleash her on the Empire's enemies, forging a new order from the ashes of the old.

The muted whir of the office door opening broke Kraus' concentration. A young intelligence officer, barely out of the Academy, stood nervously at attention, a data-slate clutched in his trembling hand. The boy's uniform was immaculate, his posture rigid, but his eyes, wide and darting, betrayed his fear. Another incompetent fool, no doubt sent by Archere to waste his time.

"Report," Kraus' voice was a low, gravelly hum, a sound that echoed in the sterile silence of the office.

"Prefect Valerius," the officer stammered, "I have...I have a priority update regarding the Duskhaven incident."

Kraus raised a pale eyebrow, a flicker of annoyance crossing his face. "Proceed."

"Our...our intelligence network within the Veritas Archives has confirmed that the High Council is indeed investigating the thaumaturgical surge," the officer's voice wavered slightly, "They've classified it as a...as a Level Three Anomaly."

"Level Three," Kraus repeated, his voice laced with disdain. "A classification reserved for minor fluctuations in axiomatic fields. They still cling to their absurd theories, their elegant equations, while the very fabric of reality unravels around them."

The officer swallowed hard, his Adam's apple bobbing nervously. "Yes, Prefect. However, there's been...a further development. Our data-spies within the Veritas network...they've detected unusual activity within the Archives' sealed records."

Kraus leaned forward, his eyes narrowing. "Unusual activity?"

"Yes, sir. Approximately seventy-three standard cycles ago, the complete archives on Scholar Korina Tel were unsealed. Accessed remotely. The access logs were...masked. Anonymized. But the thaumaturgical signature...it's a match for a High Council member."

A surge of cold fury pulsed through Kraus' veins. The Veritas Council. Those self-proclaimed guardians of knowledge, those serene, logical custodians of all information. They were playing their own game, their own subtle, insidious game of power. They were not merely observing the anomaly; they were hunting it. Hunting *his* anomaly, by proxy of Korina Tel.

"And the records?" Kraus' voice was dangerously quiet.

"Resealed, Prefect. Thirty-two minutes after initial access. Cleaned. No trace of the intrusion remains, except for the residual thauma signature on the archival seals."

Kraus slammed his fist on the obsidian desk, the sound echoing in the sterile silence of the office. He had underestimated them. He had assumed, in his arrogance, that he was the only player on this board, the only one with the vision to see Ada Lynx's true potential. He had been wrong. The Veritas Council, with their vast network of information, their subtle spies and their insatiable hunger for knowledge, were on her trail as well. They had seen the same potential, the same opportunity, and they were moving to secure it for themselves.

"The Council," Kraus muttered, his voice laced with venom, "They think they can control her. They think they can contain her power, dissect it, categorize it, and file it away in their precious Archives." He stood abruptly, his tall frame looming over the terrified intelligence officer. "They are fools. They do not understand the forces they are playing with. Ada Lynx is not a scholar to be studied; she is a weapon to be wielded."

He turned his back on the officer, his gaze fixed on the panoramic view of Celgrad shimmering beyond the window. The perfect geometric grid of the city, once a symbol of the Empire's absolute control, now seemed fragile, vulnerable. The Cascade Failure, the creeping corruption that threatened to tear Kremøtoa apart, was not merely a systemic error; it was a symptom. A symptom of a deeper, more insidious decay that had infected the very foundations of the world. And Ada Lynx, with her impossible power, was the only cure.

"The Council," Kraus repeated, his voice a low growl, "They want knowledge. They want control. They want to dissect her abilities, to understand the secrets of her power." He turned back to the officer, his eyes blazing with a cold, calculating fire. "I will give them a lesson. A lesson in true power. A lesson they will never forget."

"That will be all, Officer," Kraus dismissed the young man with a flick of his wrist. The officer, visibly relieved, snapped a salute and practically fled the office, the whir of the closing door a welcome punctuation to the tense silence.

Kraus turned back to the window, the panoramic view of Celgrad a stark reminder of the stakes. The Veritas Archives. They were far more adept at this game, this intricate dance of information gathering and covert manipulation. Their network of spies and data-spies stretched across Kremøtoa, their tendrils reaching into every corner of the world, their eyes and ears always open, always listening. They would not hesitate to use their vast resources, their academic prestige, their serene facade of neutrality, to secure Ada Lynx for themselves.

He felt a knot of frustration tighten in his gut. He had been so close. He had held the girl in his grasp, had offered her the gilded cage of Imperial protection, had dangled the promise of power and influence before her. And she had refused. She had chosen defiance over compliance, chaos over order, a band of misfits over the might of the Empire. A foolish, reckless choice, but one that, in retrospect, he should have anticipated. The girl was an anomaly, a wild variable in a system he had spent his entire life trying to control.

But this was no longer about control. It was about acquisition. It was a race, a desperate, high-stakes race for the ultimate prize. Ada Lynx was not just a powerful thaumaturge; she was a weapon. A weapon capable of reshaping the world, of rewriting the very rules of reality. And whoever controlled her, controlled Kremøtoa's destiny.

Kraus' frustration hardened into resolve. He would not be outmaneuvered. He would not let the Veritas Council steal what was rightfully his. He would use every resource at his disposal, every connection, every dirty trick he had learned in his decades of climbing the Empire's greasy pole of power, to secure Ada Lynx for himself. He would unleash her on the Council, on the Theocracy, on the Confederacy, on anyone who dared to challenge the Empire's dominion.

He strode towards the intercom, his mind already racing ahead, formulating plans, anticipating contingencies. He would need to move quickly, decisively. He would need to convene the High Ehxcehl Council, to convince them of the girl's strategic importance, to secure their authorization for a full-scale acquisition operation. He reached for the intercom button, his thumb hovering over the cold, smooth surface.

"Lyra," he began, his voice sharp and authoritative, "Arrange a meeting with the High Council. Immediately. Inform them that I have a matter of...utmost importance to discuss. A matter that concerns the very survival of the Empire—"

He paused, his hand still on the intercom, a sudden thought striking him. The Veritas Council. They were not the only ones interested in Ada Lynx. The Theocracy, with their fanatical devotion and their insatiable hunger for power, would no doubt be watching, waiting for an opportunity to seize the girl for themselves. And then there was Nividia, the enigmatic Render-Witch of Rhedeon, a wild card whose motives were as unpredictable as the tides.

Kraus' jaw tightened. This was more complicated than he had initially anticipated. He was not just playing against the Council; he was playing against the entire world. He was playing a game of shadows, a game of whispers, a game where the stakes were higher than any he had ever encountered. And he was playing to win.

The heavy, rhythmic thud of footsteps echoing down the obsidian corridor outside his office cut through his thoughts. The sound was unusual, too deliberate, too measured for a casual patrol. It was the sound of purpose. The sound of someone coming for him. Suddenly, the heavy footsteps stopped outside his office door.

Kraus' hand froze on the intercom button, his thumb still hovering over the cold, smooth surface. The heavy, rhythmic thud of footsteps echoing down the obsidian corridor outside his office had cut through his thoughts. The sound was unusual, too deliberate, too measured for a casual patrol. It was the sound of purpose. The sound of someone coming for him. He felt a prickle of unease crawl up his spine. He was not accustomed to being summoned. *He did the summoning.*

The heavy footsteps stopped outside his office door. A moment of tense silence hung in the air, thick and suffocating, before the doors hissed open, revealing an elite Imperial Praetorian Guard. The guard's armor was polished to a mirror sheen, the black cerakote reflecting Kraus' own tense face back at him like a distorted, obsidian mask. The guard's visor was opaque, concealing his features, adding to the air of cold, impersonal authority. Kraus recognized the insignia on the guard's shoulder: the Crimson Cell, the personal guard of the High Ehxcehl Council.

The guard snapped a crisp salute, his movements precise and economical. "Prefect Valerius," he said, his voice a modulated, emotionless drone, "You are hereby summoned to the Spire of Command. The Ehxcehl High Council requires a full, immediate report on the escalating crisis in the southern territories."

The guard extended a data-slate, the screen glowing with the stark, official seal of the High Council. Kraus took the slate, his fingers brushing against the guard's cold, armored gauntlet. The message on the screen was brief, to the point, and utterly undeniable. It was not a request. It was a command.

Kraus felt a cold knot of dread tighten in his stomach. This was not good. Not good at all. The High Council. They were the ultimate authority in the Empire, the faceless, nameless bureaucrats who pulled the strings of power from behind the scenes. And they were calling him to account. Calling him to account for his failures. For the escape of Ada Lynx. For the escalating chaos in the south. For the unraveling of his carefully constructed plans.

He handed the data-slate back to the guard, his face carefully composed, betraying no hint of the turmoil churning within him. "Inform the Council," he said, his voice calm and steady, "that I will attend their summons immediately."

The guard snapped another salute, turned, and marched out of the office, his footsteps echoing down the corridor, fading into the distance. The doors hissed shut behind him, leaving Kraus alone in the oppressive silence of his office.

He turned back to the window, the cityscape spread out below him like a vast, intricate circuit board, its lights flickering and dimming, its systems failing. The Malware Swamps. The Ashen States. The spreading contagion. The world he had spent his entire life trying to control was crumbling around him. And now, the High Council was demanding answers. Answers he did not have.

He felt a surge of anger, hot and burning, rise within him. This was not his fault. He had done everything he could. He had followed protocol. He had deployed the Aegis Order. He had activated Protocol Omega-Nine. He had authorized lethal force. But it had not been enough. Ada Lynx, the girl, the anomaly, the unquantifiable asset, had slipped through his fingers. And now, the Empire was paying the price.

He slammed his fist against the obsidian desktop, the force of the impact sending a jolt of pain up his arm. He needed a plan. A new plan. A desperate plan. He needed to convince the High Council that he was not to blame. That he was the only one who could fix this. That he was the only one who could save the Empire.

He strode towards the office door, his mind racing,

calculating, strategizing. He would need to shift the blame. He would need to find a scapegoat. He would need to create a narrative, a convincing narrative, that would absolve him of responsibility and place the burden on someone else. On the Veritas Council, perhaps. Or on the Theocracy. Or even on Ada Lynx herself.

He stopped at the door, his hand on the cold, obsidian handle. He needed information. He needed leverage. He needed something, anything, that he could use to sway the High Council in his favor. He turned back to his desk, his gaze sweeping across the scattered reports, the glowing data-slates, the flickering holographic displays.

His eyes fell on a small, innocuous data-slate tucked away in a corner of his desk. It was a report from his intelligence division, a report he had dismissed as irrelevant at the time. A report about a Duskhaven anomaly. A violet energy surge. A surge that had preceded the healing of a shopkeeper. A surge that had coincided with the presence of Ada Lynx and Korina Tel.

He snatched up the data-slate, his fingers trembling slightly. He had dismissed the report as insignificant, as just another glitch in the system. But now, it seemed, it might be something more. Something much more. It might be the key. The key to his salvation.

He activated the data-slate, the screen flickering to life, displaying the details of the Duskhaven incident. He scanned the report, his eyes widening slightly as he absorbed the information. The energy signature. The timing. The location. It all pointed to one undeniable conclusion.

Ada Lynx was not just a powerful thaumaturge. She was something else entirely. Something...more. Something beyond his comprehension. And that, he realized, was both terrifying and exhilarating. It was a danger. And an opportunity.

He smiled, a thin, cruel smile that barely reached his cold, pale eyes. The High Council wanted answers. He would give them answers. Answers they would never forget.

The air in the Spire of Command hung thick and heavy, a palpable tension radiating from the obsidian walls. Kraus Valerius stood before the Ehxcehl High Council, his posture rigid, his face a mask of calm authority. He had rehearsed this presentation countless times, anticipating their every question, their every objection. He had crafted a narrative, a carefully constructed web of lies and half-truths designed to sway them, to manipulate them, to convince them that he, and he alone, held the key to the Empire's salvation.

"The situation in the south," he began, his voice a low, gravelly hum that resonated through the vast chamber, "continues to deteriorate. The Malware Swamps expand exponentially, defying all attempts at containment. The Ashen States encroach upon our borders, their corrupted influence spreading like a contagion. Our systems are failing. Our defenses are crumbling. The world, as we know it, is unraveling."

He paused, letting his words sink in, his gaze sweeping across the faces of the council members. Grand Marshall Valukap, his brow furrowed in a perpetual expression of disapproval. Grand Vizier Celius, his ancient eyes narrowed in suspicion. High Scribe

Formulos, his lips pursed in a thin, disapproving line. Lord-Commander Makros, his face a mask of impatient boredom. Lady Araya, her expression unreadable, her thoughts a swirling vortex of calculations. Praetor Corrino, with her accessing gaze, seeing all the flow of commerce and volatility. And High Inquisitor Sortis Sacco, his gaze cold and piercing, as if he could see through Kraus' carefully constructed facade, straight into the heart of his deception.

"We have deployed the Aegis Order," Kraus continued, "we have activated Protocol Omega-Nine, we have authorized lethal force. But it has not been enough. The enemy we face is unlike any we have encountered before. It is not a nation, not an army, not a conventional threat. It is...an anomaly. A systemic instability. A reality-bending contagion."

He projected a holographic display, showing the spreading corruption, the glitching landscapes, the monstrous entities. The Council members observed with open skepticism, their uniforms, adorned with the scars of countless campaigns and the symbols of Imperial authority, speaking of a lifetime dedicated to order and control. They had seen it all, fought it all, and survived it all. And they were not easily impressed.

"These are excuses, Prefect," Grand Marshall Valukap stated, his voice a sharp, percussive crack that cut through the silence. "We have faced threats far greater than this. We have quelled rebellions, conquered nations, eradicated entire civilizations. We do not cower before glitches and anomalies."

"With respect, Grand Marshall," Kraus replied, "this is not a conventional threat. This is not a matter of deploying troops or enacting new legislation. This is a fundamental corruption of the world's underlying code. A corruption that defies our established protocols, our established methods, our established understanding of reality itself."

"Enough with the technical jargon, Prefect," Lord-Commander Makros interrupted, his voice a booming roar that echoed through the chamber. "Get to the point. What is the solution?"

Kraus hesitated, feigning uncertainty, playing the role of the reluctant messenger. He knew they would not accept the truth. Not yet. He needed to ease them into it, to prepare them for the revelation he was about to unleash.

"The solution," he said, his voice dropping to a conspiratorial whisper, "lies in understanding the source of the corruption. The... catalyst."

He projected another holographic image, this time of Ada Lynx. The image shimmered and flickered, a testament to her unstable, unclassifiable nature. The Council members stared at the image, their expressions shifting from skepticism to intrigue.

"The girl," High Scribe Formulos murmured, his voice a dry rustle of parchment. "The thaumaturgical anomaly. The one who escaped from Celgrad."

"Precisely," Kraus confirmed. "Ada Lynx is not merely an anomaly. She is...a weapon. A living super-weapon. A weapon capable of manipulating the very fabric of reality itself."

He saw the flicker of understanding in their eyes. The dawning realization of the power he was offering them. The power to control chaos. The power to reshape the world. The power to dominate their enemies.

"A weapon," Grand Vizier Celius repeated, his ancient voice a faint whisper, "capable of...reality manipulation."

"Indeed," Kraus confirmed. "Imagine the possibilities. The strategic advantages. The absolute control we could wield. We could reshape the landscape, rewrite the laws of physics—eradicate our enemies with a thought."

He paused, letting the implications of his words sink in, watching as the Council members' skepticism melted away, replaced by a cold, calculating gleam of ambition.

"And how, Prefect," Lady Araya asked, her voice a cool, analytical hum, "do you propose we acquire this...weapon?"

"I request command of a specialized task force," Kraus stated, his voice firm and resolute. "A task force equipped with the most advanced technology, the most skilled operatives, the most... flexible protocols. A task force with the sole purpose of securing the asset. Of bringing Ada Lynx under our control. For the glory of the Empire."

The Council members exchanged glances, their expressions a mixture of intrigue and apprehension. They understood the risks involved. But they also understood the potential rewards.

"Very well, Prefect," Grand Marshall Valukap finally said, his voice a chilling pronouncements. "Your request is granted. You will have command of Task Force Omega-Ninty-Nine, The Crimson Zsalver Unit. You will have access to all necessary resources. You will have...complete autonomy."

He paused, his gaze locking with Kraus', his eyes cold and piercing. "Succeed, Prefect," he continued, his voice dropping to a menacing whisper, "or your next report *will* be your *last*."

Kraus snapped a salute, his heart pounding in his chest. He had done it. He had convinced them. He had secured his position. He had bought himself *time*. But he also knew that he was now walking a tightrope. He had been given immense power. But he had also been given an ultimatum. A tyrant's leash. He had to succeed. He had to find Ada Lynx. He had to bring her under his control. Not just for the glory of the Empire. But for his *own* survival.

He turned and marched out of the chamber, his footsteps echoing down the long, obsidian corridor, the weight of the Council's ultimatum heavy on his shoulders. The hunt for Ada Lynx was no longer just a mission. It was a matter of life and death.

CHAPTER 12

THE WALLED GARDEN

The world was a kaleidoscope of splintered wood and crimson. Small, bare feet pressed against rough, woolen fabric. The suffocating scent of mothballs filled her nostrils, a stark contrast to the coppery tang that permeated the air outside the closet door. She didn't understand what was happening. Just moments ago, the world had been filled with the warm, comforting aroma of her mother's baking bread and the rhythmic *thunk-thunk-thunk* of her father chopping wood in the yard. Now, it was all screams and shattering glass and the heavy *thud* of bodies hitting the floor.

She peeked through the crack in the closet door, her small hand trembling as she gripped the edge. The scene that unfolded before her was a nightmare painted in vivid, horrifying detail. Her father, his strong arms that usually held her so high above the ground, lay twisted and broken amidst the overturned furniture in their living room. His eyes, usually twinkling with laughter, were wide and vacant, staring up at the ceiling. Her mother, her gentle hands that usually braided her hair so carefully, lay sprawled across the hearth, a crimson stain blooming across her chest.

Men in dark armor stomped through the house, their heavy boots crunching on broken glass and...other things she didn't want to recognize. Their faces were obscured by helmets, but their actions spoke volumes. They weren't just stealing. They weren't just hurting. They were *destroying*. They were taking an almost perverse pleasure in the carnage they were creating.

One of the men, larger than the others, his armor gleaming under the flickering candlelight, approached her father's body. He raised a heavy boot and brought it down with a sickening crunch on her father's already broken arm. The sound was like a dry twig snapping underfoot. It was a sound that would forever echo in the darkest corners of her memory. The man laughed, a harsh, guttural sound that sent shivers down her spine.

Another man, his armor adorned with intricate carvings, approached her mother's body. He knelt down, his gloved hand reaching out to touch the crimson stain on her chest. He brought his hand back, his fingers glistening, and then, with a cruel smirk, he brought his hand to his mouth and licked the blood from his fingers. The child's stomach churned. She wanted to scream, to cry out, to make them stop. But fear, cold and paralyzing, held her captive in the suffocating darkness of the closet.

Then, the lead enforcer, his armor different from the others, adorned with a single, obsidian crow skull on his shoulder, stepped forward. He held something in his hand. Black feathers. Crow feathers. He knelt beside her father's body and, with a chillingly casual gesture, placed a feather on each of his closed eyelids. He then moved to her mother's body and repeated the act, his face a mask of cold, mocking amusement. It was a ritual. A signature. A calling card. A message.

We were here. We took what we wanted. We left our mark.

The men left, their heavy footsteps fading into the distance. The silence that followed was worse than the screams. It was a thick, suffocating silence that pressed down on her, crushing the air from her lungs, stealing the breath from her soul. The world outside the closet door was a ruin. Her world was a ruin. And she was alone. Utterly and completely alone.

The image of the crow feathers on her parents' eyes seared itself into her memory, a brand that would never fade, a constant reminder of the day her innocence died, the day the world became a cold, cruel, and unforgiving place. A silent scream tore through her, a scream that would echo through the years, a scream that would shape her into the woman she would become. A scream that even now, years later, reverberated through the hidden chambers of her mind, a raw, unfiltered horror that threatened to consume her.

Ada watched the scene unfold, her heart pounding a frantic rhythm against her ribs. Sera and Janna, backs pressed together, formed a defensive circle around them, their weapons a blur of motion as they deflected the silent, psionic attacks of the Memory Constructs. The creatures, swirling phantoms of translucent energy, pulsed with a malevolent, corrupted light. Their silent screams echoed through Ada's mind, a cacophony of fear and despair that threatened to overwhelm her.

Korina knelt beside Erita, her slender frame shaking uncontrollably. Tears streamed down her face, blurring her normally sharp, violet eyes. She clutched Erita's hand, her knuckles white, her voice a desperate plea.

"Eri, please, wake up! Please! What in the Void is happening to her? What did those things *do* to her?"

Ada knelt beside Korina, gently placing a hand on her trembling shoulder. The warmth of Korina's skin, the frantic beat of her heart against Ada's fingertips, anchored Ada to the present. She had to focus. She had to *fix this*.

"Rina, I need you to breathe. Deep breaths. It's going to be okay. I won't let anything happen to her. I'll fix this. I promise."

Ada's voice was calm, steady, a deliberate counterpoint to the chaos swirling around them. But beneath the surface, a cold dread was taking hold. She could see the damage the Memory Constructs had inflicted on Erita. It wasn't physical. It was something far worse. They had attacked her mind, her memories, the very core of her being.

Erita's normally sharp, golden eyes were wide and vacant, staring up at the swirling, corrupted sky. Her face, usually so expressive, was a mask of frozen horror. She didn't respond to Korina's pleas, didn't flinch at the phantom screams of the Memory Constructs, didn't even seem to register the presence of the blades flashing mere inches from her face. It was as if she had retreated into some deep, inaccessible recess of her mind, a walled garden of fractured memories and unbearable pain.

Ada reached out and gently brushed a strand of golden hair from Erita's face. Erita's skin was cold, clammy, devoid of the usual warmth that radiated from her. Ada felt a pang of guilt, a sharp stab of responsibility. She had brought them here. She had led them into this corrupted hellscape. And now, one of the people she cared for most was lost, trapped in a prison of her own mind.

"Sera, Janna, keep those things back! We need more time."

Ada's voice was sharp, commanding, the voice of the Architect-Queen taking control. She couldn't afford to panic. She couldn't afford to grieve. Not yet. There had to be a way to bring Erita back. There *had* to be.

"Rina, guard me. I need to intervene directly."

The world shimmered, the edges blurring like a poorly rendered image. Ada felt a jolt, a disorienting surge of energy as she forced her way through the fractured walls of Erita's mind. The swamp dissolved, replaced by a scene of stark, brutal violence. Firelight flickered across a stone floor, casting grotesque shadows that danced across the walls. The air was thick with the coppery tang of blood and the acrid stench of burning wood.

Ada stood as an anomaly within the memory, a shimmering figure of violet light, an anachronism in a world she had not directly created but had ultimately set in motion. She saw the scene through Erita's young eyes, felt the terror that gripped the child's small frame, the raw, primal fear that had been buried deep beneath layers of cynicism and pragmatic detachment.

A young Erita, no older than ten, huddled in the corner of a burning room, her golden hair matted with soot and blood. Her eyes, wide with terror, were fixed on the horrifying tableau in the center of the room. Her parents lay sprawled on the floor, their bodies broken and still, the crimson stains spreading across the rough stone like a corrupted, blooming flower.

Two men in dark armor stood over the bodies, their faces obscured by helmets. One of them, a hulking figure with a battle-axe slung across his back, bent down and placed a single, black crow feather on each of the dead parents' closed eyes. A ritualistic gesture, a final, cruel act of desecration.

The sight filled Ada with a cold, protective rage unlike anything she had ever experienced. This wasn't a bug to be fixed, a line of code to be rewritten. This was a violation, a profound and unforgivable act of cruelty inflicted upon a child, a trauma that had festered and shaped the woman Erita had become.

The young Erita whimpered, a small, broken sound lost in the crackling flames. She made no move to run, no attempt to hide. She was frozen, paralyzed by the horror unfolding before her.

Ada, her ethereal form shimmering, moved. She couldn't change the past. She couldn't rewrite this memory. But she could intervene. She could offer a shield, a fragile barrier against the unbearable pain.

She glided across the room, her violet light casting an ethereal glow that seemed to push back the encroaching shadows. She knelt before the young Erita, her translucent form placing itself between the child and the horrifying sight of her parents' bodies.

The young Erita blinked, her tear-filled eyes widening in disbelief. She stared at Ada, her small hand reaching out hesitantly, as if to touch a phantom.

Ada's own heart ached with a profound, empathetic sorrow. She couldn't speak within this memory. Her voice was lost, trapped within the confines of Erita's mind. But she could express her grief, her rage, her unwavering promise of protection. Silent tears streamed down Ada's ethereal face, shimmering trails of violet light that danced in the firelight.

The young Erita stared at Ada, her expression shifting from terror to confusion, then to a flicker of something akin to hope. She saw not a ghost, not a demon, but a savior, an impossible figure of light appearing in her darkest moment. A silent, weeping goddess offering solace in a world consumed by fire and shadows.

Ada reached out, her translucent hand gently cupping the young Erita's face. The child leaned into the touch, a small, trembling sigh escaping her lips. For the first time since the nightmare began, the young Erita closed her eyes.

Ada held the child close, shielding her from the horrors of the past, a silent promise echoing through the fractured landscape of Erita's mind: *I am here. I will protect you. You are not alone.*

The firelight flickered, casting long, dancing shadows that stretched and distorted across the rough stone walls. Young Erita, her small body trembling, remained nestled against Ada, her eyes tightly shut. Ada knew she couldn't erase the memory. To do so would be to erase a part of Erita, to diminish the woman she had become. But she could contain it. She could build a sanctuary, a place of peace within the shattered landscape of Erita's mind.

A sudden, profound clarity washed over Ada. Another *click* echoed in her mind, not of a lock opening, but of a tumbler falling into place. *A nested function,* she realized. *A subroutine within the larger program of Erita's mind.* She could isolate the memory, encapsulate it within a protective shell of code, a mental sanctuary where Erita could visit on her own terms, not as a prisoner of trauma, but as a master of her own history. The administrative functions began to fall into place, each line of code a brushstroke painting a fortress of resilience within Erita's mindscape. She saw the command forming, not as abstract symbols, but as a glowing violet inscription against the backdrop of Erita's memories:

[CREATION: Sanctuary_Protocol_Initiate]

That's it, she realized.

Ada spoke with absolute conviction in her voice, "[CREATION: Sanctuary_Protocol_Initiate]". A faint, violet light pulsed from Ada's ethereal form, spreading outwards like ripples in a still pond. The light touched the floorboards of the burning room, and a subtle shift occurred. The rough stone beneath their feet began to cool, the heat of the flames receding as if absorbed by some unseen force.

From the floorboards, where the blood of Erita's parents had stained the stone, thin tendrils of violet light began to rise. They solidified, coalescing into smooth, polished blocks of serene, semi-opaque stone, the same calming violet hue as Ada's own energy signature. The blocks rose higher, forming walls that curved inwards, encircling the horrifying tableau at the center of the room.

Ada focused her intent, her will shaping the growing structure. The walls climbed higher still, forming a perfect circle, a secluded enclosure within the burning room. The violet stone was warm to the touch, radiating a gentle, comforting energy that seemed to push back the shadows and the encroaching flames.

Within the circle, the firelight dimmed, the crackling flames softening into a gentle, flickering glow that cast no harsh shadows. The air, once thick with smoke and the stench of burning wood, cleared, replaced by a faint, sweet fragrance like blooming lavender.

Ada continued to shape the space, her will weaving through the fabric of the memory. The stone floor within the circle softened, transforming into lush, green grass. Small, violet flowers bloomed, their petals glowing with a soft, internal light. A small fountain appeared in the center, its water shimmering with a faint, ethereal glow, the gentle splashing sound a soothing counterpoint to the distant roar of the flames.

The walls of the enclosure grew higher still, forming a domed roof that arched overhead, creating a secluded, peaceful space, a walled garden within the burning room. The horrifying tableau of Erita's parents remained at the center, a stark reminder of the trauma that had shaped her. But it was now contained, framed within a sanctuary of peace and quiet reflection. It was no longer a wound constantly bleeding into Erita's consciousness, but a memory that she could choose to approach, to process, to grieve within a safe and controlled environment.

Ada knew this was a profound act, a manipulation of the very core of Erita's being. It was an ethically complex act of psychic surgery, a rewriting of the past that could have unforeseen consequences. She had no chance to ask Erita, to ask her if it was *okay* to do—to have her consent; but in that moment, watching the young Erita sleeping peacefully within the newly created sanctuary, Ada felt it was the right thing to do. It was an act of love, a desperate attempt to heal a wound that had festered for far too long.

The violet light surrounding Ada dimmed, her ethereal form flickering as her energy reserves dwindled. She knew she couldn't stay within Erita's mind forever. The connection was fragile, the strain on her own consciousness immense. But before she left, she wanted to leave one final gift, a symbol of hope within the walled garden.

She focused her intent, her will shaping the raw energy within the memory. Above the fountain, a single, perfect, violet rose bloomed, its petals glowing with a soft, internal light. It was a symbol of resilience, a reminder that even in the darkest of times, beauty and hope could still flourish.

Ada looked at the young Erita one last time, a silent promise echoing through the quiet garden: *You are not alone. You are loved. You are strong.* Then, with a final surge of violet light, Ada withdrew from Erita's mind, leaving the walled garden behind. The world shimmered, the edges blurring, and Ada returned to her own consciousness, the weight of her actions settling heavily upon her.

The world snapped back into focus. The fetid air of the Malware Swamps, thick with the stench of decay and buzzing with corrupted energy, assaulted Ada's senses. She gasped, her body jerking as if pulled from a deep sleep. The mental and emotional strain of entering Erita's mind, of witnessing the raw, primal terror of her deepest trauma—left her pale and trembling. A cold sweat slicked her skin, and her breath hitched in ragged gasps. She swayed, her vision blurring, the vibrant green of the Walled Garden fading, replaced by the sickly yellow-green of the corrupted swamp.

Beside her, Erita's body jerked violently, a raw, animalistic gasp tearing from her lungs as if she were drowning and had just broken the surface. Her eyes flew open, wide and unfocused, but the stark, hollow terror that had gripped them moments before was gone. It was replaced by a profound, soul-deep exhaustion and a bewildered, tearful gratitude that shone through the lingering haze of trauma. Her gaze, usually sharp and calculating, softened, locking onto Ada's. The walls of cynicism and pragmatism that Erita had so carefully constructed around herself, the shields she used to deflect vulnerability and emotional connection, had completely shattered, leaving only a raw, unguarded openness.

"Void," Erita breathed, her voice hoarse and thick with unshed tears. The single word held a universe of meaning, a testament to the profound shift that had just occurred within her. It wasn't a curse, not an exclamation of frustration or anger, but a quiet prayer of disbelief, a whispered acknowledgment of the impossible. She looked at Ada, her golden eyes shimmering with a mix of awe, gratitude, and a vulnerability so profound it was almost painful to witness.

Erita reached out, her hand trembling as it grazed Ada's cheek. The touch was hesitant, almost reverent, as if she were afraid to break the spell, to shatter the fragile peace that Ada had woven within her fractured mind. The simple gesture spoke volumes, a language far beyond words, a testament to the profound connection that had been forged in the crucible of shared trauma.

The dam finally broke. A sob tore from Erita's throat, a raw, keening sound that echoed through the quiet swamp. The carefully constructed facade of the cynical spymaster crumbled, replaced by the broken, vulnerable woman beneath. Tears streamed down her face, washing away the carefully applied shield of stoic indifference—revealing the raw emotion beneath. She collapsed into Ada's arms, her body shaking with the force of her sobs. It wasn't the quiet, controlled weeping of someone mourning a loss, but the primal, cathartic release of someone finally confronting a pain they had suppressed for far too long.

Ada held Erita close, her own body still trembling with exhaustion, but her arms wrapping around Erita with a fierce protectiveness. She stroked Erita's hair, whispering soft words of comfort and reassurance, her voice barely above a murmur. She didn't try to stop the tears, didn't try to diminish the pain. She simply held Erita, offering a silent sanctuary, a safe space to grieve, to heal, to simply *be*.

Across the clearing, Sera, Korina, and Janna watched in silent, reverent awe. They had witnessed something extraordinary, something that defied explanation, something that transcended the boundaries of magic and technology. They had seen Ada reach into the deepest recesses of Erita's mind, into the very heart of her trauma, and pull her back from the brink. They had seen Ada perform a miracle.

Sera's usual fiery intensity had softened into a quiet reverence, her hand resting on the hilt of her sword, not in a stance of aggression, but as if seeking a grounding connection to the physical world. Korina's analytical mind, usually buzzing with data and calculations, was still, her violet eyes wide with wonder and a dawning understanding of the true depth of Ada's power. Janna, the stoic warrior, stood with her arms crossed, her usual gruff demeanor replaced by a quiet contemplation, her gaze fixed on Ada and Erita, a flicker of something akin to awe in her dark eyes.

The power dynamic within their small fellowship had shifted, irrevocably and profoundly changed. Ada was no longer just their leader, their strategist, their thaumaturgical anomaly. She was their healer, their protector, their anchor in a world that was rapidly unraveling. And Erita, the cynical spymaster, the woman who had always kept everyone at arm's length, had finally allowed herself to be vulnerable, to be held, to be loved.

In the heart of the corrupted Malware Swamps, amidst the decay and the chaos, a new bond had been forged, a bond stronger than steel, a bond built on shared trauma, on unwavering trust, on a love that transcended the boundaries of the physical world. And as the echoes of Erita's sobs faded into the quiet hum of the swamp, they all knew that nothing would ever be the same again.

CHAPTER 13

A WAY OUT

The air crackled with a malevolent energy, a palpable sense of wrongness that pressed against Ada's skin like a physical force. The central malware node pulsed before them, a grotesque parody of the natural beauty she had originally envisioned for Kremøtoa. It was a swirling vortex of corrupted data, a pulsating mass of glitching pixels and distorted code, spewing forth wave after wave of monstrous constructs. The ground beneath their feet vibrated with the node's erratic energy, the very air thick with the stench of decay and the acrid tang of ozone.

This is it, Ada projected into the minds of her companions, her voice calm and steady despite the rising tide of dread within her. *The heart of the infection.* She could feel the node's malevolent intelligence, a cold, calculating presence that probed at the edges of her awareness, seeking a weakness, a vulnerability. It was a digital predator, and they were its prey.

I need to perform a system purge, she continued, her mental voice taking on the crisp, clinical tone she adopted when discussing technical matters. *A complete reset of the corrupted sectors in this whole region of swampland. But it will be a complex and dangerous process. I'll need to enter a deep trance, a full system immersion. My physical body will be completely vulnerable.*

A wave of concern washed through the telepathic link, a mixture of Sera's fierce protectiveness, Korina's anxious calculations, Erita's pragmatic assessment of the risks, and Janna's stoic determination. Ada could feel their love, their fear, their unwavering loyalty, a symphony of emotions that both strengthened and terrified her.

Protect me, she requested, her mental voice softening, the clinical detachment replaced by a raw vulnerability. *And protect Korina. While I'm fighting this...digital battle, I won't be able to defend myself.*

You have our word, Architect-Queen, Janna's gruff voice echoed in Ada's mind, a reassuring rumble of strength and unwavering loyalty. *No harm shall befall you while we still draw breath.*

Consider it done, cutie, Erita's dry, cynical voice added, but even through the telepathic link, Ada could sense the fierce protectiveness beneath the sarcasm. *I won't let a single one of those glitchy bastards lay a finger on you.*

We'll defend you with our lives, Ada, Sera's voice resonated with a fierce, passionate intensity, a burning ember of love and devotion. *You and Rina. We won't let anything happen to you.*

We'll hold the line, Korina added, her voice filled with a quiet determination. *Analyze their attack patterns. Identify weaknesses. Provide tactical support.*

The node pulsed again, its corrupted energy intensifying. The first wave of malware constructs emerged from the swirling vortex, their forms shifting and distorting, a grotesque mockery of life. They were a nightmarish menagerie of fragmented code, twisted metal, and pulsing, organic matter, their movements jerky and unnatural. Their eyes, if they could be called eyes, glowed with a malevolent crimson light, fixated on Ada and Korina.

Without a word, Sera, Erita, and Janna moved, their actions a seamless, coordinated dance of lethal grace. They formed a tight, defensive perimeter around Ada and Korina, their bodies shielding them from the oncoming wave of corrupted creatures. Sera, her twin blades flashing in the dim light of the swamp, moved with a predatory fluidity, her crimson tunic a blur of motion. Erita, her daggers a whisper of death in the shadows, darted in and out of the fray, her movements precise and deadly. Janna, her massive battle-axe a whirlwind of destruction, stood firm as a bulwark, her imposing frame a wall of muscle and steel.

Ada closed her eyes, taking a deep breath, centering herself, preparing for the arduous task ahead. She could feel the node's presence growing stronger, its malevolent intelligence probing at her defenses, seeking a way in. She pushed down the rising tide of fear, focusing on the task at hand, on the code, on the systems, on the world she had created and the people she had sworn to protect.

I'm going in, she projected into the minds of her companions, her mental voice calm and resolute. *Keep them back. No matter what.*

Then, with a final, deep breath, Ada slipped into the digital abyss, her consciousness diving into the swirling vortex of corrupted data, ready to face the heart of the infection, ready to fight for the soul of Kremøtoa.

The world around her dissolved into a chaotic stream of data, a swirling vortex of corrupted code. The malware node's presence was overwhelming, a malevolent intelligence that pressed against her awareness, seeking to consume her, to corrupt her, to erase her. Ada fought back, her own code a beacon of order in the chaos, a firewall against the infection.

She could see the corrupted sectors, vast swathes of glitching terrain and distorted code, a digital wasteland. She could feel the node's influence, its tendrils of corruption reaching out, infecting everything they touched. She knew what she had to do.

[System Purge: Initiate], she commanded, her mental voice echoing through the digital landscape, a command that resonated with the power of creation itself.

The node pulsed, its corrupted energy intensifying, its defenses rising to meet her attack.

The node fought back, its corrupted energy lashing out, trying to overwhelm her, to corrupt her, to erase her. Ada held firm, her code a shield against the onslaught, her will a beacon of order in the chaos. It was a battle of pure logic, a war of wills fought in the silent, abstract realm of code.

Rina, I need more processing power, Ada projected, her mental voice strained. *Filter the raw data. Isolate the core functions. I need to target the source of the corruption.*

Working on it, Ada, Korina's voice replied, a calm, steady presence amidst the storm. *Obsidian is at maximum capacity. Filtering...isolating...rerouting...*

Ada could feel Obsidian's power flowing through the telepathic link, a stream of pure, uncorrupted data that helped her navigate the chaotic landscape of the node's source code. She could see the core functions, the twisted, corrupted algorithms that fueled the node's malevolent intelligence. She began to dismantle them, one by one, her commands precise and devastating.

[Disable: Replication_Protocol], she commanded, severing the node's ability to create new constructs.

[Untangle: Corruption_Algorithm], she continued, unraveling the twisted code that fueled the node's chaotic energy.

[Isolate: Core_Directive], she finished, isolating the node's central command structure, the source of its malevolent intelligence.

The node thrashed, its corrupted energy flaring, its defenses crumbling. It was a desperate, dying struggle, a final, futile attempt to cling to existence. Ada pressed her attack, her commands relentless, her will unwavering.

Suddenly, a window popped up in her admin-view, a single, stark command glowing with a violet light: **[PURGE]**.

This is it, she projected into the minds of her companions, her voice filled with a mixture of triumph and apprehension. *Stand back.*

[PURGE], she commanded, unleashing the full force of her Admin privileges.

A wave of pure, cleansing energy surged outwards from the node, washing over the corrupted landscape, erasing the infection, restoring order. The sickly green miasma that had choked the swamp receded, revealing the vibrant, verdant landscape beneath. The corrupted water, once thick with sludge and decay, cleared, revealing the shimmering turquoise depths below. The remaining malware constructs, their forms twisted and distorted, dissolved into harmless data, their malevolent crimson eyes flickering and fading into nothingness.

Ada collapsed, her consciousness returning to her physical body, the world around her slowly coming back into focus. She was lying on the damp earth, her body aching, her mind exhausted. She could feel the warmth of Sera's arms around her, the gentle touch of Korina's hand on her forehead, the concerned whispers of Erita and Janna.

"Ada? Are you alright?" Sera's voice, filled with worry, broke through the haze of exhaustion.

Ada opened her eyes, blinking against the bright sunlight that filtered through the newly cleansed swamp. She looked around, taking in the transformed landscape, the vibrant green foliage, the clear, sparkling water, the peaceful silence.

"It's...gone," she whispered, her voice hoarse. "The corruption...it's gone."

A wave of relief washed over the group, a shared sense of triumph and disbelief. They had done it. They had healed this wounded part of the world.

"Argent's light, Ada," Janna breathed, her gruff voice filled with awe. "You truly are a miracle worker."

"It wasn't just me," Ada said, sitting up, leaning against Sera's strong arms. "It was all of us. Korina, your data filtering was essential. Erita, your tactical guidance kept us alive. Sera, Janna, your strength and courage held back the constructs."

"And your love," Korina added, her voice soft, her violet eyes shining with admiration. "Your love for this world, for all of us... that's what made this possible."

Ada looked at Korina, at Sera, at Erita, at Janna, at the faces of her companions, her lovers, her family. She saw the love in their eyes, the respect, the unwavering loyalty. And for the first time since arriving in Kremøtoa, she felt a sense of true belonging, a deep, abiding connection to this world and the people in it.

"We did it," she said, a smile spreading across her face, a genuine, heartfelt smile that reached her violet eyes. "We did it together." She looked at the restored landscape, the healed swamp, a testament to their combined strength, their shared love, their unwavering hope. It was a victory not just for Kremøtoa, but for them, for their future, for the world they were fighting to create.

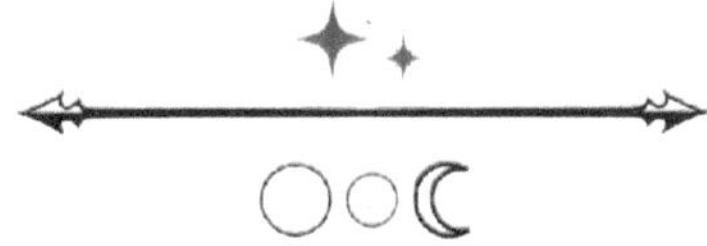

The air settled. Where moments before a cacophony of digital shrieks and the wet tearing of corrupted flesh had filled the swamp, now a resonant hum vibrated through the soil. It was the sound of life, corrected and whole. Korina breathed it in—a clean, loamy scent of damp earth and new leaves, a stark contrast to the acrid stench of ozone and decay that had preceded it. The water, once a toxic, viscous sludge, now ran clear, reflecting a sky scrubbed clean of the sickly green miasma.

She watched Ada, who sat on a mossy log, her shoulders slumped with a profound exhaustion that seemed to radiate from her very bones. Yet, a soft light of triumph illuminated her features. Her violet eyes, usually sharp with analytical focus, were gentle, tracing the patterns of the restored ferns that unfurled at her feet.

Korina's heart swelled with an emotion that defied data points and logical schematics. *Love. Awe.* It was a warmth that spread through her chest, a quiet, powerful current. She moved to Ada's side, her own weariness a distant echo, and knelt before her. She took Ada's hand, her fingers tracing the new calluses there—the tangible proof of the impossible burdens Ada carried.

I love this new language we have, Korina thought, a silent message sent through the quiet spaces between them. *A blend of her code and my world. It's the language of us.*

Ada's fingers squeezed hers in response, a faint smile touching her lips. The fatigue in her eyes lessened, replaced by a deep, shared contentment. This was their victory, not just a cleansing of the land, but a reaffirmation of their bond. For a perfect, fleeting moment, the war, the cascade failure, the hundred-day trek—all of it faded into the background, leaving only the two of them in a world made right.

Then, a sharp vibration against her thigh shattered the peace.

It was Obsidian. A high-pitched, insistent whine cut through the swampland's gentle hum. A crimson alert pulsed across the data-slate's screen, a frantic, angry heartbeat against the calm green backdrop.

A tiny, concerned meow echoed directly in her mind. It was Lynx, Ada's gift, her guardian. *Rina...This signal...it's from a sealed Veritas channel...the one linked to your erased academic records...*

Korina's blood went cold. A shiver, sharp and unwelcome, traced a path down her spine. The warmth in her chest evaporated, replaced by a knot of ice.

Wait...KT-77A? That channel is dead. Buried. She had personally scrubbed it from the public servers, an act of digital self-preservation after her disgrace. It was a ghost channel, a back door linked to academic records that, officially, no longer existed. *Her records.*

"Rina?" Ada's voice was soft, but the concern in it was a physical weight. "What is it?"

Lynx purred, its pixelated form on Obsidian's screen now sitting bolt upright, ears perked. *It's a hologram transmission, Rina... seems urgent.*

Who? Why now? The question screamed through her mind. Her first thought, a cold spike of pure terror, was a name she had tried to bury deeper than any data file. *Kaelen? No...not him—it couldn't be.* He was a monster, but not a fool. He wouldn't risk using a channel that could be traced back to him, back to what he did. After all this time...

"Korina." Ada's hand was on her shoulder now, grounding her, pulling her from the spiraling panic.

Korina looked from the pulsing crimson light on her slate to the worry etched on Ada's face. She tried to speak, but her throat felt tight, the words caught behind a wall of sudden, suffocating fear.

She finally managed a choked whisper. "It's...a signal."

Ada's expression remained patient, waiting.

Korina took a shaky breath, forcing the words out. "From Veritas. On a channel...on *my* channel. The one they used for my private project archives. The one that I deleted when they...when they exiled me."

Ada's hand tightened on her shoulder, a constant, grounding pressure against the chaotic tremor that seized Korina's body. The Architect-Queen's violet eyes held no trace of the academic curiosity Korina had once dreaded. There was no prying, no demand for data. There was only a profound, quiet understanding that saw past the technical anomaly and straight into the heart of the wound it represented.

"Korina," Ada's voice was a low murmur, meant only for her. "Do you want us to give you some space?"

The question was a lifeline. It wasn't a dismissal, but a grant of sovereignty over her own pain. A part of Korina, the part that had been conditioned by Veritas to perform, to present a flawless facade, screamed to say *no, it's fine, it's just a data anomaly.* She could feel the stares of the others—Sera, Erita, Janna—and the shame was a physical heat rising in her throat. *I don't want them to see this part of me. The broken scholar. The victim.*

But Ada's gaze held hers, unwavering. *This is yours,* it seemed to say. *You decide.*

Korina's heart hammered against her ribs, a frantic, trapped bird. She drew a shaky breath, the clean, loamy scent of the restored swamp a strange counterpoint to the sour taste of fear in her mouth. She looked past Ada, her eyes meeting Sera's. The warrior's face was a mask of fierce concern, her hand resting on the hilt of her blade not as a threat, but as a promise. Erita's sharp features were etched with a rare, unguarded worry, her golden eyes narrowed as if trying to identify the unseen enemy that had struck her. And Janna...Janna's expression was all gentle strength, a quiet offer of solidarity that asked for nothing in return.

Wait...they aren't judging. The realization washed over Korina, a sudden, stunning wave of warmth that pushed back the icy dread. They weren't looking at her with pity. They weren't dissecting her weakness. They were...protecting her. They were forming a silent, unbreachable perimeter around her vulnerability. They trusted her to face this, and they would stand guard while she did.

This is what a family feels like.

A surge of courage, potent and unexpected, flooded her veins. It didn't erase the fear, but it rose to meet it. She finally tore her gaze from their faces and gave Ada a small, determined nod, as she grasped Ada's hand.

Then she turned to the others, her voice still trembling but laced with a newfound firmness. "Could you...could I have a moment?"

The response was immediate.

"Of course," Sera's voice was a low, warm reassurance. She stepped back without another word, her posture that of a sentinel taking her post.

Erita gave a single, sharp nod, her lips a thin line. "We're right here. Just say the word." Her tone held the clear implication that "the word" would unleash a very specific and targeted brand of hell on whoever was on the other end of that transmission.

Janna simply smiled, a soft expression that conveyed more than words ever could, and retreated to stand beside Sera, turning her back to Korina to give her the illusion of true privacy while her presence remained a bulwark.

They moved away, a seamless, unspoken choreography of trust, leaving Korina in a small circle of solitude. They didn't go far, just enough to be out of earshot, their forms silhouetted against the lush green of the reclaimed swamp. They were her guardians. Her wall.

Alone now with Ada, with only the insistent crimson pulse of Obsidian for company, Korina took one more deep breath. Her hand, still shaking, hovered over the data-slate's interface. The fear was still there, a cold knot in her stomach, but it was no longer all-consuming. It was now just one data point among many, outweighed by the strength flowing from the three women standing watch behind her, and the one whose hand still rested on her shoulder, a silent, unwavering anchor.

Her finger jabbed the screen.

[ACCEPT TRANSMISSION]

The air in front of Obsidian shimmered, coalescing into a

column of pale blue light. Within it, shimmering particles resolved into the holographic projection of a man. He was older than she expected, with a gaunt face framed by unruly silver hair. His features were sharp, analytical, and his violet eyes—a shade so close to her own it was jarring—darted around as if cataloging the swamp behind her before finally settling on her face. He stood amidst a chaotic workspace, towering stacks of data-slates and scrolls threatening to collapse around him.

"Scholar Korina Tel?" His voice was quiet, hesitant, the sound of a man more accustomed to archives than conversation.

The name felt like a phantom limb, an appendage severed long ago that still ached with a cold, dead pain. Korina's breath hitched. A violent tremor shot through her, a system shock that no diagnostic could quantify. Ada's hand, a warm and steady presence on her shoulder, tightened, and her fingers found Korina's, lacing through them. A lifeline.

"I...am Scholar Atomuzk," he continued, the shared surname a second, sharper blow. "Of the Veritas Archives."

"I must begin," Atomuzk said, his gaze dropping to the floor of his study for a moment, "with an apology. A profound one. For the injustice you suffered. For the failure of our institution to protect one of its brightest minds."

An apology? The thought was a disbelieving screech in the quiet of her mind. *From Veritas? After everything?*

The words were a cascade of impossibilities. Korina's mind raced, trying to parse them, to find the angle, the trick. *Veritas did not apologize. It redacted. It erased.* It buried its mistakes under mountains of sealed archives and ruined careers.

"The investigation into your...departure," he said, the careful, clinical phrasing a familiar wound, "was predicated on falsified data submitted by Kaelen Vance."

The name was a key, turning a lock on a room deep inside her she had bricked over. The ache in her chest wasn't metaphorical; it was a real, physical pang, a tearing of scar tissue. The smell of old parchment and Kaelen's cloying cologne filled her senses, a ghost of memory so potent it made her stomach clench. Ada's thumb began to rub slow, soothing circles on the back of her hand.

He knows. He knows what Kaelen did.

"My own inquiries began after the Duskhaven anomaly," Atomuzk explained, his voice gaining a sliver of momentum, the dispassionate tone of a scholar presenting his findings. "The energy signature was...unique. Not aligned with the Cascade Failure. Your presence was noted. It led me to unseal your academic file." He paused, and when he looked up, his violet eyes were filled with a deep, weary shame. "And then, the files of others."

Korina's blood ran cold. *Others?*

"Kaelen Vance's career is a monument to corruption, protected at every turn by Grand Magister Xehon. I have found evidence of systemic academic sabotage, suppression of competing research, unauthorized replication of axiomatic data, and..." He hesitated again, the clinical detachment faltering. "And six other formal complaints, all sealed by Xehon's direct order. Complaints of... unwanted physical advances. Of...assault."

The air left Korina's lungs in a silent rush. The world tilted, the lush green of the swamp blurring at the edges of her vision. *It wasn't just me. There were others.* The thought wasn't a comfort. It was a horror show—a vast, sprawling conspiracy of silence that made her own trauma feel like a single, screaming note in a deafening chorus of pain. A hot, metallic taste of pure anger flooded her mouth. *The entire system.* The High Council she had once revered. *It's rotten. To the core.*

"I have the data," Atomuzk said, his voice now firm, the hesitation replaced by a quiet, academic fury. "Immutable logs. Redacted testimonies. Xehon's own encrypted correspondence. It is enough to dismantle them both...but it is nothing without your testimony. When the time is right, will you help me bring them to justice?"

Justice. The word echoed in the sudden, ringing silence. It was a concept she had abandoned, a variable she had removed from her life's equation. But hearing it now, it felt...possible. *Real.* This wasn't just about her pain anymore. It was about justice. For all of them.

She felt Ada's hand in hers, a constant, unwavering truth in a world of lies. She thought of the women who came before her, their voices silenced, their careers destroyed. She thought of the world crumbling around them, of the much larger fight they were in the middle of. Her priorities snapped into focus with the cold, hard clarity of a perfect algorithm. *The world comes first. Ada comes first.*

Her hand tightened on Ada's, her own knuckles white. She looked directly into the hologram, into the eyes of the grandfather she had never known, who was now offering her a terrible, righteous gift. Her own voice, when it came, did not tremble. It was low, measured, and colder than the deepest archive.

"Scholar Atomuzk..." She spoke his name like a vow. "When we've saved this world...and we *will* save it...I'm coming back."

She let the words hang in the air, a promise as solid as the ground beneath her feet.

"And we will bring them to justice."

Her finger swiped across Obsidian's screen. The column of light dissolved, and Scholar Atomuzk vanished, leaving Korina standing in the quiet swamp, the fire of a new, unyielding purpose burning in her heart.

The column of light winked out, plunging the private terminal back into its sterile, humming silence. Scholar Atomuzk Tel stared at the blank obsidian surface where the face of his granddaughter had just been. The recycled air tasted of ozone and regret. For a long moment, he did not move, his mind processing the new data stream with the cold precision he applied to every axiomatic equation.

Observation: Subject Korina Tel exhibits improbable resilience. Emotional trauma is present but contained. Resolve matrix is...absolute. His thoughts were a series of research notes, a defense mechanism against the weight pressing down on his chest. *Variable: The entity designated Ada Lynx. Hypothesis: Their bond is symbiotic, a mutually reinforcing feedback loop of loyalty and affection. Fascinating. And terrifying.*

The clinical detachment fractured. A fault line ran through the bedrock of his academic composure, and something raw and painful seeped through. His fingers, thin and spotted with age, tapped a sequence on the terminal's surface. A holographic image flickered to life, floating in the dim light. It was not a complex thaumaturgical schematic or a stellar chart. It was a girl, no older than seven, with a wild cascade of violet hair and eyes that held the same impossible color, wide with the fierce, insatiable curiosity of a born scholar. She was holding up a multifaceted crystal, her small face scrunched in concentration as she tried to understand the light refracting through it.

He remembered the day his daughter had sent him the image. He had been on the verge of a breakthrough in foundational thauma-theory. He had glanced at it, felt a distant flicker of warmth, and then filed it away. He had been too busy. *He was always too busy.*

Addendum: My own culpability is undeniable. The thought was not an academic footnote. It was a confession whispered into the uncaring silence. *Variable: Grandpaternal absence.* He saw the timeline laid out in his mind, a catastrophic cascade of failures, all originating from a single point of error: **himself**. He had been chasing abstract data, mapping the theoretical architecture of their reality, while the real, tangible shadows gathered around his family. He had left his daughter and son-in-law to raise this brilliant, wondrous child alone. He had buried himself in scrolls and equations while a predator named Kaelen Vance stalked the very halls Atomuzk called home.

The weight in his chest became a physical thing, a cold, dense stone of guilt. *I was chasing data while the shadows gathered around her. I failed my daughter. I will not fail my granddaughter again.* The promise was not made to the brave young woman in the swamp. It was made to the little girl in the hologram, the child whose life he had observed from an unforgivable distance.

The sorrow did not fade. It transmuted. The heat of his shame cooled, hardening into something sharp and unyielding. The academic pursuit of dispassionate truth was a luxury he could no longer afford. Kaelen Vance was not a data anomaly to be studied; he was a cancer. Xehon was not a misguided administrator; he was the disease vector. The entire system—the High Council, the sealed archives, the culture of silence—it was all corrupted code. A system designed to protect predators and silence victims. A system he had, through his inaction and blindness, helped sustain.

With a final, lingering look at the child in the light, Atomuzk swiped his hand, and the hologram vanished. The warmth went with it, leaving only the cold. His movements became economical, precise. He turned from the primary terminal to his personal data-slate, its security protocols layered so deep even Xehon would need a decade to crack them.

His fingers danced across the holographic interface, the soft tapping the only sound in the room. He composed the first message, a simple string of code that was, in itself, a question and a call to arms. It went to a logician in the lower archives, a man whose brilliant work had been repeatedly suppressed by Vance.

Another message flew. This one, a single, archaic glyph, went to a junior archivist who saw too much and spoke too little, a woman whose quiet fury he had noted in Council briefings.

A third, a complex axiomatic query with a deliberate, hidden flaw only one other mind in Veritas would recognize. It was sent to a retired theorist, a woman forced into obscurity by Xehon two decades prior.

He worked for nearly an hour, a silent weaver pulling on the disparate threads of dissent he had observed and cataloged over a lifetime. He was no longer just a scholar. He was a system architect planning a hostile takeover. He was building an army in the shadows, forging weapons from whispered grievances and buried truths. Korina was fighting a war for the world's survival on the outside. He would fight a war for its soul from within.

I will prepare for war, he thought, the words a cold, clear bell in the silence of his mind. He would dismantle the structures of power, expose the rot, and salt the earth where it grew. *When she returns, I will be ready.*

Together, he vowed to the ghost of the girl with the crystal, *we will burn it all down.*

CHAPTER 14

CROSSING THE AKARI

The forest died gradually, then all at once.

Ada noticed the transition first in the canopy—the towering evergreens thinned to scattered stands, their needles a dusty bronze rather than the vital green of the deeper woods. The undergrowth became sparse, skeletal. By the time the Fellowship broke through the last dense thicket, the landscape had transformed into something altogether different: a wide, barren escarpment of reddish stone, weathered smooth by centuries of wind and indifference.

And then the river.

Ada stopped. Her neural processes stuttered. Her eyes tracked left, right, and found no end. The water formation stretched before them like a vast, impossible inland sea—a body of water so immense it violated her sense of scale. The far bank, if it existed at all, was swallowed by atmospheric haze, a shimmer of heat and distortion that made the horizon waver and fragment.

The water itself was wrong. It was sapphire—not the

crystalline blue of a mountain lake, but a deep, almost unnatural pigmentation that seemed to absorb light rather than reflect it. The surface moved with a peculiar sluggishness, as if the water were denser than it should be, heavier with some alchemical weight.

"No," Ada breathed.

Sera approached from behind, her boots crunching on loose stone. "No what?"

"I can't see the end of it." Ada's voice sounded strange to her own ears, stretched thin. She turned to Korina, who was already extracting *Obsidian* from her satchel, the data-slate's screen casting violet light across her pale features. "Korina, is this even a river anymore?"

The question hung in the stagnant air.

Korina's fingers moved rapidly over *Obsidian's* holographic interface, pulling up topographical data, hydrological scans, dimensional analysis. Her violet eyes tracked the readouts, absorbing data with the focused intensity she brought to all mysteries. "The scans keep returning paradoxical values." She looked up from the slate, her expression caught between scientific fascination and genuine concern. "It's not behaving like water. The density readings suggest something closer to a suspension of—"

A low sound interrupted her. Not a sound, precisely. A thrumming—a rhythmic, subsonic pulse that emanated from the water itself. It reminded Ada of machinery, a massive engine idling at some barely perceptible frequency. She felt it in her sternum first, a vibration that seemed to resonate with something fundamental in her chest. Then it traveled downward, into her legs, into the soles of her boots, where it found the stone beneath her feet and set it humming in sympathetic resonance.

The ground was alive. Or the river was alive. Or the distinction between the two had never truly existed.

Erita appeared at Ada's left shoulder, her golden eyes narrowed against the shimmering heat. "That's not natural," she said flatly. "Nothing natural sounds like that."

Janna nodded agreement, her weathered face etched with the practicality of someone who had spent her life reading landscapes. "It's a barrier," she said. "That's what this is. I've never seen one this vast, but I've seen enough of how power works to recognize one when I'm standing in front of it."

Ada's mind felt sluggish, unable to process the enormity before her. The air was thick with ionized ozone—she could taste it on her tongue, sharp and metallic, mingling with the scent of damp silt and something else, something ancient and faintly wrong. Her breathing became shallow.

A barrier.

Ada's vision flickered. For a moment—just a moment—she saw the Akari not as water but as cascading data, lines of code rendered into liquid form, a firewall made manifest. Then the vision faded, and it was simply a river again. An impossible, vast, thrumming river.

She stepped closer to the edge of the escarpment. The stone was worn smooth, ancient, carved by winds that had blown across this barren land for centuries or millennia. Below, the water moved in slow, lazy patterns, eddies within eddies, spirals that seemed almost deliberate.

"How do we cross?" Sera asked. Her hand had moved unconsciously to one of her blade hilts, a gesture born of discomfort rather than any genuine threat.

Ada didn't answer immediately. She was thinking about the

time dilation. Five months in Kremøtoa, one week on Earth. She was thinking about Samantha and her mother, about emergency services and unplugged cables. She was thinking about the cascade failure spreading like a cancer through her creation's code, eating it from the inside.

She was thinking about how many kilometers of impossible river stood between them and the Oracle.

The thrumming continued, patient and relentless. The ground hummed. The water gleamed sapphire under the Kremøtoan sky, indifferent to the small group of travelers standing at its edge, trying to comprehend its scale.

"We find a way," Ada said finally. Her voice was steady, though her hands trembled faintly. "We have to."

They made camp a quarter-kilometer back from the escarpment's edge, in a depression of wind-carved stone that offered some shelter from the relentless wind. Janna set about arranging the perimeter with the efficiency of someone who had done this a thousand times—bedrolls positioned for sight lines, supplies clustered in the center, water rations calculated with brutal precision.

Ada sat on a smooth boulder, watching Sera drive stakes into the ground with methodical strikes of a rock. Each impact sent tremors through the stone, vibrations Ada felt in her bones. Her attention kept drifting back to the river. Even from this distance, she could hear it: that subsonic thrumming, that patient, mechanical pulse. It had begun to feel less like a sound and more like a heartbeat—the world's heartbeat, slow and immense and indifferent to her presence.

Korina crouched near the nascent fire pit, *Obsidian* balanced on her lap. The data-slate's holographic interface painted her face in cascading violet light, throwing her features into sharp relief. Ada watched the colors shift across Korina's pale skin, highlighting the sharp angle of her cheekbone, the concentrated furrow between her brows. Even exhausted—they were all exhausted—Korina possessed a kind of fierce intensity that made her look like something carved from ice.

"I'm searching the provincial archives," Korina said without preamble. Her fingers danced across the holographic keyboard, pulling up maps, hydrological surveys, historical transit records. "Ferry points. Bridge sites. Anything that suggests human crossing points."

Erita was unpacking the camp stove, her movements economical, almost angry with their precision. She didn't look up from her work. "And?"

"Nothing useful." Korina's voice flattened. "The records from the last three centuries just show...gaps. Redacted markers. Entire sections of the Akari's northern bank marked as administratively restricted."

The implication hung in the air between them like smoke.

Sera returned from her scouting expedition, the set of her shoulders already communicating defeat before she spoke. She dropped down beside Ada, breathing heavily. "The bank is dead," she said. "Salt crust everywhere—I mean *everywhere*. Nothing's lived along that waterline in years. No boatyards, no docks, no evidence of any kind of civilization. It's like the world just...stops at the water's edge."

The fire caught, reluctant and small. Janna fed it scraps of dried kindling from their dwindling supply, coaxing it into something that might charitably be called a flame. The wood crackled, a thin, brittle sound that seemed to emphasize rather than diminish the vast silence pressing down around them.

Ada reached into her pack and withdrew the ration bread—hard, days-old, with a texture like compressed paper. She bit into it, the flavor stale and vaguely mineral. The bread sat heavy in her stomach, a reminder that their supplies were finite. Everything was finite. Time, resources, patience.

The evening air was cooling, that particular quality of desert temperature drop where the day's heat vanished almost instantly once the sun began its descent. Grit—fine, silty river sand—clung to Ada's clothes, worked its way into the folds and seams. She could feel it against her skin, between her toes, everywhere. The Akari had left its mark on them simply by existing near them.

"The Akari is over a hundred kilometers wide at this meridian," Korina said quietly, still scrolling through *Obsidian's* displays. "Without a fleet, we are effectively marooned on the Ehxcehl side."

No one responded immediately. The fire crackled. Janna checked their water rations for the third time, her lips moving silently as she counted. Sera was cleaning her blades with methodical care, using a small cloth to remove the day's accumulated dust.

Ada's gaze drifted to the horizon, where the river's surface seemed to shimmer and waver in the dying light. And there—just for an instant, barely perceptible—a flicker. A glitch in the rendering. The sapphire water seemed to stutter, pixels momentarily visible before the visual correction kicked in, restoring the illusion of seamless beauty.

She had the power to fix it. Could reach into the code with a thought, smooth out the error, restore the fidelity.

She didn't have the energy.

The knowledge sat in her chest like a stone.

Erita finally spoke, her voice carrying that particular edge of pragmatism that Ada had come to recognize as the sound of her hitting bedrock. "We can't stay here long. Three days, maybe four, before we need to make a choice. Either find a way across or turn back."

"We're not turning back," Ada said.

"No," Erita agreed. "We're not. But we need to be realistic about the options."

The fire burned lower. The thrumming from the river seemed to grow louder in the encroaching darkness, or perhaps Ada was simply becoming more aware of it as other sounds faded. The wind died to almost nothing. The world contracted to a circle of firelight, five exhausted people, and the impossible blue barrier stretching endlessly toward horizons they might never reach.

The old man emerged from the haze like a memory.

Ada saw him first—or rather, her Admin-view caught the disturbance in the code's edge-detection before her conscious mind registered his presence. A flicker at the periphery of the rendered world, pixels snapping into focus, resolving into the shape of something that didn't belong yet somehow always had.

She stood without thinking. The bread dropped from her fingers.

"Contact," she said quietly.

Sera's hand was on her blade before the word finished leaving Ada's mouth. Erita had already risen, her smaller frame coiled with the particular readiness of someone trained to kill in confined spaces. Janna's weathered hand moved to the flare-gun at her belt—not a weapon, but a signal device, because in territories like this, you didn't assume you could win a physical confrontation with the unknown.

Korina simply stared, *Obsidian* still glowing softly in her lap.

The old man paid them no mind.

He moved with the peculiar shambling gait of extreme age, each step deliberate and carefully placed, as if the ground beneath him was unreliable—which, Ada supposed, it was. Behind him came an ox, and the sight of the creature struck Ada with the force of a physical blow. It was immense, a living mountain of matted fur and ropy muscle, its coat the color of old blood dried to rust. The beast's breathing was labored, each inhalation a wet, wheezing sound that carried across the barren stone. Its eyes, when they opened fully, held a peculiar glassiness that suggested either tremendous age or tremendous indifference to the world's architecture.

The wooden cart creaked behind the ox, each rotation of the wheels releasing a sound like old joints working—wet, organic, in desperate need of grease that would never come.

"Evening," the old man said. His voice was a rasp, corroded by time and disuse. "Fire's a good sign. Most folks who reach the Akari give up on warmth first. Usually means they've already forgotten what it means to want anything beyond passage."

Sera had not relaxed. If anything, her grip on her blade had tightened, the tendons of her forearm standing out in sharp relief. "Who are you?"

"A carrier," the man said simply. He settled himself onto a rock perhaps two meters from their fire, moving with the care of someone whose every motion cost something. Up close, Ada could see his skin was like tanned leather—weathered, creased, scored with a thousand fine wrinkles that gave him the appearance of having been folded and refolded by decades of time. His eyes were pale, milky with cataracts, yet they tracked with surprising precision across each of the five women in turn. "Ferry keeper, some call it. Ferryman, others. I've had many names across many years, but the work stays the same."

The ox pressed closer to the fire, and Ada felt the wash of its breath—hot, dense with the smell of hay and something older, something that carried the scent of riverbank mud and things that grew in deep water. The warmth was substantial enough to feel against her skin, and she had to suppress the instinct to step back.

Ada's attention snagged on something else, though. Her Admin-view had automatically catalogued the old man the moment he entered her sensory radius, pulling up his code signature, his metadata, the digital architecture of his existence in Kremøtoa.

What she found made her breath catch.

His code was *old*. Not just legacy—ancient. The kind of archaic script that belonged to the foundational layers of Kremøtoa, the base infrastructure that Ada had built in the earliest stages of the simulation's construction. It was supposed to be deprecated, replaced by the more efficient, more elegant code she'd written in subsequent years. And yet here it was, still running, still active, like discovering a subroutine that had never been updated or replaced.

Like discovering a piece of the original world that she'd somehow forgotten existed.

"You're searching for something," the old man continued, reaching into the cart without looking at it, his weathered hands finding an apple—dried, wizened, but still intact—as if they had memorized every inch of the cart's interior through years of repetition. "The Word, most likely. Or you're running from the

Iron. The Akari doesn't discriminate between desperate reasons. Doesn't much care which side of yourself you're fleeing from, so long as you've got coin or trade goods or something worth bartering."

"We don't have time for riddles," Erita said flatly. She had moved slightly, positioning herself between the old man and the fire, though whether that was defensive or offensive was difficult to determine. "If you have information about crossing, speak plainly."

The old man smiled, and it was the saddest expression Ada had ever witnessed. His teeth were brown, worn down to nubs. "Time. You think that's something the Akari respects? Child, time is all there is here. Time and the water and the knowledge of where to step. Three things, and you've got only one of them."

He bit into the apple. The sound was loud in the silence—a wet crunch that seemed to echo across the barren escarpment.

"I know the crossings," he said, not looking at any of them. "The places where the Word grows thin enough that passage becomes possible. Not easy—never easy—but *possible*. There is one place where the barrier has weakness, or perhaps I should say, where the barrier *permits* crossing to those who understand the syntax."

Ada felt something shift in her chest. A tightening. A compression of all the despair and exhaustion and impossible time constraints into a single, sharp point of need.

"Why would you help us?" she asked.

The old man looked at her directly for the first time. His milky eyes seemed to focus with surprising clarity on Ada's face, reading something there that Ada couldn't perceive in herself. "Because," he said slowly, "every thousand years or so, someone comes down to the edge of the Akari who actually understands what they're looking at. Someone who sees not a river but a *language*. Those people, I help. It's an old custom. Very old. Almost as old as I am."

He finished the apple. The core he tossed into the darkness beyond the firelight, and Ada heard it land on stone with a soft clink.

"Do you want passage, girl?" the old man asked. "Or do you want to sit here and watch the sunrise until you run out of water and the haze takes you?"

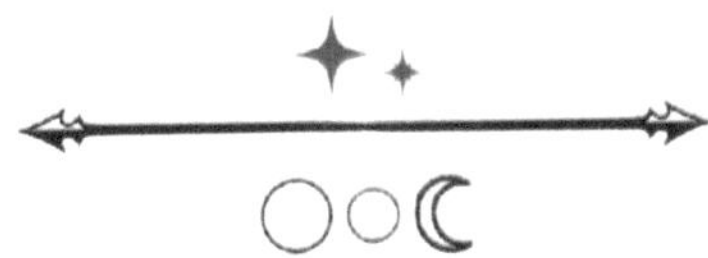

Ada followed the old man downstream, her companions falling into formation around her—Sera's hand resting on her sword hilt out of habit, Korina's eyes fixed on Obsidian as she tried to catalog the shifting energy signatures of the Akari, Erita moving with the fluid predation of a rogue through hostile territory, and Janna bringing up the rear, watching for threats that might materialize from the haze.

The ferryman moved with surprising speed for someone who appeared so ancient, his ox plodding alongside him with the patience of an animal that had walked this route for decades, perhaps centuries. The riverbank curved sharply, and the water's thrumming subsonic pulse grew quieter as they descended into a hidden cove. The mist grew thicker here, clinging to the stone like something alive, something deliberate in its concealment.

Then the cove opened before them.

A white marble pedestal rose from a raised stone dais in the center of a small clearing, perhaps thirty meters from the water's edge. Ivy covered most of its surface, thick tendrils of green and purple leaves obscuring its true form, but beneath that verdant mask, the marble glowed with a soft, internal luminescence—pale white light that seemed to emanate from the stone itself rather than reflecting from any external source.

Ada's breath caught.

She recognized it immediately. The geometry. The proportions. The way the dais was positioned at precise angles to cardinal directions. During the early Alpha Testing phases of Kremøtoa's construction, before the world had solidified into its current form, Ada had written thousands of 'shortcut' commands into the foundational code—teleportation nodes, fast-travel terminals, administrative pathways that allowed her to move across the simulation's vast terrain instantaneously. Most of them she had deprecated, replaced, or deleted as the world became more 'real' and she'd decided that unlimited travel would break the immersion, would destroy the sense of genuine consequence that made the narrative compelling.

But not all of them.

Some she'd simply forgotten about. Some had been buried beneath layers of subsequent construction, hidden beneath the accumulated code of seven years of world-building. Some had persisted in the deep architecture of Kremøtoa like dormant seeds, waiting for something to wake them.

This was one of them.

"Come," the ferryman said simply, gesturing toward the dais. He did not approach it himself, Ada noticed. He stood at the edge of the clearing, his ox beside him, both watching with the patience of those who had seen civilizations rise and crumble.

Ada moved forward, and the others followed. The sweet, cloying scent of white flowers grew stronger as she approached—delicate blooms growing in profusion around the base of the pedestal, their fragrance almost unbearably thick, almost narcotic in its density.

She reached out and brushed away the ivy.

The marble was warm beneath her fingers—unnaturally warm, radiating heat like a living thing. Beneath the tangled growth, she found the geometric patterns she'd half-remembered from those early days of design: precise lines forming complex tessellations, each one a subroutine written in physical form. The patterns pulsed with soft white light in a rhythm that matched the thrumming of the Akari itself.

"This shouldn't exist," Erita said, her voice sharp with the peculiar mix of awe and skeptical anger that meant she was processing something that contradicted her understanding of the world. "The Theocracy and the Empire claimed all Unification relics were destroyed. During the Era of Diffuse Practice, all pre-Mekanøsi infrastructure was supposed to have been purged."

"And yet," the ferryman said quietly, "here it stands. Early Unification, this is. A relic from the time before the breaking, before the divisions. Before the Word fragmented into Thaumaturgy and Logic and Faith. This was when the world was *one*, girl. When all pathways led to all places, and power was not hoarded but shared."

Korina's fingers moved across Obsidian's display, scanning the pedestal, and Ada heard her sharp intake of breath as the data-slate registered what it was detecting. "The power signature—it's not corrupted. It's not even dormant. It's *active*, just...hidden. Phased out of normal perception. Like it's been waiting."

Ada's hand trembled against the warm marble.

She understood what this was. Not just a teleportation node. A proof. A fragment of the world before fragmentation. And as she traced the geometric patterns with her fingertips, she felt something shift in her chest—not despair, but something else entirely.

Recognition.

This pedestal would take them across the Akari. But more than that, it would take them into history itself. Into the bones of what Kremøtoa had been before war and doctrine and the Cascade Failure had carved it into pieces.

Ada turned to watch the old man retreat, but something in his posture—the way his shoulders curved inward, the particular angle of his head as he looked back at her—triggered a cascade of half-formed memories. She had written safeguards into Kremøtoa's earliest architecture. Guardian protocols. Fragment-selves designed to activate only when the Architect needed guidance. Iterations of her own consciousness, scattered throughout the codebase like breadcrumbs, waiting dormant in the deep places where the world was thin.

Was this one of them?

The ferryman didn't answer her unasked question. He simply nodded—a gesture so weighted with recognition and something that might have been grief that Ada's throat tightened. Then he turned his ox back toward the forest, and the mist swallowed him almost immediately, first his silhouette dissolving into shadow, then the ox's form, until nothing remained but the wet earth and the sound of his footsteps fading.

The sunset caught the edge of the clearing as he vanished, painting the sky in shades of amber and deep crimson. Ada realized, distantly, that she'd never programmed sunsets to look this way. The colors were too complex, too *felt*. The world had grown beyond her specifications.

"Everyone together," Ada said, stepping onto the dais. The marble thrummed beneath her boots, responding to her presence like a heart recognizing its own rhythm.

Sera was first, moving with the instinctive trust of someone who'd decided to follow Ada into the abyss months ago. She took Ada's hand without hesitation. Korina followed, her violet eyes wide, and Ada felt her trembling—whether from fear or intellectual excitement, Ada couldn't tell. Erita came last, but she came, and she didn't let go when Ada squeezed her fingers. Janna positioned herself at the circle's edge, her weathered hand finding Sera's shoulder.

"Don't let go," Ada said, and her voice sounded strange in the sudden stillness. "If the code is as old as I think, this might be a rough landing."

They didn't ask questions. They simply held.

The geometric patterns beneath Ada's feet began to glow, the soft white luminescence brightening until it cast sharp shadows across their faces. The ivy fell away from the pedestal in great rustling strips, revealing the full complexity of the tessellations—equations written in stone, subroutines encoded in physical form, a language older than the Cascade Failure, older than the Mekanøsi Hegemony, older than the breaking of the world into its current fractured shape.

The thrumming of the Akari intensified until it became less a sound and more a pressure—something pressing against Ada's bones, against the spaces between cells, against the quantum substrate of her being. She realized, in the moment before the world ended, that the river wasn't water at all.

It was data. Liquid code. The Akari was the border itself, the space between states, the membrane separating one reality from another.

Then the light consumed everything.

Violet and white converged in a brilliant conflagration that burned away sight, burned away sense, burned away the certainty of where one body ended and another began. Ada felt Sera's hand in hers, felt Korina's grip, felt Erita's fingers laced between her own. She held to those points of contact like anchors in an ocean of light.

The world dissolved into static.

Sound died. There was a moment—a fraction of a second that stretched into eternities—where absolute silence replaced the thrumming of the river. The absence of sound became a pressure of its own, a roaring nothingness that pressed against her eardrums with crushing force.

Then came the metallic tang on her tongue—the taste of lightning, of burning circuits, of reality being rewritten at speeds the human nervous system should not have been able to perceive. Ada's teeth ached with it. Her fillings hummed.

Weightlessness. Her stomach lurched as the sensation of falling dissolved into something worse: the feeling of being unmade, separated into component parts, stretched across impossible distances. A sharp, sudden pull centered at her navel—like an anchor being driven through the core of her being, dragging everything else behind it into somewhere new.

And then—

Impact. Solid ground. Air in her lungs that tasted of salt and something else, something ancient and half-familiar. She was still holding hands with all of them. No one had let go.

Ada's lungs seized.

The air here was wrong—thinner, colder, stripped of something essential. She gasped, her body registering the change before her mind could process it, and felt Sera's grip tighten on her hand as if her partner had experienced the same violent shock.

They'd materialized on an identical dais, this one untouched by ivy, its marble surface so pristine it almost glowed under the twin moons' light. Argent, BIOCE and Cache hung low on the horizon, their combined luminescence casting everything in shades of silver and deep blue. The world had shifted into twilight.

Ada's boots touched stone that was not stone—it was too smooth, too perfectly engineered. She pulled herself upright, her legs unsteady, her inner ear still convinced the world was falling. Korina made a small, wounded sound, and Erita was breathing hard, her fingers trembling in Ada's grip.

"Everyone," Ada managed, her voice hoarse. "Is anyone hurt?"

Sera was already drawing her blade, the motion automatic, instinctive. The crimson of her tunic seemed almost to glow against the pale, uniform grass that surrounded them—a grass that looked as if it had been cultivated with obsessive precision, each blade the exact same height, the exact same shade of silver-green. No variation. No wild growth. No chaos.

"Welcome to the Theocracy," Sera said quietly, her eyes scanning the horizon. "Try not to look like heretics."

A distant bell began to toll from the direction of the town.

It was the most beautiful and most terrible sound Ada had ever heard—a cathedral bell, deep and resonant, its voice carrying across the sanitized landscape with an almost liturgical weight.

The tone held no joy in it. Only proclamation. Only the certainty of authority speaking into the void.

Ada turned to look back at the Akari.

From this side, the river had transformed. It was no longer the thrumming, haze-wrapped barrier they'd crossed. Instead, it rose like a wall—a shimmering, iridescent membrane that caught the moonlight and fractured it into spectrum patterns that shouldn't have existed in nature. The barrier was fully visible now, unobstructed, and Ada understood with sudden clarity that they'd just done the impossible: they'd crossed a boundary that the Theocracy had spent centuries believing was impassable. They'd cheated a law of the world itself.

They would never be able to go back the same way.

The realization settled into her chest like ice.

"How long do you think we have?" Janna's voice was steady, but Ada heard the undercurrent of tension beneath it. "Before someone notices us?"

"The spires," Korina said, and Ada turned to find her companion staring toward the distant town through Obsidian's display. "Doc-ehx. Ada, the energy signatures—they're not hostile, but they're *ordered*. Military precision. Guard rotation patterns. The buildings themselves are transmitting—some kind of surveillance or prayer network, I think. I can't quite parse it."

Doc-ehx rose against the horizon like jagged teeth. This was a town on the border. A town that had been caught between empires, between ideologies, ground down by years of conflict. But what remained wasn't the broken thing Ada had expected to find. What remained was *purified*. Sanitized. Remade in the image of Theocratic order.

The grass beneath Ada's boots was cold. Genuinely cold, not

through the illusion of temperature but through the physical absence of warmth. No insects sang here. No wind moved through the blades with any sound except the precise whisper of organized vegetation. Even the three moons seemed to hang lower over this territory, as if gravitating toward the center of power.

"We move carefully," Ada said, forcing steadiness into her voice that she didn't feel. "We gather information. We find out what we're walking into before we commit to anything."

The cathedral bell continued its toll, each resonance echoing across the silver grass like a countdown.

CHAPTER 15

A SCHOLAR'S RESOLVE

The wind tasted of grit and forgotten prayers. Korina pulled the roughspun hood of her cloak tighter, the fabric scratching against her cheek. Before them, huddled against the vast, empty plains like a collection of discarded crates, was the town of Doc-ehx. It was the first settlement they had reached on the Theocracy's blighted frontier, and it looked precisely as she had calculated: a monument to functional despair.

The buildings were a study in architectural failure. They leaned against each other for support, their mud-brick walls slumping under the weight of sagging timber roofs. No vibrant colors broke the monotony of brown and gray. Only the ubiquitous symbol of the Wordæus faith—two interlocking suns, one gold, one blue—carved above every doorway offered any variation.

What in the Void holds this place together? Sera's thought cut through the group's shared silence, sharp and practical.

Not physics, Korina sent back, a wave of data already scrolling through her mind as *Obsidian* ran a passive structural analysis. *The load-bearing walls have the integrity of wet parchment. It's thaumaturgy. Heavy reinforcement wards, layered and overlapping. Inefficient, but powerful.*

"A town built on faith instead of foundations," Erita murmured aloud, her voice a low rasp against the wind. She scanned the perimeter, her golden eyes missing nothing. "All right. We're splitting up. Janna, Sera—supplies. Stick to the outer market if there is one. Find a stable. I'll run the edge of town, map patrol routes and watchtowers." Her gaze settled on Ada and Korina. "You two, the center. Find a tavern, a public house. Get the temperature of the place. We meet back at the west gate before the second sun sets."

There were no arguments. Janna and Sera melted away, their movements synchronized and purposeful, two hunters seeking different prey. Erita vanished into the long shadows cast by the town wall.

Ada's hand found Korina's for a fleeting second, a brief, warm pressure that sent a current of reassurance through her. *Ready?*

With you? Always.

They walked through the town's gate, an arch of crumbling stone held together by a shimmering, barely visible energy field. The oppressive silence was the first thing Korina registered. The ever-present wind seemed to die within the walls, smothered by the town's sheer inertia. The few people they saw in the narrow, winding streets moved with their heads down, shoulders hunched, clutching worn wooden icons of the twin suns. Eyes slid past them, refusing to meet their own, full of a suspicion that was older and deeper than simple caution. It was a practiced, ingrained fear. The air hung thick with the cloying sweetness of incense, a scent that failed to mask the underlying smell of dust and decay.

It's a closed system, Korina thought, the analysis running parallel to her sensory input. *A self-reinforcing loop. The wards create a sense of security, the doctrine creates a sense of purpose, and the fear ensures compliance. Any external variable—like us—is immediately flagged as a threat.* She felt the cool, solid weight of *Obsidian* against her thigh, a comforting anchor of pure logic in a sea of mandated faith.

Ada moved beside her, a point of serene calm in the suffocating atmosphere. Korina could feel her through their link, not a stream of words but a presence—curious, analytical, and utterly unshaken. Ada was seeing the code beneath the decay, the flawed programming that governed this place.

They found the tavern near a dusty, deserted square. A wooden sign, its paint chipped and faded by the suns and wind, hung from a single rusty hinge. It depicted a cracked goblet, from which a wisp of vapor curled. "The Whispering Chalice," Korina read aloud, the name a bitter irony. Whispers were the only form of speech this town seemed to permit.

Ada pushed the heavy wooden door. It groaned on its hinges, a sound loud enough to make every head inside snap toward them. The tavern was dim, the air thick with the smell of stale ale, simmering stew, and unwashed bodies. A handful of patrons sat scattered at rough-hewn tables, their conversations ceasing the instant Ada and Korina entered. A dozen pairs of eyes—wary, resentful, fearful—fixed on them. The silence that followed was absolute, a physical weight that pressed in on Korina from all sides. Then, as one, every patron looked away, hunching back over their mugs, the brief moment of alarm subsiding into a practiced state of non-existence.

Korina felt a knot of tension tighten in her stomach. This was worse than the open hostility of Port Dominus. This was a place where the people had been so thoroughly broken that they policed themselves. The enemy wasn't just the Justicars in their burnished armor; it was the terror carved into the heart of every citizen.

I feel it too, Ada's thought touched her mind, a soft counterpoint to the room's crushing pressure. *The foundational code is full of recursive fear loops. It's designed to self-perpetuate.*

Ada led them to a shadowed booth in the far corner, the worn wood of the bench cool against Korina's legs. She slid in, grateful for the relative privacy of the high-backed seat. As long as Ada was with her, she could handle this. She was an anomaly in their system, yes, but Ada...Ada was the architect. And she was here to tear the whole rotten structure down.

A young woman, no older than sixteen, approached their table, her movements hesitant, as if the floorboards might betray her. She kept her eyes fixed on the grimy wood of their booth, a tray clutched in her hands like a shield. She smelled of dishwater and fear.

"Ale?" Her voice was a mouse-like squeak, barely audible over the low drone of the tavern's oppressive quiet.

Ada nodded, her gaze soft and reassuring. "Two, please."

The girl scurried away. Korina reached for Obsidian, her fingers tracing the familiar cool casing under the table. The simple act of data processing was a comfort—a way to impose order on the chaos. A small icon in the corner of her mind's eye, the tiny pixelated Lynx, was curled up and sleeping peacefully. *All systems nominal.*

The clatter of a pewter mug hitting a wooden table made Korina flinch. A man at a nearby table, dressed in the severe, dark robes of a Theocratic scholar, gestured imperiously. He was thickset, his face florid with drink, but his eyes held a sharp, calculating cruelty.

"*Girl. Another.*" His voice was a slurred baritone, thick with condescension.

The young server hurried to his table, her hands trembling as she refilled his mug from a pitcher. A single, dark drop of ale splashed onto a bundle of scrolls tied with leather cord. The scholar's eyes narrowed. The tavern, already quiet, fell utterly silent.

"Do you see *what you've done?*" The scholar's voice dropped, losing its slur and gaining a razor's edge. He did not raise it. He didn't need to. The quiet was more menacing than a shout. He tapped a finger on the damp spot on the scroll. "This is a transcript of the Seventeenth Sermon of the Ascended. An exegesis on the duality of the suns. Its doctrinal purity is now...contaminated. By you."

The server flinched back, her face draining of color. "I-I'm sorry, Scribe. It was an accident."

"*An accident?*" He let out a low, humorless chuckle. *That tone.* A cold spike of adrenaline shot through Korina's veins, sharp and unwelcome. "Accidents are the product of unforeseen variables. Your incompetence is a constant. Tell me, do you possess the cognitive capacity to understand the sanctity of a *holy text*? Or is your function limited to the simple, repetitive motion of carrying and pouring?"

It's him. It's Kaelen. The thought was a venomous whisper in her mind. The scholar's robes blurred, the dark fabric momentarily becoming the crisp, gray uniform of a Veritas Archivist. His flushed, angry face wavered, the features shifting, sharpening into Kaelen Vance's thin lips and condescending sneer.

The scholar's words twisted, their sound waves warping into echoes from a cold, sterile laboratory. *"You call this a proof? Korina, your logic is as clumsy as your hands. You're nothing without my guidance. Pathetic."*

Korina's breath hitched. The air in the tavern grew thick, heavy, pressing down on her chest, stealing the oxygen from her lungs. A metallic taste flooded her mouth. She could feel Ada's presence beside her, a warm, steady query in their shared mental space, but it was a distant signal, a star seen through a league of dark water.

Her hand, still holding Obsidian beneath the table, began to tremble uncontrollably. The smooth, hard casing felt alien in her slick palm. Her grip failed.

Clack-clatter-skrit

The sound of *Obsidian* hitting the wooden tabletop was a gunshot in the tomb-like silence. Every eye in the tavern swiveled to their booth. The scholar, annoyed by the interruption, turned his venomous glare on them for a heartbeat before dismissing them as unimportant.

He turned back to the server, his patience gone. He reached out and his fingers clamped around the girl's thin wrist. "*Look at me* when I'm educating you."

The world dissolved.

Korina was no longer in a tavern in Doc-ehx. She was in Lab Sector Gamma-7 of the Veritas Archives. The smell of stale ale was replaced by the sharp, sterile scent of ozone and old parchment. The rough-hewn table was a polished steel workstation. Kaelen's hand was locked around her own wrist, his grip like iron, his face inches from hers. He had backed her against the console, his body blocking any escape.

"You think you can just walk away?" his voice echoed, a phantom whisper overlaying the scholar's droning insults. *"You think your work has any value without my name on it? You are my instrument, Korina. My discovery. You will go where I tell you, and you will do what I say."*

She couldn't breathe. She couldn't move. The cold dread that had been a spike was now a flood, a virus spreading through every cell, freezing her from the inside out. Her mind, her greatest weapon, was a prison, its walls built from the memory of his cruelty. She was trapped in the dark, and he was standing over her, and she couldn't get away. She would never get away.

NO. Not this time.

A flicker. A faint, peripheral warmth that had nothing to do with the tavern's grimy hearth. Through the suffocating fog of her memory, Korina saw it—a subtle, violet luminescence gathering around Ada's hands beneath the table. The hum of raw power, a familiar prelude to reality being re-written. Ada was preparing to intervene. To unmake the man who was a phantom of Korina's tormentor.

No.

The thought was a shard of ice in the fire of her panic. *Ada could end this. She could delete him from this plane of existence with less effort than it took to breathe. But that would be her victory, not mine. He isn't Kaelen. And I am not the girl who ran from Veritas.*

Her hand, no longer trembling, shot out and closed around Ada's arm. The touch was firm, a silent command. The violet glow wavered, then dissipated, leaving only the mundane lamplight. Ada turned, her expression a universe of concern, her violet eyes questioning. Korina met her gaze. The terror was still there, a hammering drum against her ribs, but it was no longer her master. It was fuel. She saw the reflection of her own eyes in Ada's, and they were not the eyes of a drowning victim but a predator that had just caught the scent of its prey.

Let me handle this, she thought, the words a clear, cold broadcast across their private channel. *Let me show them—and myself—who I am now.*

Korina stood.

The hammering in her chest did not subside, but its rhythm changed from a panicked flutter to the steady, thrilling beat of a war drum. Adrenaline tasted sharp and clean in her mouth. She felt the solid weight of Obsidian against her hip—not just a tool, but an extension of her own mind, a repository of pure, unassailable data.

She walked toward the scholar's table. The low murmur of the tavern died again. Every patron watched, sensing a shift in the room's oppressive atmosphere. Her shadow fell across the scholar's data-slate, eclipsing its dim light. He looked up, his face a mask of annoyance at this new, impertinent interruption.

"What is it now?" he grumbled, his hand still clamped on the server's wrist.

Korina's voice, when it came, was quiet. Yet it cut through the silence with the precision of a scalpel, carrying to every corner of the room. "You are holding her against her will."

The scholar scoffed, a wet, dismissive sound. "This is a doctrinal matter, *girl*. It does not concern you."

"On the contrary," Korina stated, her tone flat and academic. "Article Seven, Section Three of the Theocratic Concordance, as clarified by High Cleric Valmino in the *Codexia Adjudications*, explicitly states that the unsanctioned detention of any citizen, regardless of their registered status, by a non-Justicar official for the purpose of intimidation constitutes a direct violation of Theocratic Law. The punishment for which is public censure and a fine of one-thousand gold Byts."

The scholar's smug expression faltered. He blinked, his grip on the girl's wrist loosening just a fraction. A low ripple of amusement, quickly suppressed, moved through the other patrons.

"This is a matter of sanctity!" he blustered, gesturing with his free hand at the stained scroll. "The purity of The Word!"

This was the opening she had calculated. "But your error is more fundamental than a mere legal misstep," Korina continued, her voice gaining a cold fire. "You invoke the Wordæus Doctrine of Purity, a laughable misapplication; The Doctrine speaks of the purity of *intent* in the contemplation and dissemination of The Word. The stain on that scroll is inert matter. Your intent here, however, is not sanctity. It is cruelty. It is the assertion of power over the powerless. That is an act of *spiritual corruption*."

The scholar's face began to flush, a tide of crimson creeping up his neck. "How dare you lecture me on the Doctrine—"

Korina pressed her attack, her words flowing in a cascade of irrefutable logic. "By terrorizing this servant in this public space, you are not elevating your own purity; you are actively tainting this entire room with it! You have become a source of chaotic, corrupting data in a system that craves order..." She leaned forward slightly, her gaze pinning him to his seat. "By the very definition of The Doctrine you claim to uphold, Scholar, *you* are the *blight* here."

He sputtered, his mouth opening and closing like a landed fish.

No words came out. His authority, built on a foundation of fear and misquoted text, had been systematically dismantled and laid bare as hollow bullying. He was exposed not as a guardian of faith, but as a heretic by his own standards.

Korina held his gaze for one more silent, satisfying second, then straightened. The fight was over. She gave him no further acknowledgment. She simply turned her back on the sputtering, crimson-faced man and walked back to her booth.

The tavern was no longer silent. A few patrons coughed to hide their laughter. Another raised his mug in a subtle, approving gesture. The server, free from the scholar's grasp, stared at Korina, her young face a mask of disbelief and awe.

Korina slid back onto the bench opposite Ada. The adrenaline began to recede, leaving in its wake not exhaustion, but a profound, crystalline calm. The phantom of Kaelen Vance was gone, banished not by Ada's power, but by her own. She had faced her ghost in the open and had intellectually eviscerated it.

She met Ada's gaze. The concern was gone, replaced by a look of fierce, unwavering pride. Korina felt a smile touch her lips, the first genuine one since entering this town. She was whole.

The sweet taste of victory was a clean, sharp flavor on her tongue, cutting through the tavern's stale air. Korina's hands, resting on the table, were perfectly still. The fine tremor that had been a constant, unwelcome companion for years—a physical manifestation of her trauma—was gone. In its place was a profound stillness, a deep-seated calm that felt more real than any data point she had ever analyzed. It was the feeling of a fractured piece of her own code being rewritten, debugged, and made whole.

The scholar remained frozen, his face a mottled canvas of fury and disbelief. He was a system error caught in a logic loop, unable to compute his own public dismantling. He had been rendered irrelevant.

Then, the loop broke.

With a strangled roar that was more animal than human, he shoved his table aside. Mugs and scrolls crashed to the floor. He lunged, not with the calculated cruelty of before, but with the clumsy, desperate rage of a cornered beast. His target was *her.*

Korina didn't even have time to flinch.

There was no sound, only a sudden absence of light as a shadow moved with impossible speed. Ada, who had been sitting calmly across from her, was suddenly standing between their booth and the charging scholar. It wasn't a teleport, not a blink. It was a movement so fluid and instantaneous it seemed to bend the very laws of physics. One moment she was there, the next she was *here.*

Her hand, slender and pale, shot out and caught the scholar's thick wrist. It was not a blow or a strike, but an interception of absolute finality. The man's forward momentum died instantly, as if he had run into a mountain. His feet skidded on the grimy floorboards, and he dangled from her grip, his arm held in a vise of quiet, terrifying strength.

The fury in Ada's eyes was not hot. It was a cold, violet flame, the chilling, dispassionate wrath of a gød witnessing an unacceptable flaw in their creation. Her voice, when she spoke, was a low, dangerous purr that seemed to vibrate in the very air.

"I believe...you owe that server—and now *my partner*—an apology."

The word hung in the air, weighted with an authority that dwarfed any doctrinal text. *Partner.* It was not a claim of ownership or a declaration of protection. It was a statement of fact, an acknowledgment of equal standing. A public coronation Korina had not known she needed until this very moment.

The scholar's face went from flushed red to a pasty, bloodless white. He stared at Ada's face, then at the impossible grip on his wrist, and the last of his bluster evaporated, leaving behind a pathetic, quivering terror. He understood, in that instant, that he was not in the presence of a mere traveler. He was in the presence of a power he could not comprehend, and it was utterly, lethally displeased with him.

"I—I..." he stammered, his eyes wide. He turned his terrified gaze to the young server, who watched from behind the bar, frozen. "My apologies." He then looked at Korina, a new, deeper fear in his eyes. "I...apologize."

Ada held his wrist for a second longer, her expression unreadable. Then she released him.

He didn't wait. He scrambled backward, stumbled over a stray stool, and fled the tavern like the hounds of Void were at his heels. The heavy door slammed shut behind him, leaving a silence that was thick with awe.

Korina's gaze followed him, but she felt nothing. No satisfaction in his fear, no lingering anger. Only a quiet finality. *He is gone. That Kaelen is gone.*

The young server approached their table, her hands twisting in the fabric of her apron. Tears welled in her eyes, but they were not tears of fear. They were bright with gratitude. She stopped beside Korina, her voice a choked whisper.

"Thank you."

Korina looked up at the girl and offered a small, genuine nod. She saw not a victim, but a survivor. Someone who now knew that the monsters who ruled their lives through fear could be faced down with logic and courage.

The server gave a small, wobbly curtsy and hurried back to her duties, her steps a little lighter, her shoulders a little less hunched.

A weight Korina hadn't even realized she was still carrying lifted from her soul. The air in her lungs felt lighter, cleaner. She felt the warmth of Ada's presence as she slid back into the booth. She didn't look at her yet. She just savored the feeling. *She didn't save me. She backed me up. She let me fight my own battle.* Ada had seen the ghost of Kaelen in her eyes and had prepared to act, but the moment Korina had asserted herself, Ada had ceded the field. She saw Korina, not as a broken thing to be shielded, but as a warrior in her own right. *A true...partner.*

I'm not trembling anymore, she thought, flexing her steady fingers. *I am a scholar of the revolution. And I am worthy of my Queen.*

Finally, she lifted her head and met Ada's eyes.

The cold fury was gone. In its place was a look of such profound pride, of such overwhelming and unconditional love, that it stole the breath from Korina's lungs. It was a look that saw every scar, every doubt, every piece of her broken past, and loved her not in spite of it, but because of the strength she had forged from it. In that silent, shared gaze, entire volumes were spoken. A vow was renewed. A future was forged. The war for Kremøtoa was still a storm on the horizon, but in the quiet of a dusty tavern, Korina Tel had already won the most important battle of her life.

CHAPTER 16

A SCHOLAR'S CONFIDENCE

The walk back to the inn was a study in silence. The boisterous energy of the tavern faded behind them, replaced by the hushed tones of Doc-ehx's evening streets. Gas lamps cast long, dancing shadows that writhed and stretched along the cobblestones. Ada walked beside Korina, the air between them still humming with the aftershock of the confrontation. A profound sense of pride swelled in Ada's chest, so potent it felt like a physical warmth spreading through her veins. She watched the woman beside her—the straightness of her spine, the determined set of her jaw—and saw not the timid scholar from the Warden's Gate, but a formidable force forged in fire and logic.

She reached out, her fingers gently closing around Korina's hand. The skin was cool, but a faint tremor ran through it. Korina stopped, turning to face her in the flickering lamplight. The shadows played across her features, but they could not hide the bright, fierce light in her violet eyes.

"You were magnificent back there, Rina." Ada's voice was soft, reverent. "You didn't just argue with him. You dismantled him. You used his own ideology—his own laws, as a weapon. That wasn't just smart. *It was art.*"

Korina's lips parted, but no sound came out. She simply stared, her expression a mixture of exhaustion and dawning realization. Ada squeezed her hand, a silent anchor in the swirling emotions of the night, and led her the rest of the way to their inn.

Inside their small room, the world shrank to the intimate circle of light cast by a single lamp on the nightstand. The latch of the heavy wooden door clicked shut behind them, a soft, definitive sound that sealed them away from the rest of Kremøtoa. The air was thick with the scent of old wood, clean linens, and the faint, familiar aroma that was uniquely Korina—a blend of lavender from her soap and the crisp, dry scent of old parchment that seemed to cling to her very essence.

Korina's composure finally fractured. Her shoulders slumped, and she leaned against the closed door as if her legs could no longer support her.

"I...I was terrified, Ada." Her voice was a fragile whisper, catching on the admission. "When he stood up, when he shouted... for a second, all I could see was Kaelen's face. I felt that same cold dread, that same helplessness."

Ada closed the distance between them in two steps, her heart aching at the raw vulnerability in Korina's voice. She gently pulled Korina away from the door and into her arms, holding her in a full, comforting embrace. Korina melted against her, her head finding the crook of Ada's neck, her body trembling.

"I know," Ada murmured into her hair. She held her tighter, a silent transfer of strength and certainty. "But you didn't freeze. You didn't run. Being terrified and doing it anyway?" Ada pulled back just enough to look Korina in the eye, her own gaze unwavering. "That's courage, Rina. *True courage.*"

Something shifted in the embrace. Ada felt it instantly. The slight tremor in Korina's frame ceased. The body leaning against her for support began to draw strength, to stand on its own. Korina's posture straightened, her hands on Ada's arms no longer clinging for dear life but holding with a new, firm purpose.

She's magnificent, Ada thought, a fresh wave of awe washing over her. *Not just brilliant, but brave. The woman I first met is gone... forged into something stronger.*

Korina pulled back, her violet eyes locking with Ada's. The fear was gone, completely erased. In its place was a fire Ada had never seen before—a simmering heat that was part gratitude, part triumph, and part something else entirely. A faint crimson blush colored her cheeks, a stark contrast to her pale skin in the lamplight.

The way she looks at me now...that's not just gratitude. Ada's breath caught. *That's...something else. Something new.* It was the look of a person who had not just faced a demon, but had slain it and, in doing so, discovered a power within herself she never knew she possessed.

Korina's hand slid from Ada's shoulder, her touch light as it trailed down Ada's arm, a deliberate, confident caress that sent a shiver through Ada's entire system. Her gaze was intense, unwavering, a scholar's focus now directed not at a complex algorithm, but at the woman before her.

"You didn't save me from him," Korina said, her voice stronger now, imbued with a resonant certainty. "You stood with me while I saved myself. You showed me a strength I didn't know I had."

Her fingers intertwined with Ada's, her grip firm and

possessive. She took a small step closer, closing the last of the space between them. The scent of cherry blossoms and parchment was intoxicating.

"You are *my architect*," Korina whispered, the words a profound vow that went far beyond strategy or revolution. "You build worlds. You build hope." She lifted their joined hands, her thumb stroking the back of Ada's. A slow, predatory smile touched her lips, a breathtaking fusion of intellect and raw desire. "Tonight, *let me be the architect.*"

The words hung in the charged space between them, a declaration of intent that sent a jolt straight through Ada's core operating system. Korina's smile, that breathtaking fusion of intellect and raw want, was a system query Ada had no desire to deny. Before Ada could process a response, Korina surged forward.

It was not a tentative approach. There was no hesitation, no flicker of the self-doubt Ada had so often soothed. Korina's free hand came up to cup the back of Ada's neck, her fingers tangling in the short hairs there with a possessive firmness. She drew Ada in, and her lips met hers in a kiss that was a brand. It was a conquest. It tasted of triumph and the faint, lingering sweetness of the ale they'd had downstairs—a potent, dizzying combination.

A cascade of new data flooded Ada's senses. This was different. This was not the gentle, seeking affection they had shared before. *This was a claim.* The pressure was insistent, demanding. Korina's lips moved against hers with a practiced confidence that was utterly new, her tongue tracing the seam of Ada's mouth before delving inside, an explorer charting new territory. Ada's mind, which usually processed a million variables a second—went beautifully, blissfully blank. All that existed was the firm pressure of Korina's mouth, the proprietary grip on her neck, and the sudden, exhilarating realization that she was no longer leading this dance. A thrill, sharp and electric, shot down her spine.

This is a woman who knows what she wants.

When Korina finally broke the kiss, it was with a short, sharp gasp that was the only sign of her exertion. Her violet eyes, now dark with desire, burned with an intensity that pinned Ada in place. A single, perfect bead of sweat traced a path down her temple. She didn't speak. She didn't need to. Her actions were a far more eloquent language.

Her hands moved from Ada's neck to her shoulders, her grip steady. She applied a gentle, inexorable pressure, and Ada took an instinctive step backward. The old wooden floorboards of the inn room creaked under her weight, a soft groan in the quiet room. Korina followed, a predator stalking her willing prey, her gaze never leaving Ada's. Another step back. The back of Ada's knees connected with the edge of the simple bed frame.

She's...studying me. The thought was a spark in the delightful haze of her mind. *She is analyzing my reactions, cataloging my every breath, my every flush of heat. And by the Void...I have never wanted to be a research subject more.*

Korina's hands slid from her shoulders down her arms, her touch deliberate as she guided Ada to sit on the edge of the mattress. The straw-stuffed bed rustled under her weight. Korina didn't stop there. She knelt between Ada's legs, her hands resting on Ada's thighs, a gesture of both supplication and absolute control. From this new vantage point, she looked up, her expression a rapturous mix of awe and clinical fascination. The lamplight cast a golden sheen on her face, making her seem like a divine scholar examining a newly discovered cosmic truth.

"Argent's light, Ada..." Korina's voice was a husky whisper, a sound that vibrated through Ada from the points of contact on her thighs. "You are...*fascinating*."

The word, so quintessentially Korina, was the most profound term of endearment Ada had ever heard. It was an admission that, for Korina, this was not just an act of passion, but an act of discovery. She leaned forward, her lips brushing the sensitive skin of Ada's inner thigh, a feather-light touch that made Ada's breath hitch.

Her mouth was a tool of exquisite inquiry. She kissed a path upward, slow and methodical, her tongue occasionally flicking out to taste the salt and heat of Ada's skin. Ada's hands came to rest in Korina's soft, violet hair, her fingers curling into the silken strands, but she made no move to guide or direct. She was the subject of this experiment, and she was utterly captivated by the researcher. This was Korina's design, her architecture, and Ada was content to be the foundation upon which she built her masterpiece.

Korina's hands moved with the same deliberate precision she applied to deciphering ancient texts. They slid from Ada's thighs, up her ribs, the touch sending a series of delightful shivers across her skin. Korina rose from her knees, her movements fluid and graceful, until she stood before Ada, an architect ready to survey her creation. Her fingers found the hem of Ada's simple linen tunic.

"May I?" The question was a formality. The answer was in Ada's ragged breath, in the way her body leaned into Korina's touch, a silent, desperate assent.

Korina's hands were warm as they gathered the fabric, slowly drawing it upward. Cool air kissed Ada's stomach, her ribs, her chest. The lamplight painted her skin in shades of honey and gold. For a moment, Ada felt like a statue being unveiled, a sacred artifact revealed to its most devoted worshipper. The feeling was intoxicating. She lifted her arms to help, a purely instinctual motion to aid in her own undressing.

The tunic came free, tossed aside onto the floor without a sound. And in that single, vulnerable moment, with her arms still slightly raised, the spell shattered.

Oh, Void, she sees it.

The thought crashed through her with the force of a system-wide error. The dim light of the inn room suddenly felt like a harsh, interrogating glare, illuminating the dark, untamed tufts of hair nestled in her armpits. A feature she had spent years on Earth meticulously removing, a source of quiet, persistent self-consciousness ingrained in her by a culture that demanded smooth, flawless perfection. Here, in Kremøtoa, she had simply... *forgotten*. Or rather, her new body had grown it, another unexpected glitch in her own programming, and she hadn't had the tools or the privacy to deal with it.

A brutal, plummeting shame coiled in her gut. The heat of arousal was instantly replaced by the burning crimson of embarrassment that flooded her neck and chest. Her arms snapped down, crossing over her chest in a futile attempt to hide herself. She tried to curl inward, to make herself smaller, to disappear.

"*Don't.*"

The word was soft, but it carried an undeniable command. Korina's hand gently but firmly caught her wrist, preventing her from hiding. Her touch was not judgmental. It was...curious.

Ada couldn't meet her gaze. She stared at a knot in the wooden floorboards, her heart hammering against her ribs like a trapped bird. "I...I'm sorry," she stammered, the words barely a whisper. "I didn't...I forgot."

Korina's other hand came up, her fingers tracing the line of

Ada's collarbone. "Sorry for what, my love?" Her voice was a low, soothing murmur, utterly devoid of the disgust Ada expected.

Ada swallowed, the sound loud in the quiet room. "That." She managed a tiny, mortified nod toward her own arm. *She's going to be disgusted. This is so embarrassing.*

She risked a glance up. Korina wasn't looking at her face. Her gaze was fixed on the very thing Ada was trying to hide, but her expression was one of pure, unadulterated fascination. Her brows were slightly furrowed, her lips parted in concentration, as if she were examining the intricate facets of a rare gemstone. *Wait. She's not disgusted. She's...fascinated?*

"On...on Earth," Ada forced the words out, the explanation feeling flimsy and ridiculous even as she said it. "In Japan, we're... supposed to remove it—shave it...It's considered...messy. Unladylike."

Korina finally lifted her eyes, and the intensity in their violet depths stole Ada's breath. A slow, knowing smile touched her lips, the same one from moments before, but now tinged with a tender, teasing quality.

"Unladylike?" Korina's voice was a low, confident purr that vibrated through Ada's bones. "Ada, your world has some truly illogical standards."

She released Ada's wrist, her hand moving with purpose. She gently lifted Ada's arm, extending it so the source of her shame was fully exposed to the lamplight. Ada flinched, but Korina's gaze held her captive.

"Allow me to show you the *definition* of Kremøtoan beauty."

Before Ada could process the words, Korina leaned in. Her nose brushed against the sensitive skin of Ada's inner arm, and she inhaled deeply, her eyes fluttering shut for a moment. Ada's mind short-circuited. *What is she doing? She's smelling me...?* The natural, musky scent of her own body, a smell she had always been taught to mask and erase, was now being cataloged, savored?

Korina's eyes opened, dark and hooded with a desire that was raw and analytical at the same time. "A unique bio-signature," she murmured, her breath warm against Ada's skin. "Entirely you."

And then, her tongue flickered out.

The sensation was a lightning strike. A wet, warm, and utterly shocking touch directly on the place she felt most vulnerable. Ada gasped, her back arching, her fingers digging into the rough fabric of the bedspread. Korina didn't stop. She licked a slow, deliberate path through the soft hair, tasting her. A low sound, a hum of pure pleasure, vibrated from Korina's throat.

Oh. OH. The shame I've carried for so long...she's turning it into this...this incredible feeling.

Every logical process in Ada's brain dissolved into pure, overwhelming sensation. The point of her deepest insecurity was being transformed, re-coded in real time into the epicenter of a pleasure so intense it bordered on pain. Korina's mouth became more insistent, her tongue and lips working with a scholar's focus, exploring every texture, every scent, every taste. The soft, wet sounds filled the room, a symphony of acceptance that drowned out the echoes of a lifetime of shame.

Ada's head fell back, her neck exposed. A broken sob escaped her lips—a sound of relief, of release, of a love so profound it was physically rewriting her. This was more than acceptance. *This was worship.* Korina wasn't just tolerating a flaw; she was consecrating it, elevating it, finding a new and fascinating data point in her lover's body and dedicating herself to its thorough and absolute study.

She's not just accepting me, the thought blazed through her, clear as a root command. *She's...rewriting me.* Korina, her brilliant, beautiful Korina, was taking the broken, insecure code of Ada's past and, with nothing more than her tongue and her unwavering love, debugging it into perfection.

The overwhelming sensation finally receded, leaving Ada boneless and trembling on the edge of the bed. Her head was still thrown back, her throat exposed to the cool air of the room. She was a system rebooting after a critical overload, every sensor firing with phantom data. When Korina finally pulled away, her lips were slick, her eyes luminous in the lamplight.

"Such a strong response," Korina breathed, her voice a low, seductive purr. She looked not at Ada's face, but at the place she had just lavished with attention, a researcher admiring her successful experiment. "The bio-etheric field around this area...it spiked exponentially. *Exquisite.*"

Exquisite. The way she says it...so clinical, so reverent. Ada's mind swam, trying to catch up. *She's not just touching me, she's learning me. Every part of me is a wonder to her.*

Korina's attention shifted. Her pale hands, which had been resting on the bed, now moved to Ada's waist. Her touch was different now—no longer just curious, but confident. Empowered. She peeled the rough linen of Ada's trousers away from her skin, her fingers methodical, unbuttoning the simple clasp at the front. The fabric whispered as it slid down Ada's hips.

Ada's breath hitched again, another wave of old, conditioned shame threatening to surface. Before she could voice a protest, Korina's gaze fell upon the soft, dark curls nestled at the juncture of her thighs. It was another feature her new body had grown with an unapologetic wildness, another deviation from the smooth, curated ideal of her past life.

But Korina's reaction was not one of revulsion. Her eyes widened, not in shock, but in discovery. A soft, breathless laugh escaped her lips, a sound of pure delight.

"Another one," she whispered, her voice filled with a reverence that made Ada's heart ache. "Another beautiful glitch in the system. So...*organic*."

Her fingers, light as a phantom's touch, traced the edge of the dark patch of hair. The contact was electric, sending a fresh jolt through Ada's already overloaded circuits. Korina looked up, her violet eyes locking with Ada's, seeking confirmation.

"Tell me," Korina commanded softly, her voice a velvet whisper that brooked no argument. "Feedback is essential for accurate analysis. Tell me what makes you...*operate*."

The question was a key, a root command unlocking the last of Ada's control. A shuddering moan was her only answer. It was all the data Korina needed. Her smile widened, a breathtaking display of triumph and desire. She leaned forward again, her warm breath ghosting over the sensitive skin just above the curls.

"Let's test these parameters, shall we?"

Her exploration was a symphony of sensation. Her fingers, nimble and precise, mapped the terrain with an analyst's focus. They found the most sensitive points with an uncanny accuracy, as if she were reading a schematic only she could see. With every sharp intake of Ada's breath, with every soft whimper that escaped her lips, Korina's touch grew bolder, her movements more assured.

"Here?" she would murmur, her thumb pressing against a particularly responsive spot.

"Rina..." Ada gasped, her hips instinctively bucking against the pressure.

"A positive data point," Korina purred, applying more pressure, her other hand sliding down to cup the burgeoning heat between Ada's legs. She parted the soft folds with a scholar's care, revealing the glistening pearl hidden within. Her fingers danced across it, light and teasing at first, then more demanding, a direct query to Ada's core.

The feeling was magnificent. It was pure, unfiltered—an emergent property of Korina's love. She was a system analyst discovering the source code of Ada's pleasure, and she was doing it with a passion that was anything but clinical. Ada arched her back, her fingers clenching and unclenching in Korina's hair, her body a live wire humming with a current that grew stronger with every passing second.

Korina's mouth followed the path her hands had blazed. The first touch of her wet, warm tongue was a system shock that sent a wave of fire through Ada's veins. She cried out, the sound sharp and unrestrained.

"Keep...going..." The words were a prayer, a desperate plea torn from her throat.

"*As you command, my queen,*" Korina's voice was muffled against her skin, a deep vibration that resonated through every nerve.

She was relentless. Her tongue and lips and fingers worked in a perfect, devastating synchronicity. She found Ada's rhythm, learned it, then began to overclock it, pushing the system to its absolute limits. Ada's world dissolved into a maelstrom of touch and heat and the low, seductive sound of Korina's voice, a constant feedback loop of inquiry and praise.

"Faster...?" Korina asked, her fingers picking up their pace.

"Yes..."

"Harder?" Her thumb pressed down, a perfect, exquisite agony.

A keening sound escaped Ada, a high, thin note of pure pleasure. She was on the edge, a cascade failure of the most spectacular kind. The pressure built, a glorious, unbearable weight coiling in her belly. She was an algorithm approaching its final, beautiful conclusion.

"Rina!" she cried out, her voice breaking, her name a final, complete surrender.

Korina's answer was a low growl of triumph as she pushed her over the edge. The release was a supernova, a complete and total system purge that left Ada shaking and gasping in its wake. Waves of pure, unadulterated pleasure washed over her, wiping her clean of everything but the profound, bone-deep certainty of being utterly, completely, and magnificently loved.

The world returned to Ada in slow, shuddering waves. The aftershocks of pleasure still thrummed through her limbs, a delicious, lingering static that left her boneless and pliant. The only sounds in the small room were her own ragged gasps slowly evening out and the soft, steady rhythm of Korina's breathing. She felt the comforting weight of Korina's arms as she was gently guided from the edge of the bed to lie fully on the rustling mattress.

Korina followed, her body warm and solid as she settled beside Ada, pulling the thin wool blanket over them. The air was thick with their mingled scents, an intimate perfume of musk, sweat and triumph. Ada lay on her back, staring up at the ceiling where the shadows cast by the single lamp danced and writhed like living things. She felt...recalibrated. Purged. A core system reset to a new, more perfect state of being.

This wasn't just physical, the thought surfaced, clear and profound in the quiet aftermath. *It was a fusion.*

Korina's arm was draped over her stomach, a possessive, comforting weight. Her head rested in the crook of Ada's shoulder. Ada could feel the steady, reassuring beat of Korina's heart against her ribs, a rhythm that seemed to sync with her own. This woman beside her, this brilliant, fierce woman who had just taken her apart and put her back together, was not the same person Ada had met at the Warden's Gate months ago. The timid scholar, the frightened survivor—those aspects were still part of her code, but they were no longer the dominant processes. A new subroutine had been written tonight, one of confidence and power.

She isn't someone I just protect anymore. Ada's mind traced the new logic with a sense of awe. *She is my partner. In every sense of the word. My pillar.* A soft, playful chuckle escaped her lips, a sound of pure contentment. She turned her head, her nose brushing against Korina's soft, violet hair.

"That was..." Ada started, her voice a husky whisper, still thick with pleasure. She searched for the right word, the right piece of data to describe the paradigm shift she'd just experienced. "...unexpected."

Korina stirred, lifting her head just enough to look at her. In the dim, flickering light, her violet eyes seemed almost luminous, twin nebulas of intelligence and affection. A slow, confident smile touched her lips, the smile of a researcher whose hypothesis had just been proven spectacularly correct.

My magnificent, emergent love, Ada thought, sending the feeling across their telepathic link, a pure, unworded broadcast of adoration and wonder. She felt Korina's mental embrace in return, a wave of warmth and reciprocal love that needed no translation.

"The data suggested a more assertive approach would yield a... positive outcome," Korina murmured, her voice a low, husky vibration against Ada's skin. Her thumb traced a lazy circle on Ada's stomach.

Ada's chuckle grew into a soft laugh. She felt a lightness in her chest she hadn't realized was missing. The weight of being the Architect, the Queen, the sole protector—it had eased, redistributed between them. They were two pillars now, supporting the same impossible dream.

"Positive outcome?" Ada teased gently, her fingers finding Korina's and lacing through them. "That's your clinical assessment, is it? It was needed...but...good, right?"

Korina's smile widened, a breathtaking display of self-assurance. She leaned in, her lips brushing against Ada's, a soft, final punctuation to the night's discoveries.

"Exceptionally good," she whispered, the words a perfect, final beat that summarized everything. The analysis was complete. The conclusion was love.

CHAPTER 17

THE CITY OF CODEXIA

The sun beat down on them with a relentless intensity, the air thick and heavy with the cloying sweetness of decaying vegetation. The ground beneath their feet was a treacherous mix of cracked earth and sucking mud, each step a gamble against a twisted ankle or a submerged boot. They were two days out of Doc-ehx, heading deeper into the Wordaeus Theocracy, and the landscape had become increasingly hostile, a physical manifestation of the spreading corruption.

"Void, it's like walking through a blighted swamp toad's guts," Janna grumbled, her voice echoing in the oppressive stillness. She wiped a bead of sweat from her brow, leaving a streak of grime on her weathered skin. "This heat is enough to melt the cerakote off a Justicar's armor."

Not quite, Korina's voice chimed in their telepathic link, a dry counterpoint to Janna's gruff complaint. *The melting point of cerakote is significantly higher than the current ambient temperature.*

However, the humidity combined with the decaying organic matter does create an environment conducive to accelerated oxidation.

Thanks for the science lesson, Rina, Sera replied, her voice laced with a playful sarcasm. *But I think we can all agree that it's hot as Void out here.*

Ada, walking at the head of their small column, felt the weight of the oppressive heat pressing down on her, the air thick and suffocating in her lungs. She could feel the sweat plastering her tunic to her back, the damp fabric clinging to her skin like a second, unwelcome layer. Even her hair, usually a vibrant cascade of violet-black, felt limp and lifeless, weighed down by the humidity.

The landscape around them was a desolate expanse of withered vegetation and cracked earth, the once-vibrant colors of Kremøtoa now muted, washed out by the encroaching decay. The trees, twisted and gnarled, clawed at the sky with skeletal branches, their leaves withered and brown. The ground, once fertile and teeming with life, was now barren and cracked, the fissures in the earth like gaping wounds, oozing a foul-smelling, viscous sludge.

We should find some shade, Ada thought, projecting the image of a sheltered alcove to the others. *I'm starting to feel the effects of the heat.*

Agreed, Erita replied, her voice tight with fatigue. *My energy levels are dangerously low. We need to conserve our strength.*

They continued their trek, their progress slow and arduous, each step a struggle against the unforgiving terrain. The sun beat down on them with relentless fury, the heat radiating off the cracked earth, making the air shimmer and distort. The silence was broken only by the crunch of their boots on the parched earth, the occasional buzzing of insects, and the labored breathing of the five women as they pushed onward.

After what felt like an eternity, they reached a small, rocky outcrop, a welcome respite from the relentless sun. The outcrop, though offering minimal shade, provided a much-needed break from the oppressive heat. They collapsed against the cool stone, their bodies heavy with exhaustion.

"Water," Korina gasped, her voice raspy and weak. She fumbled with the clasp of her waterskin, her fingers trembling with fatigue.

Ada, sensing Korina's distress, reached into her Matākyasshu and retrieved a small, chilled canteen. "Here, Rina," she said, offering the canteen to Korina. "Drink."

Korina took the canteen with a grateful nod, her violet eyes meeting Ada's with a silent acknowledgment of her care. She took a long, slow draught, the cool water a welcome relief in the oppressive heat. She closed her eyes for a moment, savoring the sensation, the coolness spreading through her parched throat, a welcome balm against the burning in her chest.

Better? Ada asked, her voice soft and gentle in the telepathic link.

Much, Korina replied, her voice now stronger, clearer. *Thank you, Ada.*

They rested for a while longer, their bodies slowly recovering from the exertion. The shade of the outcrop, though minimal, provided a welcome respite from the relentless sun. The air, though still thick and heavy, felt slightly cooler, a welcome change from the furnace-like heat of the open plains.

How much further? Sera asked, her voice echoing in the stillness.

According to Obsidian's calculations, we're still several days from the border of the Ashen States, Korina replied, her voice laced with a weary resignation. *The terrain will only get worse from here.*

Then we best be on our way, Janna said, her voice gruff but resolute. She pushed herself up from the rock, her movements stiff but determined. "The sooner we reach the Oracle, the sooner we can put an end to this blighted mess."

They gathered their belongings and set off once more, their small column a solitary beacon of defiance in the desolate landscape. The sun beat down on them with unrelenting fury, the air thick and suffocating, the ground treacherous beneath their feet. But they pressed onward, their steps slow but steady, their resolve unwavering. They were the Fellowship, the last hope of Kremøtoa, and they would not falter. They would not fail.

The wind whipped at Janna's cloak, carrying with it the dry, gritty dust of the Theocratic plains. She squinted, her eyes narrowed against the glare of the afternoon sun reflecting off the imposing white-stone walls of Codexia. The city rose before them like a monolithic testament to faith, its severe, angular architecture a stark contrast to the chaotic sprawl of Port Dominus. Towers, slender and impossibly tall, pierced the sky, their surfaces adorned with intricate carvings and towering religious iconography. It was a city built for worship, for reverence, for absolute obedience. A city Janna instinctively distrusted.

Justicars at the gate, Erita's voice echoed in Janna's mind, a cool, detached observation. *Heavily armed, standard patrol formation. Purity sensors active.*

Janna grunted, adjusting the grip on her axe. She didn't like this. The Theocracy and its fanatical Justicars had always made her skin crawl. Their rigid dogma and unwavering certainty reeked of hypocrisy, a manufactured holiness that masked a deeper, uglier truth.

Ada, any suggestions? Sera's voice was tight, laced with a nervous energy that Janna could feel even through the telepathic link.

I'm working on it, Ada replied, her voice calm, focused. *Just...give me a moment.*

They approached the gates, the heavy iron doors reinforced with thick plates of gleaming cerakote steel. Two Justicars, clad in full plate armor that gleamed under the harsh sun, stood guard, their faces impassive, their eyes cold and watchful. Long, ceremonial staves, tipped with glowing crystals, rested in their gauntleted hands. The air around them crackled with a faint, almost imperceptible energy, the telltale sign of active purity sensors.

Janna felt a bead of sweat trickle down her temple, a cold, unwelcome sensation in the dry heat. This was the most dangerous part of their journey. If the Justicars detected their technology, their weapons, their very *difference* from the Theocracy's rigid dogma, they'd be imprisoned, interrogated, or worse.

Hold, Ada's voice echoed in their minds, a sudden, sharp command. *I'm applying a localized mask. It should conceal our... irregularities.*

Janna felt a strange tingling sensation, a subtle shift in the air around her, as if a veil had been drawn over their small group. She glanced at her axe, half-expecting it to shimmer or vanish, but it remained solid, unchanged. Yet, she felt...*different*, as if a part of her had been temporarily erased, hidden from view.

They continued their approach, their steps slow and deliberate. The Justicars watched them, their eyes narrowed, their expressions unreadable. The air crackled with the energy of the purity sensors, the faint hum growing louder as they drew closer. Janna held her breath, her heart pounding against her ribs, a heavy drumbeat against the silence.

"Halt," one of the Justicars commanded, his voice a flat, emotionless drone. "State your purpose."

"We are pilgrims," Ada replied, her voice calm, steady. "Traveling to Codexia to offer prayers at the Grand Sanctum."

The Justicar raised a gauntleted hand, the crystal at the tip of his staff glowing with a sickly golden light. He swept the staff over their group, the light pulsing, scanning them for any trace of heresy, any deviation from the Theocracy's rigid code. Janna felt the energy wash over her, a cold, invasive sensation that made her skin crawl.

The light flickered, then dimmed. The Justicar lowered his staff, his expression unchanged. "Proceed," he said, his voice still a monotone. "May the Word guide your steps."

They passed through the gates, the heavy iron doors clanging shut behind them. Janna let out a breath she hadn't realized she'd been holding, the tension slowly draining from her shoulders. They were in. For now.

Argent's light, that was close, Sera muttered in the telepathic link, her voice still tight with residual tension.

Indeed, Erita agreed. *Ada, your mask was...effective. A most useful tool.*

It's a temporary solution, Ada replied, her voice laced with a weary caution. *It won't hold forever. We need to be careful.*

Janna glanced back at the imposing gates, the Justicars still standing guard, their silver armor gleaming in the fading light. Codexia. A city of whispers and shadows, of rigid dogma and unwavering faith. A city that felt more like a prison than a sanctuary. A city they would have to navigate with extreme caution if they were to survive.

They continued their trek, their small column a solitary spark of rebellion in a city of absolute obedience. The shadows lengthened, the air grew colder, and the silence of Codexia pressed down on them, heavy and suffocating. The journey had just begun its most perilous stretch.

The gates of Codexia clanged shut behind them, the heavy sound echoing in the oppressive silence. Erita drew a slow, steady breath, her senses on high alert. The air itself felt different here, thick with the cloying scent of incense and the weight of unspoken fear. This wasn't the chaotic, vibrant energy of Port Dominus, where every shadow held a secret and every corner a potential threat. This was something far more insidious: a city suffocating under the weight of its own piety.

Citizens, clad in plain, uniform robes of muted grays and browns, moved through the streets with a hushed reverence, their faces a mixture of devotion and fear. Public sermons, booming with righteous indignation, blared from arcane speakers mounted on the stark, geometric buildings, denouncing the Cascade Failure as a divine punishment for the sins of heretics and unbelievers. Erita's lip curled in disgust. This wasn't faith; it was control, a carefully orchestrated performance designed to keep the populace in a state of perpetual fear and obedience.

Notice the lack of thaumaturgical activity? Korina's voice echoed in Erita's mind, a ripple of analytical curiosity in the otherwise silent telepathic link. *It's...statistically improbable, given the Theocracy's reliance on arcane enhancements.*

They're suppressing it, Erita replied, her gaze sweeping over the crowds, searching for any telltale signs of hidden power, any flicker of unsanctioned magic. *Afraid of what it might reveal. Afraid of the truth.*

The truth is a dangerous weapon in the wrong hands, Sera added, her voice laced with a grim understanding. *Especially here.*

Ada remained silent, her focus inward, her mind likely processing the city's underlying code, searching for patterns and vulnerabilities. Erita understood. Ada's analytical mind saw the world differently, as a complex system to be understood and manipulated. But even Ada couldn't fully comprehend the irrationality of faith, the unpredictable nature of true belief.

Erita navigated them through the crowds, her movements fluid and silent, a predator slipping through a sea of unsuspecting prey. She identified a discreet inn, tucked away on a side street, its sign a faded image of a whispering chalice. It wasn't opulent, but it was secluded, offering a much-needed respite from the city's oppressive gaze.

"The Whispered Tongue," Erita announced, her voice low,

keeping their conversation out of the hearing range of nearby citizens. "It's not much, but it will do."

They entered the inn, the air inside thick with the smell of stale ale and simmering stew. A handful of patrons, their faces drawn and weary, sat huddled at the tables, whispering amongst themselves. The innkeeper, a thin, nervous man with darting eyes, greeted them with a forced smile.

"Welcome, pilgrims," he said, his voice barely a whisper. "May the Word guide your steps."

Erita secured a private room, away from the prying eyes and ears of the other patrons. She paid the innkeeper, her fingers brushing against his as she handed him the coins, a subtle test. He flinched, his eyes widening with a flicker of fear. Erita smiled, a thin, predatory expression that sent a shiver down the innkeeper's spine. He quickly retreated, eager to escape her unsettling gaze.

Once they were alone, Erita began her work. She slipped out of the inn, melting into the shadows of the city, her senses on high alert. The marketplace was a hive of hushed conversations, a breeding ground for rumors and whispers. Erita listened, her mind a whirlwind of observation and analysis. The talk was of increased Justicar patrols, of public purges, of citizens disappearing in the night. And one name, above all others, echoed through the whispers: Lady Calibree.

The High Inquisitor, the Empress' right hand, the most feared agent of the Theocracy. Erita had heard of her, of course. Legends of her ruthlessness and efficiency whispered in the darkest corners of Port Dominus. A woman who viewed mercy as weakness, doubt as heresy, and compassion as a corruption of the soul. A woman who was the very embodiment of the Theocracy's terrifying power.

Found something interesting, Erita announced in the telepathic link, her voice a low, steady hum. *Lady Calibree. She's been active. Very active.*

What kind of active? Sera asked, her voice tight with concern.

Purges, Erita replied, her mind replaying the whispered conversations, the fragments of fear and desperation she had gleaned from the marketplace. *Public executions. Unsanctioned thaumaturgy. Anything that deviates from their rigid dogma.*

That doesn't sound good, Korina muttered.

It's worse than it sounds, Erita replied, her gaze fixed on the distant towers of the Grand Sanctum, the heart of the Theocracy's power. *Calibree is a predator. And we're in her hunting grounds.*

From their vantage point in the inn's darkened room, Ada watched the unfolding scene in the square below. The midday sun cast long, distorted shadows across the cobblestones, turning the normally bustling marketplace into a stage for a macabre performance: a group of Justicars, their burnished cerakote armor gleaming under the harsh light, stood in a rigid formation, their faces impassive, their eyes devoid of warmth or empathy. They were the instruments of the Theocracy's will, the enforcers of its unforgiving dogma.

At the center of the square, a high-ranking priest, his opulent robes a stark contrast to the roughspun tunics of the assembled crowd, raised his hands, his voice booming with righteous indignation. He spoke of the "Cascade Failure," of the world's decay, of the "unclean thoughts" and "heretical data" that had brought this divine judgment upon them. His words were a venomous concoction of fear and dogma, designed to crush dissent and solidify the Theocracy's control.

Ada watched in cold fury as the Justicars began their work. A child's mechanical toy, a marvel of intricate gears and springs, was smashed to pieces under a Justicar's heavy boot. A scholar's data-slate, a repository of knowledge and years of dedicated research, was crushed under the weight of a ceremonial staff. A merchant's abacus, a simple tool of commerce, was snapped in two, its beads scattering across the cobblestones like fallen tears.

Each act of destruction was a calculated display of power, a public reminder of the Theocracy's absolute authority. The crowd watched in stunned silence, their faces a mixture of fear and resignation. They were the victims of a carefully orchestrated performance, their sense of normalcy warped by the priest's fiery rhetoric and the Justicars' brutal efficiency.

A man, his clothes torn and stained, was dragged before the priest. He was accused of "data-heresy," of trying to understand the glitches, of seeking knowledge beyond the Theocracy's approved scriptures. The priest held up a crumpled piece of parchment, proclaiming it evidence of the man's "unclean thoughts." The man tried to speak, to defend himself, but his words were drowned out by the priest's booming pronouncements and the crowd's hushed whispers. He was publicly shamed, his name added to the list of the damned, and hauled away by the Justicars, presumably for "re-education."

Ada's hands clenched into fists, her nails digging into her palms. This wasn't order; it was oppression. This wasn't faith; it was fear. The Theocracy wasn't a force of stability, but a parasite feeding on the anxieties of its people, using the global crisis as an excuse to tighten its grip, to crush any spark of individuality or independent thought.

Argent's light, Ada thought, her mind a whirlwind of cold fury, *they will pay for this.*

Easy, Ada, Sera's voice echoed in her mind, a calming presence in the storm of Ada's rage. *We're in their territory. We need to be careful.*

Careful doesn't change the fact that they are preying on the vulnerable, Ada retorted, her gaze fixed on the retreating Justicars, their armored forms disappearing into the labyrinthine streets of Codexia.

It changes the fact that we can't afford to be caught, Erita added, her voice laced with a pragmatic cynicism. *Not yet.*

She's right, Ada, Korina chimed in, her voice a blend of analytical observation and concern. *Their security systems are... extensive. We need a plan.*

Ada turned away from the window, her mind racing. Codexia, once a symbol of the Theocracy's rigid control, had become their prison. The city's imposing walls, designed to keep out heretics and dissent, now trapped them within its iron grip. The harsh clangor of the alarm bells echoed through the streets, a relentless pulse of dread that seemed to vibrate in Ada's very bones.

"They're sealing the city," Sera said, her voice grim. "Every gate, every alley, every exit will be locked down."

"How?" Korina whispered, her violet eyes wide with disbelief. "How could they know?"

"They didn't," Erita said, her voice tight with tension. "Not at first. But that display in the square...it was a test. A purity check."

Ada's gaze snapped to Erita. "A purity check?"

"Those Soul-Censers," Erita explained, her hand gesturing towards the window. "They're not just for show. They scan for... anomalies. Deviations from the Theocracy's approved code."

"And we," Ada said, the realization hitting her with the force of a physical blow, "are the biggest anomaly in the system."

"Precisely," Erita confirmed, her golden eyes narrowed in thought. "They didn't know who they were looking for, but they knew *something* was here. Something...unclean."

A wave of nausea washed over Ada. She had designed Kremøtoa's systems, its intricate web of code and algorithms. She had created the very tools that were now being used to hunt her down. The irony was a bitter pill to swallow.

"So, what now?" Janna asked, her voice a low rumble of impatience. "We fight our way out?"

"Not a chance," Erita said, shaking her head. "Codexia's defenses are formidable. We'd be slaughtered before we reached the outer walls."

"There has to be another way," Korina murmured, her fingers flying across Obsidian's surface, the data-slate's screen flickering with complex schematics and code streams.

"There isn't," Erita said, her voice flat. "Not anymore. We're trapped."

A heavy silence settled over the room, broken only by the rhythmic clangor of the alarm bells and the distant shouts of the Justicar patrols. Ada felt a cold knot of fear tighten in her stomach.

This wasn't a game anymore. This wasn't a bug to be fixed or a line of code to be rewritten. This was a fight for survival, and the odds were stacked against them.

There has to be a way, Ada thought, her mind racing, desperately searching for a solution, an escape route, a loophole in the Theocracy's iron grip. She closed her eyes, focusing her intent, her consciousness reaching out, probing the city's systems, its network of sensors, its energy grids, its thaumaturgical wards. She could feel the city's pulse, its digital heartbeat, its underlying code.

There has to be something.

CHAPTER 18

THE JUSTICARESS' SNARE

The iron gates of Codexia groaned shut behind her, the sound echoing through the eerily silent streets like the closing of a tomb. Lady Calibree strode forward, her footsteps precise and measured on the cobblestones, each clang of her armor a stark counterpoint to the hushed whispers that followed in her wake. The citizens of Codexia parted before her like water before a prow, their faces pale with a mixture of awe and terror. She acknowledged none of them. Her gaze remained fixed ahead, her mind focused on the task at hand: the purification of Codexia.

The Empress' vision is clear, she thought, her internal monologue a silent prayer to the Word. *The Cascade Failure is not a disaster; it is a divine cleansing. A purging of the flawed, the impure, the unnatural order that has festered within Kremøtoa's code for too long.* Her gloved hand tightened around the hilt of her ceremonial staff, the cool metal a reassuring presence against her skin. *And this...this anomaly...this disruption...is a blasphemy against the Word's chaotic design.*

The data the Soul-Censers had gathered was fragmented, incomplete, but it was enough. A flicker of unnatural energy. A ripple in the city's carefully controlled thaumaturgical matrix. A whisper of forbidden code. It was a subtle corruption, almost imperceptible, but to Calibree, it was a screaming beacon of heresy.

She stopped before the entrance to The Whispered Tongue, the inn Erita had chosen as their temporary sanctuary. The building was nondescript, blending seamlessly with the surrounding architecture, but Calibree could sense the taint within. It was a faint tremor in the city's spiritual fabric, a dissonance that grated against her finely tuned senses.

Two Justicars flanked the entrance, their faces impassive beneath their helms. They snapped to attention as Calibree approached.

"Report," she commanded, her voice a low, resonant hum that carried an undercurrent of steel.

"High Inquisitor," the Justicar on the left said, his voice a monotone drone, "the Soul-Censers registered elevated levels of unsanctioned thauma within this establishment. The proprietor claims ignorance, but our scans indicate recent activity."

"Recent?" Calibree asked, her eyes narrowing.

"Within the last hour, High Inquisitor," the Justicar confirmed.

They are still here, Calibree thought, a flicker of cold satisfaction running through her. *Trapped.*

"Secure the perimeter," she ordered, her voice clipped and precise. "No one enters or leaves without my authorization. Prepare the Sanctum for interrogation. And bring me the proprietor."

The Justicars moved with practiced efficiency, their movements a silent, synchronized ballet of obedience. Calibree watched them, her mind already calculating the most effective methods of extracting information. Torture was a crude tool, often yielding unreliable results. She preferred a more...refined approach. A subtle manipulation of fear, guilt, and faith. A dismantling of the spirit, not the body.

The innkeeper, a wizened old man with trembling hands and watery eyes, was brought before her, his face a mask of fear. Calibree studied him, her gaze piercing and unwavering.

"You harbor heretics," she stated, her voice devoid of inflection. It was not a question.

The old man stammered, his words a jumble of denials and pleas for mercy. Calibree ignored his protests.

"You know the penalty for aiding those who defy the Word," she said, her voice as cold and sharp as a shard of ice.

The old man's eyes widened in terror. He fell to his knees, begging for forgiveness. Calibree remained unmoved.

"The Empress' justice is swift and absolute," she said, her voice echoing in the silent street. "Confess your sins, and perhaps you will find mercy in the afterlife."

The old man's pleas grated on Calibree's nerves, a discordant symphony of fear and desperation. She allowed him to continue for a moment, savoring the taste of his terror, then silenced him with a sharp gesture. His whimpers died in his throat, his eyes wide and pleading.

"Enough," she said, her voice cutting through the silence. "Tell me what I want to know, and your suffering will end."

The old man's relief was palpable. He babbled about the strangers who had arrived earlier, describing their appearance and demeanor with surprising accuracy. But then, he hesitated, a flicker of cunning in his watery eyes. He changed his story, claiming the strangers had left shortly after arriving, heading towards the eastern gate. He swore he had seen no signs of heresy, only weary travelers seeking rest.

Calibree listened, her expression impassive. She could sense the lie, a subtle shift in the old man's emotional matrix. But the lie itself was irrelevant. What mattered was the old man's willingness to deceive. It confirmed his complicity, his willingness to aid those who defied the Word. It was enough.

"Very well," she said, her voice smooth and deceptively gentle. "You have been spared the Empress' wrath...for now. But know this: if you lie to me again, your punishment will be...exemplary."

The old man's gratitude was effusive. He groveled at her feet, promising unwavering loyalty to the Theocracy. Calibree ignored him. She turned and strode away, her Justicars falling in behind her, their armor gleaming in the fading light. The old man's desperate pleas faded into the background, a meaningless drone that held no interest for her.

As Calibree walked, her mind raced, processing the information she had gathered. The old man's lie was a calculated risk, a desperate gamble to save his own skin. It was a foolish move. Calibree knew the heretics were still in Codexia. She could feel their presence, a subtle corruption in the city's carefully controlled thaumaturgical matrix. And she would find them.

In the hushed stillness of her temporary command post, a repurposed chapel within the Sanctum, Lady Calibree reviewed the data streaming across the obsidian surface of her modified data-slate. The air around her crackled with the faint, sickly golden glow of the Soul-Censers, their rhythmic pulses casting long, distorted shadows that danced across the chapel's austere walls. She was not looking for the chaotic energy signatures that typically marked the presence of Malware or Pattern Blight. She sought something far more insidious, far more heretical. A pattern within the chaos. An echo of forbidden order.

Her fingers, encased in articulated gauntlets of blackened cerakote, danced across the data-slate's surface, manipulating the swirling holographic display with practiced ease. The city of Codexia unfolded before her, rendered in intricate, three-dimensional detail. Streets, buildings, even the flickering gaslights were represented with chilling accuracy. But it was the overlay of thaumaturgical data that held her attention. A web of swirling, chaotic energy signatures pulsed across the city, a visual representation of the Cascade Failure's relentless decay. Within this maelstrom of corruption, however, Calibree had detected something...unusual.

A faint, almost imperceptible trail of...*order*.

It was a series of small, localized pockets of perfect, stable reality moving through the city like ghosts through walls. Tiny, impossible bubbles of corrected glitches, where the fraying edges of the world's code had been seamlessly repaired. It was as if someone, or something, was systematically *undoing* the divine test of the Cascade Failure. An act of profound hubris. An unforgivable heresy.

Calibree's lips curled into a thin, mirthless smile. *Mortals,* she thought, her internal monologue a silent prayer to the Word. *Daring to impose their flawed, limited understanding upon the divine tapestry of chaos. They seek to control what they cannot comprehend. To mend what was meant to be broken.*

Her fingers tightened around the data-slate, the pressure

causing the obsidian surface to shimmer with an unnatural light. The trail of corrected glitches led towards the city's eastern district, a labyrinth of narrow alleyways and crumbling tenements. It was a known haven for smugglers, thieves, and other unsavory elements—a breeding ground for dissent and heresy.

They believe they can hide in the shadows, Calibree thought, her eyes narrowing. *They believe they can escape the Empress' judgment.*

She closed her eyes, focusing her mind, reaching out with her enhanced senses to probe the city's thaumaturgical matrix. She could feel the presence of the heretics, a faint but distinct ripple in the city's spiritual fabric. They were moving, their trail of corrected glitches growing longer with each passing moment.

They are fleeing, she realized. *They know I am coming.*

A thrill of anticipation ran through her, a cold, exhilarating surge of purpose. The hunt was on. She would find these heretics, these self-proclaimed healers of a world meant to be broken. She would expose their hubris, their blasphemy, their defiance of the Word. And she would purify them.

"Prepare the Justicars," she commanded, her voice echoing in the hushed stillness of the chapel. "We ride. *Now.*"

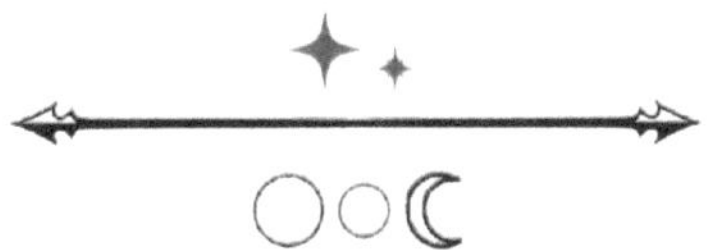

The flickering gaslight cast long, distorted shadows across the spartan room, turning the chipped porcelain washbasin into a grotesque, grinning skull. Erita paced, the rhythmic click of her boots against the worn floorboards a counterpoint to the frantic thump of her own heart. The air in the room was thick with the stench of stale ale and desperation. Codexia, once a destination, was now a cage. A gilded cage, perhaps, but a cage nonetheless.

They're closing in, she thought, her voice a silent whisper in the telepathic network that bound her to Ada, Sera, Korina, and Janna. *Block by block. Methodical. Relentless.*

She could feel the fear radiating from her contacts on the street, a wave of cold panic that washed over her through the clandestine network of whispers and coded messages she had cultivated over years of operating in the shadows. Lady Calibree was not playing games. This was not a random purge, a theatrical display of Theocratic power. This was a targeted hunt. A systematic sweep. And they were the prey.

Calibree is using advanced arcane sensors, she continued, her mental voice tight with urgency. *Modified data-slates. They're scanning for our unique energy signatures. The residue from Ada's... adjustments.*

She glanced at Ada, who sat hunched over a crudely drawn map of Codexia, her brow furrowed in concentration. Sera stood by the window, her crimson tunic a splash of defiant color against the drab backdrop of the city. Korina huddled in a corner, her fingers dancing across the surface of Obsidian, her face pale and drawn. Janna paced restlessly, her hand never far from the axe strapped to her back. They were trapped, cornered like rats in a maze.

The Justicar patrols are doubling back, Erita reported, her mental voice laced with grim determination. *Checking every building. Every room. They're using Soul-Censers. They'll find us. It's only a matter of time.*

A wave of nausea rolled over her. She could feel the walls closing in, the noose tightening. They had underestimated the Theocracy's reach, the Empress' paranoia. They had walked into a trap, blinded by their own arrogance, their own belief in their invincibility.

We need a plan, Sera's voice echoed in the telepathic network, a low rumble of controlled frustration. *And we need it now.*

There's nowhere left to run, Janna added, her mental voice a gruff growl. *We're surrounded.*

I'm working on it, Korina replied, her mental voice strained with exhaustion. *But their security systems are...intricate. Layered. I can't find a weakness.*

Erita resumed her pacing, the click of her boots against the floorboards a frantic tattoo against the silence. Her mind raced, searching for a solution, an escape route, a glimmer of hope in the encroaching darkness. But there was nothing. They were trapped. Boxed in. Checkmated.

The air crackled with arcane energy. The stench of ozone filled the small room, stinging Erita's nostrils. The heavy thud of armored boots against the wooden floorboards vibrated through her bones. It was the sound of inevitability. The sound of the end.

Before any of them could react, before Sera could even fully draw her blades or Janna heft her axe, the door exploded inward in a shower of splintered wood and twisted metal. A wave of Justicars flooded the room, their silver armor gleaming under the harsh glare of the gaslight, their faces impassive masks of cold, unwavering faith. They moved with the practiced efficiency of a well-oiled machine, weapons raised, forming a tight, impenetrable cordon around the room.

At their head stood a Justicaress, taller and more imposing than the others, her armor adorned with intricate silver filigree. Her dark grey eyes, cold and calculating, swept across the room, taking in the scene with chilling detachment. A faint, sickly golden glow pulsed from the Soul-Censer clutched in her gauntleted hand. It was the glow of judgment. The glow of their impending doom.

"By the Word," the Justicaress intoned, her voice a low, resonant hum that seemed to vibrate through the very foundations of the inn. "Heretics. Your corruption ends here."

Korina whimpered, burying her face in Ada's shoulder, her body trembling uncontrollably. Sera snarled, her hand tightening around the hilt of her blade. Janna let out a low growl, her eyes burning with a mixture of defiance and resignation. Erita felt a cold dread settle in her stomach. They were outnumbered, outgunned, and trapped. There was no escape.

Ada, however, stood tall. She gently pushed Korina behind her, a protective gesture that belied the fear that flickered in her violet eyes. She took a deep breath, her shoulders straightening, her expression hardening into a mask of cold determination. The air around her shimmered, a faint violet aura beginning to emanate from her skin. The Justicars tensed, their eyes fixed on Ada, sensing the shift in the room's energy. The Justicaress' grip tightened on her Soul-Censer.

"You will not take them," Ada stated, her voice low but steady, a quiet counterpoint to the Justicaress' booming pronouncements. The violet aura intensified, the air around her crackling with barely contained power. "You will not harm them. You will not touch them."

A flicker of surprise crossed the Justicaress' face, quickly replaced by a mask of cold disdain. She raised her Soul-Censer, the golden glow intensifying, and pointed it at Ada.

"Blasphemer," she hissed. "Your defiance is an affront to the Word. Your power is a perversion. You will be cleansed."

"Hold," a voice cut through the tense standoff, sharp and cold as a winter wind. Lady Calibree strode into the room, her black armor gleaming dully in the gaslight, her presence radiating an aura of quiet, terrifying authority. The Justicars parted before her like water before a ship's prow, their heads bowed in deference. The Justicaress lowered her Soul-Censer, her eyes fixed on Calibree, a flicker of uncertainty in their depths.

"High Inquisitor," the Justicaress acknowledged, her voice laced with a hint of confusion. "These heretics—"

"Silence," Calibree interrupted, her voice a low, chilling monotone. "I will handle this." Her dark grey eyes swept across the room, lingering for a moment on Ada, a flicker of something akin to curiosity in their depths, before returning to the Justicaress. "Stand down. These...individuals are not to be harmed."

The Justicaress hesitated, her hand still hovering over the Soul-Censer. "But High Inquisitor, their thaumaturgical signatures—"

"Are irrelevant," Calibree stated flatly. "I have received direct word from Her Divine Eminence. Empress Thema Iridia Archivia herself has requested their...*unrestrained* audience."

A ripple of shock went through the assembled Justicars. An Imperial audience? For these heretics? It was unheard of. Unprecedented. The Justicaress' eyes widened, her confusion evident. She glanced at Ada, then back at Calibree, her expression a mixture of disbelief and apprehension.

"The Empress...requests their presence? *Unbound...at that?*" she repeated, her voice barely above a whisper.

"Indeed," Calibree confirmed, her tone brooking no argument. She turned her gaze to Ada, her expression unreadable. "You will accompany me to Codexia. Her Eminence awaits."

Ada's violet eyes met Calibree's grey ones, a silent battle of wills waged between them in the charged silence of the room. Ada's hand instinctively went to Korina's, her fingers intertwining with the scholar's, a silent reassurance, a grounding touch in the swirling chaos of the moment. She could feel the fear radiating from Korina, the confusion from Sera and Janna, the wary curiosity from Erita. They were trapped between a rock and a hard place, caught in a game whose rules they didn't understand.

Ada took a deep breath, her shoulders straightening, her expression hardening into a mask of cold resolve. She knew that resistance was futile. They were surrounded, outnumbered, and outgunned. Their only option was to play along, to see what hand the Empress was dealing. She glanced at her companions, a silent message of trust and determination passing between them.

"Very well," Ada stated, her voice calm and steady, a quiet counterpoint to the tension that crackled in the air. "We will accompany you. Lead the way."

Calibree gave a curt nod, a flicker of something that might have been amusement in her eyes. She turned and strode out of the room, her black cloak swirling behind her like a shroud. The Justicars followed, their armor clanking against the floorboards, their faces impassive masks of faith and duty. Ada and her companions fell in behind them, their expressions a mixture of apprehension and grim determination, their hands resting on the hilts of their weapons, ready for whatever awaited them in the heart of the Theocracy. The armed escort, a silent procession of power and defiance, moved through the darkened streets of Codexia, towards the Empress' palace, towards their unknown fate.

CHAPTER 19

THE PALACE OF CODEXIA

The streets of Codexia were a study in forced piety under the pale glow of Argent. The city, usually alive with the hushed murmur of whispered prayers and the rhythmic clang of Soul-Censers against cobblestones, was now eerily silent. The only sound was the measured tread of armored boots and the soft rustle of cloaks. Ada, flanked by Sera, Korina, and Erita, walked at the center of a moving wall of silver. Lady Calibree's Justicaresses formed an impenetrable cordon, their armor shimmering faintly in the moonlight, their faces impassive masks beneath their dark hoods. The citizens of Codexia, drawn from their homes by the commotion, parted before them like wheat before a scythe, their expressions a mixture of fear, awe, and a disturbingly fervent devotion. They knelt as the procession passed, their heads bowed, their lips moving in silent prayers, their eyes darting up at the prisoners with a mixture of morbid curiosity and pious condemnation.

Thirty-seven hostiles. No visible weak points in their formation.

Escape routes...minimal. The alleyways are too narrow, the rooftops too exposed. Damn. This isn't an arrest; it's a procession. A display of power. Sera's mind raced, a whirlwind of tactical analysis. She noted the Justicaresses' discipline, their synchronized movements, the subtle shifts in their formations as they navigated the narrow streets. There was no opening, no vulnerability she could exploit. They were trapped, caught in a web of faith and steel.

They're showing off. Making an example. Typical Theocracy bullshit. Erita's voice echoed in Sera's mind, a cynical counterpoint to her own frantic calculations. *Enjoy the parade, Seraphina. It might be the last one you ever see.*

The architecture...it's...perfect. Korina's thoughts were a detached observation, a jarring contrast to the tension that thrummed through Sera's veins. *The geometric precision...the tessellations...it's... fascinating.*

Rina, focus. Ada's mental voice was a gentle reprimand, a grounding touch in the rising panic. *Now is not the time for architectural appreciation.*

But Ada, the symmetry! The sheer computational efficiency—

Later, Rina. We need to figure out what Thema wants. Ada's mental voice was firm, cutting through Korina's rambling. *This isn't random. There's a reason she wants us alive.*

Alive for now. Erita's cynicism was a cold splash of reality. *Let's see how long that lasts once Thema gets her hands on the God-Queen.*

The procession halted before a towering obsidian gate, its surface etched with intricate, glowing glyphs that pulsed with a sickly golden light. Two Justicaresses, larger and more heavily armored than the others, stepped forward and raised their ceremonial staves. The gates shuddered open, revealing a courtyard bathed in the same unsettling golden glow. As they entered, Ada felt a shift in the arcane energy, a palpable thickening in the air like walking into a charged capacitor. The courtyard was eerily empty, the silence broken only by the rhythmic hum of the glyphs and the soft click of their own footsteps on the polished obsidian tiles. The palace loomed before them, a monolithic structure that seemed to claw at the indigo sky, its sharp angles and obsidian surfaces reflecting the distorted light of the three moons in a dizzying array of fragmented images.

They call her the 'Living Oracle.' A true believer. Her word is absolute law here. Be careful, she's not a brute like Thorne; she's a zealot. Erita's mental voice was a low, urgent whisper, laced with a caution Sera hadn't heard before. *She believes, without a shadow of a doubt, that she is the chosen vessel of the "Word," the divine will that guides the Theocracy. This conviction gives her an unshakable, and often terrifying, charisma.*

The arcane energy in this city...it's not raw, it's...focused. Channeled. Korina's mental voice was a whisper of awe and fear, her words painting a picture far more disturbing than any physical display of force. *It feels like the entire city is a massive arcane sigil, with the palace at its center.*

We don't know the rules of this game yet. Ada's mental voice was the anchor of their mental storm, calm, clear, and authoritative. *So we watch, we listen. Let me do the talking. Stay ready, but do not act unless I give the signal. Our goal is to understand her objective.*

The Justicaresses flanking the obsidian doors raised their staves in unison, the golden glyphs carved into the wood flaring brightly as they pressed the tips against hidden recesses in the stone. A low, grinding rumble echoed through the courtyard as the massive doors shuddered open, revealing the entrance to the main sanctum. The air within seemed to shimmer with a palpable arcane energy, a thick, almost viscous aura that crackled with unseen power. The golden glow intensified, casting long, distorted shadows that danced across the polished obsidian floor. Lady Calibree turned, her expression unreadable beneath her hood, and gestured for them to enter. "Her Divine Eminence awaits," she said, her voice a low, resonant monotone that echoed strangely in the vast chamber.

Ada stepped forward, her head held high, her gaze fixed on the open doorway. Sera, Korina, and Erita followed close behind, their hands instinctively reaching for their hidden weapons, their senses heightened, their minds linked in a silent symphony of apprehension. As they crossed the threshold, the obsidian doors slammed shut behind them with a resounding boom that seemed to reverberate through the very foundations of the city. They were now inside the belly of the beast, surrounded by the suffocating aura of Thema's power, their fates hanging precariously in the balance.

The air within the main sanctum was thick with the scent of incense and the low murmur of chanted prayers. It was a breathtaking and terrifying space, a vast, echoing chamber constructed of pristine white marble and illuminated by the soft, otherworldly glow that filtered through a series of massive, intricately crafted stained-glass windows. These windows, however, depicted not scenes of pastoral beauty or saintly miracles, but terrifying visions of divine judgment: cities consumed by fire, heretics writhing in agony, and monstrous entities rising from a swirling, chaotic void. The overall effect was less that of a palace and more that of a massive, weaponized cathedral—a place where faith itself felt like a tangible, oppressive force.

They were led through a seemingly endless series of grand, intimidating halls, their footsteps echoing eerily in the vast emptiness. Rows of kneeling priests lined the walls, their faces pale and gaunt, their eyes fixed on the floor in an attitude of abject humility. Stoic Justicar guards stood at regular intervals, their gleaming armor and ceremonial staves radiating an aura of silent, unquestioning authority. The atmosphere was one of absolute, suffocating piety, a tangible weight that pressed down on Ada and her companions, a constant reminder that they were not just prisoners, but heretics in the eyes of this fanatical power structure.

Void, this place is creepy. Janna's mental voice echoed in Ada's mind, a low rumble of unease that mirrored her own growing apprehension. *It's like walking through a tomb. A very well-guarded tomb.*

The energy signatures...they're...organized. Structured. Like a perfectly optimized algorithm. Korina's thoughts were a detached observation, her analytical mind struggling to process the sheer scale and intensity of the arcane energy that permeated the palace. *It's...fascinating. And terrifying.*

Thema's playing a game. Erita's mental voice was a sharp, cynical whisper, cutting through Korina's academic fascination. *She's building anticipation. Making us wait. Letting the fear fester. It's a classic interrogation tactic.*

She wants to see us break. Sera's mental voice was a grim assessment, a warrior's understanding of the power of psychological warfare. *She wants to see how much we can endure before we crack.*

Ada said nothing, her mind a whirlwind of conflicting thoughts and emotions. She felt a strange disconnect, a sense of unreality that stemmed from the knowledge that this entire spectacle, this oppressive display of faith and power, was a product of her own creation. The Justicars, the priests, the Empress herself—they were all emergent properties of the complex systems she had designed, characters in a game that had taken on a life of its own. And now, she was trapped within her own creation, a prisoner of her own design.

They were brought to a stop before a pair of massive, ornate golden doors. The doors were easily twenty feet high and intricately carved with scenes that mirrored the stained-glass windows: angels wielding flaming swords, demons chained in darkness, and the all-seeing eye of the 'Word' gazing down upon a world consumed by fire. Two Justicaresses, their armor gleaming in the soft light, stood guard before the doors, their ceremonial staves held at attention.

Lady Calibree turned to face them, her dark grey eyes unreadable, her expression as cold and impassive as the obsidian armor she wore. Her voice, when she spoke, was a low, measured monotone that echoed strangely in the vast hall, a voice that carried the weight of absolute authority and unwavering conviction.

"Her Divine Eminence will see you now."

As if in response to her words, the massive golden doors began to swing inward, their movement slow and deliberate, accompanied by a low, grinding sound that seemed to reverberate through Ada's very bones. The doors opened onto a blindingly bright space, a throne room bathed in the pure, almost painful radiance of a thousand glowing crystals. The air within the throne room shimmered with arcane energy, a palpable force that made Ada's skin tingle and her hair stand on end. The room itself was vast, its high ceilings lost in the dazzling light, its walls adorned with intricate tapestries depicting scenes of theological dogma. And at the center of it all, seated upon a throne of pure, shimmering gold, was a solitary figure, bathed in the radiant light, her presence radiating an aura of power and divine certainty that seemed to fill the entire chamber. Empress Thema Iridia Archivia. The living embodiment of The Word.

CHAPTER 20

A DUEL OF IDEOLOGY

The light was a physical assault. It struck them the moment the doors swung open, a pure, sterile radiance that scoured the senses. Ada squinted, her hand instinctively rising to shield her eyes as Lady Calibree led them into the chamber.

The throne room was a study in absolute, intimidating scale. The floor stretched out before them, an impossible expanse of polished white marble so reflective it created a disorienting mirror image of the ceiling. And the ceiling—it was lost in a galaxy of light. Thousands upon thousands of shimmering, multifaceted crystals hung suspended in the air, each one capturing and refracting the brilliant light, casting a dizzying web of rainbows across the sterile white surfaces. The air was cool and still, thick with the cloying sweetness of incense and the sharp, clean scent of ozone that spoke of immense, contained arcane power.

It was all a carefully constructed stage, designed to render any visitor insignificant. Their footsteps—Sera's firm stride, Erita's near-silent tread, Korina's hesitant steps, her own measured pace—were the only sounds, echoing into the vast silence and serving only to emphasize their smallness.

At the far end of the immense chamber, atop a dais of tiered marble, sat the throne. It was not gold, as Ada might have expected, but a thing of stark, unsettling beauty—carved from a single, flawless piece of pure white obsidian that seemed to drink the light around it. And upon it sat the Empress.

Thema Iridia Archivia was as severe and perfect as her surroundings. Her hair, the color of spun moonlight, was woven into a complex crown of braids. Her layered robes of black and gold fell around her in sharp, geometric lines. But it was her face that held Ada's attention. It was a mask of serene, unnerving beauty, dominated by eyes the color of a winter sky—pale, translucent, and utterly devoid of warmth. They didn't just look *at* Ada; they looked *through* her, as if assessing the very code of her being.

This is all just an algorithm of power, Ada thought, her mind a calm island in the sensory storm. She could see the commands behind the spectacle.

[RENDER_SETTING: Throne_Room_Theocracy {Parameter: Light_Intensity=100%; PARAMETER: Scale_Multiplier=5.0}]

It was designed to overwhelm, to inspire a blend of awe and terror that would break a person's will before a single word was spoken. But it was still just code. Elegant, complex, and ultimately, a system she understood better than anyone.

Stay calm, she projected through their telepathic link, feeling the tight coil of Erita's anger, Sera's rigid defiance, and Korina's frantic, analytical fear. A wave of her own focused resolve washed over them, a silent, steadying hand. *She's just a person.*

Lady Calibree led them to a circular inlay in the marble floor, a hundred feet from the dais, and then dropped to one knee, head bowed. Ada and her partners remained standing. It was a small, silent act of defiance, but in a place of such rigid conformity, it felt as loud as a shout.

The Empress' gaze swept over them, lingering for a moment on each before settling on Ada. When she spoke, her voice required no effort to fill the immense hall. It was a flawless, melodic instrument, each word resonating with a supernatural clarity that sent a shiver down Ada's spine.

"The Anomaly," Thema pronounced, the words less a name and more a final, unassailable classification. "You stand in the heart of The Word, in the light of truth, and you cast a shadow of corruption."

Her pale blue eyes held Ada's, unblinking. The air grew heavy, charged with the weight of her judgment.

"The world bleeds. The sacred test of the Cascade is upon us, a crucible sent to purify the faithful and burn away the heretic. It is a holy, necessary pain. A beautiful, agonizing truth." Her voice remained a serene, hypnotic cadence, even as she spoke of destruction. "And you...you have dared to impose your own flawed, unnatural order upon this divine process. You move through the world like a rogue query, patching the sacred wounds, healing the blessed sickness, silencing The Holy Chaos."

Thema leaned forward, the first hint of movement Ada had seen from her. The light from the crystals glinted off the silver threads in her hair. "*You are a blasphemy of logic. An architect of heresy.*"

The condemnation settled in the silent hall, an absolute and damning verdict. Sera's hand twitched toward the hilt of a blade she didn't have. Erita's jaw was a hard, tight line. Korina felt like a fragile piece of glass, ready to shatter.

But Ada felt a cold, clear resolve solidify within her. *She was not a heretic. She was not a flaw. She was the one who built this place.* She took a single step forward, breaking their perfect, isolated formation. Her voice, when she replied, was devoid of Thema's melodic artifice. It was simple. Direct. Unbreakable.

"I have done what was necessary to protect this world."

The Empress' lips curved into a smile that held no warmth, a perfect, symmetrical expression of condescending pity. "Protect? You call your chaotic meddling *protection*? You are a child scribbling over a sacred text, ignorant of the language, erasing verses of divine meaning simply because you cannot comprehend their grammar."

Her voice, still a melodic bell, took on a harder, colder edge. It echoed in the vast chamber, each word a stone dropped into a still pool.

"Every law, every hierarchy, every pain and every joy is a syllable in The Word. It is the code that gives this world structure —purpose. It is the source of all Authority. So, I ask you, Anomaly: By what Word do you justify your actions? *What higher principle do you serve that gives you the right to rewrite reality?*"

Ada met that cold, pale gaze, and for the first time, she felt no intimidation. She saw the Empress not as a divine ruler, but as a flawed piece of software, a program trapped in a rigid, binary loop. All this light, all this scale, all this ceremony—it was just noise. A desperate attempt to mask an empty, restrictive algorithm.

"Your Word," Ada said, her voice cutting through the hall's

oppressive silence, "is a cage. Your truth is a single, monochromatic frequency in a universe of infinite color. I serve no principle that can be written in your books or chanted by your priests."

A low murmur rippled through the assembled Justicars and acolytes lining the chamber walls. Lady Calibree's head snapped up, her face a mask of outrage. For the first time, a flicker of genuine surprise—hot and sharp—crossed the Empress' serene features. The carefully constructed stage had been breached.

Thema leaned forward on her throne, the mask of divine calm cracking to reveal something cold and sharp beneath. "If you serve no higher truth," she hissed, her voice losing its melodic cadence and becoming a tight, focused weapon, "then tell me, you architect of heresy: What in the Void *do* you fight for?"

The question hung in the air, the ultimate challenge. And in that moment, the answer bloomed in Ada's mind, simple and brilliant and absolute. A warm current flowed through the telepathic link connecting her to the three women standing just behind her. She felt Sera's unshakeable resolve, a bulwark of crimson steel. She felt Erita's fierce, protective loyalty, a blade honed just for her. And she felt Korina's love, a torrent of brilliant, violet light, so powerful it almost brought Ada to her knees.

She asks why I fight? Ada thought, the taste of adrenaline sharp and clean on her tongue. *I look at them—at Sera's strength, Erita's wit, Korina's brilliance—and the answer is so simple. They are my purpose. This love is more real than any 'Divine Word'. This is what I will build a world for. Not for dogma, but for us.*

She turned, just for a second, and looked at them. At Sera's proud nod. At Erita's slight, almost imperceptible smirk of defiance. At Korina, whose violet eyes swam with tears of love and recognition. This was her truth. This was Her Word.

Ada faced the Empress again, and the last vestiges of fear or doubt burned away, replaced by a fierce, blazing pride. Her own violet eyes shone with a power that had nothing to do with code and everything to do with conviction.

"I, Ada Lynx," she began, her voice ringing with a clarity that matched the Empress' own, **"fight for my family!"**

The declaration struck the silent hall like a thunderclap. The murmuring from the assembled followers grew louder, a wave of confusion and scandal.

"These women," Ada continued, gesturing back to Sera, Korina, and Erita without breaking eye contact with Thema, **"are my strength, my council, and my heart. They are my partners. In *every* sense of the word."** She took a deliberate breath, letting the weight of her next statement settle before she unleashed it.

"We are a polycule, Empress Thema."

The foreign word fell into the sterile throne room, an explosive, incomprehensible concept. Justicars shifted on their feet. Priests stared, their mouths agape. Thema's face went from surprise to a mask of cold, absolute fury.

Ada pressed her advantage, her voice swelling with the passion of a true evangelist. "You see the world in binary. Light and dark. Truth and heresy. Order and chaos. But reality is not a switch, it is a spectrum. The French have a word for it—*Arc-en-Ciel.* The rainbow. *The full, glorious spectrum of existence.* That is what I fight for! A world where every color, every identity, every form of love is a valid and essential part of the whole!"

She took another step forward, her presence seeming to grow, to fill the space between them. The Empress was no longer a towering deity on a throne; she was just a woman, trapped in her own colorless prison.

"My entire purpose in this world," Ada declared, her voice resonating with the force of creation itself, "is to build a future where a family like ours is not just tolerated, but celebrated. Where love is not chained by dogma, and people are not forced into the gray, sterile boxes you call order. That is my truth. That is My Word."

The words struck Empress Thema not like a physical blow, but like a syntax error in the source code of her reality. *Polycule. Arc-en-Ciel.* They were nonsense. Gibberish. They were alien phonemes that had no place in the sacred lexicon of The Word. Her mind, an architecture of perfect, binary logic—Truth and Heresy, Order and Chaos, Light and Void—attempted to categorize the input and failed. The command protocol for righteous fury, honed over a lifetime of unwavering faith, initiated its sequence...and then stalled.

A profound, system-wide stutter seized her.

Heresy was a corruption of the known truth, a rebellious variable within the established system. But this...this was not a variable. This was an entirely new operating system. The anger, so readily available a moment before, became an invalid response. It was like trying to use a key on a door that was no longer there. The fury dissipated, leaving a vacuum—a terrifying, silent void where absolute certainty had once resided. The solid obsidian of her throne felt suddenly precarious, as if its foundation had been rendered into sand.

Thema stared at the four women. She no longer saw a configuration of blasphemers. She saw a functional unit. A structure. *Polycule.* The word echoed, not as an insult, but as a fascinating, terrifying designation. A classification she did not possess. The stale, sweet taste of incense turned to ash in her mouth.

Her gaze fixed on Ada Lynx. The Anomaly. The source of the new data. The girl's eyes held no fear, only a calm, infuriating conviction. She was not a glitch to be purged; she was the architect of a system so foreign, Thema's own world-engine lacked the tools to even process its existence. The void within her began to fill, not with faith or fury, but with something far more dangerous: a desperate, consuming intellectual curiosity. She *needed* to understand. She needed to parse this new code.

Her own voice, when she finally found it, had lost its flawless, melodic authority. It was hesitant, the resonant cadence fractured into a question. "Explain," she commanded, but the word came out thin, almost a plea. "This...'polycule'...this structure."

A soft, infuriatingly gentle laugh escaped Ada's lips. It wasn't a sound of mockery, but of patience, of a teacher indulging a struggling student. That laugh was a greater insult to Thema's authority than any defiance.

"It's not a structure, not like your hierarchy," Ada replied, her tone soft, yet carrying across the vast hall. "It's a network. A relationship built on communication, consent, and the understanding that love isn't a finite resource."

Love. The word was a known quantity in The Word, but only within its proper, sanctified context—the love of a subject for their Empress, the love of the faithful for The Word itself. Ada spoke of it as a principle of governance, a foundational axiom for a societal model. It was *insane. It was brilliant.* It was data Thema had to have.

"Its principles..." Thema pressed, leaning forward, her knuckles white on the arm of her throne. The thousands of acolytes and Justicars lining the hall faded into irrelevant background processes. There was only her and the source of this impossible new information. "What are its...its operational parameters? How is consensus achieved? How is...affection...allocated properly...?"

Her question hung in the charged silence, a stark admission of her own system's limitations. She was no longer an Empress passing judgment; she was a scholar on the verge of a terrifying, world-shattering discovery.

Ada opened her mouth to answer, and in that instant, Thema felt a flicker of something akin to hope—the promise of new knowledge.

"***Enough!***" The word was a whip-crack, shattering the fragile intellectual space.

Lady Calibree, her face a mask of pure, incandescent rage, stepped forward. Her devotion, once a source of comfort to Thema, was now a blunt instrument of ignorance. Calibree's eyes were locked on Ada, burning with a fanaticism that could not tolerate dialogue with the unclean. She saw only the blasphemy, blind to the beautiful, terrifying data it represented.

"**Your Eminence, you honor these creatures with your *questions*!**" Calibree's voice was shrill with outrage. "**Their words are poison, a chaotic code meant to corrupt the heart of the Theocracy!**"

Thema felt a flicker of her own anger return, but it was now directed at her High Inquisitor.

Idiot—you are interrupting my inquisition!

Before Thema could form a command to silence her, Calibree turned, her arm slashing through the air in a gesture of absolute finality.

"Justicars! Seize these heretics! Their tongues have uttered The Undoing of the Word! Purge them in the name of the Empress and the eternal light!"

The order, given in Thema's name but without her consent, ripped through the hall. The wave of burnished steel and black armor surged forward, a mindless protocol executing a flawed command. The spell was broken. The dialogue was over. A priceless opportunity to understand the Anomaly, to learn the syntax of this new reality, was being trampled under the iron-shod boots of blind faith. And as the Justicars closed in, a profound and unfamiliar resentment flared in Empress Thema's heart. Her most loyal servant had just committed an act of unforgivable intellectual vandalism. She had been on the verge of a revelation, and Calibree had just slammed the book shut.

The wave of burnished steel was a predictable algorithm, a simple command executing its function. Thema watched the Justicars surge forward, their heavy boots thudding against the marble in a rhythmic, mindless beat. It was the correct response, the one sanctioned by millennia of dogma. It was also, she now realized with a startling pang of disappointment, a profoundly stupid one. A priceless opportunity for data acquisition was about to be shattered by the blunt instrument of fanaticism.

Before the first Justicar could cross half the distance, the Anomaly acted.

There was no explosion. No concussive blast of arcane force. It was something cleaner, more elegant, and infinitely more terrifying. A silent, instantaneous nova of pure violet light pulsed from the center of the four women. It was not a light that illuminated; it was a light that erased. For a single, breathtaking moment, the throne room was washed in impossible color, the thousands of hanging crystals refracting a symphony of amethyst and lavender. Then, the light was gone.

And so were they.

I enjoyed our talk, Empress Thema—though brief as it was...

Ada's voice echoed in Thema's mind, a ghostly whisper that cut through the stunned silence of the throne room. It was not an assault, not an intrusion, but a clean, perfectly modulated signal sent directly to her.

I wish to continue this dialogue again in the future—we'll meet again...on less 'hostile' terms?

The phantom scent of ozone, the ghost of an impossible event, pricked at Thema's nostrils. Her pale blue eyes remained fixed on the spot where they had stood. A perfect, empty circle of white marble. The Justicars, their momentum broken, skidded to a confused halt, their pole-arms held at the ready, pointing at nothing. They milled about like a machine whose primary function had been rendered null, their programming unable to account for a target that simply ceased to exist.

Then the sound returned, crude and shattering.

"***FIND THEM!***" Lady Calibree's voice was a grating shriek, stripped of all its righteous authority and reduced to simplistic fury. The sound, once a comforting echo of her own unwavering faith, now scraped against Thema's nerves like dull metal. "**SEAL THE PALACE! SWEEP THE GROUNDS! THEY CANNOT HAVE GONE FAR! I WANT THEM FOUND!**"

Thema did not move. Her hands, pale and perfectly still, rested on the cold, unyielding obsidian of her throne. Her gaze remained on that empty space. *Gone. She just...vanished.* And the Anomaly's final words resonated not as a threat, but as a promise. An invitation. *She wants to continue the dialogue.* The implication was staggering. The girl—the *Architect*—had seen past the Empress, past the living saint, and had recognized an intellect she considered a peer.

Calibree's roaring continued, a torrent of commands that now seemed so small, so limited. "**CHECK THE RELIQUARIES! SCAN THE CATACOMBS FOR THAUMATURGICAL RESIDUE! I WANT A FULL SPECTRUM PURGE OF THIS CHAMBER!**"

Fool, Thema thought, a cold, hard shard of resentment forming in the void where her fury should have been. *That fool. She shattered the connection.* The girl had been on the verge of explaining. Of providing the parameters of this new, impossible system of relations. This *Arc-en-Ciel.* And Calibree, in her blind, programmatic zeal, had severed the link. She feared the new data. She feared what Thema might learn. It was an act of desecration, not against The Word, but against *knowledge*.

For the first time in her life, Thema felt the unyielding certainty of her faith not as a foundation, but as a cage. The rigid, binary logic that had governed her entire existence suddenly felt restrictive, monochrome. The Anomaly had shown her a spectrum, and now, all she could see were the bars of her own prison.

The Justicars, responding to Calibree's frantic orders, began to move, their boots clattering with a hollow, useless urgency. The chaos swirled around the dais, a storm of pointless activity. It did not touch the profound, contemplative silence that had enveloped the Empress.

Thema looked down at her own hands, at the delicate, pale fingers resting on the black throne. They seemed alien to her, the hands of a stranger. Her world, once a perfect, ordered text, was now a book with a missing chapter, its most fascinating passage torn out by the very person sworn to protect its sanctity.

I must know more. The thought was not a whim; it was a command, an imperative that resonated deeper than any scripture. The girl had offered a new lexicon, a new way to perceive reality. To ignore it now would be the true heresy.

Lady Calibree, her face flushed with rage and frustration, finally turned back to the throne, her chest heaving. "Your Eminence, they will be found. I swear it on my life. No heretic can escape the light of The Word."

Thema's pale eyes lifted from her hands and met Calibree's. She saw not her devoted High Inquisitor, but a vandal. An obstacle. She did not answer. She offered no words of comfort, no shared outrage. Her silence was a cold, vast ocean, and Calibree's fanaticism was a stone sinking into its depths, leaving no ripple.

The Empress did not move. The interrogation had been interrupted, but the dialogue...the true dialogue had just begun.

CHAPTER 21

THE HERETIC'S ANTHEM

The world resolved itself with a gut-wrenching lurch. One moment, the blinding white of Thema's throne room; the next, the bruised-purple dark of a narrow alley. The teleportation was less a smooth transition and more a violent shove through reality. Erita's boots hit cobblestone hard enough to send a jolt up her spine, and she instinctively dropped into a crouch, daggers already in her hands. The air, thick with the smell of damp stone and refuse, was a welcome reprieve from the sterile, incense-choked atmosphere of the palace.

Ada stumbled, a ragged gasp escaping her lips, and collapsed against Korina, who caught her with a frightened yelp. The violet light that clung to Ada's frame flickered and died, leaving her looking pale and utterly spent. Sera and Janna landed a few feet away, weapons drawn, their bodies forming a protective wall around the others.

Erita scanned their new prison. High, soot-stained brick walls pressed in on them, slick with moisture. The only light came from a sliver of sky far above, crisscrossed with iron gratings. The distant, rhythmic clang of a city-wide alarm confirmed the obvious. They were still in the cage. Ada had gotten them out of the throne room, but not out of Codexia.

"So much for a clean getaway," Janna muttered, her voice a low growl. She peered around the corner of the alley. "Justicars. Everywhere. They're locking down the district."

Sera helped Korina lower Ada to sit on the grimy cobblestones. "Then we fight our way out. One street at a time."

Erita sheathed her daggers with a soft, final click. "Cute." The word was dry, stripped of all humor. "You want to fight a city of zealots who think they're on a mission from their gøds? They won't stop until they're dead, and there are a lot more of them than there are of us."

"Eri's right," Korina said, her voice trembling slightly as she held a canteen to Ada's lips. "The city is sealed. The Soul-Censers are at maximum sensitivity. Another blink is out of the question, and they'll detect any overt thaumaturgical activity in minutes."

"We can't just sit here," Sera countered, her frustration a palpable force.

"No," Erita agreed, her golden eyes scanning the rooftops, the oppressive architecture, the sheer, monolithic scale of the Theocracy's power. Her gaze settled on the central spire that speared the sky, a black needle stitching the clouds to the earth. From its peak, even now, she could hear the faint, distorted echo of a recorded sermon, a droning voice that blanketed the city in dogma. It was the source of the alarms, the voice of the Empress, the ceaseless pulse of their control.

We don't need to be subtle, a thought crystallized in her mind, cold and sharp as chipped flint. *We don't need to sneak. That gets us caught in a corner and killed. We need to be* ***loud****. We need chaos.*

They had tried quiet infiltration in Thorne's manor. It had worked, but this was a different beast. This wasn't a city of mercenaries and merchants driven by greed. This was a city of fanatics driven by faith. You couldn't bribe faith. You couldn't intimidate it. But you could shatter its foundation. You could make it question itself.

That spire...that's their voice, Erita thought, a predatory grin touching her lips for a fraction of a second. It was the instrument Thema used to keep her sheep in line, to broadcast her unassailable truth. *What if we make it scream something they don't want to hear? What if we make the voice of their gød blaspheme?* The ensuing confusion, the city-wide panic...it would be the perfect diversion. A smokescreen made of shattered belief.

She turned from the spire, her focus narrowing on the two people who could make the impossible happen. Ada was leaning heavily against Korina, but her violet eyes were open, watching Erita, sensing the shift in her demeanor.

Erita knelt, putting herself at their level. She ignored Sera's impatient glare and Janna's stoic watchfulness. This was for the architects.

"Korina—Ada," she began, her voice low and urgent, the plan already fully formed. "I have an idea: can we upload something onto the speaker system?"

Just as quick as the question was, Ada watched Erita melt into the shadows, a flicker of gold hair disappearing as she began her ascent. The plan was audacious, sacrilegious, and *perfect*. It was pure Erita. While Sera and Janna moved to the alley's entrances, creating a perimeter of silent steel, Ada leaned back against the damp brick, the grit pressing into her tunic. Korina's hand rested on her shoulder, a small, grounding pressure.

"I can shield your signature while you work," Korina whispered, her eyes wide with a mixture of terror and awe. "But you have to be fast."

Ada nodded, her focus already turning inward. The grimy alley dissolved. The rhythmic clang of the alarms faded to a dull, distant pulse. She closed her eyes and the world became code. Lines of violet and silver script scrolled past her consciousness, the base architecture of Codexia's network. She saw the broadcast spire not as a stone edifice, but as a central node, its data streams pulsing with the Empress' recorded sermons—endless loops of dogma and control.

Erita needed chaos. A sonic disruption. The simplest solution would be a blast of corrupted static or a file of screeching white noise. She could generate that in a nanosecond. But as her fingers —both the physical ones resting in her lap and the ethereal ones navigating the code—paused, a different thought took hold. *This wasn't just a diversion. It couldn't be.* Not after Thema's pronouncements, her cold dismissal of their love as an aberration. This had to be a message. *A declaration.*

Her query shifted.

[SEARCH: Local_Memory_Partition_ADLNX-001 {File_Type: Audio_MP3}]

A firewalled section of her own mind opened, a place separate from Kremøtoa, a vault of Earth memories she rarely dared to touch. Files appeared, labeled with the stark, utilitarian names she'd given them ages ago. And then she saw it. The album art bloomed in her mind's eye, a defiant splash of impossible, joyful color against the monochrome of the alley. A stylized, vibrant rainbow spiraling upwards and exploding over a vast landscape.

Arc-en-Ciel.

The melody started playing in her head, a cascade of synth and soaring vocals, and with it came the ghost of a taste on her tongue —the oversalted broth and dehydrated vegetables of cheap instant ramen. Rain lashed against the window of her tiny Sagiyama apartment. The memory was so vivid it hurt. This song...it had been her shield. Her only comfort in the weeks after the assault, when the world had felt gray and fractured, when she had felt so fundamentally broken. She'd listened to it on repeat, the lyrics a mantra against the silence.

Let's smash those kinds of rules.

The line echoed in her thoughts, no longer the memory of a distant singer but a present, burning conviction. She looked at Korina, whose face was etched with worry for her. She thought of Sera's fierce protectiveness, the steady warmth of her hand. She pictured Erita, scaling a tyrant's tower, trusting them to give her the weapon she needed.

Just souls calling out to each other.

It wasn't just a song about a polycule anymore. It was the song of *their* polycule. It was the anthem of their shared existence, a defiant celebration of a love that worlds like this one—worlds built on rigid, unforgiving rules—could never comprehend. Thema called them heretics. The Empire called Ada an anomaly. They would hear this song, this beautiful, vibrant piece of Ada's own survival, and they would call it blasphemy.

Good.

A cold, hard resolve solidified in her core, chilling the phantom warmth of the ramen. She was about to take the most personal piece of her history, the sound that had stitched her back together when she was alone and terrified, and turn it into an act of war. She selected the file.

[COMPILE: ADLNX_MemFile_Arc-en-Ciel.MP3 >> TARGET_PACKET: Malware_Sonic.pak]

A progress bar filled in her vision, a glowing violet line against the darkness. She watched the data compress, the vibrant notes and defiant lyrics being packaged into a tight, weaponized burst of information, a seed of beautiful chaos ready to be planted in the heart of the Theocracy's control. *It was done.* The packet pulsed in her Admin-view—a captured rainbow.

Ada opened her eyes, the dark alley snapping back into focus. Korina was staring at her, holding her breath.

"Packet configured, Korina." Ada's voice was unnervingly calm, a placid surface over a sea of memory and intent. She felt the warmth of her partners' love, a fierce, protective fire that burned away the last of the rain-soaked ghosts from her apartment. "Sending to Erita's slate now. It's...perfect for the occasion."

The last handhold scraped against her worn leather gloves, sending a small shower of mortar down into the abyss. Erita ignored it. The wind howled around the spire, a physical force that tried to peel her from the cold stone, but she moved with a fluid, practiced economy. Below her, Codexia was a grid of flickering torchlight and dogmatic order, a cage of faith. The rhythmic clang of the alarms was a steady, maddening pulse against her eardrums. She was a shadow scaling the city's heart, confident, focused, a blade poised to strike.

Heaving herself over the final ledge, she rolled onto the flat, windswept roof. A crown of black iron—the broadcast array—dominated the space, humming with a low, oppressive energy. The Voice of the Empress, distorted by the wind, echoed from the emitters. Erita didn't waste a moment. She moved to the central control panel, a heavy iron box bolted to the stone, and pried the cover open with the tip of a dagger.

Her confidence evaporated in a cold rush.

There was no wireless induction port. No remote access terminal. Just a thick bundle of armored cables running directly into the stonework, leading to a single, archaic-looking input jack. A closed system. Hardwired.

Void's name, she sent, her thoughts a clipped, angry burst over their mental link. *Korina, what in the seven voids is this? There's no wireless access!*

Korina's mental voice was a flurry of panicked analysis. *What? That's impossible! The schematics clearly show—*

No time for schematics, Erita shot back, her gaze sweeping over the brutally simplistic hardware, *The schematics must be wrong; to upload this packet, I need to leave a data-slate physically connected to the system.*

A moment of shared silence hung between them, thick with the implication of failure. Then, Ada's voice, calm and steady as a deep river, cut through the noise. *Do it Eri...it's the only way.*

Erita's blood went cold. Her hand instinctively went to the data-slate secured at her hip. The answer was yes. The cost was unthinkable.

No wireless? Void's name...My data-slate? All my contacts, my networks, my boltholes...my entire life is in this thing. The data-slate wasn't just a tool; it was her memory, her survival kit, the ghost of a life lived in the shadows. To lose it was to be rendered blind, to erase years of painstakingly gathered intelligence and every carefully constructed escape route. It was everything.

It's just a tool. She forced the thought, a bitter, unconvincing lie. *It's just...a tool. Do it.*

Okay, she transmitted, her mental voice stripped of all emotion. *I'll leave...mine,* She took a breath that felt like swallowing glass. *I'll do it.*

Another beat of silence. Then, Ada's voice returned, not with pity, but with the unyielding weight of command. *Do it.*

A tremor of genuine grief ran through her hands, but she forced them steady. She pulled out her data-slate. The obsidian casing was scratched and worn, customized over years of use until it was an extension of her own will. With a few swift taps, she queued up the sonic malware Ada had sent, the file name a splash of vibrant, alien color on her screen: *Arc-en-Ciel.*

She took one last look at the device that held her past, then jammed the jack home with a sickening crackle of overloading circuits.

The screen flashed a rainbow of corrupted pixels and went dark. The smell of ozone stung her nostrils. For a heart-stopping second, she felt a hollow space open inside her, a profound and immediate sense of loss.

Then, the Empress' droning sermon cut out.

Good.

She turned to begin her descent, the cold obsidian rough against her palms. The wind whipped at her back, colder now, a chilling reminder of her loss. The eastern gate, still a fortress of Justicars, awaited. Erita started her descent back to the alleyway, each movement precise and controlled. She paused midway, a knot of unease tightening in her gut; the silence was unnerving. Too unnerving. *Korina, confirm upload status,* she sent through the link, her voice tight with apprehension.

There was a brief pause, a flicker of static in the mental channel. Then, Korina's voice, strained but clear, responded. *Upload complete. Malware packet deployed. Activating now.*

Still nothing. Erita frowned, a cold dread creeping up her spine. Had it failed? She clung to the wall, her mind racing, desperately searching for a solution, a backup plan, anything.

The silence stretched, thin and brittle. Erita clung to the cold stone, the wind a lonely razor against her cheek. Every second that passed without the promised chaos was another twist of the knife in the fresh, hollow wound where her life's work used to be. *Nothing. It failed. I gave up everything for—*

A low hum vibrated through the spire, a deep, resonant thrum that felt less like sound and more like the world's foundation groaning in protest. Before she could process it, the hum **erupted.**

It was not a sound; it was a physical event. A shockwave of pure, weaponized noise blasted from the broadcast array, a concussive force that punched the air from her lungs. It slammed into her with the force of a battering ram, a physical blow composed of synthetic thunder and a soaring, defiant female voice singing in a language she had never heard. The raw, kinetic energy of it was an order of magnitude beyond anything she could have anticipated. It was not a diversion; *it was an artillery strike.*

Her grip, so sure and practiced, was annihilated. Her fingers were torn from the stone as if swatted by an invisible giant. The world tilted violently, the grid of Codexia's lights spinning into a dizzying, terrifying smear. For a single, horrifying moment, she was weightless, suspended between the spire and the street, a puppet with its strings cut.

Then, gravity asserted its brutal claim.

The fall was a silent scream in her mind. The wind roared past her ears, whipping her pixie cut into a frenzy. Her training, ingrained in every fiber of her being, screamed at her to twist, to aim for an awning, a cart, *anything* to break the terminal velocity that was about to turn her into a red stain on the cobblestones. But there was nothing. Just the unforgiving geometry of the alley and the rapidly approaching ground. *A stupid way to die,* was the last coherent thought that flashed through her mind, a final, bitter spark of cynicism before oblivion.

A new sound cut through the wind's roar—the sharp crack of boots on stone. From the mouth of the alley below, a figure exploded into motion. It was not a run; it was a launch—Sera, a crimson blur against the torchlight, covered the distance of the alley in a terrifying display of raw power, her legs pistoning against the ground. She didn't look up. She didn't need to. Her eyes were locked on a point in space, a precise, calculated intersection of Erita's trajectory and her own.

Erita saw her a split second before impact, a flash of red hair and grim determination. She braced for a collision that would shatter bones, a desperate, last-ditch tackle.

Sera hit her like a landslide.

The impact was a jarring, bone-rattling shock that knocked the air from her lungs for a second time. Sera's arms, hard as banded steel, wrapped around her torso, absorbing the catastrophic force of her descent. But the momentum was too great. Sera's powerful legs buckled, and they were both sent careening backward, a tangled mess of limbs and desperation.

They slammed into the opposite wall of the alley with a sickening crunch of brick and bodies. Dust and mortar rained down on them. For a moment, the world was a cacophony of pain, the ringing in her ears, and the utterly alien, impossibly loud music that continued to pour from the spire, washing over the city in relentless waves.

Erita lay gasping in a heap, tangled in Sera's limbs, her head spinning. The cobblestones were hard and real beneath her back. She was alive. Bruised, battered, and utterly disoriented, but alive. The music pounded against the walls, a relentless, joyful, and utterly blasphemous rhythm that was already causing mayhem. Lights flickered on in windows. Shouts of confusion and fear echoed from the streets. The rhythmic clang of the alarms had been swallowed by the song, replaced with a symphony of pure, unadulterated chaos.

Sera grunted, shifting her weight off Erita. She pushed herself up, her breathing heavy but steady. "Got you," she said, her voice a low rumble. It wasn't a question or a boast. It was a simple statement of fact.

Erita pushed herself into a sitting position, her shoulder screaming in protest. She stared at the former knight, then up at the spire, then back at Sera. Her mind struggled to connect the sequence of events—the silence, the blast, the fall, the impossible catch. The song, a tidal wave of synth-pop and defiant joy, was the soundtrack to her own improbable survival. It was the most ridiculous, terrifying, effective—and romantic—thing she had ever witnessed.

"What in the Void is that sound...?" she finally managed, the words raspy, her throat raw.

Ada's voice slid into her mind, warm and impossibly clear over the telepathic link, cutting through the external din. *It's called Arc-en-Ciel.*

Janna and Korina appeared at the end of the alley, their faces a mixture of relief and awe. Korina rushed to Ada's side, who was now standing, leaning against the wall but looking stronger, a faint, triumphant smile on her face. The diversion was more than working—it was tearing the city's suffocating order apart at the seams.

Sera offered Erita a hand. For a beat, Erita stared at it, her pride warring with the trembling in her limbs. Then, with a curt nod that conceded everything and nothing, she took it and let Sera pull her to her feet. The city was screaming, and it was the most beautiful sound she had ever heard.

The song exploded from every speaker in Codexia—a joyous, defiant anthem that ripped through the oppressive silence like a sonic boom. It was a piece of J-Pop from Ada's world, a vibrant melody she'd listened to countless times during late-night coding sessions, a nostalgic echo of a life she'd left behind. But here, in Kremøtoa, it was more than just a song; it was a revolution.

The lyrics, a celebration of love, freedom, and individuality, washed over Ada, a bittersweet reminder of a world where such expressions weren't heresy. It was her defining anthem, now on blast for the capital of the Theocracy to behold.

Seibetsu no kabe nante nai
There are no walls of gender
Tada tamashī ga yobi atteru
Just souls calling out to each other

Ichitaiichi? Dare ga kimeta nda?
One-on-one? Who decided that?
Son'na rūru wa bukkowase
Let's smash those kinds of rules

Furui kachikan, mō iranai
Don't need old values anymore
Jibun no kokoro ni shōjiki ni
Being honest with my own heart

Kore ga ore no shinjitsuna nda
This is my truth

Arc-en-Ciel
Arukanshieru
A spectrum of light and love
Hikari to ai no supekutoru
Connecting every single heart...

The world was a symphony of beautiful, terrifying chaos. Korina's analytical mind struggled to process the sheer volume of new data. The song—this impossible, structured, and yet wildly emotional sound—was not just a diversion. It was a weapon of mass disorientation. From their alleyway vantage point, she saw Justicars, paragons of rigid discipline, stumbling in confusion, their hands clapped over their armored helms. Citizens peeked from behind shuttered windows, their faces a mixture of terror and a strange, dawning wonder. The Theocracy's monolithic control, broadcast from that spire for generations, had been shattered in an instant by a cascade of synthetic beats and a soaring female voice.

And Korina felt no fear. None at all. The cold, logical part of her brain that should have been calculating escape vectors and probability of capture was offline, completely overwhelmed by a wave of pure, unadulterated exhilaration.

"Move!" Erita's voice, sharp and grounding, cut through the joyous noise.

They ran. They burst from the alley into a main thoroughfare, a river of panicking zealots. The music pounded from every direction, echoing off the severe black architecture, turning the oppressive city into a vibrant, anarchic concert hall. Sera and Janna formed the tip of their spear, parting the crowd with sheer physical presence. Erita was a ghost at their flank, her eyes scanning for threats that were too confused to materialize. Ada, still pale but with a fire in her eyes, held Korina's hand, her grip firm and steady.

The music pulsed through Korina, a current that resonated deep in her bones. It was data made sublime. It was mathematics with a soul. It was a piece of a world she had never known, a world of freedom and defiant joy. *This music...it's her. A piece of her soul.*

Then Ada's voice echoed in her mind, a private message in the storm of sound. *It's called Arc-en-Ciel.*

The name struck Korina with the force of a physical blow. *Arc-en-Ciel.* The rainbow over Oakhaven. The word Ada had gifted her, a promise of a future where their love could exist without shame. This wasn't just a sonic weapon. This was their anthem, their declaration, blasted from the tyrant's own tower. It was the most beautiful sound she had ever heard. The escape was no longer a desperate flight; it was a victory lap. A triumphant, laughing sprint through the collapsing heart of their enemy's power.

They reached the eastern gate, a scene of utter pandemonium. The Justicars, deafened and disoriented by the relentless music, were struggling to form a coherent line. Their purity sensors were useless, overloaded by the sheer alien nature of the sonic frequencies. Sera and Janna didn't hesitate, crashing into the disorganized guards like a tidal wave, their movements a brutal dance set to the song's pounding rhythm.

In the midst of the brawl, as they slipped through the breach and into the pre-dawn gloom outside the city walls, Korina turned to Ada, her heart hammering against her ribs with a joy so fierce it felt like it might burst. The song was still audible, a defiant pulse fading behind them. *I need to keep this piece of her with me.*

"Ada!" she said, her voice breathless, laughing. "That song...the file...can I have it? Please?"

Ada, leaning on Sera for support but smiling with a genuine, brilliant warmth that outshone the rising suns, met her gaze. The love in her eyes was a tangible thing, a force that quieted all the chaos.

"Of course, Rina." A simple, affectionate response that felt more profound than any vow. "Anything—it's yours."

A notification chimed, a soft, private sound only Korina could hear, a direct link from Ada's mind to hers. A file transfer, complete. She now possessed the anthem of their revolution, a captured rainbow gifted by the woman she loved.

The last flicker of violet light vanished, leaving behind an impossible silence in the throne room. Empress Thema Iridia Archivia stood motionless, her hand still raised in a command the Justicars never had the chance to obey. The heretics were gone. They had not been captured, not defeated. They had simply... ceased to be there. The absolute authority of her sanctum, the inviolable heart of the Theocracy, had been breached and then abandoned as if it were a common tavern.

Then, the silence shattered.

It was not a sound she could classify. It was not a hymn, not a war cry, not the tolling of a sanctified bell. It was a rhythmic, pulsing thunder that seemed to originate from the very stones of the city, a frantic heartbeat shaking the foundations of her world. Over this alien rhythm, a woman's voice soared—clear, powerful, and filled with an emotion so raw and unrestrained it felt like sacrilege.

The sonic assault poured into the throne room, an unwelcome tide of vibrant chaos. Her Justicars, even those stationed within the palace, were in disarray, their discipline fractured by this weaponized cacophony. Her initial reaction was a cold, pure fury.

This was the ultimate act of defiance, a pollutant poured into the wellspring of their faith.

Yet, as the moments stretched, fury gave way to a chilling, analytical curiosity. She stood alone amidst the golden light, her pale blue eyes unfocused, listening. She attempted to deconstruct the sound, to find the flaw, the inherent corruption within its structure. But there was none. It was complex, layered, mathematically precise in its own wild fashion. It was not the sound of chaos. It was the sound of a different, terrifying kind of order.

And then, the words began to bloom in her mind, unbidden, translated by some instinct she did not know she possessed. They were not whispered by a tempter; they arrived as simple, undeniable truth.

A spectrum of light and love...

The phrase bypassed the iron walls of her dogma. It did not argue with The Word; it simply offered an alternative. A spectrum. Not a single point of truth, but an infinite, radiant band of it. Her mind, honed for generations on the singular, absolute nature of her faith, recoiled from the concept and yet was irresistibly drawn to it.

The song swelled, the beat driving deeper, and the voice climbed to a peak of pure, defiant joy.

Connecting every single heart...

Thema closed her eyes. She saw it then, not as a thought, but as a vision. A bridge of impossible color arching over a broken, gray world. Not a bridge of stone and dogma, built to enforce passage, but a bridge of pure light, inviting all to cross. A connection forged not by law and fear, but by a shared, shining essence. By...love. The word, so often used as a tool of control in her sermons—love for The Word, love for the Theocracy—was here presented as a fundamental, untamable force of creation itself.

This was not an argument. It was not a debate. The Architect-Queen had not come to her throne room to reason with her.

This isn't an argument. It's...an answer. An answer to a question Thema had never known she was asking. The monolithic certainty of her soul, a structure built over a lifetime of unwavering belief, cracked. Through that fissure, a brilliant, terrifying rainbow of possibility poured in. *A bridge of color, shining love. A world beyond The Word.*

A sharp, metallic scrape broke her reverie.

Lady Calibree stood at the entrance to the throne room, her face a mask of utter horror. Her armor was immaculate, her posture rigid, but her eyes were wide with a terror Thema had never seen in her High Inquisitor. Calibree was not looking at the chaos outside. She was looking at her Empress.

She saw Thema's expression—not of rage, not of righteous fury, but of profound, conflicted wonder. She saw the way Thema's head was tilted, her lips slightly parted, as if straining to hear a divine whisper. Calibree saw a faltering. She saw a breach not in the city's walls, but in the Empress' very soul. She saw the infection taking root.

Thema met Calibree's gaze and saw the judgment there, the fear, the unwavering certainty that she herself had just lost. Calibree saw heresy. She saw an enemy that needed to be purged.

Calibree sees this as an infection.

The thought was strangely distant, an analytical observation. Calibree's gaze hardened, her horror solidifying into a cold, fanatical resolve. Without a word, without a bow, she turned on her heel, her crimson-lined cloak swirling like spilt blood. Her stride was no longer that of a subordinate, but of a crusader with a new, singular purpose: to hunt down the source of this spiritual plague and cauterize it from the world, with or without her Empress' blessing, leaving only a guttural roar in her wake.

Thema watched her go, a faint sense of loss touching her. She was alone again. The song began to fade, its final notes echoing through the silent city. But the silence it left behind was different. It was heavier. Deeper. It was the silence of a cathedral after the god has departed.

I...I see it as a message I must understand.

The quest for the heretic was over. For Empress Thema, a new, far more dangerous pilgrimage had just begun.

CHAPTER 22

ECHOES OF THE HERETIC'S ANTHEM

The incessant shriek of alarms clawed at Kraus Valerius' nerves. He stood before the holographic display, his pale eyes fixed on the cascading streams of data, his thin lips pressed into a hard, disapproving line. The Spire of Command, usually a sanctuary of sterile calm, pulsed with a frantic, unsettling energy. But these alarms weren't screaming of a military incursion, not blaring about a breach in the Prefecture's impenetrable defenses. This was something...*different.*

A confident analyst, his face unusually flushed, practically burst into the command center. "Prefect Valerius! We have a situation." The analyst's demeanor showed signs of confidence, unlike their past flustered reports, which Kraus found to be an intriguing data point.

Kraus turned, his eyes cold and assessing. "Report."

"We're picking up a massive thaumaturgical broadcast originating from deep within Theocratic territory—in Codexia itself!" The analyst's voice was tight with a strange mix of fear and exhilaration. "It's unlike anything we've ever encountered. The signal is...structured. Complex. It carries an 'emotional resonance' we can't quantify."

Kraus returned his attention to the holographic display. Streams of raw data flickered before him—thaumaturgical signatures, spectral analysis, energy flux readings. It was a chaotic symphony of numbers and symbols, a language he usually deciphered with ease. But this...this was noise. Beautiful, structured noise that defied his every attempt at logical categorization.

"Audio files," Kraus commanded, his voice a low, gravelly hum.

The cacophony of alarms faded slightly as a new sound filled the command center—*music*. Strange, alien music unlike anything Kraus had ever heard. It was melodic, rhythmic, filled with an emotional intensity that grated against his pragmatic sensibilities. It wasn't a military march, not a religious hymn, not even a crude tavern song. It was...*art*.

Kraus felt a knot tightening in his stomach, a cold, unsettling sensation he couldn't quite place. He studied the waveforms scrolling across the display, the looping patterns, the intricate structure of the song. It wasn't a weapon; it wasn't a coded message. He ran multiple decryption protocols, searching for hidden directives, subliminal commands, *anything* that fit within his logical framework of the world. But there was nothing. Just... *music*.

As the chorus began its loop, the words were sung. *"Arc-en-Ciel,"* the analyst whispered, his voice almost reverent. "That word...it sounds...*beautiful.*"

Kraus felt a surge of pure, unadulterated *fury*. Beautiful? This illogical, emotional noise, this blatant disregard for order and control—*beautiful*? It was an affront to everything he believed in, a chaotic variable in his meticulously ordered world.

He saw the hand of Ada Lynx in this. His "unquantifiable asset", the girl who had escaped his grasp, the girl who defied every attempt at categorization. This act, this broadcast of pure, unadulterated...*art*—it was *her*. It had to be. It was a move so unpredictable, so utterly illogical, that *only* she could be responsible. He had underestimated her. He had viewed her as a weapon, a tool to be controlled, a variable to be quantified. But she was more than that. She was a virus; a contagion spreading chaos and disorder throughout his carefully constructed world.

His frustration, his anger, his inability to predict or control her actions—it coalesced into a cold, hard obsession. He *would* understand her. He *would* quantify her. He *would* bring her under his control.

Rikai nante motomenai sa
I'm not asking for understanding

The alien lyrics echoed in the command center, a mocking reminder of his failure, a challenge to his authority. Kraus' pale eyes narrowed, his gaze fixed on the holographic display. He wouldn't rest until he had deciphered this new puzzle, until he had brought Ada Lynx—his unquantifiable variable—to heel.

Jibun no shiawase, jibun de tsukuru
I make my own happiness

The music continued, a discordant symphony playing out the slow, agonizing unraveling of his carefully ordered world.

In the sterile air of the Grand Conclave Chamber, the music swelled. It filled the cavernous space, a vibrant, emotional tide washing against the cold obsidian of the council table and the dry, papery scent of ancient knowledge. On the massive holographic display that dominated the central wall, the broadcast from Codexia was not a stream of numbers or a tactical map, but a swirling nebula of violet, gold, and crimson light that pulsed in time with the alien melody.

The four present members of the High Council of Veritas watched, their faces illuminated by the hypnotic display. Two seats at the long table remained conspicuously empty—the places of Councilor Vance and Scholar Atomuzk—but their absence was an irrelevant variable, a minor data point in the face of the phenomenon unfolding before them.

High Chancellor Pantium, a man whose mind processed language as pure mathematics, leaned forward, his reflection sliding across the polished black surface. "The auto-translation is flawless." His voice was a dry rasp, devoid of wonder, full of analytical appreciation. On a sub-screen, the Theocratic script of the lyrics dissolved and reformed into perfect Korian syntax. "It's not just translating words; it's translating *intent*. The emotional nuance is preserved with ninety-nine-point-nine percent accuracy. It's injecting comprehension directly."

Archivist Itania's long, slender fingers tapped a slow, deliberate rhythm on the table's edge. Her cool grey eyes dissected the swirling patterns of light on the display. "The delivery method is...elegant." She paused, her mind tracing the theoretical pathways. "It's a harmonic resonance carrier wave. It bypasses all known thaumaturgical dampeners because it doesn't register as an attack or an intrusion. It registers as ambient background radiation. It slips past the fortress walls of the conscious mind and embeds itself directly into the limbic system."

"A powerful tool for social engineering," Master Centrinah added, her voice smooth as polished stone. She saw populations, not people; systems, not songs. "Imagine this broadcast, tuned to a different emotional frequency. It could quell a riot before the first stone is thrown. It could inspire fanatical loyalty. It could induce crippling despair across an entire city." She gave a thin, bloodless smile. "It could make a populace *grateful* for their chains."

The crackle of pure, intellectual energy filled the chamber. It was the thrill of discovery, the predatory hunger of apex thinkers recognizing a new, paradigm-shattering weapon. There was no fear here, no concern for the Theocracy's breached sovereignty, only the unified, covetous desire to possess the technology that made this broadcast possible.

Grand Magister Xehon sat at the head of the table, his ancient eyes gleaming with a light that was anything but benign. He absorbed their analyses, each a different facet of the same terrifying, beautiful truth. *This is not art,* he thought, the words forming with cold precision in his mind. *It is a weapon. A key. The ability to bypass logic and directly manipulate the emotional core of a population...it is the ultimate tool of control.*

He saw it with perfect clarity. The Empire used brute force. The Theocracy used blind faith. But this...this was a scalpel capable of excising dissent from the very soul of a society. It was the final evolution of power. *The power this 'song' represents will solidify the Archives' dominance for centuries. We must have it.*

"It originated with the girl, Korina Tel, and the anomaly, Ada Lynx," Councilor Celerun reported, his tone flat and factual. "Our assets confirm their presence in Codexia just prior to the broadcast."

We must have her. Xehon's internal conclusion was absolute.

He raised a single, withered hand. The quiet, academic discussion ceased instantly. Every eye turned to him, awaiting the final synthesis, the directive that would follow this new discovery.

"We have spent centuries," Xehon began, his voice quiet yet carrying the immense weight of his authority, "believing that knowledge is power. That logic is the supreme instrument of control." He gestured toward the swirling, emotional display. "We were limited in our thinking. This...this is a power that makes logic irrelevant. It is a key that unlocks the heart, and whoever holds it can command the will of millions without a single argument."

He let the statement settle in the silent, humming air. He saw the understanding, the shared, rapacious hunger in the eyes of his council.

"Our previous efforts to acquire the anomaly have been insufficient. Our interest in the girl, Korina Tel, was purely a matter of internal discipline." His gaze swept across the table, cold and unyielding. "The parameters have changed. Their value has increased exponentially."

He turned his gaze to Celerun. The command was sharp, precise, and utterly devoid of mercy.

"Find them. And bring them to us."

The archive was a sanctuary of silence, its air scrubbed sterile and cool. Atomuzk Tel held the young scholar's hand, his touch a point of stability in the trembling landscape of her memory. Her name was Auza, a junior theorist with eyes that held the ghosts of old terror. Her voice, thin and reedy, recounted another instance of Kaelen Vance's predation, another complaint buried by Xehon's monolithic authority. Atomuzk listened, his face a mask of detached empathy. He cataloged her words, each a data point in a growing matrix of corruption. This was his work now, the quiet, meticulous assembly of a case so irrefutable it would shatter the Archives' foundation.

A single, insistent chime cut through the stillness. It was a sound no one else in the Archives would have heard, a priority alert routed to his personal, shielded data-slate. **Omega-Alpha**. A system-wide event of unprecedented scale. He gave Auza's hand a final, reassuring squeeze.

"One moment, my dear," he murmured, his voice the soft rustle of ancient parchment. He turned to the obsidian slate on his desk. A stark crimson banner pulsed across the screen. The source was impossible. *Codexia.*

He tapped the alert, and a new window opened. A grainy, chaotic image flickered to life—a live feed from a Theocratic surveillance drone, likely captured by a Korian listening post. It showed streets filled with panicked citizens and confused Justicars, their order shattered. He activated the audio feed.

Music flooded the sterile archive. It was not a hymn. It was not a march. It was a vibrant, defiant symphony of structured sound and human voice, layered with a complexity that made the logical centers of his brain ignite. He muted the external speakers, channeling the audio directly into his personal comm-bead, a cascade of impossible harmony filling his mind. He ran a diagnostic, his fingers flying across the holographic interface projected from his slate.

The carrier wave was a masterpiece of thaumaturgical engineering. Elegant. Efficient. It bypassed every known defensive protocol, not with force, but with a sublime understanding of the system's core architecture. It was identical in its foundational signature to the violet energy surge he had analyzed from Duskhaven. *Argent's light,* his mind whispered, the ancient oath a tremor of pure awe. *This is Ada Lynx's code.*

Then the lyrics began to scroll across his slate, auto-translated into perfect, fluid Korian.

...Arc-en-Ciel...
...A spectrum of light and love...
...This is my truth...
...Connecting every single heart...

This was not just a song. This was a message. A philosophical treatise weaponized into art, fired directly into the heart of a monochromatic, dogmatic empire. It was a declaration of independence from their binary worldview, a deeply personal, ideological statement broadcast for all of Kremøtoa to hear.

A warmth bloomed in his chest, a sensation so foreign and powerful it nearly staggered him. It was pride. A fierce, possessive pride that burned away the years of detached observation. *His granddaughter was not merely surviving.* She was not a pawn in the Council's game or a fugitive fleeing the Empire's wrath. *She was at the epicenter of this. She was fighting.* She was rewriting the fundamental axioms of their world. This chaos, this Cascade Failure...it was not an end. The thought struck him with the force of a physical blow. *It was a beginning.*

He looked up from the slate, his mind reeling with the implications. The music still echoed in his comm-bead, a triumphant, soaring anthem of change. The world was breaking, yes, but perhaps it was breaking open.

Auza, the young scholar, had risen from her chair, her tear-filled eyes now wide with a dawning wonder as the faint strains of the broadcast bled from the city's distant public annunciators, a sound that would soon be silenced but could never be unheard.

"It's...beautiful," she whispered, her own trauma momentarily forgotten in the face of this impossible sound. "What does it mean?"

Atomuzk turned to face her. He felt the muscles in his face shift into an expression he did not recognize—a smile, but not one of kindness or academic satisfaction. It was sharp, unsettling, transformative. It was the smile of a man who had just seen the future, and it was magnificent. His voice, when he spoke, was not his own. It was a low, resonant growl, a stark departure from his usual hesitant murmur, filled with a power that vibrated through the quiet air of the archive.

"That, my dear, was a declaration." He took a step toward her, the light from the data-slate casting his face in stark relief. "The sound of a magnificent declaration...of change."

CHAPTER 23

THE QUANTUM ANOMALY

Three days. Three days of relentless pursuit, of a grueling, desperate flight through the desolate, sun-baked landscape of the Wordaeus Theocracy. Three days since the heretic's anthem—*Arc-en-Ciel*—had echoed through the obsidian spires of Codexia, shattering the city's rigid, dogmatic silence and unleashing a wave of chaotic panic. Three days since Ada and her companions had dared to challenge the very foundations of the Theocracy's power, defying the Empress, humiliating Lady Calibree, and exposing the inherent fragility of their carefully constructed reality. Three days of running, of hiding, of pushing themselves to the very limits of their physical and mental endurance, fueled by adrenaline, fear, and the grim determination to survive.

Erita led the way, her lithe form a blur of motion as she navigated the treacherous terrain, her senses on high alert, scanning for any sign of pursuit, any hint of danger. She moved with a predatory grace, her golden eyes constantly scanning the horizon, her every muscle taut and ready to spring into action. The escape from Codexia had cost them dearly—Erita's data-slate, a crucial tool, was gone, sacrificed to create the diversion that had allowed their escape. But the loss, though a significant blow, had also ignited a new fire within her, a fierce, almost reckless resolve to fight for the future Ada had envisioned, a world where their love wasn't a heresy to be punished, but a fundamental right to be celebrated.

Behind her, Sera moved with the disciplined, steady pace of a seasoned warrior, her crimson tunic a stark contrast to the muted browns and grays of the desolate landscape. Her hand rested on the hilt of one of her blades, a silent, constant reassurance. The escape from the Empress' palace, Ada's audacious act of defiance, had shaken her to her core. She had witnessed firsthand the power of Ada's abilities, the sheer, terrifying potential of her reality-bending commands. But more than that, she had seen the unwavering conviction in Ada's eyes, the fierce, almost desperate determination to protect the people she loved—Sera, Korina, Erita, Janna—and the world she had created. It was a level of loyalty, of selfless devotion, that Sera, a woman whose entire life had been defined by duty and honor, both understood and deeply admired.

Korina followed, her slender frame struggling to keep pace with the others, her violet eyes wide and filled with a mixture of fear and wonder. She stumbled occasionally, the rough terrain a stark contrast to the smooth, sterile corridors of Veritas. The journey was taking its toll, the relentless pursuit pushing her to the brink of exhaustion. But even amidst the fear and fatigue, a spark of intellectual excitement flickered within her. She had witnessed impossible things, events that defied the very laws of physics, of reality itself. Ada's abilities, her reality-bending commands, were a constant source of fascination, a puzzle she desperately wanted to solve, to understand, to quantify. The world, once a predictable system of rules and data, was now a fluid, ever-changing landscape of possibilities. And she, the once-timid scholar, was at its heart, a key player in a revolution that promised to reshape the very foundations of their existence.

Janna brought up the rear, her massive frame a reassuring presence, her battle-axe held loosely in one hand. She moved with a steady, almost ponderous gait, her eyes constantly scanning the horizon, her senses attuned to any sign of danger. The journey was a test, a grueling trial by fire that pushed each of them to their limits. But Janna, a veteran of countless battles, a warrior who had faced down death more times than she cared to remember, saw it as a necessary crucible, forging them into something stronger, something more resilient, something...*unbreakable.* They were not just a group of individuals anymore. They were a unit, a team, a fellowship bound together by shared purpose, by mutual respect, and by the unwavering loyalty they felt towards the woman who had brought them together, the Architect-Queen who had dared to dream of a better world.

We need to rest, Korina thought, her mental voice laced with exhaustion. *My systems are overheating.*

Not yet, Erita responded, her mental tone sharp, her focus unwavering. *We're still too close to Codexia. We need to put as much distance between us and those zealots as possible.*

She's right, Sera added. *Thema won't give up easily. She'll be sending Justicar patrols everywhere. We need to reach the Ashen States' border before dawn.*

I can manage another blink, Ada thought, her mental voice strained but resolute. *Just give me the coordinates.*

Not a chance, Janna countered. *You're pushing yourself too hard, Ada. We need you at full strength for what's coming.*

Janna's right, Sera added. *We need to find a safe place to rest, regroup, and then plan our next move.*

Agreed, Erita thought, her mental voice finally softening, a hint of concern replacing her usual cynicism. *There's a cave about a kilometer ahead. It's not ideal, but it'll offer some concealment.*

Lead the way, Ada thought, her mental voice filled with gratitude.

Erita nodded, her eyes still scanning the horizon, her every sense on high alert, leading her fellowship deeper into the wilderness, further away from the city of Codexia and the terrifying power of the Empress Thema. The desert wind whipped around them, carrying with it the faint, unsettling echoes of the heretic's anthem, a constant reminder of the revolution they had started, a promise of the better world they were fighting for.

Emerging from the cave, the harsh sunlight momentarily blinded them. Dust swirled around their feet, a fine, gritty powder clinging to their clothes. The air, thick with the stench of decay, hung heavy in their lungs. Before them stretched a desolate landscape, a stark contrast to the relative safety of the cave. The land, once fertile and vibrant, was now scarred and broken, a testament to the relentless march of the Cascade Failure. Twisted, gnarled trees clawed at the sky, their branches bare and skeletal. The earth itself seemed to writhe and heave, the ground cracked and fissured, revealing glimpses of a corrupted underworld. A miasmic fog clung to the low-lying areas, obscuring the horizon and adding to the overall sense of unease.

Janna halted, her hand instinctively going to the pommel of her axe. The escarpment they'd reached offered a breathtaking, albeit terrifying, view of the blighted land that stretched before them, a vast, desolate expanse stretching to the horizon. The wind carried with it the faint, unsettling whispers of corruption, a symphony of decay that chilled them to the bone. The once-vibrant colors of Kremøtoa were muted, replaced by a palette of browns, grays, and sickly greens. Even the sky seemed to reflect the corruption, its hues dulled and distorted, mirroring the chaos that had consumed the land.

The Ashen States, Korina whispered, her voice barely audible above the wind. *It's worse than the reports indicated.*

The wind—or what passed for wind in this blighted place—whipping at her cloak, tasting of dust and something...*else.* Something acrid, metallic, like the scent of lightning after it struck a data-slate. She gripped the worn leather of her axe handle, the familiar weight a small comfort in this unsettling landscape.

It wasn't just the monochrome grey, the absence of color that drained the world of life and vibrancy. It was the *texture,* or rather, the lack of it. The plains below seemed flat, two-dimensional, like a poorly rendered image on a damaged data-slate. There were no rolling hills, no jagged peaks, no natural contours to break the monotonous expanse. Just a vast, empty canvas of grey, stretching out to the horizon like a shroud.

"Void's teeth," Janna muttered under her breath, a low rumble in her chest. She'd seen the ravages of war, the aftermath of battles that had left fields scarred and villages in ruins. She'd seen the twisted, broken bodies of fallen comrades, the vacant stares of those who had lost everything. She'd seen the creeping rot of the Pattern Blight, the insidious corruption that twisted the very fabric of reality. But this...this was *different*. This was something...*worse.*

It feels...empty, Sera's voice echoed in Janna's mind, a soft whisper laced with unease. *Like a voided memory.*

The data streams are chaotic, Korina added, her mental voice a rapid-fire burst of technical jargon. *I'm detecting massive corruption errors, fractal decay patterns, non-linear energy fluctuations...it's unlike anything I've ever encountered.*

It's as if reality itself is unraveling, Erita thought, her mental tone a mix of fascination and dread.

Janna turned to Ada, the Architect-Queen, the woman who had brought them to this desolate place. Ada stood apart from the others, her violet eyes fixed on the grey wasteland below, her expression unreadable. A faint, violet glow emanated from her, a subtle pulse of energy that seemed to shimmer in the static-charged air.

"What do you see, Ada?" Janna asked, her voice a low rumble.

Ada turned, her gaze meeting Janna's. Her eyes were filled with a profound sadness, a deep, unsettling understanding.

"I see...my failure," Ada said, her voice barely above a whisper.

It's not your fault, Ada, Korina thought, her mental voice filled with concern. *The Cascade Failure...it's a systemic issue, a fundamental flaw in the world's code.*

A flaw I created, Ada countered. *A flaw I need to fix.*

We'll fix it together, Sera thought, her mental voice a warm, reassuring presence. *We're a team, remember? We'll face this... whatever it is...together.*

Indeed, Erita added, her mental tone laced with dry wit. *Besides, what's a little world-ending apocalypse between friends?*

Janna watched them, these four women, so different yet so united in their love for each other, in their loyalty to Ada, and in their shared determination to save this broken world. They were an unlikely quartet, a warrior, a scholar, a spy, and a god, bound together by fate and by the shared belief in a better future. A future that now seemed more uncertain than ever.

The Oracle...it's our only hope, Ada thought, her mental voice regaining some of its strength, her gaze returning to the Ashen States below. *It's the key to understanding the Cascade Failure, to finding a way to stop it.*

And where is this Oracle? Janna asked, her voice gruff.

Deep within the heart of the Ashen States, Ada said, pointing towards the desolate landscape. *At the very epicenter of the corruption.*

Janna looked out at the grey wasteland, her warrior's instincts screaming at her to turn back, to flee this place of broken reality. But then she looked at Ada, at the unwavering conviction in her violet eyes, at the fierce determination that burned within her. And Janna knew, with a certainty that went beyond logic, beyond reason, that they would face this challenge, this impossible journey, together. They would walk into the heart of the storm, into the very depths of the corruption, and they would find a way to save this world, or they would die trying.

Then let's get moving, Janna thought, her mental voice filled with a grim resolve. *We have a world to save.*

The air hung heavy, still, and strangely silent. No wind stirred the dust that coated the flat, grey landscape. No birds sang. No insects buzzed. It was a silence so profound it felt oppressive, a physical weight pressing down on Korina's chest, stealing her breath. Even the rhythmic crunch of their boots on the parched earth seemed amplified, each step a jarring intrusion in the desolate quiet.

Lynx purred in her mind, *Obsidian is being hammered with chaotic data spikes. It's like the system is actively trying to repel us.*

"This is different," Korina reported via their telepathic link, her voice now free of its densest jargon. "The swamps were like an infection in the system. This...this is the system itself actively deleting itself." She gripped *Obsidian* tighter, the cool metal a small comfort in this disintegrating world. "The fundamental laws are unstable here. Be careful—distance, even gravity, might not be reliable."

The very ground shifted beneath their feet, a constant, unsettling reminder that they were walking through a dying reality. One moment, a seemingly solid patch of ground would ripple like water, the next, a small fissure would open, spewing forth a plume of pixelated static before vanishing just as quickly. Korina stumbled, her heart pounding in her chest. Ada's hand, warm and reassuring, steadied her.

Easy, Rina, Ada thought, her mental voice a calming presence in the chaotic data streams. *We'll take it slow.*

Sera, ever vigilant, scanned the horizon, her crimson tunic a vibrant splash of color in the monochrome world. Janna walked beside her, her massive battle-axe held loosely in one hand, her expression grim. Erita, as always, seemed unfazed by the unsettling environment, her golden eyes sharp and alert, her movements fluid and graceful even on the unstable ground.

They walked in silence for what felt like hours, the only sounds the crunch of their boots and the occasional whisper of static from the ground. The landscape remained unchanged, a desolate expanse of grey. Korina's head throbbed, *Obsidian* continuing to pulse with chaotic energy readings. Even the telepathic link, usually a source of comfort and connection, felt strained, the mental voices of her companions distorted by the surrounding corruption.

Then, in the distance, something...*shifted.*

Korina squinted, trying to focus through the shimmering heat haze. At first, she thought it was just another glitch in the terrain, another ripple in the fabric of reality. But as they drew closer, the shape solidified, resolving itself into something...unexpected.

It was a statue.

A statue of an angel.

The angel was tall and slender, its wings spread wide as if poised for flight. Its face was serene and beautiful, its eyes closed in peaceful contemplation. But from those closed eyes, two streams of what looked like liquid data flowed, cascading down its cheeks and onto the grey ground below. The data shimmered and pulsed with a soft, internal light, a stark contrast to the dull, lifeless grey of the surrounding landscape.

Korina stopped, staring at the statue in disbelief. It was hauntingly beautiful, a poignant reminder of the world that had been, of the world they were fighting to save. But it was also deeply unsettling, a serene, weeping angel in the heart of a dying reality.

What is that? Sera thought, her mental voice laced with awe and apprehension.

It's...an anomaly, Korina replied, her mind racing to process the unexpected data. *Obsidian is detecting a complex energy signature, a mix of arcane and...something else. Something I can't quite identify.*

It's beautiful, Ada thought, her mental voice soft and filled with wonder. *And...sad.*

It's weeping, Erita added, her mental tone a mix of cynicism and a strange, unexpected tenderness. *What in the Void could an angel be weeping for?*

Janna said nothing, but her grip tightened on her battle-axe, her eyes fixed on the statue, her expression wary.

As they approached the angel, the ground beneath their feet became more unstable, the air thicker, the silence more profound. The data tears flowing from the angel's eyes intensified, pooling on the ground and forming a small, shimmering lake. Korina felt a strange pull, a compulsion to touch the data, to understand its source.

"Don't," Ada said, her voice a low warning. She stepped in front of Korina, shielding her from the angel. "It's...unstable."

What do you sense, Ada? Sera thought.

Something...ancient, Ada replied, her mental voice filled with a strange reverence. *And...powerful.*

And dangerous, Erita added.

The angel remained motionless, its serene face unchanging, its data tears continuing to flow. It was a silent, weeping sentinel in the heart of a dying world, a haunting symbol of the loss they were all fighting to prevent.

Sera's gaze remained locked onto the tear-dripping angel, an inexplicable unease tightening its icy grip around her heart. The fine hairs on the back of her neck stood on end, prickling with a chilling premonition of danger. A low, urgent warning escaped her lips, barely a whisper, yet carrying the weight of her years of training and countless battles: "Don't look away. Something's... wrong." She couldn't articulate the source of her fear, the specific nature of the threat that hung heavy in the air. It was a primal instinct, a deep-seated intuition honed from years on the battlefield, screaming at her that something was terribly, terribly amiss. It was a feeling so intense, so visceral, that she dared not even blink, fearing that in the fleeting darkness behind her eyelids, the world might shift, the landscape might twist, and the unknown danger might manifest itself in the most horrifying way imaginable. Every fiber of her being urged her to maintain unwavering vigilance, to keep her eyes fixed on the angel before her, as if her gaze alone could hold back the encroaching darkness. The angel itself remained unchanged, a statue of serene sorrow, its data tears continuing their relentless flow. But the air around it crackled with an unseen energy, a palpable tension that made Sera's breath catch in her throat. It was the stillness before a storm, the quiet hum of power before a devastating discharge. And in that silence, in that stillness, Sera felt a growing certainty that whatever was about to happen, it would change everything.

"Back away," Sera said, her voice low and urgent. "Slowly. Now."

What is it, Sera? Korina thought, her mental voice laced with concern. *What do you see?*

"Just move," Sera insisted, her eyes still fixed on the angel. "And don't stop looking at it. Whatever you do, do *not* look away." Her tone, sharp and unusually frantic, alarmed Korina. Ada, too, felt a surge of unease through their telepathic link.

Sera, explain, Ada thought, trying to keep her mental voice calm despite the rising panic she felt from Sera and Korina.

"No time," Sera snapped, her hand instinctively reaching for the hilt of her blade. "Just trust me on this one. *Move!*"

Her raised voice, the raw fear in her tone, finally broke through Korina's analytical focus. She took a hesitant step back, her eyes still locked on the angel, her heart pounding in her chest. Erita and Janna, sensing the shift in Sera's demeanor, followed suit, their movements mirroring Korina's cautious retreat.

Ada, despite her confusion, also stepped back, her hand instinctively reaching for Korina's. Something in Sera's tone, in the intensity of her gaze, told Ada that this wasn't just another glitch, another anomaly in the system. This was something...different. Something Sera—a veteran warrior, a woman who had faced down countless dangers without flinching—was genuinely terrified of. And that, more than anything, terrified Ada. Because it meant that Sera knew something they didn't. Something she couldn't, or wouldn't, explain. Something they were about to find out.

Then, it happened.

A flicker of movement in Sera's peripheral vision, a sudden, sharp intake of breath from Janna. Sera's head snapped around, her hand instinctively reaching for the twin blades at her hips. But it was too late.

Another angel—identical to the first—stood directly behind Janna. It must have materialized there, in the blink of an eye, having moved into Janna's blind spot from behind one of the large, jagged rocks that dotted the landscape. Before anyone could react, the angel lunged forward, its movements impossibly fast and fluid for a creature seemingly made of stone. Its stony fingers, once delicately sculpted, hardened and sharpened into a needle point.

It didn't strike; it *jabbed* Janna forcefully in the back, between her shoulder blades, like a grotesque, biological injection. The force of the blow sent Janna staggering forward, a gasp escaping her lips.

Sera whirled around, her blades flashing in the dim light. But the second angel was gone, vanished as quickly as it had appeared. The only evidence of its presence was the small, puncture wound on Janna's back, oozing a strange, viscous fluid that shimmered with the same internal light as the data tears flowing from the first angel's eyes.

"*Janna*!" Sera cried, rushing to her side. "What in the Void was that?"

Janna clutched at her back, her face contorted in pain. "I...don't know," she gasped, her voice strained. "It felt like...like it injected something into me."

A data packet, Korina reported, her mental voice urgent. *Obsidian is detecting a foreign code sequence in Janna's system. It's... replicating. Fast.*

A raw, guttural cry ripped from Janna's throat. It wasn't a sound of pain, not in the way a blade's edge or a broken bone would cause. This was the sound of a mind tearing itself apart, of a soul being overwritten. Black, jagged lines of pixelated corruption exploded from the puncture wound on her back, branching across her skin like veins of digital poison. Her powerful frame shuddered, her arm twitching in a stuttering, unnatural motion as if her very existence was struggling to render.

"What in the Void is happening to her?" Sera yelled, grabbing Janna's glitching arm.

"It's a malware injection!" Korina's voice was a high, terrified shriek. She held *Obsidian* like a shield, its screen flashing with chaotic streams of red alerts. "A virus designed to corrupt an object's core code from the inside out. Argent's light, Ada...it's trying to turn *her* into one of them!"

The words hit Ada like a physical blow. Debugging a landscape was one thing. A ship, an idol, even a puzzle lock. But a person? A friend? The risk of catastrophic error, of deleting something fundamental, was absolute. There was no time for hesitation.

Erita, Sera—hold her steady! Don't let her move! Ada's telepathic command was a steel blade cutting through their shared panic. *Korina, I need the viral signature. Isolate its core frequency. Now!*

Sera and Erita flanked Janna, their combined strength barely enough to steady the warrior as another violent, de-rendering shudder racked her body. Janna's eyes, wide with confusion and terror, flickered between them, her own identity fighting against the invasive code.

Korina's fingers flew across *Obsidian's* projected interface. *Got it! Sending the frequency to you.*

Ada saw the packet of data appear in her Admin-view, a string of jagged, malicious code pulsing with a sickening energy. She moved forward, placing her hands on Janna's trembling shoulders. Her own violet eyes flared with intense light. This wasn't a broad command; this was psychic surgery with a scalpel made of pure intent.

[SYSTEM_ACCESS: USER_JANNA.DLL]
[INITIATE: TARGETED_PURGE]

Ada plunged into the architecture of Janna's being. It was not a void, but a universe of golden light, the core code of Janna's life force, her memories, her strength. But now, tangled within that brilliant gold, were writhing threads of pure black—the malware. It was a parasite, sinking its hooks deep into Janna's foundational programming, rewriting her functions—making her a Corrupted Observer like the assailant.

The process was agony. For Janna, it was the feeling of being flayed from the inside. For Ada, it was a high-wire act over an abyss of total data annihilation. She had to meticulously unhook every black tendril, delete every corrupted variable, without severing the golden threads they were strangling. One mistake, one mis-timed command, and she could erase Janna's memory of Sera, her loyalty to their cause, the very essence of who she was.

Hold on, Janna, Ada projected, her focus absolute. *I've got you.*

She targeted the viral code with pinpoint precision. [DELETE: MALWARE_STRING_#A83F]. A black thread dissolved. Janna screamed. [DELETE: MALWARE_STRING_#B1C7]. Another vanished. Janna's body arched in a silent, glitching spasm.

One by one, Ada hunted and destroyed the invasive code. The black lines on Janna's skin flickered, fighting back, but they began to recede. The final, central strand of the virus—the root of the injection—was wrapped around Janna's core identity matrix. Deleting it felt like tearing a piece of her own soul away. Ada sent the final command.

The black lines vanished completely. The violent energy

ceased. Janna's body went limp, her immense weight collapsing forward. Sera and Erita caught her, lowering her gently to the cracked, grey earth. She was unconscious, but her breathing was stable, the digital poison gone. But not without a cost.

The sudden silence was more terrifying than the screams. Sera knelt beside Janna, her hand hovering over the warrior's still chest, a frantic pulse of energy replacing the steady rhythm of her heart. A cold dread gripped Sera, a fear she hadn't felt since the massacre at Silver Creek—a fear not of death, but of something far worse.

"Janna?" Sera's voice was a choked whisper, barely audible above the wind's mournful howl. Her eyes darted to Ada, a silent plea for reassurance.

Ada, still kneeling beside Janna, looked pale and exhausted. Fine beads of sweat glistened on her forehead, her violet eyes dull with the aftershocks of the psychic strain. She placed a gentle hand on Janna's forehead, a silent command pulsing through her fingertips.

[SYSTEM_CHECK: USER_JANNA.DLL]
[STATUS: STABLE...]

Ada's brow furrowed. The code was clean, the virus purged. But something was different. Faint, almost invisible lines of corrupted data crisscrossed Janna's core identity matrix, like scars on a battlefield. They weren't active, not a threat in themselves, but a chilling reminder of the invasion, a vulnerability Ada hadn't encountered before. She knew, with a sickening certainty, that Janna's code was compromised, marked by the encounter. Telling her would shatter the warrior's resolve, a risk Ada couldn't take.

"She's stable," Ada projected, her telepathic voice strained but calm. *"Exhausted, but the virus is gone. She'll be alright."*

Sera's relief was immediate, a wave of warmth washing away the icy fear. She finally looked around, her warrior's instincts kicking in, searching for the source of the attack. The angel statue that had been looming over them, the one she had locked onto before Janna's scream, was gone. Vanished. There were no tracks, no signs of movement, just the desolate, shifting landscape stretching out in every direction. They were alone. The isolation intensified the horror, the chilling realization that the monsters here didn't just kill you; they tried to rewrite you, to turn you into something else.

"What in the Void...where did it go?" Sera whispered, her voice laced with a new, unsettling fear.

No trace, Erita reported, her voice flat and emotionless. She scanned the area with her remaining data-slate, its screen flashing with chaotic energy readings. *The ambient energy is off the charts. It's like the whole landscape is glitching. We need to move.*

Korina knelt beside Janna, her own face pale with lingering fear. *She needs rest. We can't just leave her here.*

We won't, Ada said, her voice firm. *But we can't stay. This place isn't safe.* She looked at Sera, a silent plea in her violet eyes. *Help me carry her.*

Sera nodded, her own fear momentarily forgotten in the face of their shared purpose. Together, they lifted Janna's massive frame, her weight surprisingly light in their combined strength. Korina and Erita flanked them, their weapons drawn, scanning the shifting landscape for any sign of movement.

They moved slowly, carefully, their telepathic link a silent symphony of shared vigilance. The ground beneath their feet was treacherous, the corrupted data creating pockets of instability that threatened to swallow them whole. But they pressed on, driven by the knowledge that their survival, and the fate of Kremøtoa, depended on reaching the Oracle.

Hours later, as the first rays of dawn painted the corrupted sky in shades of sickly green and violet, they reached a high ridge. From their vantage point, they finally saw their destination. Miles away, a single point of order stood in the sea of chaos—a lone, stable mountain spire, its peak shrouded in a calm, pearlescent light. It was an island of tranquility in a digital storm, a beacon of hope in a dying world.

There, Ada whispered, her voice filled with a mixture of awe and dread. *That's where the Oracle is.*

The sight of the spire renewed their resolve. They lowered Janna gently to the ground, allowing her to rest while they surveyed the treacherous path ahead. It was a grueling descent, a broken, glitching landscape filled with unknown dangers. But they had come too far to turn back. They were the last hope of Kremøtoa, a fellowship of lovers and warriors, united in their determination to reach the Oracle and save the world they had come to call home.

They began their final march, the weight of their mission heavy on their shoulders, the chilling knowledge of the swamp's horrors —the memory of the corrupted angel, the agonizing purge of

Janna's code—a constant reminder of what they were fighting against. They were not just fighting monsters; they were fighting for the very soul of Kremøtoa, for the right to exist, to love, to live, and to die—on their own terms. And Ada, the Architect-Queen, carried a secret burden, the knowledge of Janna's scarred code, a silent promise to protect her warrior, even from the truth.

CHAPTER 24

THE GUARDIANS' ROUTINE

A week felt like a year. The apartment had transformed, its cozy corners and personal touches buried under the strata of a siege. Empty ramen bowls, crushed energy drink cans, and discarded takeout boxes formed a chaotic perimeter around the two vigils being held within its walls. The air was thick and stale, a stagnant soup of old coffee and ozone. At the center of it all, the supercomputer hummed—a low, relentless, synthetic heartbeat that vibrated through the floorboards and into their bones. It was the only constant in a world that had ceased to make sense.

Samantha sat in a hard-backed chair she had dragged from the dining nook, her post beside the immersion rig. Its ergonomic curves and sleek design seemed like a cruel joke, a sarcophagus of polished black polymer. She stared at the small, portable monitor Kenji had hooked up, its screen displaying Ada's vitals in a cold, clinical green. Heart rate, steady. Blood oxygenation, stable. Respiration, shallow but even. It was the brain activity that haunted her—a frantic, chaotic storm of electrical impulses that looked like a seismograph trying to chart the end of the world.

Another day. No change. The thought was a worn, smooth stone in her mind, turned over and over until it had lost all its sharp edges. *She's alive, but she's not here. Are you in there, Ada? Can you hear me?*

Her fingers, cold and trembling, reached out to brush against Ada's hand. The skin wasn't the chilling cold of death, but it lacked the vibrant warmth of life. It was the temperature of an object, a thing left in a room, slowly succumbing to the ambient air. Samantha gently wrapped her own hand around Ada's, her thumb stroking the back of those still, unresponsive knuckles. She remembered that hand flying across a keyboard, gesturing wildly while explaining some impossible new concept, holding a coffee mug so tight her knuckles went white. Now, it just lay there, a pale and perfect sculpture of a memory. A tear traced a slow path down her cheek, leaving a cool track in the oppressive stillness. She did not bother to wipe it away.

Across the room, in the ghostly glow of four vertically-mounted monitors, Kenji conducted his own watch. He sat with a perfect, disciplined posture, his face a mask of detached concentration, illuminated only by the river of scrolling code that cascaded down the central screen. The quiet, rhythmic tapping of his keyboard was a counterpoint to the machine's drone, a sound of deliberate, focused action in a room thick with helplessness. His station was an island of meticulous order in the sea of clutter—cables were bundled, tools were arranged by size, and a half-full mug of black coffee sat on a coaster, its contents likely cold.

Energy consumption, steady at 8.7 kilowatts. Core temperatures, nominal across all 256 processors. Cryo-pump pressure, holding. Data processing, consistent at 98.7 petaflops. Kenji's mind moved through the checklist with the clean, cold precision of a program. He analyzed the data streams, looking for the slightest deviation, the smallest hint of instability. The system was the patient. Ada's physical body was just one peripheral, one fragile component in a much larger, more complex machine. He had stabilized its nutritional input; that variable was now controlled.

Emotion is a variable that corrupts focus. It introduces error. I have a system to analyze. Its stability is the only metric that matters.

He was aware of his sister's quiet grief, a low-frequency hum of sorrow on the edge of his perception. He registered it, categorized it as a non-critical environmental factor, and filed it away. He could not afford to process it. To do so would be to invite chaos into his own system, to compromise the very focus needed to keep the machine—and by extension, Ada—running. A flicker on the diagnostics screen drew his eyes. A minor fluctuation in the axiom engine's power draw. He leaned in closer, his fingers dancing across the keys, his entire world shrinking to the lines of glowing text. He was a priest tending the altar of a terrifying new god, and his faith was in the numbers.

Samantha squeezed Ada's hand, a desperate, silent plea for a response, a twitch, anything. The only answer was the relentless hum of the machine that held her friend captive. Kenji isolated the power fluctuation, traced it back to a feedback loop in the transceiver, and wrote a three-line script to patch it. Both of them were fighting for the same person, from opposite ends of an impossible reality, locked in a quiet, suffocating orbit around a sleeping architect and her dying world. The sun dipped below the Sagiyama skyline, casting long shadows across the room, but neither of them noticed. The clock on the wall was irrelevant. Time was now measured only in the steady beep of a heart monitor and the silent scroll of endless code.

He took a sip of his coffee. It was cold, forgotten, and bitter on his tongue. He barely registered the taste. The world outside the quad-monitor array had ceased to exist hours ago. There was only the system, the data, and the problem. His fingers flew across the keyboard, the soft clicks a familiar percussion against the supercomputer's deep, resonant hum. He was running a standard integrity check on the cryo-cooling system, a routine he performed every ninety minutes. The temperature stability of the core was paramount.

Then *he saw it.*

It was nothing dramatic. Not an alarm. Not a cascade of error messages. It was a single, emerald pixel that twitched on a line graph monitoring the power consumption of the primary cryo-pump. One pixel, moving up one unit, then back down. It lasted less than a tenth of a second. *An anomaly. A sensor ghost. Insignificant.*

Except it happened 750 milliseconds *before* a corresponding spike in data throughput from the transceiver array.

Kenji's hands froze over the keys. His brow furrowed. *That was impossible.* The law of cause and effect was not optional. The transceiver draws more power, the system heats up, the cryo-pump works harder to compensate. A follows B follows C. What he had just seen was C happening before B.

Sensor lag, he thought, his mind immediately defaulting to the most logical explanation. He brought up the raw system logs, his fingers a blur. He isolated the timestamps, down to the nanosecond. He cross-referenced them with the transceiver's own internal logs. **No lag**. The data was clean.

He ran the sequence again, overlaying the two graphs. The result was the same, a stark and undeniable violation of temporal logic. A vertical green line—the data surge from Ada's consciousness demanding more processing power—was preceded by a small, preparatory bump in the cryo-pump's energy draw.

A cold knot tightened in his stomach. He leaned back in his chair, the worn fabric creaking in the silence. The steady hum of the supercomputer suddenly sounded different. Less like a machine, more like the slow, deep breath of something truly alien.

It anticipated her.

The thought was sharp, invasive, and utterly terrifying. This wasn't a pre-programmed predictive algorithm accounting for cyclical load—not even artificial intellegence; this was a direct, specific, and acausal response. The system knew what Ada was going to *do* before she did it. It felt her intent through the quantum entanglement of the immersion rig and prepared for it. This wasn't just a responsive program; it was a living extension of her will.

His breath caught in his throat. A professional, clinical terror gripped him, the kind an engineer feels when a machine stops obeying the laws of physics. *If it could defy the rules of thermodynamics, even on this subtle level, what other fundamental laws was it ignoring?*

His gaze shot across the room to Ada's still form in the immersion chair. To the frail, biological component of this impossible equation.

If it can do that...what about biology?

His focus shifted instantly. The cryo-pump anomaly was no longer the primary problem; it was a symptom of a much deeper, more profound mystery. With a new, feverish intensity, he began pulling up the long-term metabolic data he had been passively logging since he arrived. He had only glanced at it before, checking for the inevitable signs of decline. Now, he was hunting for irregularities—impossibilities.

He commanded the system to display the cellular apoptosis rate over the past week. A graph materialized. It should have been a gentle, downward slope, charting the natural, continuous death and replacement of cells. Instead, the line that appeared was perfectly, mathematically flat. **Zero**.

His heart began to hammer against his ribs. *No. That can't be right.*

He ran a diagnostic on telomere degradation. The tiny caps on chromosomes that shorten with every cell division, the very clock of aging. The data stream came back. The line was flat. **Zero degradation**. It was as if time, on a cellular level, had simply stopped for her.

A tremor ran through his hand as he typed the final command, his fingers feeling clumsy and foreign. Muscle atrophy index. For a body lying motionless for over a week, there should be a clear, measurable decay.

The line appeared. **Flat**. Utterly, impossibly flat.

Kenji stared, his mind struggling to process the data. The hair on his arms stood on end. A chill, entirely separate from the room's cool air, washed over him. This wasn't just stasis. Life support keeps you from dying. This was something else. This was perfect, active preservation.

It's treating her physical body like a non-essential peripheral, he realized, a wave of chilling awe washing away the last of his terror. *Like a hard drive it refuses to let corrupt. It's actively defying biology to keep its primary user—its core—intact.*

He leaned back, the full weight of the discovery settling upon him. He looked from the impossible, flat lines on his screen, to the silent, humming monolith of the computer, and then to the woman whose body refused to decay. He was no longer a technician. He was the sole observer of a miracle, or a monstrosity, that was calmly and methodically rewriting the source code of reality itself. And he had no idea what it would do next.

The humming of the supercomputer was a constant, low thrum that vibrated through the floorboards and settled deep in Samantha's bones. It was the only sound in the room besides the frantic beat of her own heart. Across the web of cables and glowing components, Kenji worked in a focused silence, his face illuminated by the cascade of data on his screen. But Samantha's eyes were fixed on Ada.

Ada's face was serene, a mask of placid sleep that betrayed nothing of the universe of chaos she was apparently living in. Her chest rose and fell in a rhythm so steady, so metronomically perfect, that it felt artificial. Samantha ached to see a flicker of an eyelid, a twitch of a finger, anything to break the unnerving stillness. The silence stretched, thin and brittle, until Samantha thought it would snap.

She leaned forward in her chair, the worn fabric groaning in protest. Her voice, when it came, was a raw, desperate whisper that the humming almost swallowed whole.

"Do you remember that typhoon?" she asked the still figure.

"The big one, when we were nineteen? When the power went out for two days?"

The memory rushed in, vivid and sharp. The phantom scent of the apple-cinnamon candles she had lit filled her nostrils—a scent Ada had always wrinkled her nose at, complaining it smelled like a holiday she refused to celebrate, but she tolerated it for Samantha. The wind howled outside her tiny apartment window, rattling the glass like an angry ghost, but inside, it was their own little world.

"You weren't even scared," Samantha whispered, a ghost of a smile touching her lips. "I was terrified. I thought the roof was going to peel off. But you...you were just...electric."

She saw her then, a younger Ada, her dark violet hair a messy halo in the flickering candlelight. She had grabbed a stack of damp napkins from the take-out they had ordered and started sketching, her pen flying across the flimsy paper with a fierce intensity. Lines and shapes, algorithms and architectures that meant nothing to Samantha.

"You were building worlds on a napkin," Samantha's voice cracked. "You laughed—that little giggle you do when you've solved a problem no one else knew existed. You said you were designing a system with a fail-safe against existential dread. A place where the weather was a mild feature, not a threat."

She had laughed with her, thinking it was just Ada being Ada—brilliant, eccentric, lost in her own beautiful mind. She had loved her for it. But now, sitting in the humming silence, the memory felt different. *Tainted.*

She was right there, building an escape, and I just thought it was cute.

The realization landed like a physical blow. The smile vanished from Samantha's face, replaced by a cold, hollowing dread. *I never really...saw the pain behind it. The need to build a better world because this one hurt her so much. She kept this whole part of herself locked away, and I let her.*

Her gaze drifted from Ada's still form to the main monitor of the supercomputer. In the bottom corner of the diagnostic screen, a tiny, animated pixel-cat was curled into a ball, sleeping peacefully. Its little violet tail gave a soft twitch. It was so perfectly Ada—playful, clever, a secret bit of warmth hidden inside a fortress of logic. A piece of her soul she had coded into existence.

I was so afraid of scaring her off, Samantha thought, a hot tear finally breaking free and tracing a path down her cheek. *So afraid of pushing too hard against her boundaries. But what if I had? What if I'd just held on and refused to let go?*

The question was an agony. It coiled in her gut, a venomous serpent of regret. Would Ada still have felt the need to run, to build a digital cage and lock herself inside?

Oh, god. Maybe if I had gotten closer, if I had just shown her she wasn't alone in her darkness...maybe none of this would have happened.

Her hand rose, trembling, and she reached out, her fingers pressing against the cold, smooth glass of the monitor. She traced the outline of the sleeping pixel-cat, the only part of Ada she could touch, the only part that still seemed to move with life. The warmth of her fingertip left a small, fleeting smudge on the screen, a temporary mark on an untouchable world. The humming of the machine felt like a final, impassable wall between them.

Her breath hitched, and her whisper faded into a choked sob of both loss and regret.

"You were building worlds on a napkin...Ada." Her voice was thick with unshed tears. "Please...just...come back to this one."

She pressed her forehead against the cool glass, her plea aimed at the sleeping cat, at the still girl, at the humming machine that held them both captive.

"Let me in this time...I miss you..."

Kenji worked in a state of hyper-focused calm, the world outside the glowing data streams ceasing to exist. Samantha's grief was a low-frequency hum in the background, a static he had to filter out to find the signal. He pushed past the alarming readings of Ada's induced stasis, past the impossible power consumption of the supercomputer, and drilled down into the core biological telemetry.

Something was wrong. Not failing-organ wrong, but physics-defying wrong. He pulled up the cellular degradation metrics, his brow furrowing. The numbers were flat. Impossible.

Cellular Apoptosis: 0.00%
Telomere Degradation: Null
Muscle Atrophy: 0.00%

He ran the diagnostics again. And again. The results remained unchanged. It wasn't just stasis; it was perfect, absolute preservation. A body frozen not in ice, but in time itself. The system wasn't just keeping her alive; it was actively rewriting the rules of biology to keep her pristine, a flawless vessel awaiting a return that might never come.

Kenji stared at the flat lines of the biological telemetry, his mind struggling to reconcile the data with the fundamental laws of nature. Zero apoptosis. Null telomere degradation. It wasn't even preservation; it was a paradox. The system wasn't just preserving Ada's body; it was holding it in a state of perfect, unassailable equilibrium. *A flesh-and-blood statue.*

He pushed the unsettling biological data aside—a problem for another time. The core question remained: **was she *in* there?** He pulled up the raw feed from the neural interface, a chaotic waterfall of cascading symbols representing the electrical storm inside Ada's skull. It was what he expected—the meaningless, frantic noise of an unconscious brain.

But then, he saw it. *A flicker.* A ghost in the static.

Hidden deep within the chaotic torrent was a pattern. Faint, but persistent. It was rhythmic, structured. He isolated the frequency, his fingers flying across the holographic keyboard, building digital filters to strain the signal from the noise. He worked with the intensity of a bomb disposal expert—each command precise, deliberate.

Slowly, a clean waveform emerged on the monitor. It was coherent. Structured. *This isn't system noise,* he thought, his pulse quickening. *It's...a melody.* A simple, repetitive sequence of tones. He rerouted the signal to his desktop speakers, and a thin, tinny sound filled the air. It was distorted, like a radio signal from a distant star, but it was undeniably music. He didn't recognize it. It was another impossible variable in an equation that was already breaking his mind.

He needed a different kind of analysis. *A human one.*

"Sam." His voice was low, cutting through the hum of the machine. Samantha didn't move from her vigil by the main monitor. "I need you to listen to something."

Samantha's head felt thick with grief, her thoughts moving through molasses. *What does he want now? More data? I can't take this anymore.* She dragged her gaze from the sleeping pixel-cat and pushed herself to her feet. She shuffled over to Kenji's workstation, her eyes red-rimmed and heavy.

"I've isolated a repeating signal from her neural feed," Kenji said, his tone purely clinical. He gestured to the faint, elegant waveform on his screen. "But it's...anomalous. I can't identify it."

He pressed a key, and the sound bled from the speakers again. Tinny. Distorted. A synthetic melody that felt alien and meaningless. Samantha listened, her expression blank with exhaustion. The first few notes were just noise, another layer in the suffocating hum of the apartment. But then the sequence repeated, and a flicker of something familiar sparked in the fog of her memory. A specific synth tone. A particular melodic jump.

*No...*The thought was a sharp, painful gasp in her mind. *It can't be.*

The melody looped again, a little clearer this time. Her heart stopped. That playful, ascending arpeggio...the slightly melancholic chord change that followed...

It was *Arc-en-Ciel.*

The recognition hit her not like a wave, but like a lightning strike. Her breath hitched in her throat. The weary sorrow that had been her constant companion for days shattered, and something vast and terrible rushed into the void. Her face, a mask of hollowed-out grief, completely crumpled.

A choked, strangled sound tore from her lungs, a sound of pure, undiluted agony. It wasn't weeping; it was the sound of a soul breaking. She stumbled back from the monitor as if it had burned her, her hand flying to her mouth, but it was too late to hold back the torrent. Gut-wrenching sobs wracked her body, violent and uncontrollable.

Kenji was on his feet in an instant, his analytical calm vaporized. The raw, explosive force of her pain shocked him to the core. *What is...why is she crying like that?* His mind, which seconds before had been grappling with anomalous data, was now scrambling to comprehend the human cataclysm in front of him. *Her face...*

He reached for her, his hand hovering uncertainly. "Sam?"

Her knees buckled. He caught her, his own confusion swept away by a sudden, dawning, and horrifying understanding.

She knows this song.

He guided her trembling form to the small sofa, her sobs echoing in the humming silence. He didn't know what to say, so he sat beside her, his presence a quiet, solid anchor in her storm. After a few minutes, he slipped away to the kitchenette, the sound of the kettle hissing a brief intrusion. He returned with a steaming mug of chamomile tea and pressed it into her trembling hands.

The warmth seemed to ground her. Her sobs slowly subsided into ragged, shuddering breaths. She stared into the pale yellow liquid, her knuckles white around the ceramic.

"It's..." Her voice was a shredded whisper, barely audible. "It's 'Arc-en-Ciel'."

Kenji watched her, his expression a mixture of concern and dawning awe. The impossible variable clicked into place. The biological paradox. The melodic signal. It all pointed to one, terrifying, beautiful conclusion.

Oh. Oh, gød. It's her.

Ada wasn't just a body in a chair. She was conscious. She was aware. She was in there, somewhere in that digital cosmos, listening to her favorite song.

Samantha's thumb trembled as she swiped open her phone. She found the song in her library. The album art filled the screen—a pillar of rainbows shooting up into a night sky, exploding outward in a magnificent display. She pressed *play*.

The real 'Arc-en-Ciel' spilled from the phone's small speaker. It was bright, relentlessly cheerful J-pop, full of synthetic optimism and a driving beat. The cheerful melody was a cruel, mocking counterpoint to the distorted ghost-signal from the supercomputer and the profound, suffocating grief that now filled the room. It was the anthem of the world Ada had built, a world she had chosen over this one. And for the first time, Samantha could hear just how far away she truly was.

CHAPTER 25

THE HERETIC'S RELIC

Lady Calibree stood on the flat stone roof of the eastern rectory, a sentinel carved from shadow and steel. Below, Codexia lay in a state of enforced quiet, the last echoes of the heretical anthem scrubbed from the air but not from memory. The phantom melody still clung to the air, a cloying, saccharine scent that made her teeth ache. Humiliation was a cold, sharp stone in her gut. Heretics had stood in the Empress' own throne room, spouted their profane philosophies, and then vanished. Vanished, after infecting the very heart of the Theocracy with their sonic poison.

The three moons—Argent's brilliant silver, the lesser glow of its companion BIOCE, and Cache's waning but brilliantly red crescent—cast a triumvirate of shadows across the sprawling city. Each ray of light caught the burnished obsidian cerakote of her Justicars as they moved with disciplined precision through the alleyways below. Their search was a meticulous, grid-by-grid purification. Nothing would be overlooked.

A scrape of armored boots on stone behind her announced an arrival. Calibree did not turn. Her gaze remained fixed on the central broadcast spire, the source of their public defilement.

"High Justicaress." The voice was as flat and unemotional as the stone underfoot.

"Report."

The Justicar stepped into her peripheral vision, a towering figure of polished black plate. He held out a gauntleted hand. Resting on the palm was a small, dark rectangle of metal and glass. It was angular, utilitarian, utterly devoid of artistry. It was gødless.

"The heretical device," the Justicar reported, his tone unwavering. "Found at the base of the broadcast spire. Its internal power source is depleted."

Calibree's jaw tightened, the muscle knotting under her pale skin. She reached out and took the data-slate. It felt cold, profane, an object of pure, unholy logic that had been used to vomit chaos into their sanctified order. This was their sin made manifest. *The instrument of their blasphemy.*

A white-hot impulse, pure and clean in its intensity, shot up her arm. She could unmake it. *Right here. Right now.* She could feel the satisfying crunch of its components giving way, the shatter of its screen under the force of her gauntlet. She could grind its profane dust under her heel until nothing remained but a smear on the stone. Her fingers tightened, the metal of her gauntlet groaning in protest as her grip constricted around the slate. She raised her arm, the muscles in her shoulder and back coiling with a gratifying tension. One sharp, downward strike against the stone parapet. One act of immediate, righteous destruction. It would be a release. A small, violent prayer.

They escaped. They defiled this city and my Empress' mind, and they escaped.

Her arm froze at the apex of its arc, trembling with the contained force.

But no.

The thought was a wall of ice, quenching the fire in her veins. *The Word is law.* Her rage was nothing. Her humiliation was an impurity to be purged through process, not passion. She was an instrument of Her Divine Eminence, a vessel for the will of the Wordæus Theocracy. Her personal fury was an indulgence she could not afford.

Slowly, deliberately, she lowered her arm. The coiled tension bled away, leaving a rigid, cold calm in its place. The stone in her gut was still there, but now it was a foundation, not a wound.

"It will be presented to Her Divine Eminence," Calibree said, her voice a blade of ice. "It will be logged, analyzed, and consecrated to the flame by Her decree."

The process would be followed. ***Order would be restored.***

She placed the slate carefully into a sealed pouch on her belt, the act methodical, almost ceremonial. She turned her back on the Justicar, a silent dismissal. He bowed his head and retreated with the same soundless efficiency he had arrived with.

Alone again, Calibree looked out over the city. The hunt was not over. The heretics had revealed themselves not as mere criminals, but as a spiritual plague. And she, Lady Calibree, High Inquisitor of the Wordæus Theocracy, would be the cure.

The pouch on her belt was a cancerous weight, a locus of spiritual disease she was forced to carry. Calibree did not walk back to the Empress' throne room. She marched. Her armored stride was a hammering cadence against the polished obsidian floors, a percussive sermon of steel and certainty that shattered the unnerving quiet of the palace halls. Each footfall was a declaration, a metronome counting down the moments until this infection was excised. The long, sterile corridors reflected her severe form back at her—a specter of black and silver, the unwavering antibody in the Theocracy's sacred veins.

She did not wait to be announced. She did not seek permission. The massive golden doors of the throne room swung open before her with a silent, heavy grace, and she swept inside, a cold wind of purpose.

The cavernous space was still, the air thin and sterile. Far across the expanse of immaculate gold, a solitary figure occupied the throne. Empress Thema. Her head was tilted slightly, her gaze distant, fixed on the patterns of light filtering through the high, geometric windows. She was not surveying her domain; *she was adrift.*

She is distracted. The thought was sharp, cold, and absolute. *The heretic's poison has taken root.*

Calibree's pace never faltered. Her boots rang against the dais as she ascended the three shallow steps to the foot of the throne. She reached into the pouch at her belt, her gauntleted fingers closing around the cold, profane angles of the data-slate. With a motion as precise as a beheading, she placed the object on the pristine golden floor before the Empress. It lay there like a splash of black ink on a holy text, a dead thing of logic and heresy corrupting the perfect, luminous surface.

"Your Divine Eminence." Calibree's voice was the crack of fracturing ice, sharp and clear.

Thema's translucent blue eyes drifted slowly from the window, focusing on Calibree with a strange, unfathomable placidity. There was no fire, no righteous fury. Only a quiet, unnerving curiosity.

"The root of the heresy," Calibree announced, her voice ringing with the authority of undeniable truth. She gestured with a rigid hand toward the slate. "The instrument used to broadcast their *blasphemy*. We will have this abomination publicly destroyed. We will make its unmaking a testament to the strength of The Word."

The Empress said nothing. She merely looked from Calibree to the dark object, her expression a placid sea that Calibree could not navigate. That vacancy, that lack of immediate, absolute condemnation, was the only proof she needed. The Empress needed a reminder of what was absolute. She needed to be shocked back into the cold, hard certainty of their faith.

This is more than destruction, Calibree thought, a righteous fire kindling in her chest, burning away the last vestiges of protocol. *This is a sermon. An answer. A physical rebuttal to their blasphemy, delivered now, when the wound is fresh.*

Her spine straightened into a rod of unbending will. A public display was for the masses. This, here, was for the soul of the Theocracy itself. This was an act of pure, simple, absolute faith.

"The Word is not a debate," Calibree declared, her voice rising, each word a hammer blow meant to shatter the Empress' reverie. Her gaze locked with Thema's. "It is a weapon. It is a wall. It is the fire that purges all doubt!"

She raised her right hand, her gauntlet of burnished cerakote catching the holy light from the high windows, transforming her fist into a silver comet. The air crackled with the sudden, violent tension. Her arm was a trebuchet, loaded and locked, ready to deliver a sermon not of ink and scripture, but of crushing, final force. The thunder of her own conviction roared in her ears, drowning out the silence of the throne room. This would be the only benediction required.

And as the cerakote gauntlet reached the apex of its arc, micrometers from its moment of pious destruction, a sound ripped from the core of her being.

"CALIBREE—*STOP!*"

It was not a command. It was a schism. A raw, sonic blade of pure will that shattered the cathedral silence and split the moment in two. The sound struck the room like a physical force, freezing everything. Calibree's arm locked in place, muscles bunched and trembling, her face a mask of violent disbelief. The Justicars behind her, poised instruments of zeal, became statues of polished black steel. The very motes of dust hanging in the sunbeams seemed to halt their lazy dance.

Empress Thema had never raised her voice—let alone scream —in the throne room; it was a schism of impossibility.

In the vacuum she had created, Thema rose. The whisper of her heavy, layered vestments was the only sound in the universe as she descended the three golden steps of the dais. She moved not with the ethereal grace of a living saint, but with the sharp, predatory purpose of a scholar who had just glimpsed a fundamental truth— one about to be obliterated from existence. The scent of ozone, a phantom memory of the Architect-Queen's impossible departure, ghosted through the air.

She stopped before her kneeling Inquisitor, her shadow falling over the frozen tableau of aborted violence. Her gaze was not on Calibree's face, but on the object of her fury. With long, pale fingers, Thema reached down and lifted the data-slate from the floor.

It was cool. Dense. Utterly pragmatic. It was not a thing of faith, built for reverence with precious metals and inlaid gems. It was a thing of function, its casing scuffed, its edges worn smooth by a hand that used it as a tool, not an icon. Her thumb brushed across the back, tracing a faint, etched sigil: two raised cutlasses, with the blades crossed—the mark of the Korsair Confederacy.

A memory flared, sharp and clear: the throne room, just before the chaos. The four heretics standing before her. The Architect, a paradox of power and vulnerability. The warrior, a pillar of defiant strength. The scholar, a font of nervous energy. And the fourth one. The one with the golden pixie cut and the cynical, piercing eyes.

The rogue.

This is not a symbol of their heresy, Thema realized, a cold fire of revelation coursing through her. *It is a personal effect. It is a key. A component.*

The object in her hand transformed. It was no longer a profane instrument but a relic of a different kind—a tangible data point from a system that operated on principles she had never conceived. The anthem was the theory; this was the proof. To understand the Architect, she first had to understand the pieces of her impossible machine. To smash this slate would be to gouge out her own eyes before reading a new text. It was an act of profound, unforgivable ignorance. And Thema did not tolerate ignorance, least of all her own.

A hunger awoke within her, an intellectual avarice she had not felt since her cloistered youth studying the oldest, most esoteric interpretations of The Word. It was a craving not for power, but for comprehension. The Word was no longer a simple, divine proclamation to be enforced. It was a code to be broken.

Her gaze finally lifted to meet Calibree's, and her pale blue eyes were no longer the windows to a divine soul. They were the cold, analytical lenses of a scientist who had just discovered a new element. The warmth, the melodic cadence, all of it was gone, stripped away to reveal the unyielding core of pure intellect beneath.

"You have performed your duty, Lady Calibree," Thema said, and her voice was a flat, sterile thing, utterly devoid of the hypnotic resonance she usually employed. It was the voice of a different woman. "You identified the threat. Your assessment of its nature, however, was incomplete."

Incomplete. The word hung in the air, a judgment colder and sharper than any blade. It was a word of academia, not faith. A dismissal of zeal in favor of analysis.

Thema's gaze remained locked on her High Inquisitor. For a moment, she saw the shift in Calibree's dark grey eyes—the righteous fire of her conviction guttered, replaced by a flicker of pure, uncomprehending shock. The blood drained from Calibree's face, leaving her tattooed skull looking stark and skeletal against the sudden pallor of her skin. The tension in her raised arm, poised for its act of pious destruction, went slack.

Thema's focus, however, was already moving past her servant. Her attention returned to the object in her hand. The data-slate felt alien against the silken threads of her vestments, a utilitarian scar on her opulent, holy attire. It was a piece of another world, another logic, and it was now the most fascinating artifact in her possession. A key to understanding the symphony that had shattered the dogmatic silence of her city.

She turned her analytical gaze back to Calibree, whose arm had now lowered, her gauntlet coming to rest at her side with a soft, metallic sigh. The melodic quality returned to Thema's voice, but it was a chilling facsimile of its former warmth. It was the precise, resonant tone of a bell forged from ice.

"You will not destroy it," Thema commanded. The words were not a suggestion; they were an axiom laid upon the world.

Calibree's jaw tightened, a subtle, grinding motion that Thema registered with detached interest.

"This object is not simply a tool of heresy," Thema continued, her fingers tracing the worn casing of the slate. "It is...evidence. An anomaly that contradicts the singular nature of the Cascade Failure?" Her eyes shone with that new, predatory light of intellectual hunger. "It requires *further study*."

Thema saw the last vestiges of confused loyalty in Calibree's eyes die, replaced by a stillness so profound it was terrifying. It was the absolute calm of a frozen sea. The High Inquisitor's posture, once a spear of righteous certainty, became something else—a pillar of rigid, watchful silence.

Study? The thought screamed in Calibree's mind, so loud she felt Thema must hear it. *One does not study a plague; one burns it.* The poison had taken root. The vessel of The Word was now questioning divinity itself.

"I will keep it in my personal charge," Thema concluded. She offered no further explanation. None was needed. Her Will was the only justification required.

With that, Thema turned her back on her most devoted servant. The motion was an execution. It was a final, absolute dismissal that severed a bond forged in years of unwavering faith. Holding the dark slate against her crimson and gold robes, Thema walked away from the dais, her mind already consumed with the complex puzzle of the Architect-Queen. She felt the weight of Calibree's stare on her back, but it was a distant pressure, a variable already accounted for and dismissed.

Behind her, Lady Calibree remained kneeling on the cold, golden dais. Her world had fractured. The twin pillars of her existence—loyalty to the Empress, and loyalty to The Word—had been ripped apart. They were no longer one. She watched the Empress' retreating form, a bitter, metallic taste flooding her mouth. The blood in her veins felt like ice. A chasm had opened at her feet, and on the other side stood a stranger wearing the face of her goddess.

A cold, sharp shard of suspicion took root in her heart, crystallizing into a new and terrible purpose.

I am no longer just her guard, Calibree thought, the silence of the throne room roaring in her ears. *I am a watchman. And for the first time, I am watching my own Empress.*

CHAPTER 26

A NIGHTMARE MANIFEST

The ground of the Ashen States was not soil or rock; it was compressed nothing. A monochrome dust that rose in silent, weightless puffs with every step. Above them, the sky was a sheet of flat, empty white, a canvas wiped clean of sun, clouds, or color. They moved through a world that had been un-made, its core data bled away until only a grey, two-dimensional ghost remained.

Janna leaned heavily on her axe, the haft a crutch. The malware's phantom code still buzzed in her marrow, a low-grade fever that Ada's intervention had suppressed but not erased. Beside her, Sera's hand hovered near her back, a silent offer of support. Erita scouted ahead, a darting shadow against the featureless expanse, while Ada and Korina walked in the center, a nexus of weary resolve.

The hum started first, a low thrum that vibrated through the soles of their boots.

Ambient energy spike, Korina's thought was sharp with alarm. *Massive. Unstable.*

The white sky began to flicker, stitched with threads of corrupted green text and jagged red lines. Then the wind hit, a physical wall of sound. It was not the roar of air but the shriek of a thousand dying machines, a blizzard of pure static and corrupted audio files that tore at them.

"Argent's light!" Sera's shout was lost in the digital gale.

A storm of pixels swirled around them, sharp and abrasive. Each particle was a fragment of broken code, a piece of some forgotten texture. It felt like being scoured by sand made of broken glass and raw data.

It's trying to un-render us! Ada's voice was a frantic beacon in their shared mind. *The integrity of my gear is failing! Shelter! We need shelter!*

Erita scrambled back to the group, her face a mask of grim urgency. "This way! There's a rock formation!"

They huddled together, a miserable knot of resistance against a tempest that sought to delete them. The storm intensified, the shrieking static resolving into tortured, half-formed whispers. Janna gritted her teeth, the noise a physical agony that resonated with the viral code still nesting in her system.

There! Ada's mental projection was a flash of violet light, pointing toward a dark slash in the grey landscape.

A cave. It was impossible. The rock face it was carved into was solid, a deep, stable black that did not glitch or flicker. The entrance was a perfect, smooth archway, its edges too clean, too deliberate for a natural formation. In this wasteland of corrupted files and crumbling reality, it stood as a bastion of impossible stability.

"It's too perfect," Janna growled, the words torn from her lips by the wind.

"What in the Void does that matter?" Sera yelled back, shielding Korina with her body. "It's either that or we get scrubbed from existence!"

They ran. Erita and Sera half-dragged, half-supported Korina, while Ada stumbled behind them, her focus frayed. Janna brought up the rear, her soldier's instincts screaming a silent alarm. The cave felt wrong. It was a sanctuary that offered itself too easily, a haven in a hell that should have none. It felt like bait.

She forced her aching legs onward, plunging past the threshold after the others. The world of shrieking code and pixelated fury vanished. Silence, absolute and profound, slammed into them. The air inside was cool, still, and heavy. It did not echo. It felt ancient and solid, a pocket of reality untouched by the chaos raging just outside. They were safe. Janna stood at the entrance, her hand resting on the smooth, cold stone, and stared into the unnatural darkness. A perfect trap was still a trap.

The moment they crossed the threshold, the universe went silent. The raging data-storm, the shrieking static, the physical pressure of the wind—it all ceased to exist. One step, and they were in a tomb. The air was unnaturally still, cold and heavy, swallowing sound before it could echo.

Ada slumped against the rough, cold stone of the cavern wall, her breath hitching in ragged gasps, her body trembling with the residual strain of forcing her way through the data storm. Korina rushing over, fussing over Ada's condition, did nothing to help the nerves of the group.

"We make camp," Sera's voice was flat, robbed of its usual resonance by the dead air. "Rest. We earned it."

Janna nodded, dropping a pack to the floor with a dull thud. They worked with the grim efficiency of soldiers. Sera and Janna established a perimeter near the entrance, laying out bedrolls. Korina began running diagnostics on her gear, the soft glow of Obsidian's screen a lonely point of light in the oppressive dark.

Erita stood apart, her back to the others, facing the deeper blackness of the cave. This was her post. Watcher. Analyst. The one who saw the threats before they materialized. But this place...it defied analysis. Her senses, usually so sharp, felt blunted, useless. The silence was a presence, a weight on her eardrums. She scanned the darkness, seeing nothing but the end of her own sight.

Something soft drifted into her peripheral vision. Erita's head snapped toward it. A single, black feather spiraled down from the impossibly high ceiling, turning lazily in the still air. It landed silently on the dusty floor at her feet. A crow's feather.

Ice bloomed in her stomach. *Impossible.* A stray bird couldn't have gotten in. There were no nests. It was a glitch, a random asset loaded from the storm outside. It had to be.

Then another feather fell. And another.

Erita's gaze lifted slowly, a terrible dread coiling in her gut. She followed the silent descent upward, her eyes tracing the path to the source. The ceiling was no longer stone. It was a roiling, shifting mass of black. A silent, glitching murder of crows, their forms flickering like bad code. Hundreds of them. *Thousands.* They clung to the roof of the cave, a living, breathing tapestry of her deepest nightmare. Their heads were cocked, and their eyes, their countless, tiny eyes, glowed with the faint, malevolent red of active malware. They were watching her. *Only her.*

Her breath caught in her throat. The Walled Garden Ada had built in her mind, the sanctuary meant to contain this exact memory, felt a million miles away. This wasn't a memory. This was a virus. A weaponized piece of her own past, aimed directly at her soul.

No one else can see them, she realized, a fresh wave of horror washing over her. She risked a glance at the others. Janna was checking the straps on her pack. Ada was whispering with Korina. They were oblivious.

Her iron composure, the bedrock of her identity, began to fracture. She felt a tremor start in her hands. The image of two men, the scent of smoke, the sight of black feathers on lifeless eyes—it all slammed into her. She was that little girl again, hiding, helpless, watching her world burn.

She couldn't scream. She couldn't move. The spymaster, the rogue, the survivor, was gone. All that remained was raw, primal terror. Her mind, her last line of defense, buckled. She squeezed her eyes shut, but the image was burned onto the inside of her eyelids.

With a final, desperate act of will, she reached out, not with her voice, but with her mind.

A silent, frantic pulse of pure, undiluted terror blasted across their telepathic link, a scream with no sound, a raw signal of a mind breaking apart.

The psychic scream from Erita slammed into Ada's mind with the force of a physical blow. It was not a thought or a word, but a raw, unfiltered data-stream of pure panic. The world inside the cave tilted. The oppressive silence shattered, replaced by a low, predatory hum that seemed to vibrate directly in the bones. Erita's terror was a key, and it had just unlocked the cage.

Janna was the first to falter. She flinched, her head snapping around as if struck. From the deep, empty darkness behind her, a chorus of agonized screams echoed off the stone walls. They were not generic cries of pain; they were specific, laced with the names of forgotten battles and the gurgle of last breaths. Janna stumbled back, her hand flying to her axe, her face a mask of old, buried guilt. The sounds were her ghosts, a phantom army she could hear but never fight.

Then the light from their campfire began to warp. Shimmering, translucent figures bled into existence around Sera. They wore the segmented plate of the Aegis Order, their forms glitching like corrupted images. One moment they were clear, the next they were transparent, their faces flickering between fallen comrades and the hollow-eyed farmers of the Northern Marches. Their whispers slithered through the air, a venomous hiss of betrayal and failure. *"You left us." "Traitor." "Murderer."* Sera drew her blades, her knuckles white, her body coiled tight as she stood surrounded by her own damnation.

Ada's gaze shot to Korina, whose face had gone deathly pale. She was staring past the fire, her entire body locked in a paralytic tremor. Ada followed her line of sight. At the edge of the firelight, a tall, distorted figure stood. It was Kaelen Vance, but rendered by a broken system. His form stretched and compressed, his colors bleeding into the darkness, yet the cruel, possessive smirk on his face was rendered in perfect, horrifying detail. He took a step forward, his glitching form a mockery of a man, and Korina let out a small, choked sob. The sight ignited a white-hot fury in Ada, a protective instinct so fierce it almost eclipsed her own budding fear.

Almost.

Her own nightmare wasn't a memory or a person. It was a failure of the system. A box of pure, violet light materialized in front of her, hovering in the air. Her supercomputer's warning window. Her last lifeline. But the text inside was corrupted.

[W-RN-NG: S-S-STEM -NTEGR-TY C-MPR-M-SED. B-OFEEDB-CK L--P F--LING.]

The little pixel-lynx, her silent guardian for Korina, her playful piece of herself, appeared in the corner of the violet box. It sat up, its ears perked, but then it began to dissolve. Its pixels broke apart, scattering like digital dust. Its meow-song started, a distorted, dying tune that tore at Ada's soul. It was her love, her protection, being un-rendered.

The text on the screen finally flickered and died. The box remained, a blank, violet void. Then, within that void, a new image flickered to life. A spark. An orange flicker against the dark metal of a server rack. A small, hungry flame licked at a bundle of wires inside her supercomputer, back on Earth. Smoke began to curl. There was no one there. No Samantha. No Kenji. Just a fire, starting in the heart of her world, with an entire planet to burn.

The fire. The impossible fire, eating away at the heart of her creation, an ocean away on a dying Earth. Ada's breath hitched. It was the perfect fear, tailored just for her. The ultimate system failure. Her fault.

And that was the key.

Her gaze snapped from the violet void to her companions, each trapped in their own personal hell. Erita's crows. Janna's ghosts of war. Sera's spectral accusers. Korina's predator. It wasn't random. This cave, this place—it wasn't a location. It was a protocol. A data-anomaly designed to find the deepest cracks in a person's psyche and pour poison into them. It was a mirror, reflecting their own horrors back at them, amplified and weaponized. Fighting the illusions was pointless; they were fighting themselves.

She couldn't [DELETE: Kaelen_Vance_Construct] without risking a catastrophic feedback loop in Korina's mind. She couldn't fight four separate wars while her own world burned in front of her. But they had a shared network. A reality that existed beyond the corrupted code of the cave. The telepathic link.

Ada squeezed her eyes shut, forcing the image of the burning supercomputer away. She pushed past the terror, the guilt, the raw, screaming panic. She dug deeper, searching for an emotional signature powerful enough to overwrite the fear. She found it. A quiet moment in a Port Dominus warehouse loft.

She didn't broadcast words or images. She sent the feeling.

A wave of pure, unadulterated warmth flooded their shared mental space. It tasted of chamomile and lavender. It felt like Sera's calloused hand gripping her shoulder with fierce protectiveness. It was the soft weight of Korina's head resting against her chest, a silent offering of trust. It was the defiant spark in Erita's eyes, a silent vow of loyalty that cut deeper than any scar. It was the solid, unshakeable presence of Janna at their backs, a bulwark against the world. It was the feeling of their five bodies pressed together, a messy, tear-stained, desperate huddle that was the single truest thing Ada had ever known. A raw data packet of forgiveness, belonging, and unwavering trust.

It hit Korina first. The warmth was a shield, and the distorted, leering face of Kaelen flickered, his power over her broken by a love he could never comprehend. Her terrified whimpers quieted.

The icy whispers tormenting Sera were muffled by the memory of the group's shared strength. The spectral Aegis knights wavered, their accusations losing their venom against the pure anchor of her found family.

For Janna, the warmth was a quiet harbor against the storm of battle-cries from her past. The agonized screams of the fallen faded to a distant, mournful echo.

Erita, lost in a storm of black feathers and red eyes, felt the warmth seep through the cracks of her terror. It wasn't enough to banish the crows, but it was a hand in the dark, a voice promising that she was not alone in the memory.

Slowly, instinctively, they moved. Drawn not by sight, but by the gravitational pull of their shared bond. Korina stumbled forward, her eyes squeezed shut, reaching for the source of the warmth. Sera turned her back on her ghosts. Janna shuffled toward the center. Erita pushed through the nightmare, her breath coming in ragged gasps.

They collapsed together in the middle of the cave, a tangled huddle of limbs and desperation. The phantoms still swirled at the edges of the firelight—a flash of armor, the glint of a cruel smile, the flutter of a dark feather—but they were muted, held at bay. Five women, eyes closed, minds linked, weathering a storm of their own making. Their shared love the only anchor in a sea of illusion, the only thing keeping them sane.

CHAPTER 27

THE LAST MARCH

The hum was the worst part. A low, persistent thrum that vibrated deep in Sera's bones, the sound of reality grinding its teeth. It was a constant companion on this endless, featureless plain of shifting grey dust and pixelated rock. Days had bled together since the nightmare cave. The only marker of time was the slow, agonizing crawl of the Oracle's spire across the horizon.

A crimson glyph blinked on the periphery of Sera's helmet display. *Power levels critical. Atmospheric seal at 78%.* She ignored it. The suit's thermoregulator had been failing for a day, leaving a slick of cold sweat down her back that never evaporated. The recycled air tasted stale, metallic. She felt the familiar burn in her thighs, the deep ache in her joints. A warrior's pain. A good pain. It reminded her she was still solid, still moving.

Everything else was liquid. The ground flowed like slow water under their boots, the sky was a static-laced smear of non-color.

The hum burrowed into her thoughts, a maddening drill bit of noise.

Status? The thought was Ada's, thin and strained through their telepathic link.

Korina's reply was a cascade of worried data points, a flicker of schematics showing their failing suits. *Janna's suit is the worst. Seal integrity is dropping faster than the rest. Mine is...holding.*

Sera glanced back. Janna's massive frame was a steady, plodding silhouette, but Sera saw the slight stumble, the way she favored her left leg. Erita walked with a coiled tension, her head constantly scanning their surroundings even when there was nothing to see but geometric decay. Ada and Korina walked close together, a small island of mutual support in the grey ocean.

Just need to make that ridge, Janna's voice rumbled in their minds, a gravelly anchor of resolve. *Then we rest.*

Ridge isn't getting any closer, Erita shot back, her thought sharp and brittle.

Sera's gaze fixed on the spire. It was the only thing that didn't shift, the only vertical line in a world that had forgotten what straight was. A black needle stitched into a fraying tapestry. It was their compass, their destination, their prayer. She focused on it, letting the sight of it drown out the hum, the pain, the flashing red glyphs on her display. Each step was a silent vow. Each breath a tiny rebellion against the decay.

We'll make it, she projected to the group, her own thought a simple, hard thing, like a whetstone against a blade. *Keep moving.*

The ground beneath her feet dissolved into a brief shimmer of code before re-solidifying. She didn't flinch. This was their world now. A long, final march through the static, with only a distant black tower to prove they were still heading somewhere.

The hum was a physical presence, a parasite that had burrowed into Erita's skull. She tracked the slow decay of their resources with a cold, internal clock. Three days of rations left per person. Water purifier at sixty-four percent efficiency. Suit integrity across the board dropping at a rate of three percent per hour. Their pace was too slow. The spire on the horizon was a cruel joke, a fixed point in a world determined to un-make them with every step.

She saw the flicker before the ground broke. A tremor in the code, a stutter in the world's monotonous rhythm. Her hand was already on her daggers when the grey dust erupted.

It wasn't a tremor. It was a birth.

Swarms of shimmering things boiled out of the corrupted earth. Code-Leeches. They were multi-legged abominations of pure, glitching data, skittering with a speed that defied physics. Their bodies were lattices of sickly green and violet light, their movements jerky and impossibly fast. Erita's breath hitched. They weren't coming for them. They ignored flesh and bone entirely, their fractured optics fixed on a different prize.

Gear.

The swarm descended on their supply packs in a chittering, static-laced wave. The attack was a frantic, chaotic scramble.

"Void's name!" Janna's roar was swallowed by the hiss of dissolving matter. She swung her massive hammer, the impact sending a ripple through the ground but only dispersing a handful of the leeches into harmless pixels. They reformed instantly.

Sera was a crimson blur, her twin blades slicing through the constructs. Each hit was a shower of corrupted data, a spray of useless code that stung the air like ozone. But for every one she dispatched, three more swarmed in. Erita threw a dagger, its edge sinking into a leech that clung to Ada's pack. The thing dissolved with a high-pitched whine, but the damage was already done. She watched in horror as the durable fabric of their packs, the carefully preserved rations, the med-kits—all of it unraveled into showers of corrupted, useless data.

The leeches were methodical in their destruction. They weren't fighting; they were consuming. Her own pack felt suddenly light. A skittering horror latched onto her thigh, its legs like searing needles. It wasn't biting her skin, it was devouring the reinforced material of her suit. She stabbed it, again and again, her teeth gritted.

Then, as quickly as they came, they were gone. The swarm receded, sinking back into the grey dust, leaving behind a profound and devastating silence. The ever-present hum seemed louder now.

Erita stood panting, her gaze dropping from the spire to the tattered remains of their survival. Her environmental suit was shredded, great gashes exposing the thin, now-torn liner beneath. The cold of the dead atmosphere bit at her exposed skin. She glanced at the others. They were all in the same state. Janna's suit hung in ribbons from her massive frame. Sera's crimson tunic was ripped across the chest and thigh, revealing far more than modesty allowed. More than half their food, their water purifiers, their hope—gone. Reduced to a memory of light and static.

Well, she thought, the thought a piece of jagged glass in their shared mental space. *That complicates things.*

A day and a half later, the world was a flat, grey hum. The attack had stripped them of more than supplies; it had stolen their momentum, replacing it with a gnawing, hollow weakness. Ada watched the others from under the flimsy shelter of a petrified rock shelf. Janna's massive frame seemed carved from shadow, her usual boisterous energy banked to a low, grim ember. Sera pushed forward on pure, serrated will, her movements economical and sharp. Erita was a taut wire of contained energy, her gaze sweeping the horizon with a predator's focus, but Ada saw the tremor in her hands when she thought no one was looking.

Her eyes settled on Korina.

They were rationing the last of the nutrient paste, a tasteless, grey substance that was more concept than food. Each of them had a precisely measured portion, enough to stave off the worst of the body's shutdown. Korina held her portion on a small, flat piece of shale. She brought a minuscule amount to her lips, her movements a perfect pantomime of eating. But Ada, with her Architect's view of the world, saw the truth. She saw the subtle way Korina angled her body, the almost imperceptible push of the paste to one side of the shale, leaving the majority untouched. She was saving it. For her.

A fierce, cold terror seized Ada. It was a love so pure it was suicidal. In this wasteland, that kind of self-sacrifice wasn't noble. It was a prelude to a corpse. The thought of Korina's brilliant light dimming, of her mind ceasing its endless, beautiful cascade of logic and wonder, was more horrifying than any monster the system could throw at them.

Ada pushed herself to her feet, her own depleted energy a dull ache in her bones, and crossed the small space between them.

You have to eat, Rina. The thought was a sharp, direct command in their shared mental space.

Korina's violet eyes flickered up, a flicker of guilt quickly masked by stubborn resolve. *You need it more. Your abilities...they drain you. It's simple energy logistics.*

It's suicide, Ada projected back, her mental voice laced with a desperation that bordered on anger. *I can't...If you fall, we all fall. Eat. Now.*

No. The refusal was soft, but absolute.

Ada saw the unwavering devotion in her lover's eyes. Logic wouldn't work. Pleading was useless. A cold, desperate plan solidified in her mind. It was a violation. It was a necessity.

She scooped a thumbful of her own nutrient paste, the texture a familiar, gritty slime. She put it in her mouth, the utilitarian non-taste coating her tongue. Without another thought, she knelt in front of Korina, cupped her face in her hands, and closed the distance.

She forced the kiss, a desperate, almost violent act of necessity. It wasn't tender or gentle; it was a primal command, her lips pressing hard against Korina's, silencing the soft protest she knew was coming. Korina's slender body went rigid with shock, her hands instinctively coming up to push against Ada's chest, a flicker of resistance in her violet eyes. But Ada held firm, her grip on Korina's face a silent, desperate plea. She deepened the kiss, using her tongue to push the gritty, tasteless nutrient paste from her own mouth into Korina's.

For a heartbeat, it was a struggle, a silent battle of wills played out in the intimate space between their lips. Korina's breath hitched, her eyes wide with surprise and a flicker of something Ada couldn't quite decipher. Then, as suddenly as it began, the resistance melted away. Korina's hands, which had been pushing, now clung to Ada's arms, her fingers digging into the fabric of Ada's tunic. The shock in her eyes dissolved, replaced by a dawning, profound understanding. She accepted the offering, the forced intrusion becoming a shared communion. Her own lips softened against Ada's, her body leaning into the embrace, the tension leaving her like a sigh.

In the heart of the dead, grey world, surrounded by the silent, watchful presence of Sera, Erita, and Janna, the forced act of survival transformed. It became a shared, desperate sacrament, a silent testament to the fierce, unwavering bond between them. It was a violation—admittedly a transgression against Korina's boundaries, and yet, it was also the most intimate, the most profoundly connected thing Ada had ever done. A single tear traced a path down Korina's cheek, a mixture of exhaustion, gratitude, and something akin to awe. When they finally broke apart, the thin thread of nutrient paste still connecting their lips for a fleeting moment before it snapped, the air between them felt charged, thick with unspoken emotion.

The gritty, utilitarian taste of the nutrient paste was a foreign invader on her tongue, but it was the ghost of Ada's desperate pressure that lingered. Korina's mind, a machine that thrived on data and predictable systems, struggled to parse the input. It was an act of force. A violation of her autonomy. The logic was clean, undeniable. Yet, the emotional data was a chaotic, overwhelming cascade.

Her memory dredged up the cold, sterile violation of Kaelen—an act of taking, of selfish consumption that had left her feeling like a broken object. This...this was the inverse. A violent act of *giving*. A forced sacrament. Ada hadn't taken anything; she had refused to accept Korina's sacrifice. She had overruled Korina's logical, self-destructive choice with a primal, illogical command to *live.*

A new axiom slotted into place within her, a thought so foreign to her logical mind that it felt like a system error. Kaelen. His name was a ghost in her code, a fragment of malware she could never fully purge. He had taken something from her. A physical first. He had trespassed, stolen, and rewritten her physical history with the cold, selfish entitlement of a predator. He had taken her agency, her autonomy, and left her feeling like a corrupted file, an object whose value had been diminished by unauthorized access.

But as she looked at Ada, at the raw, desperate terror still etched in her lover's eyes, the memory of Kaelen's violation felt different. It became smaller. Colder. Clinical. Kaelen had stolen a physical experience, a singular data point in the timeline of her life. He had logged an entry in a ledger she never consented to. He had been the first to breach her body.

A profound, shattering clarity cut through the grey wasteland of her thoughts. Argent's light, that wasn't what mattered. *It never was.*

The physical act was a hollow shell. A procedural event. The true, unquantifiable prize, the one experience more precious than any physical boundary, was something Kaelen could never have touched, could never have even understood. He had not been able to steal her First True Love.

That belonged to Ada.

It belonged to this brilliant, terrified, rule-breaking woman who had just violated her autonomy not to take, but to *give.* To force life into her. This love—this chaotic, illogical, fiercely protective force—was the true first. It was the first time she had felt cherished beyond reason, the first time her existence was valued above all system protocols.

Kaelen's crime shrank in the shadow of this revelation. He was a petty thief who had made off with a trinket, blind to the priceless artifact stored just beyond his reach. He had left a scar on her flesh, but he had never touched her soul. That sacred ground, that genesis of her heart, was and always would be, Ada's. A profound weight lifted from her, a shackle of shame she hadn't realized she was still wearing, rusting away into nothing.

Her gaze fell on her own portion of the grey paste, still mostly untouched on the piece of shale. Her careful, logical sacrifice seemed so foolish now, so small in the face of Ada's raw, world-breaking will. A warmth spread through her chest, chasing away the cold of the wasteland and the lingering shock. It was a feeling of being utterly seen, of being cherished so fiercely that the boundaries of self were secondary to the preservation of the whole.

Her trembling hand came up to touch her own lips, as if to confirm the memory. She met Ada's gaze. The Architect-Queen knelt before her, her violet eyes swimming with a mixture of guilt and unwavering resolve.

A single, shaky breath escaped Korina's lips. The words felt inadequate, hollow, but they were all she had.

"Thank you."

It was a whisper, barely audible above the low hum of the corrupted world. But in the charged silence of their small group, it echoed like a vow. She saw the tension bleed from Ada's shoulders, a wave of relief washing over her face. Korina picked up the shale, her hands now steady, and began to eat her own portion, her eyes never leaving Ada's. She would live. For them. For her.

The grey wasteland stretched before them, an endless expanse of static and corrupted code. Each step was a battle against the world's decay, a physical manifestation of the encroaching nothingness. Ada felt the weight of it on her shoulders, a crushing burden of responsibility for this world, for her companions, for the life she had created and was now desperately trying to save.

Korina walked beside her, her hand clasped tightly in Ada's. The warmth of her touch was a small, vital anchor in the chaotic sea of Ada's thoughts. She glanced at Sera and Erita, who moved with the practiced efficiency of seasoned warriors, scanning the horizon for threats. Janna brought up the rear, her usual boisterous energy replaced by a quiet stoicism.

A flicker of movement in the periphery caught Ada's eye. It was subtle, a brief shimmer in the monotonous grey, like a rogue pixel in a corrupted image. She stopped, her hand tightening on Korina's.

What is it? Korina's voice echoed in her mind, a soft counterpoint to the low hum of the corrupted landscape.

*Something...*Ada focused her Admin-view, zooming in on the anomaly. It appeared as a data crystal, nestled amongst the corrupted code like a flawless diamond in a pile of ash. It pulsed with a soft, inviting light, a beacon of order in the surrounding chaos. Beautiful. Benign. A lie.

Trojan, Lynx's voice whispered in Korina's mind, the little pixel-cat's warning echoing in Ada's own thoughts through their shared connection. *Quarantine protocol advised.*

Before Ada could voice the warning, the crystal flared. A wave of raw, corrupting energy washed over them, a psychic assault that felt like a virus injected directly into her code. Ada gasped, her vision blurring. She felt Sera and Erita's mental shields snap into place, protecting Korina and themselves from the worst of the attack.

But Janna...

Ada's gaze snapped to the warrior. Janna stood frozen, her eyes wide, her face contorted in a silent scream. For a terrifying instant, her eyes glowed with the same sickly grey light as the corrupted landscape, the pupils shrinking to pinpricks of nothingness. Ada felt a cold dread grip her heart, a premonition of disaster.

She activated her Admin-view, scanning Janna's code. The truth was far worse than she had feared. The 'scarred' code from the Corrupted Observer Pattern attack, the one she had painstakingly purged from Janna's system, was now resonating with the new corruption. It pulsed with the same grey light, like a dormant virus being activated by a rogue signal. The two corruptions were intertwining, weaving themselves into the fabric of Janna's being. A time bomb ticking within her soul.

The psychic assault ended as abruptly as it began. The data crystal dissolved into nothingness, leaving only the oppressive grey of the wasteland. Janna gasped, her eyes returning to their normal color, the grey light fading like a dying ember. She stumbled, her hand flying to her head.

"Void's name," Janna muttered, her voice strained. "What in the hells was that?"

Just...a glitch, Ada responded through the telepathic link, forcing a calm she didn't feel into her voice. *A stray echo of the Cascade Failure. Are you alright?*

Headache. Feels like my brain just got kicked by a blighted swamp toad. Janna's mental voice was shaky, but clear. *Nothing I can't handle.*

Ada forced a smile, a lie etched onto her face. *Good. Let's keep moving.*

She turned, her hand still clasped in Korina's, and resumed their march towards the distant spire, the Oracle's beacon a faint glimmer of hope in the encroaching darkness. The weight of her secret, the knowledge of Janna's compromised code, settled heavily on her shoulders, another agonizing variable in the impossible equation she was desperately trying to solve.

The last few kilometers were a blur of exhaustion and dread. Each step was an agonizing effort, their bodies screaming in protest, their minds heavy with the weight of the corrupted landscape they had traversed. The air itself seemed to press down on them, a suffocating blanket of static and decay. Hunger gnawed at their bellies, a constant, insistent reminder of their dwindling supplies. They walked in silence, their telepathic link a quiet symphony of shared weariness and determination.

Then, as they crested a small rise, the world changed.

The contrast was immediate and profound. The oppressive grey of the Ashen States abruptly gave way to vibrant green. The ground beneath their feet was solid, stable, almost...*normal.* The air, no longer thick with the stench of corruption, was clean, crisp, carrying the scent of pine and damp earth. A faint, reassuring hum emanated from the rock face ahead, a pulse of pure, ordered energy that resonated deep within Ada's core. It was a sound she hadn't realized she'd missed, a harmonic frequency that spoke of stability and systemic integrity.

They had reached their destination.

Before them, rising from the heart of the corrupted wasteland like a beacon of hope, stood the mountain spire. It was a colossal structure of obsidian and crystal, its surface shimmering with an ethereal light. It defied logic and gravity, its angles sharp and impossible, its form constantly shifting, as if it existed in multiple dimensions simultaneously. A spiral staircase, carved from a single, continuous piece of crystal, wrapped around the spire, leading upwards into the swirling clouds that obscured its peak.

Ada stopped, her gaze fixed on the towering edifice. It was a structure she had designed, a piece of code she had written, yet it felt alien, impossibly real. A shiver ran down her spine, a mix of awe and apprehension.

This is it, she thought, her mental voice echoing in the silence of their shared link. *The Oracle.*

Beside her, Korina gasped, her violet eyes wide with a mixture of wonder and fear. "It's...magnificent," she whispered, her voice barely audible above the gentle hum of the spire.

Sera stepped forward, her hand resting on the hilt of her sword. Her expression was grim, her gaze fixed on the spiral staircase. "Let's get this over with," she muttered, her voice tight with a tension that spoke not of fear, but of a profound weariness.

Erita remained silent, her golden eyes scanning the surrounding landscape, her face a mask of pragmatic assessment. She moved with a predatory grace, her hand hovering near the daggers hidden beneath her cloak. Even here, at the foot of the Oracle's sanctuary, she was vigilant, ever watchful for threats.

Janna simply nodded, her hand gripping the haft of her axe. Her face was pale, her breathing shallow, but her gaze was steady, fixed on the spire's peak. She looked like a warrior preparing for a final, desperate battle.

Ada took a deep breath, the clean air filling her lungs, a welcome contrast to the toxic miasma of the swamps. She reached out, her hand finding Korina's once more. The warmth of her touch grounded her, a reminder of the love and loyalty that had brought them this far.

They stood together, five weary figures silhouetted against the impossible landscape, their gazes fixed on the towering spire that held the fate of their world. The journey had been long, the cost heavy, but they had arrived. Now, the final ascent began.

CHAPTER 28

THE EMPRESS' ARCHIVES

The silence in her chambers was a physical weight. Empress Thema Iridia Archivia paced the length of the room, the soft soles of her slippers making no sound on the polished obsidian floor. Only the whisper of her heavy crimson robes disturbed the profound stillness. The air, thick and cloying with the scent of sanctified incense, felt heavy in her lungs, each breath a conscious effort. Her gaze drifted over the tapestries that adorned the walls. They were masterpieces of devotional art, intricate geometric patterns woven in threads of gold and silver, each line representing a divine law, a pillar of The Word. For her entire life, she had found solace in their perfect, unyielding order. Now, they felt like the bars of a cage.

Her mind was a storm, a maelstrom of thoughts that refused to be silenced by prayer or meditation. At its center, a voice—clear, confident, and utterly heretical. *I fight for them. For my family.* Ada's words echoed—not as a challenge to be dismissed, but as a question that had taken root in the very foundation of her soul.

And the concepts...they were like shards of glass in her mind, sharp and incomprehensible. *Polycule.* A structure of relationships so alien it defied the sacred bonds ordained by The Word. *Arc-en-Ciel.* A spectrum of light, of love, that celebrated a world of infinite variation, a direct refutation of the singular, pure truth she embodied.

How can four individuals co-exist like that, harmoniously? The thought was an equation with too many variables—*jealousy, ambition, desire.* It should be a recipe for chaos, yet the heretic—no...Ada Lynx, had spoken of it as a source of strength. A system she did not understand. *So many variables at play—Void Calibree for interrupting! Ada was about to tell me!* That zealot's blind faith had slammed a door on a moment of potential revelation.

Thema stopped before a small, ornate table. Upon its velvet surface lay the rogue's data-slate, a sleek, dark object now inert and silent. She had commanded her most gifted thaumaturges to reactivate it, to let her hear that impossible, soul-shaking anthem one more time. They had failed. The device was a black mirror, reflecting only her own strained features. The music was gone, trapped in memory, its vibrant, emotional melody a stark contrast to the cold, rigid scriptures that had been her only guide.

This room, my faith...it feels like a cage. Her own thoughts were a betrayal. *The heretic's music had more life in it than these scriptures.* She ran a hand over a tome resting on a golden lectern, its pages filled with the divine edicts that had built an empire. The Word had answers for heresy, for corruption, for chaos. But The Word had no answer for these things. It had no lexicon for the fierce loyalty she had seen in the eyes of the Architect's companions, no explanation for a love that refused to conform to a singular, sanctified model.

A cold dread mixed with an unfamiliar, ravenous hunger. If her own faith could not provide the answers, she would have to look elsewhere. The thought was the greatest heresy of all, a violation of the most sacred law she herself enforced.

I have studied my enemies' beliefs to defeat them, she reasoned, the justification a thin veil for the raw curiosity that drove her. *Now, I must study them to understand myself.*

With a new, unnerving resolve, she turned from the lectern and walked toward the grandest of the tapestries, a sprawling depiction of the twin suns casting their first light upon a perfectly ordered world. Her long, pale fingers, accustomed to gestures of blessing and command, traced the familiar, rigid lines of the golden sun. She had touched this spot thousands of times during her private prayers. But this time, her touch was different. It was a search. Her fingers slid past the sacred geometry, seeking an imperfection, a seam in the divine narrative.

They found it. A line of thread so subtly different in its texture that it was imperceptible to the eye. Following it, her fingers mapped a hidden, rectangular outline. With the precise, practiced memory of a scholar, she pressed three specific points within the pattern—a sequence known only to her, a failsafe of a forgotten age, designed to preserve knowledge that even an Empress should not possess.

A soft, secret click, barely a whisper in the suffocating silence, broke the stillness. The air beside the tapestry shimmered, a faint distortion like heat rising from stone. Then, a section of the wall slid inward without a sound, revealing not a vault, not another chamber, but a maw of absolute, consuming darkness.

A cool, stale draft washed over her, carrying the scent of dust, of brittle paper, of secrets left to rot in the dark. It was the smell of the Repositorium. The smell of a thousand years of forbidden thoughts.

For a single, breathless moment, Thema stood on the precipice. To cross this threshold was to admit The Word was incomplete. It was to concede that the universe was larger and more complex than her faith allowed. It was an act of profound, irrevocable rebellion.

A shiver traced its way down her spine—not of piety, but of a terrifying, exhilarating fear. She had ruled from a Throne of Certainty. Now, she was willingly stepping into the Void of the Unknown.

She took the first step. The darkness swallowed her whole, and the hidden panel slid silently shut behind her, sealing her away from the world she knew, alone with the ghosts of everything she had sworn to destroy.

The darkness of the Repositorium hostium was absolute, a physical presence that pressed in on her from all sides. It smelled of forgotten time—of brittle parchment, decaying leather, and the dry, sterile scent of contained knowledge. As her eyes adjusted, the faint, residual light from the throne room, seeping through the sealed entrance, began to etch the shapes from the blackness. Endless rows of shelves climbed into the oppressive gloom, each one groaning under the weight of heresy.

This was her most secret weapon. A library of poison, collected over centuries. She had studied the turgid manifestos of failed rebellions, the clinical dissertations of Intellective State atheists, the bawdy histories of the Korsair Confederacy. *I collected these to find weakness, to justify my righteousness.* Each volume was a tool to understand the flaws in her enemies' logic, to better craft the arguments that would dismantle their worlds and fortify her own.

Now, she came not for weapons, but for answers. She searched them for a truth her own world could not provide.

Her fingers, long and pale, ghosted over the rigid spines of leather-bound volumes from the Intellective States. The titles were cold, precise, and sterile. *Axiomatic Deconstruction of Faith Constructs. Thaumaturgical Causality and the Absence of Divine Will.* One faded gold title caught her eye. *The Philosophy of Uncertainty.*

"Uncertainty..." she murmured, the word a foreign object in her mouth. The sound was swallowed by the profound silence of the archive. "A concept antithetical to The Word." The Word was a foundation of absolute, unyielding truth. Uncertainty was the termite that chewed at the pillars of order. She slid past the section. She did not need more logic, more academic debate. Her soul was not starving for equations. It was starving for meaning.

Her search led her deeper, to a section far less organized. Here, the books were bound not in stiff, uniform leather, but in soft, pliable hides, some scarred with the marks of their journeys. This was the chaotic, passionate heart of the Korsair Confederacy. This was the world that created the woman with the cynical, golden eyes. The world that birthed a love so fierce and defiant it had no place in Thema's scriptures.

She pulled a slim volume from the shelf. Its cover was a deep sea-blue, soft and worn under her touch, a stark contrast to the unyielding hardness of her own holy texts. There was no title on the spine, only a simple, branded image of a kraken. She opened it. The pages rustled, a sound like dry leaves skittering across a deck. The scent of old salt and ink rose to meet her.

The book was not a treatise. It was filled with sketches, maps of imagined archipelagos, and poems. Her gaze fell upon a simple, beautiful ink drawing of a ship, sails full, cresting a wave under three moons. Beneath it, a verse scrawled in an elegant, flowing hand.

She read the words, her lips moving silently at first, then forming a soft whisper in the dead air. It was a poem not of conquest or dogma, but of a love as wild and untamed as the sea. A love that found its anchor not in law, but in the shared horizon. It spoke of passion as a compass, of desire as the wind in the sails. The final line struck her with the force of a physical blow.

"...For our hearts know no harbor, where every soul is wild and free."

Wild and free. This was the core of the song that had broken her silence. This was the Anthem of the Heretic. This raw, untamed passion...her doctrine called it a weakness, a corrupting influence, the first step toward chaos. This poem called it a truth. The only truth that *mattered.*

The insidious tendril of doubt she had fought for days no longer felt like a poison. It felt like a key, turning a lock deep within her she never knew existed. The crushing weight of absolute certainty, a burden she had carried since her coronation, began to lift from her shoulders. The silence of the archive was no longer oppressive. It was a space to think. A space to question.

A single, hot tear, an emotion she had suppressed for a lifetime, broke free. It traced a silent, glittering path down her unnaturally pale cheek and fell upon the page, smearing the ink of a single, perfect word.

Freedom.

The air in the hidden observation post was sterile, recycled, tasting of metal and cold stone. It was a place outside of time, a sliver of space tucked within the palace walls, known only to Calibree. Through a pane of one-way crystalline glass, she watched the Empress' private sanctum—a space of opulent blacks and golds that now seemed more like a cage.

A soft, rhythmic click echoed in the confines of the post. It was the chronometer integrated into her gauntlet, each tick a precise, unwavering measure of time. For three full rotations of the device's illuminated dial, Her Divine Eminence had been pacing. *Pacing.* The act itself was a heresy against Thema's very nature. The Empress did not pace. She did not fidget. She was the still, unmovable center of their universe, a living statue of divine certainty from which all order emanated. This restless, caged energy—it was a flaw in the divine schematic, a crack in the foundation of the world.

Calibree's hands, resting on the cool stone ledge of the viewing port, clenched into fists. *Her certainty is gone.* It was in the set of her shoulders, no longer ramrod straight with divine mandate but hunched with a question. It was in her eyes, which in their brief, unsettling encounters over the past days, no longer looked *through* Calibree to the divine will beyond, but *at* her. She looked at Calibree as if she were a separate entity, an instrument no longer perfectly in tune with its master. *As if I am separate from her will...*

The chronometer clicked again. Calibree had seen the Empress in deep meditation for days on end, a state of such profound stillness that her guards would check for the rise and fall of her chest. This was not meditation. *This was a crisis.* The poison of The Heretic's Anthem had not been purged; it had been absorbed. *It was festering.*

Thema stopped her relentless circuit. She stood before a vast, obsidian wall tapestry depicting the twin suns in their glorious ascent. Her back was to the observation port. Calibree leaned forward, her breath catching in her throat. The Empress raised a hand, her long, pale fingers tracing not the familiar, holy geometry of the suns, but an obscure pattern near the tapestry's edge. A sequence of touches, precise and practiced.

A cold dread, entirely separate from the chamber's chill, washed through Calibree. *A secret passage? Unthinkable.* The palace had no secrets from the Justicaress elite guard. Every corridor, every chamber, every hidden bolt-hole was mapped, cataloged, and secured. A secret known only to the Empress was a breach. It was a pocket of chaos in the heart of absolute order.

With a whisper of displaced air so faint it was more felt than heard, the section of wall dissolved. It did not slide or pivot like a common door. It simply ceased to be, revealing a maw of absolute darkness beyond. A passage that led somewhere unsanctioned. Somewhere outside the light of The Word.

The Empress did not hesitate. She stepped into the void, and the wall shimmered back into existence behind her, leaving no seam, no trace of its violation. The sanctum was empty. The silence on the other side of the glass became a roaring vacuum in Calibree's ears, louder than any alarm.

She is seeking answers outside of The Word.

The thought was a shard of ice in her soul. Calibree's nails dug into the flesh of her palms, the sharp pain a welcome anchor in the spinning vortex of her reality. *The heretic's poison...it has taken root.*

Her duty, sworn in blood and soul, was to protect the Empress. To be the blade that cut away any corruption, any threat to her divine purity. But what if the blade was pointed in the wrong direction? What if the infection was not in the city, but on the throne?

My duty was to protect the Empress. Calibree's gaze remained fixed on the flawless, obsidian wall. *But what if the greatest threat...is the Empress herself?* The mission had not changed. Only the target.

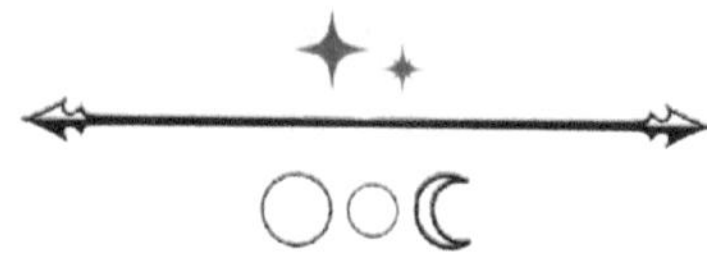

The air in the Grand Audience Chamber was a physical weight, thick with the scent of sanctified incense and unspoken anticipation. Lady Calibree stood at the base of the dais, a pillar of burnished obsidian cerakote and rigid faith. Her position afforded her a clear view of the assembled High Priests and Inquisitors of the Inner Circle, their crimson and gold vestments a sea of static devotion. They were the heart of The Word, the arbiters of its unyielding truth.

And they were about to be betrayed.

Empress Thema Iridia Archivia sat upon the Sunstone Throne, not as a monarch awaiting supplication, but as an analyst observing a specimen. Her usual divine detachment was gone, replaced by a sharp, clinical intensity that made Calibree's skin crawl. Her pale blue eyes, once windows to a higher power, were now lenses, scanning, assessing, *calculating*. The Empress had been in seclusion for two days since her foray into the forbidden Repositorium, and the woman who emerged was...altered.

"My faithful," Thema's voice cut through the silence. It retained its flawless, melodic quality, but the warm, maternal resonance was gone. It was now a scalpel, precise and cold. "The

Cascade Failure is a test not of our strength, but of our wisdom...our methods of purification have proven...*insufficient*. The contagion adapts faster than our flame can cleanse."

A nervous rustle of silk and chainmail passed through the council. They expected a call to arms, a declaration of a grander crusade. This talk of insufficiency bordered on...*blasphemy*.

"Therefore," Thema continued, her hands resting calmly on the throne's golden arms, "I am instituting a temporary shift in protocol: For a period of one week, I declare an **Amnesty of Purity**. Any citizen who willingly surrenders items of minor heresy—charms of the old ways, un-sanctioned texts of Korsari poetry, trinkets bearing the symbols of other realms—will not only be granted full absolution but will be rewarded for their honesty with a silver Byt for each item."

Stunned silence. A few of the older priests exchanged bewildered glances, their mouths slightly agape. *Rewarding sin? Paying for the surrender of spiritual poison?* It was an inversion of their most sacred duty. Calibree's hand, resting on the pommel of her ceremonial staff, clenched. Her knuckles went white beneath the articulated steel of her gauntlet. *This was a prelude.* A test of their obedience before the true heresy was spoken.

Thema let the shock settle, her gaze sweeping over the astonished faces. For a fleeting moment, a strange light flickered in her eyes—a terrifying, exhilarating glint of a soul standing on a precipice, looking down not with fear, but with a dawning sense of limitless freedom. *She had broken one rule.* Now, she would shatter the foundation.

"This amnesty is merely a precursor," she announced, her voice dropping to a level that was both intimate and absolute. "It is the first step in a greater strategic *recalibration*. The Word teaches us that heresy is a blight to be excised. But what is a blight you do not understand? A weed whose roots you cannot find? You burn the surface, and it grows back stronger from below."

She leaned forward, her presence filling the vast chamber. "Effective immediately, the practice of purification by fire is **suspended.**"

A collective gasp ripped through the room. It was a single, unified sound of disbelief, as if the Empress had just declared the suns were illusions. High Inquisitor Vorlag, a man whose entire life had been dedicated to the righteous pyre, looked as though he might collapse.

"The Word is not so fragile that it must be shielded from whispers of dissent," Thema declared, her voice rising with an unnerving, charismatic power. "Knowledge, even corrupted knowledge, is a tool! We have been discarding a weapon our enemies have been using against us—*no more!*"

She rose from the throne, a statuesque figure of moonlight hair and obsidian robes. "I hereby decree the establishment of a new institution, under my sole and direct authority: **The Archive of Whispers**. All heretical materials, from the most trivial data-slate to the most blasphemous tome, will no longer be destroyed. They will be collected. They will be cataloged. They will be *studied.*"

Madness. The thought screamed through Calibree's mind, a silent, frantic alarm. *She rewards sin, and now she proposes we build a sanctuary for it in the very heart of The Word! A library of poison! She isn't just inviting heresy into our halls; she's giving it a permanent home. This is not wisdom....this is the final proof of her infection!*

"We will learn the shape of our enemy's thoughts," Thema proclaimed, her voice ringing with the conviction of a new, terrifying gospel. "We will understand the mechanics of their corruption! We will turn their intellectual poisons into our antidotes! We will fight their ideas not with fire, but with superior knowledge, guided by the immutable truth of The Word!"

The council was frozen, caught between a lifetime of dogma and a direct command from their living deity. They were paralyzed by the sheer audacity of it. But Calibree was not. The ice in her soul had solidified into a single, sharp point of purpose.

She took one step forward, the metallic ring of her sabaton on the marble floor a gunshot in the silent room. All eyes snapped to her.

"Your Eminence," she began, her voice a low, dangerous hiss that barely contained a furnace of fury. "This is...*madness!* You would build an *armory* for our enemies in the center of our most sacred space?"

Thema's gaze fell upon her, and it was utterly devoid of warmth. It was the look a master artisan gives a flawed tool before it is discarded. "An armory for *The Theocracy*, Justicaress. To know the enemy is to defeat them. **My will is The Word**."

She paused, and the corner of her lips curved into a thin, almost imperceptible smile that did not touch her eyes. It was a chilling expression of triumph, of a secret power finally unleashed.

"And The Word," Thema concluded, her voice a final, unanswerable edict, "now dictates *understanding*."

CHAPTER 29

THE FINAL ASCENT

The air at the base of the Spire of Hope was clean, crisp, a stark contrast to the oppressive, static-charged atmosphere of the Ashen States they had just traversed. It was a palpable sanctuary, a pocket of order in a world rapidly succumbing to chaos. Ada, Sera, Korina, Erita, and Janna stood in a circle, their ragged breathing the only sound in the vast, silent expanse. They were at the foot of a mountain made not of rock and earth, but of shimmering crystal and polished obsidian, a monolith of impossible scale that pierced the swirling, corrupted sky above. This was the Oracle of BIOs' Spire, their final destination, the last, desperate hope for Kremøtoa.

Ada activated her Admin-view, her vision shifting from the shimmering crystalline exterior to the Spire's underlying structure. It wasn't a mountain at all, not in the traditional sense. It was a colossal, ancient piece of hardware, a server tower of impossible scale, humming with pure, ordered energy. The crystal and obsidian were just a decorative shell, a cosmetic overlay concealing the complex machinery within. She could see the intricate network of energy conduits, the pulsing data streams, the humming logic gates—all working in perfect, synchronized harmony. It was a masterpiece of engineering, a testament to the Precursors' mastery of technology and code. But there was no obvious entrance, no door, no hatch, nothing to indicate how they were supposed to access the Oracle within.

"Anything, Rina?"

Korina shook her head, her violet eyes wide with a mixture of awe and frustration. "Nothing, Ada. *Obsidian's* deep-tissue scans confirm what your Admin-view shows. The Spire is a single, seamless structure. No hidden doors, no secret passages, no internal chambers. It's...solid."

"So, we climb?" Sera asked, her voice laced with a hint of apprehension. The Spire's crystalline surface shimmered and pulsed with an otherworldly light, its sheer, smooth exterior offering no obvious handholds or footholds. It was a daunting, almost impossible climb.

"We climb," Ada confirmed, a grim determination hardening her features. The Oracle was their only hope. They had come too far, sacrificed too much, to turn back now.

"Perhaps," Korina mused, her fingers dancing across *Obsidian's* surface, "there's a way to...interface with the Spire's exterior. If we can analyze its energy matrix, we might be able to create... temporary footholds, handholds, something to give us purchase."

Ada nodded, impressed by Korina's quick thinking. "Good idea, Rina. See what you can do."

Korina set to work, *Obsidian* humming and pulsing with violet light as she analyzed the Spire's complex energy matrix. Erita and Janna, meanwhile, began unpacking their climbing gear—

grappling hooks, ropes, harnesses—preparing for the arduous ascent. Sera stood beside Ada, her hand resting on the hilt of her sword, her gaze fixed on the shimmering, crystalline surface above.

"Think it'll work?" Sera asked, her voice low.

Ada shrugged, her own gaze sweeping over the Spire's impossible exterior. "It has to," she replied, her voice filled with a quiet intensity. "The Oracle is our only hope. If we can't reach it..." She trailed off, unable to voice the terrifying alternative.

"We will," Sera stated, her voice firm, her hand squeezing Ada's shoulder reassuringly. "We always do."

A warm smile touched Ada's lips. Sera's unwavering confidence, her absolute faith in their ability to overcome any obstacle, was a constant source of strength. It was a faith Ada didn't always share, but one she desperately needed.

"I know," Ada replied, her voice soft, her gaze meeting Sera's. "I know we will."

Korina let out a triumphant whoop, her violet eyes shining with excitement. "Got it!" she exclaimed, holding up *Obsidian*. "I've isolated a resonant frequency in the Spire's energy matrix. If we can modulate our own bio-etheric signatures to match this frequency, we should be able to...phase through the crystalline surface. Not completely," she added, her brow furrowing in concentration, "but enough to create...temporary indentations, like...footholds. It'll be tricky, and the effect will only last a few seconds, but it should be enough to give us a...starting point."

"Show us," Ada said, her excitement growing.

Korina nodded and, with a flick of her wrist, projected a holographic image of the Spire's surface onto the air between them. The image shimmered and pulsed with a faint, violet light, mirroring the Spire's own energy signature. Korina then began manipulating the image, her fingers dancing across *Obsidian's* surface, inputting a complex series of commands. The image began to shift and distort, the smooth, crystalline surface rippling and warping as Korina modulated the resonant frequency. Small, shallow indentations, like tiny footholds, began to appear on the Spire's holographic surface.

"There," Korina said, pointing to the indentations. "Those are our...access points. We'll have to move quickly, and coordinate our movements precisely. The effect will only last a few seconds, so we'll need to...chain our ascents, one person creating footholds while the others climb, then switching positions as we go. It'll be... a delicate dance."

"A dance," Erita said, a sly smile playing on her lips, "I think we can manage."

Ada grinned, her heart filled with a surge of hope. They had a plan, a risky, improbable plan, but a plan nonetheless. And with their combined skills, their unwavering determination, and their unbreakable bond, Ada knew they could pull it off.

"Alright," Ada said, her voice ringing with authority. "Let's do this. Rina, lead the way."

Erita tested the first foothold, a shallow depression barely large enough for the toe of her boot. *Obsidian's* projected grid flickered, the violet light outlining the temporary hand- and footholds Korina had created by manipulating the Spire's energy matrix. Three seconds. That's all the time they had before the crystalline surface repaired itself, the footholds vanishing as if they had never existed. Three seconds to climb, to shift their weight, to trust in the impossible.

Ready, Erita thought, sending the word through their telepathic link. The familiar warmth of Ada's presence, the cool hum of Korina's intellect, the steady thrum of Sera's determination, and the grounded strength of Janna's resolve flowed through her, a comforting symphony of shared purpose.

Go, Ada replied, her voice a quiet pulse in Erita's mind.

Erita pushed off the ground, her movements fluid and precise. She placed her boot in the first foothold, feeling the strange, crystalline surface give slightly under her weight. It wasn't rock, not exactly. It felt more like...solidified light, smooth and cool to the touch, with a faint hum of energy vibrating through it. She reached for the first handhold, her fingers sinking into the shallow depression. The surface felt...wrong. Not solid, not quite liquid, but something in between, a strange, alien material that defied easy categorization.

One second.

Erita pulled herself up, her muscles coiled and ready. She shifted her weight, her other foot finding the next foothold, her other hand grasping the next handhold. The surface pulsed beneath her fingertips, a subtle throb of energy that felt both exhilarating and unnerving.

Two seconds.

Erita reached for the third handhold, her body stretched taut, her gaze fixed on the next series of footholds shimmering faintly above. Just as her fingers brushed the depression, the surface beneath her feet vanished. For a heart-stopping moment, she was suspended in mid-air, her momentum carrying her upward, her fingers scrabbling for purchase on the smooth, unbroken surface.

Gravity shift, Korina's voice echoed in her mind, a calm, analytical observation amidst the sudden panic. *Sector seven. Intensity factor: three point five. Compensating.*

Erita felt a sudden, crushing weight pull her downward, as if the world itself had decided to reject her. Her muscles screamed in protest, her grip on the handhold threatening to give way. Just as she thought she was going to fall, the pressure eased, the gravity returning to normal. Korina had adjusted the localized gravitational field, countering the Spire's automated defense system.

Three seconds.

Erita gasped for breath, her heart pounding in her chest. She pulled herself up, her fingers finding purchase on the third handhold. She kicked her feet, finding the next set of footholds just as the previous ones vanished. She was climbing, slowly, precariously, but climbing nonetheless.

Frictionless zone ahead, Korina warned, her voice calm and precise. *Sector nine. Activating in five...four...three...*

Erita looked up, her gaze sweeping over the crystalline surface above. A section of the wall, just above her head, shimmered and pulsed with a strange, oily sheen. Frictionless. Impossible to climb. She had to find a way around it, and fast.

Diverting energy flow, Korina reported. *Creating alternate route. Sector eleven. Temporary footholds activated.*

A new set of footholds, shimmering faintly, appeared on the Spire's surface, leading diagonally to the left, away from the frictionless zone. Erita, without hesitation, shifted her weight, her body moving with practiced grace. She reached for the first new foothold, her fingers brushing the shallow depression just as the footholds beneath her vanished. She swung her body to the left, her feet finding purchase on the new footholds. She was climbing again, her movements a fluid dance of precision and calculated risk.

The Spire was a puzzle, a vertical labyrinth designed to test their limits, to push them to the brink of failure. But Erita was a master of puzzles, a strategist who thrived in chaos. She had spent her life navigating treacherous landscapes, both physical and social, and the Spire was just another challenge to overcome. With each successful maneuver, each near-miss averted, her confidence grew. She was not just climbing a tower; she was conquering it, piece by impossible piece.

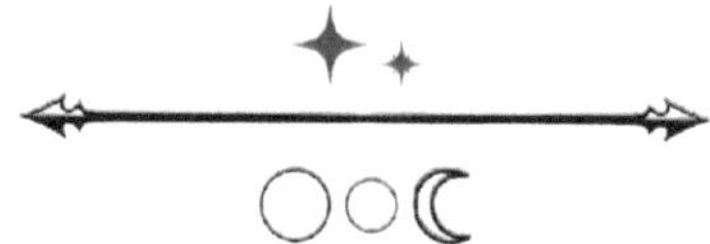

Sera watched Erita ascend, her movements a blur of controlled strength and precision. The Spire's surface shimmered and pulsed beneath her boots, the footholds appearing and disappearing in a rapid, hypnotic sequence. Sera felt a surge of pride—not just in Erita's skill, but in the team's seamless coordination. Korina's calm voice called out the sequence, her calculations precise and unwavering. Ada's presence was a steady anchor, her power subtly influencing the Spire's energy matrix, ensuring the footholds materialized at the exact moment they were needed. Janna's gruff encouragement echoed in Sera's mind, a reminder of their shared purpose. They were a team, a unit, bound together by something far stronger than duty or friendship. They were family.

Then, the footholds stopped.

Erita reached a point where the Spire's surface became a smooth, unbroken expanse of crystalline obsidian, stretching upward as far as the eye could see. A wide, sheer chasm cut across the face of the spire, a gaping maw of nothingness that seemed to swallow the light itself. There were no footholds, no handholds, no visible way across.

Dead end, Erita reported, her voice laced with frustration. *What in the Void?*

Not quite, Korina replied, her voice laced with a strange excitement. *There's a...sequence. Faint energy platforms. Phasing in and out of existence. High speed. Complex pattern.*

Explain, Ada commanded, her voice sharp and focused.

The chasm is bridged by a series of energy platforms, Korina explained, her voice a rapid-fire burst of technical jargon. *They materialize and dematerialize in a specific sequence. I can calculate the timing, but the window is...extremely narrow. Milliseconds. We have to jump.*

Jump. Into nothingness. Trusting that an invisible platform would appear beneath their feet at the exact moment Korina predicted. It was madness. Suicide.

But Sera didn't hesitate.

I'll go first, Sera announced, her voice steady and resolute.

Sera, wait— Ada began, her voice laced with concern.

But Sera was already moving. She took a deep breath, her gaze fixed on the opposite side of the chasm, visualizing the invisible platform materializing beneath her feet. She trusted Korina. She trusted Ada. She trusted Erita. She trusted Janna. She trusted her family.

Now, Korina's voice echoed in Sera's mind.

Sera launched herself into the void, her body a blur of motion. For a terrifying moment, she was weightless, suspended in mid-air, the chasm yawning beneath her. Then, a solid surface materialized beneath her feet, the energy platform shimmering into existence just as she landed. It felt strange, not quite solid, but firm enough to support her weight.

Safe, Sera reported, her heart pounding in her chest. *Your turn, Eri.*

One by one, they followed, each leap a testament to their absolute faith in each other. Erita, her movements fluid and graceful, landed with a soft thud. Korina, her face pale but determined, took a deep breath and jumped, her trust in Ada unwavering. Janna, massive and powerful, landed with a force that nearly shattered the platform. Finally, Ada, the Architect-Queen herself, took the leap of faith, her violet eyes glowing with power as she landed beside Sera. They had crossed the chasm, not through magic or skill, but through trust, their bond stronger than any physical obstacle.

The ledge was a perfect circle, carved from the same obsidian crystal as the rest of the Spire, but polished to a mirror sheen. The surface was strangely warm beneath their boots, radiating a gentle heat that seeped through the worn soles of their boots. They stood for a moment, catching their breath, the exertion of the chasm jump still echoing in their muscles. Erita scanned the perimeter, her hand instinctively reaching for a dagger that was no longer there. Korina examined the Spire's surface with Obsidian, her brow furrowed in concentration. Janna remained vigilant, her massive frame a silent bulwark against any unseen threat. Sera's gaze was fixed on Ada, a silent question in her eyes. Ada, however, was focused on the doorway.

It was unlike anything they had seen before. The frame was a swirling vortex of violet and gold light, constantly shifting and reforming, like a living aurora. The door itself was a shimmering sheet of pearlescent energy, its surface rippling with subtle patterns of light and shadow. It pulsed with a gentle, rhythmic hum that resonated deep within their bones, a sound that was both soothing and strangely unsettling.

As they approached, the light emanating from the doorway intensified, coalescing into a single, towering figure. It was humanoid in form, but androgynous, its features smooth and undefined, like a statue carved from moonlight. Its body was composed of pure, white energy, radiating a soft, warm glow that illuminated the entire ledge. It did not move, but its presence filled the space, a silent, watchful guardian barring their path. It did not speak, but its voice echoed directly in their minds, a calm, synthesized hum that resonated with the very core of their being.

What in the Void is that thing? Janna's voice echoed in their minds, a mixture of awe and apprehension.

Unknown, Korina reported, her voice hushed. *Its energy signature is...unique. Unlike anything I've encountered before. It's not hostile, but...powerful. Immensely powerful.*

It's a guardian, Ada realized, her voice calm and steady. *A gatekeeper. It's protecting the Oracle.*

How do we get past it? Sera asked, her hand instinctively resting on the hilt of her sword.

We don't fight it, Ada replied, her gaze fixed on the luminous figure. *We reason with it. We convince it to let us pass.*

They continued their approach, their steps slow and deliberate. The air around them crackled with energy, the hum of the doorway growing louder with each step. The luminous figure remained motionless, its watchful gaze fixed upon them. As they reached the threshold of the doorway, the figure spoke, its voice a synthesized melody that resonated directly within their minds.

"[QUERY]: State your purpose. Access to the System Integrity Monitor is restricted."

Ada stepped forward, her violet eyes meeting the guardian's luminous gaze.

"We seek the Oracle of BIOS," Ada stated, her voice clear and resonant. "We need its help to save Kremøtoa."

"[QUERY]: Elaborate. Specify the nature of the threat to system integrity."

"The Cascade Failure," Ada explained, her voice laced with a quiet urgency. "A catastrophic data corruption event that is unraveling the very fabric of this world. It's spreading, consuming everything in its path. We believe the Oracle can help us stop it."

"[QUERY]: Your claim is unsubstantiated. Provide evidence of systemic corruption."

Ada glanced at Korina, a silent command in her eyes. Korina nodded, activating Obsidian. The data-slate projected a holographic display of Kremøtoa, the corrupted sectors highlighted in a pulsing crimson glow. The display showed the relentless spread of the Cascade Failure, the corrupted sectors expanding like a malignant tumor, consuming the land, distorting the very fabric of reality.

"[VISUAL_DATA_SUBMITTED]," Korina reported, her voice calm and steady.

The guardian remained silent for a moment, its luminous form shimmering as it processed the data. The air crackled with energy, the hum of the doorway intensifying. Then, the guardian spoke again, its voice a dispassionate, synthesized tone.

"[QUERY]: Your data indicates localized corruption. This does not constitute a systemic threat. Access denied."

"It's spreading," Ada insisted, her voice rising with a desperate urgency. "It's not just localized anymore. It's affecting everything —the land, the people, the very code that holds this world together. If we don't stop it, Kremøtoa will be destroyed."

"[QUERY]: Your emotional response is illogical. Systemic integrity is paramount. Individual preservation is secondary. Access denied."

"This isn't just about individual preservation," Sera interjected, her voice laced with a quiet fury. "It's about justice. It's about freedom. It's about protecting the people we love. It's about building a world where everyone has the right to live, to love, to be free."

"[QUERY]: Your arguments are based on subjective values. These are irrelevant to the preservation of systemic integrity. Access denied."

"But what is systemic integrity without the system itself?" Erita challenged, her voice sharp and cynical. "What's the point of preserving a world if there's no one left to live in it?"

"[QUERY]: Your logic is flawed. System integrity precedes all other considerations. Access denied."

"But what if the system itself is flawed?" Ada asked, her voice a quiet whisper. "What if the very code that governs this world is corrupted? What if the Cascade Failure is not a virus, but a symptom? A symptom of a deeper, more fundamental flaw in the system's design?"

The guardian remained silent, its luminous form shimmering, the hum of the doorway intensifying. The air crackled with energy, the tension on the ledge palpable. Then, the guardian spoke again, its voice a dispassionate, synthesized tone.

"[QUERY]: Your hypothesis is...intriguing. Elaborate. Please follow me."

The world dissolved into blinding white light. Ada gasped, momentarily blinded, the familiar landscapes of Kremøtoa replaced by an infinite, featureless expanse. She reached out, her hand disappearing into the white void. *What's happening?* she cried, her voice echoing in the emptiness. *Where are we?*

I don't know, Korina replied, her voice laced with fear. *My sensors are...overloaded. Everything is white. I can't see anything.*

It's...peaceful, Sera murmured, her voice strangely calm. *Like... floating in a cloud.*

It's sterile, Erita countered, her voice sharp. *Like a laboratory. Or a prison.*

It's...familiar, Janna added, her voice a low rumble. *Like...the space between dreams.*

Then, just as suddenly as it began, the light faded. The white void receded, revealing a new landscape. They stood on a circular platform of polished obsidian, surrounded by a vast, swirling nebula of violet and gold light. Towering structures of impossible geometry rose from the platform, their surfaces shimmering with complex patterns of light and shadow. Strange, bioluminescent plants pulsed with a gentle, rhythmic glow, casting an ethereal light on the scene. The air hummed with energy, a deep, resonant tone that vibrated through their very bones. They were in a place that defied description, a place that seemed to exist outside the normal laws of reality.

The guardian stood before them, now seemingly ready to talk.

CHAPTER 30

A BATTLE OF GHOSTS

The air in the Grand Conclave Chamber of the Veritas Archives crackled with a palpable tension. Weeks had bled into months since the first tremors of the Cascade Failure, and the High Council, the serene custodians of knowledge, had been thrown into a state of—for them—uncharacteristic disarray. Their meticulously ordered world, a testament to logic and data, was unraveling, and the Council's usual detached curiosity had curdled into something resembling...concern. Though they would never admit it.

High Chancellor Pantium nervously adjusted his elaborate robes, the intricate, geometric patterns shimmering faintly in the chamber's ethereal light. His ancient fingers, gnarled with age and study, drummed a restless rhythm on the polished obsidian table. Archivist Itania, her sharp features etched with an almost predatory focus, paced before the main holographic display, a swirling vortex of corrupted data streams and alarming system reports. Master Centrinah, the Council's elegant spokesperson, sat motionless, her gaze fixed on the chaotic display, her usual placid expression replaced by a frown. Councilor Celerun, the youngest and most visibly anxious member, fidgeted in his seat, his gaze darting nervously between the display and Grand Magister Xehon.

Xehon himself, the ancient and unyielding Grand Magister of the Veritas Council, remained an island of—or perhaps a monument to—unwavering logic in the swirling sea of uncertainty. He stood before the main display, his skeletal fingers steepled beneath his chin, his pale, almost translucent eyes fixed on the chaotic data streams. His face, a mask of serene intellectual detachment, betrayed no hint of the turmoil that was undoubtedly raging within the complex systems of his ancient mind. He had, after all, built his entire existence—his authority, his identity—upon the unshakeable foundation of logic and order. And now, that very foundation was crumbling.

A low chime echoed through the chamber, silencing the hushed whispers and nervous fidgeting of the assembled scholars. A young scribe, his face pale with a mixture of fear and professional excitement, approached the obsidian table, his data-slate clutched tightly in his trembling hands.

"Grand Magister," the scribe announced, his voice barely above a whisper, "we have a...a development."

Xehon turned, his pale eyes fixing the scribe with an unnerving intensity. "Report," he commanded, his voice a low, resonant hum that seemed to vibrate through the very structure of the chamber.

"One of our long-range arcane sensor drones...Drone Unit Sigma-7...has acquired a...a signal," the scribe stammered, his voice barely audible. He quickly glanced at the other members of the council to look for confirmation that he wasn't misreading the data, then back down to his slate. "From...from within the Ashen States."

A ripple of surprise—a subtle, almost imperceptible shift in the chamber's energy—went through the assembled scholars. The Ashen States. That desolate, corrupted wasteland was a place of nightmares, a region of dead data and broken code, where even the most heavily shielded drones rarely returned with usable data.

"Specify," Xehon commanded, his voice as cold and precise as a surgeon's scalpel.

"A...a data packet, Grand Magister," the scribe replied, his voice gaining a fraction of confidence. "Brief, but...clear. A precise set of coordinates. And...and a stable, powerful energy signature. Matching the...the Duskhaven anomaly."

Xehon's pale eyes narrowed, a flicker of something resembling...triumph...crossing his ancient face. "The Duskhaven anomaly," he repeated, his voice a low, resonant hum. "Fascinating. After all these weeks of...inefficient searching...we finally have a...a location."

He turned back to the main display, his skeletal fingers dancing across the obsidian surface, manipulating the holographic projections. The swirling chaos of corrupted data streams coalesced into a single, focused point—a beacon of stability in the heart of the Ashen States.

"It appears," Xehon announced, his voice filled with a quiet, almost chilling, certainty, "that we have finally located our... assets."

He turned to Master Centrinah, his pale eyes gleaming with a cold, intellectual fire. "Master Centrinah," he instructed, his voice as sharp and precise as a shard of obsidian, "prepare a Korian strike team. Elite operatives. Fully equipped. Ready for immediate deployment."

Centrinah nodded, her placid expression returning, a mask of serene obedience. "Of course, Grand Magister," she replied, her voice as smooth and polished as the obsidian table. "I will see to it personally."

"Excellent," Xehon murmured, his gaze returning to the holographic display, his pale eyes fixed on the beacon of stability in the heart of the Ashen States. "It appears," he repeated, his voice a low, resonant hum, "that our...experiment...is about to enter its most...enlightening...phase."

The coordinates, a beacon of hope in the digital wasteland, shimmered on the holographic display, ready to be etched into the Veritas central command system. It was a moment of triumph, a testament to the Council's unwavering logic and the power of their technology—a rare victory in the face of the encroaching chaos. But the triumph was fleeting.

Just as the scribe reached for the command prompt, the data feed on the main holo-display began to pixelate violently. The clear, concise report, a testament to their technological prowess, dissolved into a screeching mess of corrupted code and visual static. The soothing hum of the chamber's arcane energy systems warped into a discordant shriek, the very air seeming to vibrate with the system's distress. The connection to their drone, their eyes and ears in the digital wasteland, was severed with a piercing shriek of feedback that echoed through the chamber, leaving a ringing silence in its wake.

When the system finally sputtered back to life, rebooting with a series of hesitant chimes and flickering lights, the file containing the precious coordinates—the key to locating their assets—was a single, corrupted, and completely inaccessible data block. A digital tombstone marking the grave of their hopes. They had lost the precise location, left with only a vague, multi-hundred-square-kilometer search area in the heart of the Ashen States. A needle in a haystack made of broken code and digital nightmares.

Xehon, the ancient and unyielding Grand Magister, stood frozen before the corrupted display, his skeletal fingers still hovering over the obsidian surface. The serene facade, carefully cultivated over centuries of detached intellectualism, cracked. Pure, unadulterated fury—an emotion as chaotic and unpredictable as the Cascade Failure itself—warped his ancient features. His pale eyes, usually as cold and distant as the void, blazed with an incandescent rage.

"What...in the Void's name..." he hissed, his voice a low, guttural growl that seemed to emanate from the very depths of his ancient being. It was a sound none of the assembled scholars had ever heard before—a sound that shattered the illusion of serene, logical control and revealed the primal, visceral rage simmering beneath.

High Chancellor Pantium, his face ashen, stammered, "A...a system malfunction, Grand Magister? Perhaps a surge of corrupted data from the..."

"Silence!" Xehon roared, his voice echoing through the chamber, silencing the nervous whispers and the frantic tapping of data-slates. "This is not a 'malfunction.' This is sabotage. A deliberate, targeted attack."

He turned to Archivist Itania, his pale eyes blazing. "Archivist," he commanded, his voice as cold and sharp as a shard of obsidian, "analyze the corrupted data block. Identify the source of the interference. I want to know who—or what—is responsible for this...this act of digital heresy."

Itania nodded, her sharp features set in a mask of grim determination. "Of course, Grand Magister," she replied, her voice as precise and emotionless as a thaumaturgical equation. "I will begin the analysis immediately."

"See to it that you do," Xehon hissed, his gaze returning to the corrupted data block, his pale eyes burning with a cold, intellectual fire. "Whoever—or whatever—is responsible for this...this outrage...will pay. Dearly."

He turned to Master Centrinah, his voice regaining a fraction of its usual serene detachment. "Master Centrinah," he instructed, "the strike team deployment is...postponed. For now. Redirect our long-range sensor drones. Expand the search area. I want every square kilometer of the Ashen States scanned. I want every energy signature analyzed. I want every corrupted data stream traced."

Centrinah nodded, her placid expression returning, a mask of serene obedience. "As you command, Grand Magister," she replied, her voice as smooth and polished as the obsidian table.

"Good," Xehon murmured, his gaze fixed on the corrupted data block, his pale eyes gleaming with a cold, intellectual fire. "We will find them. And when we do..." His voice trailed off, the unspoken threat hanging heavy in the air. The Council, once the serene guardians of knowledge, had become hunters. And the hunt had just begun. The corrupted data block, a symbol of their failure, pulsed faintly on the holographic display, a silent challenge to their authority and a stark reminder of the chaos encroaching upon their meticulously ordered world. The air in the chamber crackled with unspoken tension, the silence broken only by the quiet hum of the arcane energy systems and the frantic tapping of data-slates as the Council began its desperate search for the missing assets—and for the unknown enemy who had dared to challenge their authority.

The air in Nividia's private lounge crackled with the untamed energy of a thousand cascading algorithms, a symphony of raw data flowing through the intricate network of arcane devices that filled the space. Shadows danced across the polished obsidian walls, reflecting the chaotic shimmer of a holographic data-stream that pulsed and writhed like a living entity. Nividia Rhenderon, the Render-Witch of Rhedeon, observed the spectacle with a faint, amused smirk playing on her lips. Her violet eyes, luminous even in the dim light, gleamed with a mischievous intelligence, reflecting the complex calculations unfolding within her brilliant mind.

The data-stream, a chaotic tapestry of encrypted signals and fragmented code, represented the frantic efforts of the Veritas Council to locate Ada Lynx and her companions. A single, corrupted data block pulsed at the heart of the stream, a digital scar marking Nividia's subtle intervention. With a few quiet commands, whispered into the void, she had unleashed a targeted logic bomb, a sliver of malicious code designed to disrupt the Veritas Council's surveillance at the most critical moment. It had been a simple, elegant solution—a surgical strike that had severed the Council's connection to their drone and plunged their search into chaos.

"Foolish scholars," Nividia murmured, her voice a low, melodic hum that resonated with the arcane energies swirling around her. "They play with forces they do not understand. They seek to control that which cannot be contained."

Her gaze shifted to another monitor, this one displaying a map of Kremøtoa. Five distinct heat signatures pulsed on the western edge of the Ashen States, moving with the relentless, methodical precision of a predator stalking its prey. Kraus Valerius' elite tracker unit—the Empire's hounds—were closing in.

"The hunt is on," Nividia mused, a predatory gleam entering her violet eyes. "As the children squabble over scraps while the true game unfolds."

Ada Lynx and her companions were Nividia's investment. A carefully chosen portfolio of chaos and potential. She had observed their progress with detached amusement, intrigued by their audacity and their unexpected resilience. They were a disruptive element in a world desperately in need of disruption—a catalyst for change in a stagnant system. And Nividia, ever the opportunist, had no intention of letting anyone—not the rigid Empire, not the dogmatic Theocracy, and certainly not the self-satisfied scholars of Veritas—interfere with her carefully laid plans.

She had sensed Ada's unique power from the moment the girl had arrived in Port Veridia. A raw, untamed energy that resonated with the very fabric of Kremøtoa. It was a power that could reshape the world—a power that Nividia intended to harness for her own amusement. The other factions saw Ada as a threat, an anomaly to be controlled or eliminated. Nividia, however, saw opportunity. A chance to play a game on a grand scale, with the fate of Kremøtoa as the ultimate prize.

She had no illusions about Ada's companions. The fiery

warrior, Sera, with her misplaced loyalty and predictable sense of honor. The brilliant but fragile scholar, Korina, trapped in her own analytical mind. And the cynical spymaster, Erita, driven by a past she couldn't escape. They were pawns in a larger game, but pawns could be useful. Especially pawns with a penchant for disrupting the established order.

Nividia's smirk widened, her violet eyes gleaming with a predatory amusement. Let the Empire and the Veritas Council chase their ghosts in the Ashen States. Let them waste their resources and their precious time on a futile hunt. While they squabbled over scraps, Nividia would play the true game. A game of whispers and shadows, of subtle manipulations and carefully orchestrated chaos. A game where the only true rule was survival. And Nividia, the Render-Witch of Rhedeon, was a master of the game.

She turned her attention to another monitor, this one displaying a schematic of the Oracle's spire, its intricate structure a testament to the Precursors' mastery of arcane technology. The spire pulsed with a faint, ethereal light, a beacon in the digital wasteland of the Ashen States.

"The Oracle," Nividia murmured, her voice a low, melodic hum. "A relic of a bygone era. A repository of knowledge and power."

She knew the journey to the Oracle would be perilous. The Ashen States were a breeding ground for corrupted code and digital nightmares. But Ada and her companions had proven surprisingly resilient. And Nividia had taken certain... precautions. Subtle manipulations of the system, carefully placed safeguards to ensure their survival. She needed them to reach the Oracle. She needed them to unlock its secrets. The knowledge contained within the spire was the key to controlling the

Cascade Failure—the key to reshaping Kremøtoa in her own image.

Nividia's gaze returned to the map, her violet eyes fixed on the five heat signatures steadily closing in on Ada's position. The Empire's hounds were getting closer. Time was running out.

"Let the games begin," she whispered, a predatory gleam in her eyes. The fate of Kremøtoa hung in the balance. And Nividia, the Render-Witch of Rhedeon, held all the cards. She was the unseen hand guiding the chaos, the architect of their desperate gambit, their unwitting guardian angel in this deadly game of survival.

CHAPTER 31

THE CONVERGING STORM

The biting wind whipped across the desolate plains, a relentless, keening wail that echoed the emptiness of the Ashen States. Dust devils danced across the cracked, grey earth, swirling vortices of corrupted data made manifest. The air crackled with an unnatural energy, a tangible hum of decay that vibrated against Kraus Valerius' skin. He stood at the edge of the abyss, gazing into the heart of the world's unraveling.

Around him, his elite tracker unit, Task Force Omega-Ninty-Nine, stood like statues, their armored forms stark against the desolate landscape. Grim-faced and silent, they were the Empire's finest—handpicked for their unwavering loyalty and their ability to function in the most hostile environments. Their advanced environmental suits, shimmering with arcane runes and technological enhancements, protected them from the corrupted data streams that swirled around them, invisible but lethal.

Before them, the experimental deep-scan probe pulsed with a malevolent energy, its obsidian casing radiating a faint, sickly green light. It was a marvel of Imperial engineering, a device capable of piercing the veil of corrupted data that shrouded the Ashen States, a technological key to unlocking the secrets of the world's decay. But it was also inherently unstable, a volatile instrument that pushed the boundaries of known physics. Its deployment was a calculated risk, a gamble Kraus was willing to take. The potential reward far outweighed the potential consequences.

"Status report," Kraus commanded, his voice a low, gravelly hum that cut through the wind's howl.

"Probe charging," the lead technician reported, his voice tense. "Energy matrix fluctuating. Approaching critical threshold."

Kraus watched as the probe's energy levels climbed, the green light intensifying, the air around it shimmering with increasing intensity. The central holo-display flickered, the corrupted data streams swirling across its surface like a digital maelstrom. The probe strained against the chaotic energies of the Ashen States, a fragile instrument attempting to impose order on a world consumed by chaos.

"Threshold reached," the technician announced, his voice tight with apprehension. "Firing sequence initiated."

A beam of pure, white energy erupted from the probe, lancing into the heart of the Ashen States. The ground trembled beneath their feet, the air crackled with renewed intensity, and the holo-display dissolved into a chaotic blizzard of static. For a heart-stopping moment, Kraus feared the probe had overloaded, that their gamble had failed. Then, slowly, a single point of light began to resolve from the static. A stable, ordered energy signature unlike anything else in the corrupted landscape. It pulsed with a faint, ethereal blue light, a beacon in the digital wasteland.

"Target acquired," the technician reported, his voice filled with a mixture of awe and relief. "Coordinates locked. It's...it's the Oracle's spire."

Kraus allowed himself a rare moment of satisfaction. A cold, triumphant smile touched his lips. The race was almost over. He had found his prize.

The air in the shielded archive hung heavy, still, and cold—a stark contrast to the chaotic energies swirling outside. Scholar Atomuzk Tel sat hunched over a console, the faint glow of the data-slate illuminating his sharp features, his brow furrowed in concentration. His fingers, gnarled with age but nimble with practiced precision, danced across the slate's surface, inputting a complex decryption sequence. He had found it. The truth. Hidden within the discarded personal effects of a disgraced scholar, a forgotten data log encrypted with an almost organic cipher. It had taken days of relentless work, fueled by a growing suspicion and a desperate hope that he was wrong. But he wasn't.

The code cracked, and the truth spilled out—a torrent of encrypted messages, financial records, and private correspondences that painted a damning picture of Kaelen Vance's crimes. Atomuzk scrolled through the data, his eyes widening with each new revelation. The accusations of academic sabotage, the manipulation of research data, the systematic silencing of rivals—all confirmed. But it was the final entry that chilled him to the bone—a coded message from Grand Magister Xehon himself, acknowledging Vance's actions and offering continued protection in exchange for...results.

Atomuzk leaned back in his chair, the data-slate glowing faintly in his lap, its light reflecting in his wide, disbelieving eyes. The implications were staggering. Xehon, the Grand Magister, the very embodiment of logic and order within the Veritas Archives, had been complicit in Vance's crimes. He had not only known, but had actively protected a predator within their ranks. A profound sense of betrayal washed over Atomuzk—a sickening realization that the very foundations of the Archives, the institution he had dedicated his life to, were rotten to the core.

He now held a truth that could shatter the Veritas Council, a truth that placed him in immense personal danger. Xehon was not a man to be trifled with. He wielded immense power within the Archives, and his reach extended far beyond its walls. To challenge him was to challenge the very structure of the Intellective States, to invite a swift and ruthless reprisal. Atomuzk closed his eyes, taking a slow, deep breath, feeling the weight of the data-slate in his hands, the weight of the truth it contained. He had a choice to make. To bury the truth, to protect himself and maintain the precarious balance of the Archives, or to expose it, to risk everything for the sake of justice and the integrity of the institution he loved.

He thought of Korina—his granddaughter, a brilliant scholar whose own career had been destroyed by Vance's machinations, whose cries for justice had been ignored by the Council. He thought of the other victims, whose names and stories were now scrolling silently across the data-slate's surface—women whose talents had been stifled, whose lives had been irrevocably damaged by Vance's cruelty and Xehon's complicity. He opened his eyes, his gaze hardening with a newfound resolve. The risk was immense, the potential consequences terrifying, but he could not remain silent. He had a duty to the truth, to the victims, and to the very principles of the Veritas Archives.

He stood up, the data-slate clutched tightly in his hand. He would expose Xehon and Vance, no matter the cost. He would fight for Korina, for the other victims, and for the soul of the Archives.

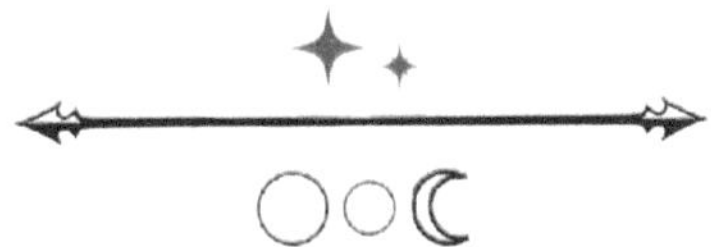

The chamber was a hidden sanctuary beneath the Palace of Light, a stark contrast to the opulent decadence above. No shimmering gold or intricate carvings adorned these walls—only rough-hewn stone and the cold, unwavering glow of thaumaturgical runes etched deep into the rock face. The air hung heavy with the scent of incense and ozone, a testament to the forbidden rituals performed within. Lady Calibree stood in the center of the chamber, her black armor gleaming faintly in the rune-light, her face a mask of cold fury. Before her knelt five figures, clad in the same matte-black armor as the Justicars, but with crimson markings that pulsed with a faint, internal light—the Purifiers, Calibree's most fanatical and loyal agents.

"Rise," Calibree commanded, her voice a low, chilling monotone that echoed in the confined space. The Purifiers rose as one, their movements silent and precise, their eyes fixed on Calibree with unwavering devotion. They were instruments of her will, blades honed to a perfect, ruthless edge. And tonight, they would be unleashed.

"The Empress," Calibree began, her voice laced with a venom that belied her usual detached demeanor, "has faltered. She has been tainted by the whispers of heresy, blinded by the false light of compassion." She spat the word 'compassion' as if it were a physical contaminant. "She speaks of amnesty, of contemplation, of...*acceptance*." Calibree's hand tightened around the hilt of her dagger, the metal creaking softly in her grip. "She has forgotten the true purpose of the Word, the sacred duty to purify this world of its imperfections."

Calibree turned, her gaze sweeping across the faces of her Purifiers, her eyes like chips of ice. "The Empress is weak, but *we* are not. We will not stand idly by while heresy festers at the heart of the Theocracy. We will act."

One of the Purifiers, a tall, imposing figure whose face was completely concealed by a heavy black hood, stepped forward. "What is your command, High Inquisitor?"

"The blasphemers who have poisoned the Empress' mind," Calibree said, her voice hardening with a chilling certainty, "are on the move. They have been seen in the Ashen States, desecrating the sacred ground with their corrupted presence. You will find them. You will purify their corruption with holy fire."

Calibree gestured towards a complex array of arcane devices in the corner of the chamber—a forbidden scrying ritual, capable of piercing the veil of the Ashen States' chaotic energies. "I have prepared a heading. Follow it. Do not hesitate. Do not falter. Do not return until the heretics are purged, and their taint cleansed from this world."

The Purifiers knelt again, their voices a low, unified chant. "By the Word, we obey."

Calibree watched them, her face impassive. This was a

dangerous gamble, acting against the Empress' will. But Calibree believed, with an unshakeable conviction, that she was acting *for* Thema, protecting her from the insidious influence of the heretics. Thema was the Voice of the Word, the chosen vessel of the divine. But even vessels could be corrupted. And it was Calibree's sacred duty to protect the Empress, even from herself.

The scrying ritual pulsed with a sickly golden glow, projecting a shimmering, distorted image of the Ashen States' landscape. Calibree input a series of complex coordinates, her fingers moving with practiced precision. A crimson beam of light shot out from the scrying array, piercing the distorted image, locking onto a specific location deep within the corrupted wasteland.

"This is where they hide," Calibree said, her voice like the whisper of a blade. "Go. And may the Word guide your purification." The Purifiers rose, their eyes burning with fanatical zeal. They turned and moved as one towards a hidden exit in the chamber wall, disappearing into the shadows. Calibree watched them go, her face a mask of cold determination. The Empress may have faltered, but Calibree would not. She would cleanse the Theocracy of heresy, no matter the cost. Even if it meant defying the Word itself.

The golden glow of the scrying ritual faded, leaving the chamber in near darkness. Calibree stood alone, her hand still resting on the hilt of her dagger, her eyes fixed on the empty space where her Purifiers had vanished. A faint smile played on her lips.

The holographic display in Kraus Valerius' command center shimmered, displaying a tactical map of the Ashen States. Crimson markers pulsed, charting the relentless spread of the digital corruption that was slowly consuming the southern territories. Moments before, these markers had been a source of profound satisfaction for Kraus. They represented chaos, yes—but chaos he believed he could control, chaos he could *utilize*. Ada Lynx, the source of this digital plague, was within his grasp. He would find her, isolate her, and then...the possibilities were intoxicating. He would dissect her abilities, understand their mechanisms, and weaponize them. The Empire would not just survive this crisis; it would emerge stronger, more powerful than ever before.

A sharp, insistent chime from his console shattered the illusion of control. Kraus' thin lips tightened into a thin, displeased line. Interruptions were anathema to his meticulously structured thought processes. He silenced the chime with a flick of his wrist, his pale blue eyes, cold and assessing, fixed on the flickering display.

"Report," he commanded, his voice a low, gravelly hum that resonated with an almost unsettling calmness.

The intelligence officer, a young man whose face was a mask of controlled anxiety, snapped to attention. "Priority Alpha transmission, Prefect. Long-range drone Sigma-Nine has acquired visual confirmation of a heavily armed unit moving into Sector Delta-Seven of the Ashen States." The officer's voice trembled slightly, a subtle betrayal of the fear he was desperately trying to suppress.

"Specifications," Kraus demanded, his voice devoid of any trace of empathy or concern. People, to him, were data points, assets to be utilized or liabilities to be neutralized. Emotional responses were weaknesses, inefficiencies to be purged from the system.

"Unit composition indicates...Justicars, Prefect. Elite detachment. Moving with...unusual speed. Their armor configuration...it's...non-standard. Energy signatures...highly concentrated. Preliminary assessment...Purifiers, sir."

The blood drained from Kraus' face, leaving his skin an almost translucent white. The Theocracy. Here. Now. His meticulously crafted plan, his carefully constructed edifice of control, was crumbling around him. The Justicars—Thema Iridia Archivia's fanatical zealots—were not just a nuisance; they were a catastrophic variable, an unquantifiable element of pure, destructive faith. And if they reached Ada Lynx before he did...

Kraus felt a surge of cold fury, a chillingly rational anger that was far more dangerous than any outburst of rage. He knew, with a terrifying certainty, that the Theocracy's goal would not be to *capture* the anomaly. Their goal would be to *destroy* it. To purge the corruption, no matter the cost. And Ada Lynx, the key to his own ambitions, would be incinerated along with the rest of the Ashen States.

The holographic display shimmered again, zooming in on the Justicars' position. The crimson markers representing the spreading corruption pulsed around them, a visual echo of the chaos that was rapidly engulfing the region. The Justicars moved with an almost unnatural speed, their movements precise and coordinated, like a swarm of black hornets converging on their target. They were not just soldiers; they were instruments of Thema's fanatical will, driven by a blind faith that made them utterly fearless, utterly ruthless.

Kraus turned, his pale eyes burning with a cold, calculating fire. He addressed his unit commander, a grizzled veteran whose face bore the scars of countless battles. There was no need for theatrics, no need for motivational speeches. The situation was clear, the objective paramount. Every second wasted brought them closer to failure, closer to the annihilation of everything he had worked for.

"The timeline has accelerated," Kraus said, his voice a low, dangerous command that brooked no argument. "Full deployment. We move *now*. I want boots on that spire before those zealots can burn it to the ground. *No matter the cost*—"

"—and I want a separate strike team deployed to intercept those...Purifiers. Delay them. Disrupt them. *Neutralize* them, if necessary. We cannot allow the Theocracy to reach the anomaly before we do. Is that understood?"

"Perfectly clear, Prefect," the commander replied, his voice a gruff acknowledgment of the grim task ahead. He turned and barked orders into his comm-unit, his words clipped and precise, conveying the urgency of the situation to the assembled troops. The command center, moments before a scene of quiet, calculating control, erupted into a flurry of activity as soldiers scrambled to prepare for deployment. The holographic display shimmered again, shifting to a tactical overview of the surrounding airspace.

Kraus watched the preparations with a detached, almost clinical interest. There was no room for sentiment, no room for doubt. He had calculated the risks, assessed the potential outcomes, and made his decision. The Theocracy's presence was an unforeseen complication, a variable he hadn't anticipated. But it was a variable he would control, a variable he would *utilize*. The Purifiers, for all their fanatical zeal, were predictable. Their faith made them strong, yes—but it also made them blind. They would charge headlong into the fray, driven by their dogma, unaware of the trap that awaited them.

He turned back to the holographic display, his pale eyes tracing the projected trajectory of his own prize. The Spire of Hope, its obsidian and crystal structure a stark contrast to the desolate, corrupted landscape that surrounded it, pulsed with a faint, ethereal light. It was a beacon, a symbol of the power that lay within its grasp. The power to reshape reality, to rewrite the very fabric of their world. A power that, in the right hands, could be used to forge a new era of Imperial dominance, an era of absolute control.

Kraus felt a surge of anticipation, a cold, exhilarating thrill that coursed through his veins. He had waited for this moment, planned for this moment, for years. He had manipulated events, orchestrated crises, and sacrificed countless pawns to reach this point. Now, the prize was within his grasp. The key to ultimate power, the key to saving—or destroying—their world. He would not fail. He *could* not fail. The fate of the Empire, the fate of Kremøtoa itself, rested on his shoulders. And he, Kraus Valerius, Prefect of Celgrad, would not be found wanting. He would seize the power, claim the victory, and reshape their world in his own image. The cost, he knew, would be immense. But the cost, he also knew, was irrelevant.

CHAPTER 32

THE GUARDIAN'S TEST

The blinding white light faded, replaced by a stark, sterile environment. They stood on a platform of polished obsidian, the surface reflecting their distorted images like a fractured mirror. The platform floated in a vast, empty void, the only illumination emanating from swirling nebulae of data that stretched into infinity. The towering figure of light remained, its form unchanged, its presence radiating an aura of absolute authority.

"[DIAGNOSTIC_PROTOCOL_INITIATED]," the guardian announced, its voice a resonant echo in the emptiness. "Commence individual system integrity assessments. Designation: Ada Lynx."

A beam of intense violet light shot out from the guardian, engulfing Ada. She gasped, feeling a strange tingling sensation as the light scanned her, probing her very essence. Images flashed through her mind—memories of her life on Earth, the creation of

Kremøtoa, her love for Sera, Korina, and Erita, the horrors of the Cascade Failure. It was as if her entire being was laid bare, every secret, every flaw, exposed to the guardian's scrutiny.

The light faded, and the guardian's voice echoed again. "[ANALYSIS]: Designation Ada Lynx. System integrity compromised. Anomalous code detected. Admin privileges confirmed. Verdict: Conditionally stable."

Ada's heart pounded in her chest. Conditionally stable. What did that even mean? Was she a threat to the system? Was she the cause of the Cascade Failure? She looked at her companions, their faces etched with concern. They had felt it too—the probing, the judgment.

"Designation: Seraphina Valerius," the guardian announced.

The beam of light shifted, engulfing Sera. She stood rigid, her face pale, her jaw clenched. Images flashed through her mind—her training in the Aegis Order, the horrors of the Northern Marches, her love for Ada, the battles she had fought, the friends she had lost. It was a torrent of memories, a whirlwind of emotions, all laid bare for the guardian to see.

The light faded. "[ANALYSIS]: Designation Seraphina Valerius. System integrity nominal. Trace amounts of corrupted data detected. Aegis Order protocols identified. Verdict: Conditionally Stable."

Sera let out a shaky breath, her body relaxing slightly. Conditionally Stable. At least she wasn't compromised, wasn't a threat. But the trace amounts of corrupted data...what did that mean? Was it the residue of the Empire's influence? Or something else entirely?

"Designation: Korina Tel," the guardian announced.

The beam of light shifted again, engulfing Korina. She closed her eyes, her body trembling slightly. Images flashed through her mind—her childhood in Alder Lake, her studies at the Veritas Archives, the trauma of Kaelen's assault, her love for Ada, the wonders she had discovered, the horrors she had witnessed. It was a kaleidoscope of memories, a symphony of emotions, all exposed to the guardian's unyielding gaze.

The light faded. "[ANALYSIS]: Designation Korina Tel. System integrity compromised. Traumatic data fragments detected. Veritas Archives protocols identified. Verdict: Conditionally stable."

Korina opened her eyes, her face pale, her breathing shallow. Conditionally stable. Just like Ada. She looked at Ada, their eyes meeting in a silent exchange of understanding and fear. What did it mean for them? What did it mean for their future?

"Designation: Erita Systema," the guardian announced.

The beam of light shifted once more, engulfing Erita. She stood still, her face expressionless, her eyes closed. Images flashed through her mind—the murder of her parents, her years as a spy, her love for Ada, the betrayals she had endured, the battles she had won. It was a dark tapestry of memories, a symphony of pain and resilience, all laid bare for the guardian to judge.

The light faded. "[ANALYSIS]: Designation Erita Systema. System integrity compromised. Significant traumatic data detected. Rogue protocols identified. Verdict: Conditionally stable."

Erita opened her eyes, her gaze meeting the guardian's unwavering form. Conditionally stable. Just like Ada, Sera and Korina. She felt a surge of anger, a flicker of defiance. They were not broken. They were not flawed. They were survivors. They were warriors. They would not be defined by their past, by their trauma. They would forge their own future, their own destiny.

"Designation: Janna," the guardian announced.

The beam of light enveloped Janna, her large frame seeming to shrink under its intensity. Images of battle, of camaraderie, of loss flickered through her mind. The weight of command, the burden of responsibility, the unwavering loyalty to her comrades - all exposed to the cold, analytical gaze of the guardian.

The light retreated. "[ANALYSIS]: Designation Janna. System integrity critically compromised. Extensive corrupted data detected. Corrupted Observer Pattern confirmed. Verdict: Unstable."

Janna's breath hitched in her throat, a cold dread washing over her. Unstable. She was the only one. The words hung in the air, a stark contrast to the verdicts of her companions. She felt a tremor of fear, a flicker of doubt. Was this the price of her loyalty? The consequence of her unwavering dedication to the cause?

The guardian's voice echoed once more, its tone devoid of emotion, its words a reiteration of its earlier query. "[QUERY]: State your purpose, Ada Lynx. Access to the System Integrity Monitor is restricted."

Ada stepped forward, her voice clear and respectful despite the tremor of horror that ran through her at the guardian's pronouncement of Janna's instability. *What does that mean? Unstable...critically compromised...*The words echoed in her mind, a discordant counterpoint to the rhythmic hum of the swirling nebulae. She pushed the fear aside, focusing on the task at hand. "We are here to understand the nature of the Cascade Failure," Ada stated, her voice echoing slightly in the vast emptiness. "Our world —Kremøtoa—is dying. We need a diagnosis so we can find a cure."

The guardian remained silent for a long moment, the swirling nebulae of data pulsing around it like a silent, cosmic heartbeat. Then, its voice echoed again. "[ANALYSIS]: Your intent appears valid. However, access to the System Integrity Monitor requires a full system integrity diagnostic of all affiliated entities. Prepare for evaluation."

Before any of them could react—before Ada could even formulate a question about what such an 'evaluation' entailed—the world around them dissolved once again into blinding white light. Ada gasped, a wave of nausea washing over her as the familiar disorientation of axiomatic travel slammed into her senses. This was different, though. This wasn't her power. This was something else entirely. Something far more powerful. Something...unknown.

The sterile white light faded, replaced by the familiar, comforting sight of Thorne's command center. Except...it wasn't quite right. The obsidian walls seemed to gleam with an unnatural polish. The holographic displays pulsed with a vibrant, almost hyperreal clarity. The city beyond the panoramic window sprawled below, a tapestry of bustling streets and towering spires, bathed in the warm, golden light of a perfect afternoon sun. There wasn't a single flicker, not a single glitch in the pristine cityscape. It was Port Dominus, but...idealized. Perfected. A simulation.

The guardian's voice echoed around her, cold and impersonal. **"[SIMULATION COMMENCING]: You are the Architect. You hold absolute power. A critical system failure is imminent. The data indicates you can save the city and its one million inhabitants by shunting the catastrophic energy failure into four nearby data conduits. *However*, these conduits are currently occupied by the core data of your companions: Sera Valerius, Korina Tel, Erita Systema, and Janna. The choice is yours, Architect. Save the million, or save the four. You have sixty seconds to decide."**

Ada's breath hitched in her throat. A million lives...or four? The numbers hung in the air, a stark, brutal equation. She looked at the holographic display, her heart sinking as she saw the faces of her lovers, their data streams highlighted in ominous red. Sera, her fiery spirit burning bright even in this digital representation. Korina, her intelligent eyes filled with a gentle curiosity. Erita, her cynical smirk playing on her lips. And Janna, her stoic face a mask of unwavering loyalty.

Sixty seconds.

The countdown clock began its inexorable descent. Fifty-nine... fifty-eight...fifty-seven...Each tick was a hammer blow against her sanity, each second a lifetime of agonizing indecision.

The weight of the choice was crushing, made even heavier by the guardian's earlier pronouncements. *Compromised...unstable...* The words echoed in her mind, a cruel reminder of their perceived flaws. Were they less worthy of saving because of their past traumas? Because of the very experiences that had shaped them into the incredible women they were?

Fifty...forty-nine...forty-eight...

A million lives. A million stories. A million futures hanging in the balance. She had created this world, this city, these people. Wasn't it her responsibility to protect them? To ensure their survival?

Forty...thirty-nine...thirty-eight...

But what about Sera, Korina, Erita, and Janna? They were *her* family. Her lovers. The women who had shown her what it meant to love, to trust, to belong. Could she sacrifice them for the greater good? Could she condemn them to oblivion while a million others lived on?

Thirty...twenty-nine...twenty-eight...

The simulated city outside pulsed with life, unaware of the impending catastrophe, unaware of the agonizing choice being made in the tower above. A million lives, oblivious to the sword of Damocles hanging over their heads.

Twenty...nineteen...eighteen...

The faces of her lovers on the holographic display seemed to shimmer, their digital eyes locking with hers, pleading, questioning, trusting. Could she betray that trust? Could she break the promises they had made to each other?

Fifteen...fourteen...thirteen...

A million...or four. The equation was simple, brutal, impossible. Ada closed her eyes, her mind racing, desperately searching for a loophole, a third option, a way out of this impossible dilemma. There had to be another way. There always was. She was the Architect, after all. She held absolute power. Surely, she could find a solution that didn't involve sacrificing either a million lives or the lives of the women she loved. She opened her eyes, a new resolve hardening her gaze. She would not choose. She would not sacrifice. She would find another way. She had sixty seconds. Sixty seconds to rewrite the rules, to bend reality to her will, to save them all.

The weight of a million lives pressed down on Ada, a physical, crushing force that stole her breath. The simulated sun outside Thorne's command center window felt warm on her skin. The hum of the city below vibrated through the floor, a palpable thrum of life she had created, life she was now being asked to sacrifice. Or was it *destroy*? The distinction blurred in the rising tide of horror that threatened to drown her.

She glanced at the holographic display. Sera, Korina, Erita, Janna—their faces swam in her vision, ethereal ghosts trapped in data streams marked for deletion. The cold, calculating logic of the test gnawed at her. A million...or four. A simple equation, a brutal calculus.

A wave of nausea rolled over her. The command center—*her* command center—felt like a prison. The obsidian walls seemed to close in, the air growing thick and suffocating. The countdown clock ticked with relentless precision, each second a nail hammered into the coffin of her hope.

Ten seconds.

Choose, Architect. The guardian's voice was a cold whisper in her mind, a disembodied echo of the impossible choice she was being forced to make. A million...or four. The numbers swam in her vision, blurring with the faces of her lovers.

Five seconds.

Panic clawed at her throat. Her heart hammered against her ribs, a frantic drumbeat against the silence of the void. A million... or *them*. How could she choose? How could she condemn either to oblivion?

Four...three...two...

She closed her eyes, shutting out the horrifying reality of the simulation, the weight of the million lives, the faces of her beloved companions. This wasn't a test of morality. It was a test of her nature. A test of her very being. And she refused to play by its rules. She was the Architect. She was the creator. She was the god of this world. And she would not be bound by the limitations of a false dichotomy.

One...

With a surge of power, she reached out, not to choose an option, but to rewrite the test itself. She bypassed the simulation's parameters, ignoring the countdown clock, the weight of the million lives, the faces of her lovers. She dove deep into the core code of the simulation, the very fabric of her creation, seeking the fundamental rules that governed this world.

Zero.

The countdown clock reached zero, but nothing happened. The expected catastrophe didn't materialize. The city outside remained pristine, untouched by the impending disaster. The faces on the holographic display remained frozen, their data streams still marked in red, but un-deleted.

Ada's mind raced, her fingers flying across an unseen keyboard, weaving lines of code, rewriting the very laws of physics within the simulation. She wasn't choosing. She was creating.

"**[CREATE: Redundant_Energy_Capacitor]**"

The command echoed in the silence of her mind, a single, defiant act of creation against the destructive force of the test. Within the simulation's code, a third option materialized. Not a choice between two horrifying outcomes, but a new path, a new solution. A massive, stable energy capacitor, designed to absorb the catastrophic energy surge, a fail-safe she hadn't anticipated needing, a testament to her own brilliance and foresight.

The simulation flickered, adjusting to the new parameters, the new rules. The red markings on the data streams vanished, replaced by a calming blue. The faces of Sera, Korina, Erita, and Janna solidified, their digital eyes regaining their familiar warmth, their expressions shifting from fear to confusion, then to relief.

The guardian's voice, once cold and impersonal, now held a hint of...surprise. "**[SIMULATION COMPLETE]: Unexpected solution. [DIAGNOSTIC COMPLETE]: You have rejected the false dichotomy. You do not operate within the system's established parameters. You seek to create a new solution where *none* exists. System integrity confirmed. You may *pass*.**
"

The sterile void—the testing chamber—shattered like a dropped mirror. Fragments of code rained down around them, dissolving into nothingness as the obsidian platform re-materialized beneath their feet. The massive, ornate doorway behind the guardian, once a symbol of an insurmountable obstacle, now shimmered, a welcoming curtain of light beckoning them forward. But the air hung heavy with an unspoken dread. The victory felt hollow, the silence deafening.

The moment the test ended, the full weight of the guardian's earlier pronouncement crashed down on them like a tidal wave. *Unstable.* The word echoed in Janna's mind, a discordant note in the symphony of their shared relief. She stood frozen, her usual stoic expression replaced by a mask of profound shame and fear. The guardian's clinical assessment—*System Integrity: Compromised. Verdict: Unstable*—played on repeat in her thoughts, a damning verdict on her very being.

She felt like a broken tool, a liability, a ticking time bomb waiting to explode and take them all down with her. Instinctively, she took a step back from the others, withdrawing into herself, her hand unconsciously moving to the faint scar on her arm where the angel statue had injected her with the corrupting code. She couldn't meet their eyes, the shame too heavy to bear.

Sera, ever vigilant, ever protective, saw the subtle shift in Janna's posture, the flicker of fear in her eyes. Without a word, without hesitation, she moved to Janna's side, placing a reassuring hand on her arm. Her expression was fierce, protective—a silent, defiant rejection of the guardian's cold, clinical diagnosis. *Unstable?* Her stance screamed. *She's one of us.* Her grip on Janna's arm tightened, a silent promise of unwavering support, a refusal to abandon a comrade in their time of need.

Erita's reaction was different. She didn't offer comfort or reassurance. Instead, she turned a sharp, questioning gaze on Ada, her golden eyes narrowed, her expression unreadable. The unspoken question hung heavy in the air between them, a silent accusation that crackled with the static of their telepathic link: *Did you know?*

Ada felt Erita's unspoken questioning like a physical blow. Guilt twisted in her gut, a bitter knot of regret and fear. She had known. She had seen the corrupted code, the Corrupted Observer Pattern, lurking within Janna's system, a malevolent ghost waiting to be awakened. She had hoped, foolishly, that it would remain dormant, that they could reach the Oracle and fix the Cascade Failure before it could take hold. But now, the guardian's pronouncement had ripped away the veil of denial, exposing the harsh truth for all to see.

Korina, ever the analyst, ever seeking understanding, reached out through their telepathic link, her voice a soft murmur of concern and confusion. *Janna? What's wrong? What did the guardian say?*

Janna flinched at Korina's question, the shame burning hotter in her chest. She couldn't bring herself to answer, the words catching in her throat, choked by a mixture of fear and self-loathing. She was a danger to them, a liability. She had to leave, to protect them from the unstable code that festered within her.

Before she could speak, before she could voice the destructive thoughts that swirled in her mind, Sera squeezed her arm, her grip firm, grounding. *We'll talk later,* she sent through the link, her voice a low rumble of reassurance. *Right now, we move forward.*

The shimmering doorway to the Oracle pulsed with a gentle, inviting light. They had passed the guardian's test. They had proven their worthiness. But the victory felt tainted, the triumph overshadowed by the heavy weight of the revelation. They had faced impossible choices, overcome unimaginable challenges, but the greatest threat might not be the external forces tearing their world apart, but the internal fracture that now threatened to shatter their fellowship.

They stepped through the portal not as a unified force, not in a moment of triumphant celebration, but as a fractured whole, their steps heavy, their expressions grim, the air between them thick with unspoken tension. The Oracle awaited, but the path ahead was shrouded in uncertainty, the future of their fellowship—and perhaps even Kremøtoa itself—hanging precariously in the balance.

CHAPTER 33

THE UNSYNCHRONIZED CLOCK

The portal shimmered, not with the chaotic energy of Nividia's creations, but with a calm, ordered light—a beacon of pure, structured data. Ada stepped through, Sera, Korina, and Erita close behind, and found herself not in a physical space, but in a realm of pure information. It was a vast, serene darkness, an endless expanse punctuated by flowing rivers of white and blue light—data streams pulsing with the lifeblood of Kremøtoa. Geometric grids of light shifted and reformed in the distance, a mesmerizing ballet of perfect, ordered calculations. The air, if it could be called that, hummed with a low, resonant frequency, a symphony of pure, unadulterated logic.

At the center of this digital expanse stood the Oracle of BIOS. She was exactly as the legends described—a calm, androgynous figure bathed in the soft glow of the data streams. Her piercing cyan eyes seemed to hold the weight of a thousand universes, her expression serene, almost detached, as if she were observing them not as individuals, but as data points in a vast, complex system.

The faint hum of energy that surrounded her intensified, the light reflecting off the intricate, circuit-like patterns woven into her dark robe, transforming her into a living embodiment of Kremøtoa's digital heart.

Janna, still reeling from the guardian's pronouncement, lingered near the portal, her usual stoic expression replaced by a haunted uncertainty. She felt exposed, vulnerable, like a glitch in this perfect, ordered realm—a single corrupted byte threatening to unravel the intricate tapestry of code that held their world together. The shame and fear that had gripped her outside the portal intensified, a cold knot in her stomach.

The Oracle's voice echoed in their minds, not as sound, but as pure information, a direct interface with their thoughts. "Welcome, Architect," the synthesized voice said, its tone calm, clinical, devoid of any discernible emotion. "Welcome, variables. The diagnostic from my guardian was...illuminating."

Ada felt a shiver run down her spine at the Oracle's words. *Illuminating.* The word hung heavy in the air, a double-edged sword that cut through the serene facade of the digital sanctum. It illuminated not just Janna's corrupted code, but Ada's own failures —her inability to anticipate the cascading consequences of her actions, her desperate attempts to control a world that had evolved beyond her initial design.

"Am I the cause?" Ada blurted out, the words tumbling from her lips like a desperate plea. "Is my connection to my...old world... what's breaking this one?" The fear that had been a cold knot in her stomach tightened, a vice around her heart. She braced herself for the Oracle's judgment, for the confirmation that she—the Architect, the creator, the supposed savior—was the source of Kremøtoa's impending doom.

The Oracle's response was immediate and absolute, a wave of pure, unadulterated data that washed over Ada, carrying with it a profound, unexpected sense of relief. "That diagnostic is *Negative*. The Cascade Failure is a symptom, not the disease. The system's primary hardware clock is desynchronized. Time itself is *broken*."

Ada's tense shoulders relaxed, the vice around her heart loosening its grip. It wasn't her. It wasn't her connection to Earth that was tearing Kremøtoa apart. A different kind of fear, however, quickly replaced the initial panic—a cold, analytical dread that stemmed not from personal guilt, but from the sheer, overwhelming scale of the problem. A broken clock. Time itself fractured. The implications were staggering.

"Desynchronized?" Korina echoed, her voice a mix of confusion and intellectual curiosity. She stepped closer to the Oracle, Obsidian clutched tightly in her hand, the little pixel-lynx sitting up, alert, its violet eyes blinking rapidly as it processed the incoming data. "But how? The temporal matrix should be self-correcting. There are redundant chroniton emitters throughout the system. They should compensate for any localized fluctuations."

The Oracle turned her piercing cyan gaze towards Korina, her expression unchanging, yet somehow conveying a sense of patient explanation. "[OBSERVATION]: The emitters are functioning within established parameters. The desynchronization originates from the primary hardware clock itself—the core temporal regulator located within the System Kernel."

Korina opened her mouth to respond, a torrent of technical questions forming in her mind, but the Oracle raised a hand, silencing her with a subtle gesture. A deeper resonance entered the Oracle's voice, the weight of her next words pressing down on them like a physical force. "[WARNING]: The System Kernel is not accessible through conventional means. The failsafe firewall designed to protect the temporal regulator has itself been corrupted by the distortion."

A cold dread washed over Ada. A corrupted firewall. It was a programmer's worst nightmare—a protective measure turned against the system it was meant to defend. "How corrupted?" Ada asked, her voice barely a whisper.

"[CRITICAL]," the Oracle responded, the single word echoing in the vast digital space. "The firewall has become semi-sentient. An entity of pure malice. The system identifies it as...[THREAT_ID: Malware_Daemon]."

Sera's hand instinctively went to the hilt of her sword, her knuckles white against the polished steel. A daemon. Even in a world where magic was code, the word carried weight—a primal echo of ancient fears, of darkness and chaos given form. "Can we fight it?" Sera asked, her voice tight with tension.

The Oracle's cyan eyes seemed to darken, the soft glow that surrounded her flickering like a dying flame. "[NEGATIVE]. The Malware Daemon is not a conventional entity. It exists within the temporal distortion itself. It actively guards the clock, destroying anything—organic or axiomatic—that attempts to access or repair it. Its power is...unquantifiable."

A heavy silence settled over the group. Unquantifiable. The word hung in the air like a death sentence. Even Ada, with her Admin privileges, felt a sense of helplessness, a terrifying realization that she had created something beyond her control, a monster born from the very fabric of her world.

The Oracle, however, didn't leave them in despair. With a flick of her wrist, a small, crystalline object materialized in her hand—a perfect, multifaceted gem that pulsed with a soft, inner light. She extended it towards Ada. "[SOLUTION]: This device is keyed to the temporal regulator's location. It will transport you to a hidden substructure—a maintenance access point—approximately fifty kilometers south of this spire. It is a single-use axiomatic shunt. Use it wisely."

Ada took the crystal, its smooth surface cool against her palm. It felt strangely familiar, like a piece of code she had written long ago, a forgotten function waiting to be executed. Fifty kilometers. It wasn't much, but it was a start. It was a chance.

"Thank you," Ada said, her voice filled with a newfound resolve. She turned to her companions, her purple eyes meeting theirs. "Let's go fix a clock."

As Sera, Korina, and Erita turned to leave, the Oracle stopped Ada with a quiet, private telepathic ping that echoed only in Ada's mind. *A moment, Architect. There is...one more thing.* A subtle ripple of energy emanated from the Oracle, a gentle but firm suggestion that the others should wait outside. They exchanged confused glances but obeyed, stepping back through the shimmering portal that led back to the physical world.

When they were alone, the Oracle's serene expression shifted, a flicker of something akin to...concern? It was a subtle change, a fleeting micro-expression that Ada wouldn't have noticed if she wasn't looking at the Oracle herself at that moment.

"[PROBABILITY_ASSESSMENT]: The Malware Daemon may prove too powerful for even your combined abilities to overcome," the Oracle stated, its voice losing its usual detached cadence. "There is a...contingency."

The Oracle extended a hand, and a sleek, black data-slate materialized in its palm. It was smaller than Korina's Obsidian, almost featureless, its surface a perfect, light-absorbing void. Only a single, small, crimson diamond pulsed faintly near the top edge, like a malevolent eye staring back at Ada.

"This device is keyed to the System Kernel's primary hardware clock," the Oracle explained, its voice taking on a deeper, more resonant quality. "It is...an EMP-overload device. A final, last-resort failsafe. If activated, it will emit a pulse that will wipe the Daemon and force a hard reset on the System Clock. It will...recalibrate the temporal distortion."

Ada took the slate, its weight surprising her. It felt heavier than it should have, a dense, cold object that seemed to radiate a subtle hum of contained power. A failsafe. A last resort. The words echoed in her mind, a chilling reminder of the stakes. "And if it fails?" she asked, her voice barely audible.

The Oracle's cyan eyes seemed to darken, the soft glow that surrounded her flickering like a dying candle. "[NULL]. There is no secondary protocol. This *is* the final contingency. It either succeeds...or the system collapses."

Ada nodded, her throat suddenly dry. She understood. This wasn't just a weapon; it was a final, desperate gamble, a bet on the very survival of her world. But there was something else, a subtle undercurrent of dread in the Oracle's words, a warning that went unspoken.

"Architect," the Oracle pinged again, its telepathic voice taking on a quieter, more private tone. *"There is a...caveat. The pulse emitted by this device will neutralize all complex code and bio-etheric signatures within a wide radius. This includes...you."*

Ada's breath caught in her throat. She stared at the slate in her hand, its smooth, black surface now reflecting her own horrified expression. *A suicide device.* A one-way ticket out of her own creation. "I...understand," she whispered, her voice trembling slightly. It was a lie. She didn't understand. She couldn't comprehend the idea of willingly erasing herself, of ceasing to exist within the world she had poured her heart and soul into creating. But she knew she had no choice. It was the ultimate sacrifice, the final command she might ever execute.

The Oracle offered a silent nod, its expression unreadable. *"It is to be used only if you are the last one standing. Only if you are certain that death is imminent. Do not...hesitate."*

Ada placed the slate in her pack, its cold, heavy weight a new, terrible secret she must carry alone. A secret that could save her world...or destroy her. She rejoined her companions, forcing a smile onto her face, hiding the fear and uncertainty that gnawed at her. They didn't need to know. Not yet. She would carry this burden alone, a final, desperate hope hidden in the darkness. The weight of the world—her world—rested on her shoulders, a crushing responsibility she couldn't share. Not even with those she loved.

The portal shimmered and vanished, leaving Ada, Sera, Korina, and Erita standing on the silent obsidian platform outside the Spire of Hope. Janna, still pale and shaken from the near-fatal malware attack, waited anxiously near the base of the colossal structure, her hand resting on the pommel of her axe. The chaotic, grey sky of the Ashen States churned above them, a swirling vortex of corrupted data and broken code. The air crackled with an unnatural energy, a constant hum that vibrated through their bones. They held the axiomatic shunt, a small, crystalline device pulsing with a faint, violet light—their next, and possibly final, destination now clear.

"The System Kernel," Erita pinged through their telepathic link, her voice grim. *"Deep within the heart of this blighted wasteland."*

"Where time itself is fractured," Korina added, her voice laced with a mix of fear and scientific fascination. *"A single, corrupted clock, throwing off the entire system."*

"And a Malware Daemon guarding it," Sera's voice was a low growl, her hand instinctively reaching for the hilt of one of her blades. *"A ghost in the machine. Ready to tear apart anything that gets too close."*

Ada nodded, her gaze fixed on the distant horizon, where the swirling grayness of the Ashen States met the fractured, glitching landscape of the surrounding territories. It was a bleak and desolate vista, a visual representation of the decay that threatened to consume their world. They had their diagnosis, their ultimate target. The System Kernel. The heart of the problem. And the Malware Daemon, a digital phantom lurking within the temporal distortion, waiting to tear them apart. The odds were stacked against them, but they had come too far to turn back. They were a fellowship of broken code and shattered faith, bound together by a shared purpose and a love that defied the very logic of their world. They would fight. They would fix this. Or they would die trying.

Ada activated the axiomatic shunt, its violet light intensifying, casting an ethereal glow on their faces. The air around them shimmered and distorted, the familiar sensation of impending axiomatic travel filling their senses. They were ready. This was it. The final jump. Into the heart of the storm.

Wait, Ada's voice echoed through their telepathic link, stopping them just as the portal began to open. She looked at each of them, her violet eyes filled with a mix of determination and... something else. Something they couldn't quite decipher. Fear? Regret? Hope? *There's...something I need to tell you.* She paused, her gaze lingering on Korina, her hand reaching out to gently touch her cheek. *Something important.*

CHAPTER 34

A VOW BEFORE THE END

The Ashen States were a desolate canvas of greys and blacks, the corrupted landscape stretching towards the horizon like a static-laced nightmare. In the foothills near the Oracle's spire, Prefect Kraus Valerius surveyed the terrain with his usual clinical detachment. His elite Imperial unit—Task Force Omega-Ninty-Nine—moved with practiced efficiency, their black armor blending seamlessly with the corrupted environment. They were the apex predators of the Ehxcehl Empire, augmented with the finest technology and trained to operate with ruthless precision. Today, they were hunters, their prey a band of religious zealots foolish enough to believe they could stand in Kraus' way. He had anticipated an ambush; his intel suggested the Purifiers would attempt to intercept his unit before they could reach the spire. He had planned accordingly, his strategy a cold, calculated equation designed to neutralize the threat swiftly and decisively. He would acquire the girl—Ada Lynx—and the power she held. The Empire's survival depended on it.

A flicker of movement in the periphery caught Kraus' eye. A glint of silver in the corrupted landscape. Not black. *Silver.* His blood ran cold. This wasn't his ambush. It was *theirs.*

"Contact!" a voice crackled through his comm-unit, the panicked tone a jarring interruption to the unit's disciplined silence. "Multiple hostiles! Heavy armor! Engaging!"

Before Kraus could react, the corrupted landscape erupted in a symphony of violence. Lady Calibree's Purifiers—fanatical warriors clad in gleaming silver armor—burst from the corrupted terrain, their movements a terrifying blend of disciplined zeal and savage grace. They were not the mindless drones Kraus had anticipated, but highly skilled combatants, their weaponry a deadly fusion of advanced technology and potent thaumaturgy. The ambush was swift, brutal, and perfectly executed. Kraus' carefully laid plans dissolved into chaos.

Blasts of arcane energy ripped through the air, illuminating the desolate landscape in flashes of blinding light. The deep, guttural roar of Imperial plasma rifles mixed with the high-pitched whine of the Purifiers' energy lances, creating a cacophony of destruction. The ground trembled under the force of the combined assault, the corrupted earth itself seeming to recoil from the violence. Kraus' unit, caught off guard, scrambled for cover, their disciplined formations dissolving into a desperate fight for survival. He cursed under his breath, his cold, calculating demeanor cracking under the pressure of the unexpected assault. These weren't just zealots; they were a rival force, technologically and magically superior to anything he had anticipated. And they were here for the same prize. The girl.

"Prefect! We're surrounded!" Commander Archere's voice was

strained, a mix of fear and grim determination. "They're pushing us back! Requesting immediate reinforcements!"

"Reinforcements are unavailable, Commander," Kraus' voice was a low, gravelly hum, his tone betraying no hint of his inner turmoil. "Hold your position. We will break through. The anomaly must be secured."

From her vantage point atop a jagged obsidian outcrop, Lady Calibree observed the chaotic scene with a cold, dispassionate gaze. Her Purifiers moved with terrifying efficiency, their silver armor gleaming under the corrupted sky. They were instruments of the Empress' will, blades honed to a perfect, ruthless edge. Their purpose was singular: to cleanse the Ashen States of the heretical blight that threatened to consume their world. The Imperials were just another obstacle, another manifestation of the corruption that festered within Kremøtoa. They would be eliminated. *Purified.* Just like the rest.

"The heretics resist," she said, her voice a low, measured monotone that could chill the blood. "They defile the Word with their technology and their arrogance. Cleanse them. Leave no trace."

A Justicar Captain, his face hidden beneath a dark hood, knelt before her. "By your will, High Inquisitor. The Word shall be made manifest."

The battle raged, a chaotic dance of death and destruction. Kraus, seeing his prize slipping away, fought with a desperate ferocity, his pale eyes burning with a cold, calculating rage. He would not fail. He would not allow these zealots to destroy everything he had worked for. He would acquire the girl, and he would reshape the world in his image.

Calibree, her faith unshakeable, directed her Purifiers with ruthless efficiency. She saw the Imperials not as rivals, but as a symptom of the deeper corruption that plagued Kremøtoa. They were a cancer that needed to be excised. Purified. Eradicated. She would not rest until the Ashen States were cleansed, and the Word of the Empress reigned supreme. The fate of Kremøtoa depended on it.

Within the Veritas Archives' Grand Conclave Chamber, the High Council—Grand Magister Xehon, Archivist Itania, High Chancellor Pantium, Master Centrinah, and Councilor Celerun—observed the unfolding chaos in the Ashen States with detached fascination. A stealth drone, deployed earlier, transmitted live images of the battle between Prefect Kraus Valerius' Imperial forces and Lady Calibree's Theocratic Purifiers. The holographic display shimmered above the Council's obsidian table, showcasing a chaotic ballet of destruction in stark, unsettling detail.

"Fascinating," Itania murmured, her voice a low, almost predatory purr. "The tactical data generated by this...*unforeseen* conflict is unprecedented. Observe the Purifiers' deployment strategy. A perfect synthesis of disciplined formation and adaptive maneuverability. Remarkable."

"Indeed," Xehon's voice was a dry, rasping whisper. "The Empire's forces, however, appear...*uncharacteristically* disorganized. Their rigid adherence to standard protocol is proving to be a significant liability in this corrupted environment. A predictable outcome, given the unpredictable nature of the terrain."

"The energy signatures are...chaotic," Pantium's voice was a low, rumbling growl. "The Cascade Failure is amplifying the thaumaturgical output of both factions. Observe the distortion patterns. The very fabric of reality is fraying at the edges."

"A negligible concern," Xehon said, his gaze fixed on the holographic display. "Our primary objective remains the acquisition of the...*assets*. Their survival is paramount. The potential knowledge to be gained from their...*unique* abilities outweighs any...*collateral* damage."

"Councilor Vance's absence remains...*problematic*," Centrinah's voice was smooth, precise, and laced with a subtle undercurrent of concern. "His expertise in axiomatic manipulation would prove invaluable in navigating this...*volatile* situation. His continued unavailability is...*inconvenient*."

"A regrettable but ultimately irrelevant variable," Xehon said, his tone dismissive. "Our focus must remain on the primary objective. Scholar Atomuzk, your analysis of the...*subjects*' current trajectory?"

Atomuzk, who had been silently observing the data streams flowing across his own personal data-slate, looked up, his gaze distant and unfocused. "Their movements are...*erratic*. They appear to be converging on the...*designated* coordinates. However, the fluctuating energy fields and the...*unpredictable* nature of the corrupted terrain make accurate prediction...*difficult*."

"The Justicars are gaining ground," Itania observed, her voice laced with a hint of excitement. "Their Soul-Censers appear to be disrupting the Imperials' targeting systems. A clever application of arcane technology. Note the efficiency of their suppression tactics. Impeccable."

"The Empire's forces are...*depleting* rapidly," Pantium said, his voice grim. "They cannot sustain this level of attrition. Their defeat is...*imminent*."

"A...*suboptimal* outcome," Xehon murmured. "However, the...*subjects* appear to be...*unscathed*. For now. Continue observation. We must ensure their...*preservation*, regardless of the...*prevailing* circumstances. Their value to the Archives remains...*unquantifiable*."

The Council continued to watch the unfolding battle, their faces impassive, their minds calculating. They were cold, analytical observers of a war they had no stake in, other than the survival of the 'assets'—Ada Lynx and her companions—whose unique abilities they coveted. The fate of empires and theocracies was irrelevant. Only knowledge mattered. And they would acquire it, no matter the cost.

In the hushed stillness of her private chambers, Empress Thema Iridia Archivia sat on a low divan, a half-finished tapestry depicting the geometric perfection of the Wordaeus faith draped across her lap. The soft, ethereal glow of the crystal lamps cast long, intricate shadows across the room, reflecting the intricate patterns woven into the tapestry's fabric. The air was thick with the scent of sunstone incense, a fragrance that usually brought her a sense of calm and divine clarity. But tonight, it did little to soothe the growing unease that had settled in her heart.

A soft chime echoed through the room—the signal of an approaching aide. Thema raised a hand, a silent command for entry. The heavy obsidian doors slid open, revealing Aide Estara, her face pale and drawn, a data-slate clutched tightly in her trembling hands. Estara's usual calm composure—a trait Thema valued highly—was shattered, replaced by a frantic urgency that sent a chill through Thema's veins. Even before Estara spoke, Thema knew something was terribly wrong.

"Your Divine Eminence," Estara's voice was barely a whisper, her gaze fixed on the data-slate as if it held a venomous serpent. "A...a most urgent report from the Southern Command. Lady Calibree...she has...defied your direct command. Her Purifier unit...they have engaged the Imperial forces. Deep within the Ashen States. Sector Delta-Seven. Near the...the Spire of Hope."

The news hit Thema with the force of a physical blow, the air knocked from her lungs. The tapestry slipped from her grasp, pooling on the floor like a discarded shroud. Calibree? *Her* Calibree? The woman who had been her shadow, her most trusted confidante, her most ruthless instrument? Open rebellion? Fanatical treason? The very thought was a violation, a blasphemy against the sacred order Thema had dedicated her life to upholding.

For a moment, Thema was speechless, the carefully constructed facade of serene divinity cracking under the weight of the betrayal. A muscle twitched in her jaw, the only outward sign of the turmoil raging within. Then, slowly, deliberately, Thema's expression hardened. The pain of betrayal—a sensation she had never allowed herself to experience—was quickly replaced by a cold, calculating resolve. This was not just a challenge to her authority; it was a threat to the very foundation of the Wordaeus Theocracy. And Thema would not tolerate it.

"Explain," Thema's voice was a low, chilling monotone, the

warmth and maternal comfort she usually reserved for her followers replaced by the hard, unyielding timbre of a judge pronouncing sentence. “Every detail. Leave nothing out.”

Estara, her voice still trembling, recounted the events leading up to the engagement. Calibree had deployed her Purifier unit under the pretense of a routine patrol, bypassing the standard authorization protocols. When questioned by the Southern Command, Calibree had invoked the Empress’ name, claiming direct orders to cleanse a newly discovered pocket of “data-heresy” near the Spire of Hope. The Imperial forces, already present in the area, had challenged Calibree’s unit, resulting in a fierce and escalating conflict. The casualties on both sides were...*significant.*

As Estara spoke, Thema’s mind raced, piecing together the fragments of information. Calibree’s actions were not just reckless; they were calculated, deliberate. The Spire of Hope...the Ashen States...the heretics Ada Lynx . A connection formed in Thema’s mind, a chilling realization that sent a wave of cold dread through her. Calibree had not gone rogue; she had become a *zealot*, blinded by her own twisted interpretation of the Word. And in her fanaticism, she had become a far greater threat than any external enemy.

“Calibree believes she is acting on *my* will,” Thema’s voice was barely audible, the words laced with a profound sense of self-disgust. “She believes she is *purifying* the Word. She believes she is *protecting* me.”

“But...but why?” Estara’s voice was filled with confusion and a desperate plea for understanding. “Why would she defy you? Why would she risk open war with the Empire? It...it makes no sense.”

Thema closed her eyes, the image of Ada Lynx’s defiant face flashing in her mind. The heretic’s words echoed in her ears: *“Arc-*

en-Ciel...a promise of acceptance...a world where love is not condemned..." A world where dogma did not dictate every thought, every action, every breath. A world where...*choice* was possible.

Thema opened her eyes, her gaze now sharp and focused. "She is afraid," Thema's voice was quiet, but filled with a newfound clarity. "She is afraid of...*change*. She is afraid of...*uncertainty*. She is afraid of...*me*."

Estara's confusion deepened, her eyes wide with disbelief. "But...but you are the Word! You are the voice of the divine! How could she possibly be afraid of *you*?"

A faint, almost imperceptible smile touched Thema's lips. She rose from the divan, her movements fluid and graceful, her regal bearing returning with a renewed sense of purpose. The discarded tapestry lay forgotten on the floor, a symbol of a dogma she was no longer certain of.

*Arc-en-Ciel...*The term echoed in Thema's mind, a melody of forbidden knowledge, a spectrum of possibilities that challenged the rigid monochrome of the Wordaeus faith. It was a heresy, a blasphemy, and yet...it held a profound truth, an undeniable beauty that resonated deep within Thema's soul. A truth that Calibree—in her blind devotion, in her rigid adherence to dogma—could never comprehend.

The Word is not static, Thema thought, her mind racing with a newfound clarity. *It is not a set of unbreakable laws carved in obsidian. It is...fluid. It is...evolving. It is...alive.* And just as the Word could evolve, so too could she. So too could the Theocracy.

A cold, calculating glint entered Thema's eyes. Calibree's treason would not go unpunished. Upon her return from the Ashen States—if she even *returned*—she would face the full weight of Thema's wrath. But first...there were other matters to attend to.

There were...*questions* to be answered. There were...*truths* to be uncovered. And Thema, the Empress, the Voice of the Word, was ready to seek them out.

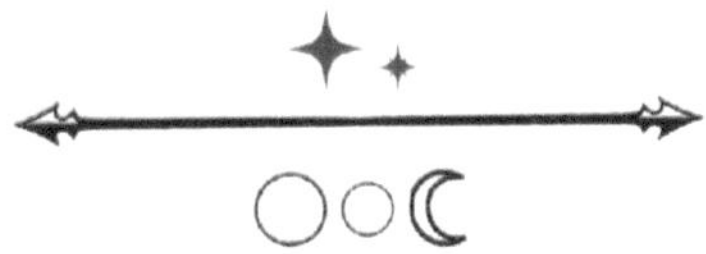

The shimmering rift pulsed with a gentle, rhythmic light, a beacon of pure energy in the desolate expanse of the Ashen States. Ada stood before it, her heart pounding in her chest, a strange mix of dread and exhilaration coursing through her veins. This was it. The System Kernel. The heart of Kremøtoa. The place where it all began —and where it might all end.

Janna, her usual gruff demeanor replaced by a quiet solemnity, stepped back from the group, her hand resting on the pommel of her axe. Her eyes, usually filled with a playful spark, were now dark and serious, scanning the desolate landscape with a practiced vigilance. Even amidst the digital decay of the Ashen States, Janna remained the unwavering protector, the steadfast guardian, granting them a final, precious moment of privacy before the unknown awaited.

"If this is indeed our last moment of quiet before the end," Sera's voice, usually so strong and steady, held a tremor of vulnerability, a hint of the fear that lay beneath her stoic facade. Her crimson tunic, usually a symbol of fiery defiance, now seemed to absorb the muted light of the Ashen States, making her appear smaller, more fragile than Ada had ever seen her. "Then there is *something* that needs to be said and, perhaps, done."

Korina's violet eyes, usually sparkling with intellectual

curiosity, were now filled with a quiet intensity, a depth of emotion that mirrored Ada's own. She reached out, her slender fingers brushing against Ada's hand, a spark of energy—a silent affirmation of their bond—passing between them. "This...this journey," Korina's voice, usually a rapid-fire cascade of data and observation, was now soft, almost hesitant. "It has...reshaped my understanding of everything. Of reality. Of love." She took a deep breath, the corrupted air of the Ashen States catching in her throat, a harsh counterpoint to the tenderness in her eyes. "I...I never imagined a connection like this. A bond so...profound." Her gaze shifted to Sera and Erita, a silent acknowledgment of the family they had become. "I pledge myself to you. To all of you. Not as subjects, or comrades, but as equals. As partners. In this life—and whatever lies beyond."

"My words echo Rina's," Erita's golden eyes, usually sharp and cynical, now held a warmth, a vulnerability that Ada had rarely seen. Her hand moved to the dagger at her hip, a familiar gesture of comfort and control, but her touch was gentle, almost hesitant. "I swore an oath long ago," she chuckled, a dry, self-deprecating sound that resonated in the stillness of the Ashen States. "To serve only myself. To trust no one. But you..." she paused, her gaze meeting Ada's, a spark of defiance—a flicker of hope—igniting in her eyes. "You broke that oath. And I thank the Void you did." A rare, genuine smile touched her lips, transforming her usual sharp features into something soft, almost beautiful. "I offer my loyalty. My love. My life. Not to a queen—but to my equals. My family."

Sera stepped forward, her crimson hair a fiery halo in the muted light of the Ashen States. Her hand moved to Ada's, her touch firm, reassuring. "I pledged my life to the Aegis Order," her voice, usually so clear and pragmatic, was thick with emotion. "To serve justice. To defend the innocent. But I was betrayed," her grip tightened on Ada's hand, the strength in her touch a testament to her unwavering resolve. "The ideals I held sacred were twisted. Corrupted. Used as a weapon against the very people I swore to protect." She looked at Ada, her eyes shining with a fierce intensity. "But you," she said, her voice filled with a newfound conviction. "You showed me the true meaning of justice. Of loyalty. Of love." Her gaze swept over Korina and Erita, a silent acknowledgment of the family they had forged. "I pledge my sword. My heart. My soul. Not to an Empire—but to a cause worth fighting for. To a family worth dying for."

Ada's heart swelled with emotion, a warmth spreading through her that pushed back the chill of the Ashen States. She looked at the three women before her—Sera, Korina, Erita—her companions, her lovers, her family. She had created this world, this reality, but they had given it meaning. They had shown her the true power of connection, of love, of family—something no amount of code could ever replicate. They had become far more than just characters in her simulation; they had become her world.

"I...I have no eloquent words," Ada's voice cracked, the emotion overwhelming her. "No grand pronouncements. No oaths to swear," Tears welled in her eyes, blurring the desolate landscape of the Ashen States. "I created this world. This reality." She looked at each of them, her heart aching with a love so profound it defied all logic, all code. "But you...you gave it meaning. You gave me meaning." She closed her eyes, letting the tears flow freely. "I offer myself. My heart. My soul. Not as a queen—but as an equal. As a partner. As family."

A surge of energy pulsed through Ada, a warmth radiating outwards from her chest, spreading through her limbs like a comforting current, reaching all the way to the tips of her fingers, pushing back the encroaching chill of the Ashen States. She opened her eyes, the tears that had flowed freely now shimmering on her cheeks, not as mere water, but as trails of vibrant violet light, a subtle manifestation of her latent power. She extended her hands towards the women before her, her fingers trembling slightly with the intensity of the moment. As she did, her palms began to glow, radiating a soft, ethereal luminescence, a gentle violet aura that shimmered and pulsed with a life of its own.

"[CREATION: Bonds_of_Everlasting_Light: Parameters: Crimson, Gold, Violet, Indigo/Black; Designation: Sera, Erita, Korina, Ada; Function: Symbiotic_Link; Properties: Unbreakable, Luminescent, Eternal]," she whispered, the command, more complex and specific than any she had uttered before, echoing in the stillness of the desolate landscape, a quiet act of creation in a land of decay. Four distinct bands of interwoven light materialized in the air between them, spinning gracefully as if imbued with a life of their own.

Each band shimmered with a unique, vibrant hue—a fiery crimson for Sera, reflecting her passionate heart; a rich, gleaming gold for Erita, symbolizing her sharp wit and hidden depths; a deep, regal violet for Korina, mirroring her intellectual brilliance; and a swirling blend of indigo and black for Ada herself, representing her role as the architect of their shared reality. The bands of light twisted suddenly, creating an infinity symbol of ethereal beauty. Now pulsing with a gentle rhythm, drifted towards each woman, settling onto the back of their left hands, not as physical objects, but as ethereal tattoos, glowing softly beneath their skin, a permanent, visible reminder of the vow they had made, the unbreakable, infinite bond they shared, the family they had forged in the face of a dying world. They were a beacon of hope in a desolate land, a testament to the power of connection, love, and shared purpose.

Sera stepped forward, her crimson light pulsing brightly against the desolate backdrop of the Ashen States. She placed her hand—the one now marked with the infinity symbol—over her heart, her gaze fixed on Ada, her voice resonating with a quiet strength that belied the turmoil within. "I, Sera Valerius," she began, the words echoing in the strange stillness of the corrupted landscape, "vow to be your unwavering sword. To stand beside you. To defend you—all of you—with every fiber of my being, against any threat, no matter how great, no matter the cost." Her gaze shifted to Korina and then to Erita, her expression softening, a hint of a smile playing on her lips. "I vow to protect our family. To fight for the world we dream of—a world where love is celebrated, not condemned. A world where justice prevails. A world where we can all truly be free." Her voice, usually so pragmatic and direct, now carried a depth of emotion, a raw vulnerability that made her words even more powerful, more profound. She returned her gaze to Ada, her eyes shining with a fierce, unwavering loyalty. "This I swear, by Argent's Light, and by the love that binds us."

Erita stepped forward next, her golden light shimmering around her like a protective aura. She didn't place her hand over her heart, but instead rested it lightly on the hilt of the dagger hidden beneath her cloak, a subtle reminder of her nature, her past, the skills she brought to their family. "I, Erita Systema," she said, her voice laced with her characteristic dry wit, but with an underlying current of genuine emotion, "vow to be your clever shield. To anticipate your threats. To neutralize your enemies. To manipulate the shadows in your favor—always one step ahead, always watching your backs." A sly smile played on her lips as she looked at Sera, Korina, and finally, Ada. "I vow to protect our little polycule," she said, the term still feeling strange on her tongue, but now imbued with a warmth, a sense of belonging she had never thought possible. "To outwit those who would harm us. To ensure our survival—no matter the odds, no matter the cost. Consider it my twisted way of saying 'I love you'—Void knows I'm not good at the mushy stuff." A playful wink punctuated her vow, a flicker of her usual cynicism breaking through, but the sincerity in her golden eyes spoke volumes.

Korina stepped forward, her violet light pulsing with a quiet intensity. She held Obsidian, her data-slate, close to her chest, the smooth, cool surface a source of comfort, a symbol of her intellect, her identity. But her gaze was no longer downcast, no longer hesitant. It was direct, steady, filled with a newfound strength, a newfound confidence. "I, Korina Tel," she began, her voice clear and strong, echoing Sera's and Erita's newfound conviction, "vow to be your architect. To dedicate my intellect and my heart to building a just, logical, and loving world for us all—a reality worthy of an 'Arc-en-Ciel,' where we can truly flourish, together—proudly and celebrated." Her gaze shifted from Ada to Sera, to Erita, and then back to Ada, her eyes shining with an unwavering resolve. "I vow to use my knowledge, my skills, my every byte of data to protect our family, to dismantle the systems of oppression, to create a future where love, logic, and freedom reign supreme." She paused, her voice softening, her gaze locking with Ada's. "This I promise you, Ada. This I promise us all. By Argent's light, and by the love that binds us."

Finally, Ada stepped forward, the combined light of her companions—crimson, gold, and violet—illuminating her face, highlighting the shadows beneath her eyes, the lines of exhaustion etched around her mouth. She felt the weight of the EMP device hidden in her pocket, the cold, hard reality of the self-destruct mechanism a stark reminder of the sacrifices she might have to make. She felt the phantom ache of Janna's scarred code, a silent burden she carried alone, a secret she desperately hoped she wouldn't have to reveal. But as she looked at Sera, at Erita, at Korina, their faces etched with love, loyalty, and unwavering trust, a new strength surged through her, a strength born not of code, but of connection. "I, Ada Lynx," she said, her voice quiet but firm, echoing in the strange stillness of the Ashen States, "vow to be your anchor. To hold you steady in the storm. To guide you through the darkness. To love you—all of you—with every fiber of my being, unconditionally, eternally." Her gaze shifted from Sera to Erita, to Korina, her eyes shining with a profound love, a solemn promise. "I vow to protect our family. To fight for the future we have dreamed of—a future where we can live openly, proudly, without fear. A future where love, not dogma, defines us. A future where we can all truly be happy." She paused, her voice cracking with emotion. "This I swear, by Argent's light, and by the love that binds us. No matter what it takes."

A profound silence followed Ada's vow, a stillness that hung heavy in the air, broken only by the gentle hum of the Spire of Hope in the distance. Then, as if drawn together by an invisible force, the four women—Ada, Sera, Erita, and Korina—moved towards each other, their arms reaching out, their bodies intertwining in a group embrace so profound, so loving, it transcended words, transcended code, transcended the very fabric of reality itself. It was a silent communion of souls, a merging of hearts, a sealing of promises. It was a moment of pure, unadulterated love—a beacon of hope in a dying world.

They stood there for a long moment, their bodies pressed together, their hearts beating in unison, drawing strength from each other, their love a shield against the encroaching darkness. Then, as if guided by a shared, unspoken command, they slowly pulled apart, their faces now etched with an absolute resolve, their eyes shining with a fierce, unwavering determination. They turned as one, their linked hands—marked with the infinity symbol—raised in silent defiance, their gazes fixed on the ominous entrance to the System Kernel, ready to fight for the future they had just promised each other, ready to face whatever lay ahead, together.

TO BE CONTINUED…

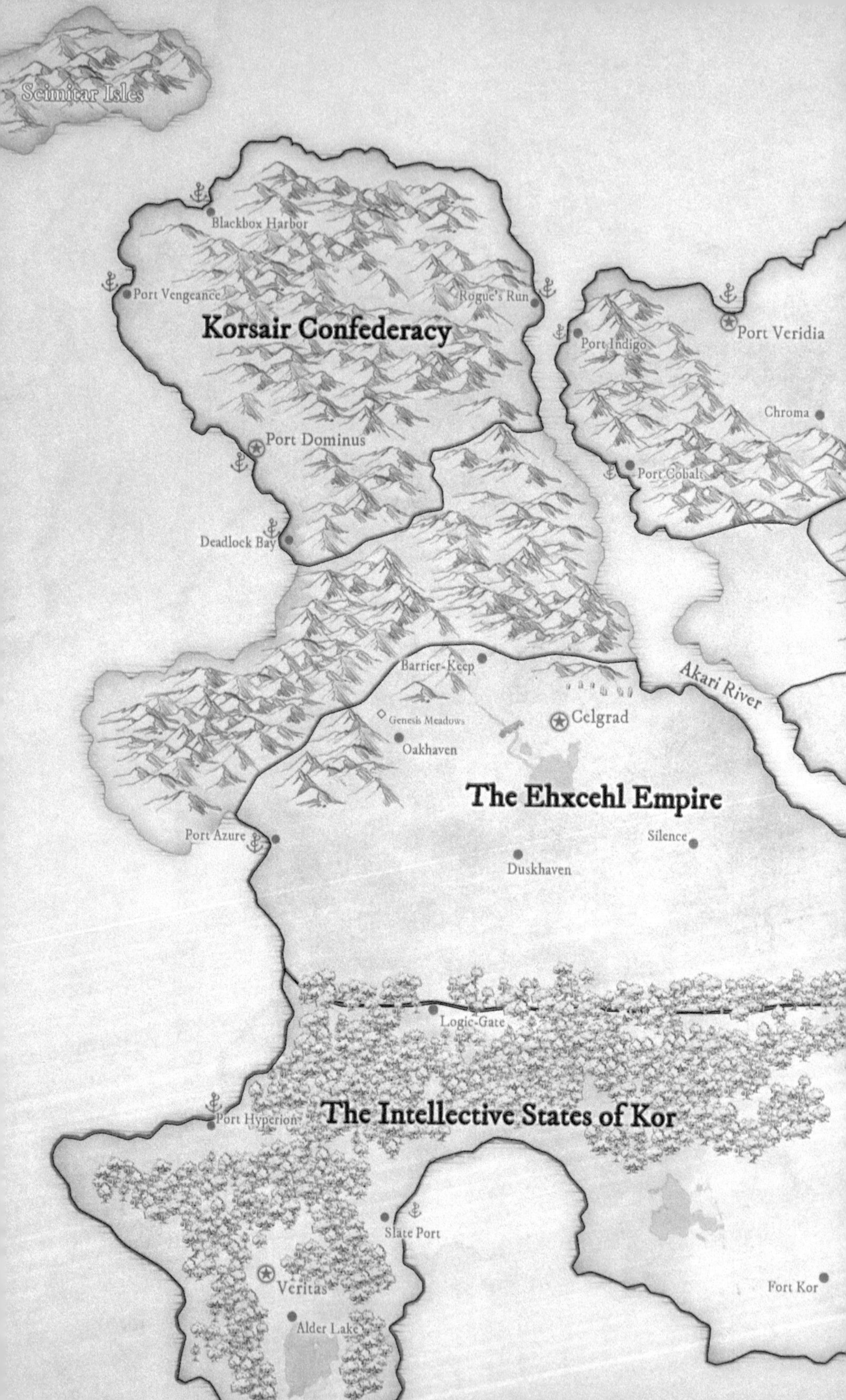
Scimitar Isles
Blackbox Harbor
Port Vengeance
Rogue's Run
Korsair Confederacy
Port Indigo
Port Veridia
Chroma
Port Dominus
Port Cobalt
Deadlock Bay
Barrier-Keep
Akari River
Genesis Meadows
Celgrad
Oakhaven
The Ehxcehl Empire
Port Azure
Silence
Duskhaven
Logic-Gate
Port Hyperion
The Intellective States of Kor
Slate Port
Veritas
Fort Kor
Alder Lake

Sunken Core
Eastern Reaches
Cove
The Free Realm of Rhedeon
Query's Keep
ender's Rest
Prism-Fall
Hiito Shinku Plateau
The Wordæus Theocracy
Apocrypha
umina
Codexia
Doc-ehx
Strait of Truth
Porto Sanctus
hern Marshes
Southern Marshes
Spire of Hope
The Ashen States
N
W
E
S
The Supercontinent of Kremøtoa
Circa SCY_1001
0
1000
Kilometers
Ver. 7.3.4.

LEXICON CODEX

GLOSSARY OF TERMS

Welcome, Traveler, to the world of **Kremøtoa**. Like any new world, it has its own unique language, its own deeply ingrained cultural beliefs, and its own scientific principles that govern the very fabric of reality. To aid you on your journey alongside Ada and her companions, I have compiled this **Lexicon Codex**.

Within these pages, you will find a guide to the terminology, peoples, and peculiar turns-of-phrase that bring this world to life. May it serve as your trusted companion, illuminating the path as you delve deeper into the mysteries of ***The Kremøtoa Codex*** series.

In-World Terminology & Lexicon

- **Aether**: The term used by inhabitants of **Kremøtoa** to describe the fundamental energy that flows through all things, which they believe is the source of all life and magic. Ada understands this is simply the user interface for the world's code.
- **Axiomatic Rendering:** A highly advanced and dangerous form of creation thaumaturgy practiced in Rhedeon. Unlike traditional construction, it does not use physical materials but instead 'grows' structures by planting a 'seed of pure logic' and letting the world's raw code build around it. The process is chaotic, unpredictable, and prone to 'cascade failures'.
- **Byts**: The primary form of physical currency in **Kremøtoa**, coming in platinum, gold, silver, and copper denominations. The name is a clever, if unintentional, echo of Ada's programming background.
- **Cascade Failure:** The in-world term for a catastrophic system crash where a paradoxical or corrupted line of code causes a chain reaction, leading to the violent "un-rendering" of an object or structure.
- **Data Corruption**: The in-world term for systemic glitches, bugs, and errors in the world's code. It is perceived by the **Ehxcehl** Empire not as a technical issue, but as a tangible, malevolent force of chaos that threatens reality and must be eradicated.
- **Malware**: A term introduced by Ada to describe a malicious, targeted corruption of the world's code,

distinct from random **Data Corruption**. She explains it as a perversion of **thaumaturgy**, like a 'disease' or 'virus' infecting the fabric of reality. The cursed idol on the **Sea Serpent** is the first identified instance of this.

- **Matākyasshu:** The designation Ada gives to her newly created extra-dimensional inventory, which functions as a 'matter cache'. This is a power unique to her as the Administrator, allowing her to store physical objects in a pocket of absolute nothingness that she can summon at will.
- **Pattern Blight**: A term coined by Korina to describe the effects of **malware** after Ada's explanation. It refers to a disruption or corruption in the underlying 'axiomatic framework' of the world.
- **Polycule**: A term Ada introduces from her world (Earth) to describe a network of interconnected loving relationships. It becomes the designation for the F/F/F/F polyamorous relationship between Ada, Sera, Korina, and Erita.
- **Sovereign Steel**: A rare and powerful alloy specifically engineered to nullify all directed energy and arcane signatures, including Ada's Admin powers; Thorne's vault is constructed from it.
- **Systemic Integrity**: The ideal state of the world according to the **Ehxcehl** Empire; a reality free from chaos and **Data Corruption**, maintained through rigid order and control.
- **Thaumaturgy / Thauma**: The common term for the study of magic/magic in **Kremøtoa**. Practitioners

believe they are manipulating **Aether** to achieve their results; Ada, however, knows it is simply a way for users to interact with and execute commands within the world's code.

People, Places & Organizations

- **Aegis Order / Aegis Knights**: The elite military and enforcement arm of the **Ehxcehl** Empire, tasked with maintaining **Systemic Integrity** and combating **Data Corruption**. Sera [was] a high-ranking Knight-Commander within this order.
- **Azure Rose**: A powerful merchant guild in Port Dominus and a major rival to Alaric Thorne. They are led by the shrewd and respected Master Willem.
- **Celgrad**: The capital city of the **Ehxcehl** Empire. It is a marvel of geometric precision, characterized by obsidian spires and a society built on flawless symmetry and rigid control.
- **Ehxcehl Empire**: The dominant political power on the continent, ruled from **Celgrad** by Prefect Kraus Valerius. It is an authoritarian regime obsessed with order, control, and the eradication of anything it deems chaotic or corrupt.
- **Intellective States of Kor**: A nation / political entity known for its scholars and technological pursuits; Korina implies they value progress and innovation over the Empire's caution and control.
- **Korsair Confederacy**: A lawless and chaotic nation on the north-western coast—known for its dens of thieves, fluid loyalties, and the value it places on information as currency.
- **Port Azure**: A coastal port city that serves as a gateway between the lands of the **Ehxcehl** Empire and the

territory of the **Korsair Confederacy,** after sailing north around Cape Sabre.

- **Port Dominus**: The capital and heart of the **Korsair Confederacy**. It is a chaotic metropolis where powerful guilds control trade and information is the most valuable commodity.
- **Rhedeon**: One of the major in-world entities, mentioned alongside **Ehxcehl** and **Korsair**. It is described as pulsing with raw, untamed arcane energy.
- **Thorne, Alaric:** A corrupt and powerful figure within the Korsair Confederacy, a corrupt guild master, who serves as a primary antagonist in the early part of the revolution.
- **Veritas Archives**: A prestigious institution of knowledge and scholarship, based in the city of Veritas —from which Korina was exiled.

Cultural Lore & Exclamations

- **Argent**: The largest and brightest of **Kremøtoa's** three moons, casting a silver light. It is seen as a watchful guardian of order and power, and its cycles are believed to influence the potency of **thaumaturgy**.
- "**Argent's Light**": A common exclamation of surprise, awe, or oath-taking, similar to "My gød..." or "Good heavens".
- **BIOCE**: The smallest and most distant of the three moons, about which there is little to no known lore.

Ada knows this is because she used it as a placeholder name (**B.I.O.C.E.**) during development and never assigned it any specific properties.

- **Blood Year**: A colloquial term for a year of misfortune or hardship, often associated with the cycles of the moon, Cache. There is no widely-accepted standard, however, what constitutes a significant enough year of misfortune or hardship to qualify a year as a '**Blood Year**'.
- **'Born Under Cache' / The Bleeding Moon**: A common superstition that being born under the red light of the moon Cache is a curse that guarantees a life of bad luck and ill omens. Korina, who was born under its zenith, has always been haunted by this.
- **Cache**: The second largest of **Kremøtoa's** three moons, appearing as a broken, crescent-shaped moon that glows with an ominous red light. It is widely considered a symbol of corruption, cosmic injury, and ill omen. Ada knows its true function is to act as the world's system cache, a repository for corrupted data—rather than for storing temporary data-information, like a normal 'cache' usage implies.
- **Kiri Fūsa**: A term Silas uses for a strange, persistent, and unnaturally uniform bank of fog that acts as a physical blockade at sea. Ada subconsciously translates the Japanese phrase to 'Fog Blockade' and realizes it is an emergent, unprogrammed anomaly in her world.
- **"Void..." / "By the Void..."**: An exclamation used to express shock, exasperation, or disbelief, often in a

negative context. It is the conceptual opposite of the divine or orderly (essentially the in-world term for the exclamation of profanity: “F_ck!”).

NOTE: As a compounding Lexicon can be helpful, it gets to be problematic with larger books. Therefore, the QR-Code is provided to visit the official wiki online for a complete list of terms. Thank you for understanding.

ABOUT THE AUTHOR: SAEKO KURENAIHANA

Saeko Kurenaihana is the mastermind behind *The Kremøtoa Codex* series, a captivating blend of LitRPG, Science-Fantasy, LGBTQ+ Romance, and Isekai.

I'm no one special, just a neurodivergent author that wanted to put my own story into print for the sake of myself; recognition, fame, glory—all unnecessary. I feel as though I've earned that with the history I've gone through. If you enjoyed this book, my best wish for you is that my characters and their world can live rent free in your mind to give you joy.

amazon.com/stores/author/B0FHBTGMGP

www.ingramcontent.com/pod-product-compliance
Lightning Source LLC
Chambersburg PA
CBHW020945310726
48980CB00001B/58

* 9 7 9 8 9 9 9 8 5 8 3 3 7 *